TWENTY OF THE FINEST IN MODERN AMERICAN SHORT FICTION

Oars bend in the swift, tremendous beat of the racing start. Kip Grant, coxswain, stares at his crew, and hates them. Harry Sylvester's **The Eight-Oared Crew** is an authentic story of character as well as varsity rowing.

Katharine Brush was the only feminine novelist who was also an expert college football reporter for a national newspaper syndicate. Her famous story, **Fumble**, is one of the football classics of all time.

Dorothy Parker's immortal **Clothe the Naked** is a quietly-told, compassionate, hotly-indignant story that sears itself on your memory.

Every Story in this Collection is a Masterpiece.

BANTAM PATHFINDER EDITIONS

A comprehensive and fully integrated series designed to meet the expanding needs of the young adult reading audience and the growing demand among readers of all ages for paperback books of high quality.

Bantam Pathfinder Editions provide the best in fiction and non-fiction in a wide variety of subject areas. They include novels by classic and contemporary writers; vivid, accurate histories and biographies; authoritative works in the sciences; collections of short stories, plays and poetry.

Bantam Pathfinder Editions are carefully selected and approved. They are presented in a new and handsome format, durably bound and printed on specially selected high quality paper.

TWENTY GRAND
SHORT STORIES

Originally published under the title
HERE WE ARE

Stories from SCHOLASTIC MAGAZINE

Edited by Ernestine Taggard with an
Introduction by Dorothy Canfield Fisher

BANTAM PATHFINDER EDITIONS

BANTAM BOOKS/NEW YORK

RLI: $\dfrac{\text{VLM } 5}{\text{IL } 7.12}$

TWENTY GRAND SHORT STORIES

This book was originally published under the title HERE WE ARE. *Bantam edition reprinted by arrangement with Dodd, Mead & Company*

Bantam edition published October 1947
New Bantam edition published January 1955
2nd printing................November 1956
3rd printing................December 1957
4th printing................November 1958
5th printing................November 1959
6th printing................September 1960
7th printing.................January 1962
8th printing....................April 1962
9th printing.................October 1962
Bantam Pathfinder edition published February 1963
11th printing
12th printing
13th printing
14th printing

Original material copyright, 1941, by
SCHOLASTIC MAGAZINE

COPYRIGHT NOTICES AND ACKNOWLEDGMENTS

Foreword

WE ALMOST called this book *The Young in Heart.* All the really important people you will meet in these twenty short stories have the spirit of adventure. Most of them are boys and girls. A few, like Young Man Axelbrod and Gran'ther Pendleton, retain the precious spark.

Young people actually chose these twenty grand short stories. They are the favorites of readers of *Scholastic Magazines*, national high school weeklies.

These stories were collected by *Scholastic's* Literary Editor, the late Ernestine Taggard, and published in a cloth-bound book called *Here We Are.* Now the adventurous young friends of these stories can be as close to you as your pocket or your pocketbook. They won't mind if you laugh with them (or at them). You can share both their triumphs and their tears. Their creators are the cream of modern American authors.

Condensation has become a great American appetite in recent years. *Scholastic* doesn't approve the appetite —doesn't encourage it. But sometimes space has demanded that the longer stories be cut to fit. Most of the stories in this representative volume are printed here as they appeared in Scholastic.

The Editors of *Scholastic Magazines*

Contents

Introduction

MY GRAY hairs are honored by being asked to write an introduction for this volume of young stories for young people. The tales are by young authors too. Half, or almost, of the excellent stories in this volume were written by people in their twenties and thirties. Pushed far back under the eaves of the attic lie the photographs which hung on the classroom walls of my school days—the venerables, bald or bearded in white, who, to the young folks of that period represented literature. That I am old enough to remember those photographs of Hawthorne, Longfellow, Whittier and Lowell, makes me a better person to write this introduction than any of the brilliant younger people whose names are in the table of contents.

For it is only set in the perspective of time that the value of such a collection of fiction for high school-age young people can be seen. One must be old enough to compare *Scholastic Magazines* with the magazine reading of adolescents forty years ago, to appreciate what it means. I'm not referring only to the fact that these are well-written tales of fine literary quality. It's not just a question of furnishing young folks with good, as well as readable, fiction. Something far more vital to our country's civilization is involved. This collection, and the five hundred tales as good as these, published in *Scholastic*, from which these were chosen, are a part of an epic change in the English teaching given to our teen-age boys and girls. A sinister barrier is being broken down which, in earlier generations, cut young people off from any notion that literary art might be a factor in their own lives, might be part of the raw material of understanding themselves and their nation.

The "classics" were the only forms of fiction recognized as literature by the school authorities of my long-ago youth. By definition a classic is a production the value of which is proved by its having passed through the sieve of public opinion and taste during several generations. Hence the subject matter of classics is the life of a period left behind in the past. It is far away from the exciting new day to which every young person opens his eyes every morning.

Fifty and forty years ago, high school-age young folks (I refer of course to the majority of them) read stories of good literary quality in order to pass their English examinations.

When they read for fun or pleasure or to be moved, they expected as a matter of course, as an inevitable result of the nature of things, to read trash, or stories which would seem very mild, superficial and childish to the mid-teens of today. The stories of college life which were written for my generation to read in the year or so before we expected to go to college would now to the keener ear of modern, pre-college-age boys and girls sound trivial, false or idiotically romantic. The stories about college life in this collection are, comparatively speaking, as rawly realistic as Zola's novels to his contemporaries. They attempt to tell something of the truth about college life. Compared to these portrayals of real human beings, struggling in college as everywhere else with material difficulties and with the complexities of human nature, the football-hero and pretty-girl romance of my youth was a shiny-paper, come-on prospectus, illustrated with posed and much retouched photographs of actors and actresses. Yet the enchantingly foolish romanticism of Saroyan's story in this collection shows that honesty in fiction does not exclude young love. We young readers could have found a poignant portrayal of early adolescent emotion such as that in "Sixteen"—and of course richer, deeper and more various—but only if we read War and Peace, which, believe me, we did not at sixteen, most of us. "Stories for young folks" always ended cheerfully in those days, with everything coming out all right for everybody. Not for us was the harsh bite of reality as in Ruth Suckow's beautiful story in this collection. This little masterpiece—for I think it no less—paints a picture as startling in its truth to each small detail of a familiar scene as a Dutch genre painting. But unspoken, implied, written between the lines with invisible ink which leaps clear and black to the eye by the end of this soberly realistic picture of a nice, every-day, ordinary, pleasant American home, is the beginning of the process of turning a whole, natural human being into a member of the "lower classes." In my youth the idea that our American democracy was not perfectly realized in every aspect was never even mildly suggested to us in any story—let alone one wringing the heart with remorseful sorrow like "A Start in Life." Publishers then expected authors to write cheerful stories with happy endings for young folks. Yet young folks were then, as now, as always, shaken to the heart by the fevers, the exaltations, despairs, joys, aspirations of adolescence. They were perfectly aware that the fairy tales written for their consumption had no connection with their own inner, or outer, lives.

Now this separation of the material of art from the stuff of daily life is the basis of the philistine attitude toward art in the most poisonous and dangerous meaning of the word. It cuts the ordinary people of the general reading public off from living art, portraying the actual life of the present; and while this is rather hard on ordinary people, it is fatal to art, for only feeble tendrils can sprout from an art-stem not rooted in acceptance by humanity.

Such a collection as this is a door cut through a stone wall which used to separate ordinary reading Americans from contemporary writing of good literary quality. People who, in their teens, have acquired the habit of getting their reading pleasure not from sentimental or sensational hokum, but from honest, vivid, thoughtful interpretations of American life and American character, cannot but form a public vastly more favorable to the development of seriously practiced literary art than were preceding generations.

The stories in this book, moving, satiric, gay, sad, romantic, realistic, the constant presentation in *Scholastic* of fiction of this quality and the work done in general by the best English teaching in our high schools—they are all milestones along a new road, undreamed of half a century ago. It leads ahead into a future, which, to my elderly eyes, looks remarkably like a golden age of writing.

And one reason I feel confident of such a golden age is that I know the kind of writing high school students themselves are capable of turning out. For years *Scholastic* has been conducting its Literary Awards—a remarkable and highly rewarding annual competition for the purpose of encouraging talent among high school students interested in creative writing. I have served as one of the judges in the short story division of the Awards and, along with the other judges, have been amazed year after year at the quality of those stories. (If you have your doubts, turn to Maureen Daly's "Sixteen" in this volume. That story won first prize in its year—and Maureen was sixteen when she wrote it!) Today these young people are reading the best that's being written; tomorrow they will write the best that's being read.

DOROTHY CANFIELD FISHER

Arlington, Vermont

A Mother in Mannville

MARJORIE KINNAN RAWLINGS

THE ORPHANAGE is high in the Carolina mountains. Sometimes in winter the snowdrifts are so deep that the institution is cut off from the village below, from all the world. Fog hides the mountain peaks, the snow swirls down the valleys, and a wind blows so bitterly that the orphanage boys who take the milk twice daily to the baby cottage reach the door with fingers stiff in an agony of numbness.

"Or when we carry trays from the cookhouse for the ones that are sick," Jerry said, "we get our faces frostbit, because we can't put our hands over them. I have gloves," he added. "Some of the boys don't have any."

He liked the late spring, he said. The rhododendron was in bloom, a carpet of color, across the mountainsides, soft as the May winds that stirred the hemlocks. He called it laurel.

"It's pretty when the laurel blooms," he said. "Some of it's pink and some of it's white."

I was there in the autumn. I wanted quiet, isolation, to do some troublesome writing. I wanted mountain air to blow out the malaria from too long a time in the subtropics. I was homesick, too, for the flaming of maples in October, and for corn shocks and pumpkins and black-walnut trees and the lift of hills. I found them all, living in a cabin that belonged to the orphanage, half a mile beyond the orphanage farm. When I took the cabin, I asked for a boy or man to come and chop wood for the fireplace. The first few days were warm, I found what wood I needed about the cabin, no one came, and I forgot the order.

I looked up from my typewriter one late afternoon, a little startled. A boy stood at the door, and my pointer dog, my companion, was at his side and had not barked to warn me. The boy was probably twelve years old, but undersized. He wore overalls and a torn shirt, and was barefooted.

He said, "I can chop some wood today."

I said, "But I have a boy coming from the orphanage."

"I'm the boy."

"You? But you're small."

1

"Size don't matter, chopping wood," he said. "Some of the big boys don't chop good. I've been chopping wood at the orphanage a long time."

I visualized mangled and inadequate branches for my fires. I was well into my work and not inclined to conversation. I was a little blunt.

"Very well. There's the ax. Go ahead and see what you can do."

I went back to work, closing the door. At first the sound of the boy dragging brush annoyed me. Then he began to chop. The blows were rhythmic and steady, and shortly I had forgotten him, the sound no more of an interruption than a consistent rain. I suppose an hour and a half passed, for when I stopped and stretched, and heard the boy's steps on the cabin stoop, the sun was dropping behind the farthest mountain, and the valleys were purple with something deeper than the asters.

The boy said, "I have to go to supper now. I can come again tomorrow evening."

I said, "I'll pay you now for what you've done," thinking I should probably have to insist on an older boy. "Ten cents an hour?"

"Anything is all right."

We went together back of the cabin. An astonishing amount of solid wood had been cut. There were cherry logs and heavy roots of rhododendron, and blocks from the waste pine and oak left from the building of the cabin.

"But you've done as much as a man," I said. "This is a splendid pile."

I looked at him, actually, for the first time. His hair was the color of the corn shocks, and his eyes, very direct, were like the mountain sky when rain is pending—gray, with a shadowing of that miraculous blue. As I spoke a light came over him, as though the setting sun had touched him with the same suffused glory with which it touched the mountains. I gave him a quarter.

"You may come tomorrow," I said, "and thank you very much."

He looked at me, and at the coin, and seemed to want to speak, but could not, and turned away.

"I'll split kindling tomorrow," he said over his thin ragged shoulder. "You'll need kindling and medium wood and logs and backlogs."

At daylight I was half wakened by the sound of chopping.

Again it was so even in texture that I went back to sleep. When I left my bed in the cool morning, the boy had come and gone, and a stack of kindling was neat against the cabin wall. He came again after school in the afternoon and worked until time to return to the orphanage. His name was Jerry; he was twelve years old, and he had been at the orphanage since he was four. I could picture him at four, with the same grave gray-blue eyes and the same—independence? No, the word that comes to me is "integrity."

The word means something very special to me, and the quality for which I use it is a rare one. My father had it— there is another of whom I am almost sure—but almost no man of my acquaintance possesses it with the clarity, the purity, the simplicity of a mountain stream. But the boy Jerry had it. It is bedded on courage, but it is more than brave. It is honest, but it is more than honesty. The ax handle broke one day. Jerry said the woodshop at the orphanage would repair it. I brought money to pay for the job and he refused it.

"I'll pay for it," he said. "I broke it. I brought the ax down careless."

"But no one hits accurately every time," I told him. "The fault was in the wood of the handle. I'll see the man from whom I bought it."

It was only then that he would take the money. He was standing back of his own carelessness. He was a free-will agent and he chose to do careful work, and if he failed, he took the responsibility without subterfuge.

And he did for me the unnecessary thing, the gracious thing, that we find done only by the great of heart. Things no training can teach, for they are done on the instant, with no predicated experience. He found a cubbyhole beside the fireplace that I had not noticed. There, of his own accord, he put kindling and "medium" wood, so that I might always have dry fire material ready in case of sudden wet weather. A stone was loose in the rough walk to the cabin. He dug a deeper hole and steadied it, although he came, himself, by a short cut over the bank. I found that when I tried to return his thoughtfulness with such things as candy and apples, he was wordless. "Thank you" was, perhaps, an expression for which he had had no use, for his courtesy was instinctive. He only looked at the gift and at me, and a curtain lifted, so that I saw deep into the clear well of his eyes, and gratitude was there, and affection, soft over the firm granite of his character.

He made simple excuses to come and sit with me. I could

no more have turned him away than if he had been physically hungry. I suggested once that the best time for us to visit was just before supper, when I left off my writing. After that, he waited always until my typewriter had been some time quiet. One day I worked until nearly dark. I went outside the cabin, having forgotten him. I saw him going up over the hill in the twilight toward the orphanage. When I sat down on my stoop, a place was warm from his body where he had been sitting.

He became intimate, of course, with my pointer, Pat. There is a strange communion between a boy and a dog. Perhaps they possess the same singleness of spirit, the same kind of wisdom. It is difficult to explain, but it exists. When I went across the state for a week-end, I left the dog in Jerry's charge. I gave him the dog whistle and the key to the cabin, and left sufficient food. He was to come two or three times a day and let out the dog, and feed and exercise him. I should return Sunday night, and Jerry would take out the dog for the last time Sunday afternoon and then leave the key under an agreed hiding place.

My return was belated and fog filled the mountain passes so treacherously that I dared not drive at night. The fog held the next morning, and it was Monday noon before I reached the cabin. The dog had been fed and cared for that morning. Jerry came early in the afternoon, anxious.

"The superintendent said nobody would drive in the fog," he said. "I came just before bedtime last night and you hadn't come. So I brought Pat some of my breakfast this morning. I wouldn't have let anything happen to him."

"I was sure of that. I didn't worry."

"When I heard about the fog, I thought you'd know."

He was needed for work at the orphanage and he had to return at once. I gave him a dollar in payment, and he looked at it and went away. But that night he came in the darkness and knocked at the door.

"Come in, Jerry," I said, "if you're allowed to be away this late."

"I told maybe a story," he said. "I told them I thought you would want to see me."

"That's true," I assured him, and I saw his relief. "I want to hear about how you managed with the dog."

He sat by the fire with me, with no other light, and told me of their two days together. The dog lay close to him, and found a comfort there that I did not have for him. And it seemed to me that being with my dog, and caring for him, had brought the boy and me, too, together, so that he felt that he belonged to me as well as to the animal.

"He stayed right with me," he told me, "except when he ran in the laurel. He likes the laurel. I took him up over the hill and we both ran fast. There was a place where the grass was high and I lay down in it and hid. I could hear Pat hunting for me. He found my trail and he barked. When he found me, he acted crazy, and he ran around and around me, in circles."

We watched the flames.

"That's an apple log," he said. "It burns the prettiest of any wood."

We were very close.

He was suddenly impelled to speak of things he had not spoken of before, nor had I cared to ask him.

"You look a little bit like my mother," he said. "Especially in the dark, by the fire."

"But you were only four, Jerry, when you came here. You have remembered how she looked, all these years?"

"My mother lives in Mannville," he said.

For a moment, finding that he had a mother shocked me as greatly as anything in my life has ever done, and I did not know why it disturbed me. Then I understood my distress. I was filled with a passionate resentment that any woman should go away and leave her son. A fresh anger added itself. A son like this one— The orphanage was a wholesome place, the executives were kind, good people, the food was more than adequate, the boys were healthy, a ragged shirt was no hardship, nor the doing of clean labor. Granted, perhaps, that the boy felt no lack, what blood fed the bowels of a woman who did not yearn over this child's lean body? At four he would have looked the same as now. Nothing, I thought, nothing in life could change those eyes. His quality must be apparent to an idiot, a fool. I burned with questions I could not ask. In any, I was afraid, there would be pain.

"Have you seen her, Jerry—lately?"

"I see her every summer. She sends for me."

I wanted to cry out. "Why are you not with her? How can she let you go away again?"

He said, "She comes up here from Mannville whenever she can. She doesn't have a job now."

His face shone in the firelight.

"She wanted to give me a puppy, but they can't let any

one boy keep a puppy. You remember the suit I had on last
Sunday?" He was plainly proud. "She sent me that for Christmas. The Christmas before that"—he drew a long breath, savoring the memory—"she sent me a pair of skates."

"Roller skates?"

My mind was busy, making pictures of her, trying to understand her. She had not, then, entirely deserted or forgotten
him. But why, then—I thought, "I must not condemn her
without knowing."

"Roller skates. I let the other boys use them. They're always borrowing them. But they're careful of them."

What circumstance other than poverty——

"I'm going to take the dollar you gave me for taking care
of Pat," he said, "and buy her a pair of gloves."

I could only say, "That will be nice. Do you know her
size?"

"I think it's eight and a half," he said.

He looked at my hands.

"Do you wear eight and a half?" he asked.

"No. I wear a smaller size, a six."

"Oh! Then I guess her hands are bigger than yours."

I hated her. Poverty or no, there was other food than bread,
and the soul could starve as quickly as the body. He was
taking his dollar to buy gloves for her big stupid hands, and
she lived away from him, in Mannville, and contented herself with sending him skates.

"She likes white gloves," he said. "Do you think I can get
them for a dollar?"

"I think so," I said.

I decided that I should not leave the mountains without
seeing her and knowing for myself why she had done this
thing.

The human mind scatters its interests as though made of
thistledown, and every wind stirs and moves it. I finished my
work. It did not please me, and I gave my thoughts to another field. I should need some Mexican material.

I made arrangements to close my Florida place. Mexico immediately, and doing the writing there, if conditions were
favorable. Then, Alaska with my brother. After that, heaven
knew what or where.

I did not take time to go to Mannville to see Jerry's mother,
nor even to talk with the orphanage officials about her. I was
a trifle abstracted about the boy, because of my work and

plans. And after my first fury at her—we did not speak of her again—his having a mother, any sort at all, not far away, in Mannville, relieved me of the ache I had had about him. He did not question the anomalous relation. He was not lonely. It was none of my concern.

He came every day and cut my wood and did small helpful favors and stayed to talk. The days had become cold, and often I let him come inside the cabin. He would lie on the floor in front of the fire, with one arm across the pointer, and they would both doze and wait quietly for me. Other days they ran with a common ecstasy through the laurel, and since the asters were now gone, he brought me back vermilion maple leaves, and chestnut boughs dripping with imperial yellow. I was ready to go.

I said to him, "You have been my good friend, Jerry. I shall often think of you and miss you. Pat will miss you too. I am leaving tomorrow."

He did not answer. When he went away, I remember that a new moon hung over the mountains, and I watched him go in silence up the hill. I expected him the next day, but he did not come. The details of packing my personal belongings, loading my car, arranging the bed over the seat, where the dog would ride, occupied me until late in the day. I closed the cabin and started the car, noticing that the sun was in the west and I should do well to be out of the mountains by nightfall. I stopped by the orphanage and left the cabin key and money for my light bill with Miss Clark.

"And will you call Jerry for me to say good-by to him?"

"I don't know where he is," she said. "I'm afraid he's not well. He didn't eat his dinner this noon. One of the boys saw him going over the hill into the laurel. He was supposed to fire the boiler this afternoon. It's not like him; he's unusually reliable."

I was almost relieved, for I knew I should never see him again, and it would be easier not to say good-by to him.

I said, "I wanted to talk with you about his mother—why he's here—but I'm in more of a hurry than I expected to be. It's out of the question for me to see her now too. But here's some money I'd like to leave with you to buy things for him at Christmas and on his birthday. It will be better than for me to try to send him things. I could so easily duplicate— skates, for instance."

She blinked her honest spinster's eyes.

"There's not much use for skates here," she said.

Her stupidity annoyed me.

"What I mean," I said, "is that I don't want to duplicate things his mother sends him. I might have chosen skates if I didn't know she had already given them to him."

She stared at me.

"I don't understand," she said. "He has no mother. He has no skates."

Without Words

ELLIOTT MERRICK

JAN MCKENZIE came over a knoll and stopped, head back, his rifle in one mitten, his ax in the other. Below him spread the river, ice-locked between the hills. A mile across, the birch bluffs were turning blue in the twilight.

He was not given to poetic fancies, for that is not the way of a Scotch-Eskimo trapper alone in the middle of Labrador. Nevertheless, it touched him always, coming out to the river after days and nights in the spruces to the east, following brooks and nameless chains of lakes that didn't lead anywhere, plowing through willow tangles and up and down wooded hills. It gave him a feeling of spaciousness, like stepping out of doors, to see the broad river again, sweeping out of sight between the hills. The river was a known thread that joined him to the nearest trapper fifty miles downstream. The river was the road to home and to his wife, Luce.

It was nine weeks now since the day in September when his canoe and the others from Turner's Harbor had swung off from the wharf and begun the upstream battle. The crowd had waved, and the double-barreled shotguns split the air in the old-time farewell, *Boomboom* . . . and a pause to load . . . *Boom*, saying, "Good-by . . . Luck." Then the trappers floating on the river in their loaded canoes raised their guns and fired one answering shot, "Luck." They picked up their paddles and disappeared around the point, to be gone five months. Sometimes, even when they'd passed around the point, and the town was lost, they could still hear the guns, *Boomboom* . . . *Boom*, like a last calling. It gave a fellow something to remember way off here where you didn't hear anything much except your own voice.

It would be pretty near three months yet before he'd be home with his fur to Luce, he was thinking as he scrambled down the bank and legged it along the ice for "the house." This cabin had a window, and a door with hinges, a good tight roof of birch bark, and, within, such luxuries as a sleeping bag, which his tiny log-tilts back in the woods had not.

It was nearly dark when he got there, but not too dark to

9

see in the cove the print of strange snowshoes. And by the point where the current flowed fast and the ice was thin, somebody had been chopping a water hole.

"Hello," he called to the cabin.

From the ridge came a silvery, mocking "hello," and faintly, seconds later, a distant hello across the river, the echo of the echo. Jan crossed the cove bent double, studying the tracks. There were three of them, a big pair of snowshoes and two smaller pairs. The smallest snowshoes had been dragging in a stick of firewood from alongshore—the women.

Jan threw off his bag and hurried into the cabin. Nobody made snowshoes of that pattern but Mathieu Su-saka-shish, the Seven Islands Indian. Nobody but Mathieu knew this cabin was here. He and his wife and daughter had come last year and begged a little tea and sugar. Now they had been here again with their Indian idea that food belongs to anybody who is hungry. Dirty dogs! Where three fifty-pound bags of flour had been hanging, only two hung now. They had dripped candle grease onto his bunk and left his big meat kettle unwashed. He dove under the bunk and pulled out his food boxes. They'd made off with some of his split peas and a few of his beans; a handful of candles too. They had sliced a big chunk of salt pork neatly down the middle.

In a frenzy of rage he ripped open his fur-bag. Every skin was there, and in addition, a black and shining otter skin lay crosswise on his bundles of mink and marten, fox and ermine. He held it up and blew the hair and felt its thickness and its length, stroking its blue-black luster. It was a prize; it would bring sixty dollars, perhaps. But the sight of it made him angrier than before.

"So!" he muttered. "Mathieu thinks one miserable skin of fur pays me for my grub, eh?" He lit a candle and his hand was trembling with rage. From now on he'd be half-hungry all the time, and hunting meat when he ought to be tending the trap line. He thought of his wife, and the blankets, and the windows, and the boat and nets and the new stove they needed at home. This was his whole year's earnings, these five months in the bush. And Mathieu thought he could steal the grub that made it possible, did he? He thought he could come every year and fit himself out, likely.

Jan took his rifle and emptied the magazine. It was only one bag of flour—but still, there were men way off here in the country who'd died for lack of a cupful, yes, a spoonful.

Slowly he reloaded with the soft-nosed cartridges he had always kept for caribou, heretofore. Would he tell Luce, would he ever be able to forget that somewhere back in the ridges, by some secret little lake that no one knew, he had shot three Indians and stuffed them through the ice? Didn't the Bible say, an eye for an eye and a tooth for a tooth?

There was bannock bread to bake and fur to be skinned. It was nearly midnight when he stoked up the stove and rolled in on the bunk for the last good sleep he expected to know for a while. At five o'clock in the starlight he was out on the river shore with a candle lantern made out of a baking-powder can, examining tracks. The polished, shallow trench which their two toboggans had left was so plain that a child could have followed it. Mathieu was ahead, taking long steps, hurrying. The two women were behind, hauling their toboggans in double harness, tandem-fashion. One of them fell and left the print of her knee going down the bank. Jay smiled as though he had seen it and heard her mutter.

He followed their tracks across the river to the top of a draw between two bare hills. There in the sunrise he turned and looked back at the ice sparkling with frost in the soft golden light, spotted with long blue shadows of the hills. As he plunged downhill into the thick country to the north he had an ominous feeling that he was leaving something. Maybe Mathieu would ambush him; it would be an easy thing to do on a track like this. Would Mathieu guess that he was being chased?

Jan studied the track, unconsciously noting every detail. Here in this book of the snow he might perhaps read Mathieu's thoughts, even a warning of an ambush. Indians were smart in the woods. Did he really think he could out-track an Indian hunter?

"By the Lord Harry, I can have a try," he whispered to himself.

Two mornings ago it was, that they passed through here under the firs, across that little brook. Two days was not much start for them. They had sleds and he had none. Mathieu had to break trail, while he had their hard frozen track to walk on. They had all their winter gear, their blankets and kettles, their tin stove and tent, traps, trout nets probably. He had nothing but the gamebag on his back, nine cakes of bread, tea and sugar, rifle and ax, a single blanket. The chances were he could travel twice as fast as they.

He passed their first fire, where they had stopped to boil tea and had thrown the tea leaves on the embers. The tea leaves were frozen stiff.

All day he swung on, parting the boughs where the spruces were thick, slipping through them as effortlessly as a weasel, trotting down all the hills with a tireless shuffle, trotting again where the way was level and open. Once he stopped for ten minutes to sit on a log and munch dry bread, light his pipe, and swing on. It was frosty, and the edges of his fur cap grew white with his breathing.

Before sunset he had long passed their first night's camp. Through the semidarkness of early twilight he pressed on, following the hardness of their track more by touch than by sight. In the starlight he made his fire and boiled tea in a ravine by a brook. Here and there a tree snapped with the frost. The brook murmured under the ice. On the western hill a horned owl was hooting.

Every hour he woke with the cold, threw on more wood, turned over and slept again. Around three o'clock he woke and could not sleep again. He sat hunched in the blanket, looking into the fire thinking what a fool he was. He should be on the trap line, not here. He had not come up the river so far away to waste time chasing Indians around the hills. Already he was hungry and wished he had brought more food. It was too bad he couldn't just shoot Mathieu, but it would be no use to leave the women to wander around and starve. At the thought of actually squeezing the trigger and seeing them drop, he shuddered.

By half-past four he had boiled his tea and eaten, and was picking his way along the track again. He should have rested another hour, he knew; it was so slow in the darkness. But he could not rest, though he was tired. He wanted to get it over with. Probably they would not bleed much; it was so cold.

The Indians were still heading northwest. Likely they were bound for the hundred-mile lake, Panchikamats, not far from the headwaters of streams that flowed into Hudson's Bay. Mathieu would feel safe there. And he would be, too. It was much farther than Jan could track him, with only three days' grub in the bag.

In the morning he passed their second night's camp. By noontime he had come to the edge of a big oval marsh that was about six miles wide at its narrowest. On its barren floor there were occasional clumps of dead sticks, juniper and fir, no higher than a man's head, the firs rotten and falling, the junipers gaunt and wind-carved. Compared to its bleak, dead savagery the greenwoods borders seemed sociable and friendly and snug. As the merciless northwest wind had stunted and killed the trees, so it could shrivel and kill a man if it caught him out there in a blizzard.

The trail was dim and wind-scoured. A mile out and there was nothing but the dully shining spots the sleds had polished; two miles out and Mathieu was veering off to the east, deviating now from his northwest course.

The marks petered out entirely, heading, at the last, straight east. If Mathieu were really heading northwest, the blue notch at the marsh's far end was the natural way for him. Then why, in the middle of the marsh, did he swing off for the steep ridges to the east?

Jan trotted about in a circle, slapping his mittens together and pounding the toes that were aching in his moccasins. The drifting snow slid by like sand, rising in little eddies as the wind rose.

He stopped and stood with his back to the wind, leaning against it. Mathieu, he figured, wanted to go through the blue notch, but it was too plain. He knew his track could be picked up there first thing. So he cut off in the middle of the marsh, thinking there'd be no mark of it left. Mathieu had just made a little circle-round, and was now right on down the valley. With the women hauling sleds, they couldn't get along in those hills. They'd have to strike the valley.

Jan picked up his gamebag and trotted off toward the now invisible notch. Lord Harry, he was hungry! In the wind he felt like singing; the wind drowned sound, sang a song of its own, saved a man from feeling that the miles of quiet woods were listening. He roared in a strong baritone:

Oh we seen the strangest sights of far-off lands,
And we conquered storm winds and stinging foam,
But the be-e-est is to see the chee-eery lights of ho-o-ome.

The drift had obscured the shores now, and he was as though alone in the middle of a white sea—snow above, below, and on all sides. But he did not think of it. The wind was compass enough for him and had been since boyhood.

He clasped his gun and ax in the crook of one elbow, put his curled mitts up around his mouth, and imitated a mouth organ, hunching up his shoulders and swinging his body, dancing on his snowshoes in the gale.

At dusk, miles beyond the blue notch, he picked up the Indians' track again. He glowed with the warmth of a hunter's pride. They'd never get away now; they were doomed, unless it snowed.

A mile farther on they had camped, and there he camped too. There was still a faint warmth in the depths of their ashes. But the sight of a bundle lashed in the low branches of a spruce made him pause. It was a hairy caribou skin, a big trout net, and a heavyish iron Dutch oven. So they were lightening loads, were they? They knew they were being tracked then. How did they know?

Jan sat on the fir brush of their tent site and thought about it. They didn't know, they couldn't know. Mathieu was just playing safe, that was all; announcing, if he should be followed, that he was still a-drivin' 'er for all he was worth, bluffing a pursuer, trying to say, "I know I am being followed"—just in case he should be followed. Mathieu would go on for a week, get his women set in a good camp, then circle back, hunting as he came, and pick up his stuff again.

That's what you think, Mathieu.

That night he ate another half a bannock, only half when he could so easily have eaten three whole ones. What a fool he was to have traveled so light. If, by some mischance, he didn't catch them now, he'd be stranded off here with nothing to eat.

Rolled in his blanket and their caribou robe, he had the best sleep yet. It was risky. He had his gun beside him. For why couldn't Mathieu come back tonight as well as in a week? All about was the ring of darkness; here was the firelight. What a perfect mark to shoot at! Yes, but Mathieu wouldn't shoot him. Why, Mathieu's father used to camp on the shore at Turner's Harbor in the summertime years ago. Mathieu's cousin used to wrestle with Jan by the hour, and Mathieu himself had been in the foot races they ran on the beach by the blue, cool bay long ago.

He sat and poked at the fire. Mathieu wouldn't shoot you, he was thinking, but you'd shoot Mathieu. Mathieu would steal his grub, but he wouldn't steal Mathieu's grub. Head in hands, he rocked to and fro, bewildered and hating this mental tangle. Oh, if Mathieu only hadn't come along at all; if only Mathieu hadn't taken a whole bag of flour, he would be so glad for Mathieu.

He settled it this way: If Mathieu wants to come along and shoot me tonight, let him, that's good luck for Mathieu, but if Mathieu doesn't, maybe Mathieu will get shot himself tomorrow night.

i

The stars paled and the east grayed the same as on other mornings. Jan did not set out until there was a little light. It would be so easy for Mathieu to wait hidden by the track.

He walked with his cap on the side, exposing one ear, and when that ear began to freeze he tilted his cap and uncovered the other. Every mile he stopped and listened, mouth open, holding his breath. Late in the forenoon as he stood examining a small valley thick with willows and boulders, he was conscious from the corner of his eye that a tuft of snow was slipping down the face of a gray boulder off to the left. Was somebody behind there? He turned and ran, dodging through the trees. Skirting the end of the willows, he stealthily approached the trail farther on. No, no one had been there. It must have been a willow twig brushing the rock in the breeze. Here were the three prints, just the three prints—Mathieu's almost indistinguishable under the women's and the sleds'. The women had given up hauling tandem. They took turns single, and when they changed places Mathieu didn't wait for them. They had to run a little to catch up, poor things. Luce could never have hauled like that.

As he tramped, he got to thinking of the otter skin Mathieu had left. It was funny the way Indian hunters would take food. They'd been hunters for so many ages they thought a bag of flour, like a caribou, was anybody's who needed it. But they wouldn't steal fur. Indians! They were like a necessary evil; they were like children. It would be better if they *did* steal fur and left the grub alone. They could pack grub as well as anybody, but they were too lazy. They let the trappers wear themselves to skin and bone struggling up the river in a canoe loaded to the gunwales, risking their lives for it in the white rapids, lugging their loads up the Great Bank, a mile long and steeper than the bridge of Satan's own nose, breaking their backs for it across twelve miles of swamps and brooks and slippery rocks on the Grand Portage where the tumplines pulled their hair out by the roots and they carried till their eyes turned black and their trembling knees sagged under them. And then—then the Indians came along and helped themselves as though flour were worth no more up here than down on the bay shore.

They won't help themselves to my grub, Jan thought grimly. Some day I'll come back to the house maybe and find it cleaned right out. And what about me, living on jay's legs and moss till I fall in the snow and die?

The sky was growing deeper gray; darkness came early. The

air was chill with a suspicion of dampness. Come a big batch
of snow to cover their track and make the walking heavy, he'd
be in a fine fix with no food. He smelled the wind and it
smelled like snow. Before dark it began to fall, and at dark he
still had not caught them. Must be getting weak, he thought
ruefully. He'd set some rabbit snares tonight. Or maybe he'd
get a partridge. And maybe he wouldn't.

He stood on the shore of a little lake and leaned against a
tree, uncertain. With the new snow and the dark, there was
only the barest sign of the track now. By morning it would be
gone. What was that sharp smell?

He threw back his head and sniffed. Wood smoke! He had
caught them. Let the snow pelt down, let it snow six feet in
the night; he had caught them and they couldn't get away.

Strange, though, that they should camp before the snow
got thick. An hour more and they would have been safe. Well,
Mathieu had made his last mistake this time.

Over a knoll in a thick clump of firs Jan built a small fire
to boil the kettle. He was ravenous, and weary to the bone.
They were camped, they would keep till he got ready for
them. And they couldn't smell his smoke with the wind this
way.

He ate the last of his bannock, drank four cups of tea, and
smoked his pipe to the last dregs. Then he left his bag and ax,
took his rifle, and stole out across the dark lake. It was black
as ink, and the new snow was like cotton wool to muffle his
steps. Just back from the far shore he saw their dome-shaped
meetchwop glimmering. They were burning a candle in there,
one of his own probably.

He crept up closer on his belly, foot by foot. The two sleds
were stuck up against a tree; there was the chopping block,
the ax, the chips. Snowshoes were hanging from a limb, the
two small pairs. The women inside were baking bread. He
could hear the frying pan scrape on the tin stove. They were
talking in their soft, musical voices, more like a brook under
the ice than like human talk. They weren't hardly human
anyway. But he could not bring himself to walk into the tent
and shoot them in cold blood. Better get Mathieu first. But
where were the big snowshoes—where was Mathieu? Behind
that black tree there with his rifle cocked?

He lay silent, scarcely breathing, ears stretched for the
slightest sound. There were only the wind and the falling
snow and the women's voices and the scraping pan.

Fifteen minutes, a half-hour, he lay thus.

He was freezing, he couldn't lie there all night. Inch by inch he crawled away. Silent as a shadow, he went back across the lake. There was danger everywhere now, every time he moved a muscle. He could feel it all around him, feel a prickling in his scalp and a supernatural certainty that as he was stalking Mathieu, Mathieu was stalking him. Cautiously, with long waits, he approached his camp. The fire was out. His fingers touched the gamebag, and drew back. Something was there, something that shouldn't be! *Something was wrong.* Chills went up and down his spine. He whirled toward a deeper patch of shadow, knowing with the certainty of panic that gunfire would belch from that shadow and blind him. His eyes roamed round in his head in the darkness and he waited, turned to stone.

There was no sound. Nothing but the soft hiss of the snow-flakes drifting down.

Then he smelled it. Bread, new-baked bread, sweet as life to his nostrils. He drew off his mitten and touched the game-bag again. His fingers counted them—seven crusty bannock cakes, still warm.

"Mathieu," he whispered to the engulfing darkness. There was no answer. He struck a match and looked at the cakes. He bit one, and shook his head, ashamed. All his muscles sagged as he slumped into the snow and took a deep, deep breath—the first, it seemed, in many days.

Everything was different now. Noisily he crashed down a big tree for his night's fire. He was sticking up a lean-to by the fireplace, he was chilled by the night's cold, not by the cold horror of that other unthinkable job. Lord, he'd rather Mathieu plugged him full of holes than to take a sight on Mathieu. It was like waking up from a nightmare. He had half a mind to go across the lake now and ask Mathieu's woman to sew up the tear in his britches, and have a good sleep in the Indians' warm tent. How they would giggle and talk with their black eyes!

But he was too ashamed. Mathieu was a better man than he was, that was all—smarter in the woods and more forgiving. I wouldn't forgive Mathieu, he mused, for taking a bag of flour, but he forgives me for trying to kill him. All the time the snow's coming down and he only had to go on a little piece farther tonight to lose me. He knows that, but he takes a chance and sneaks back to feed me, me that's chasing him to kill him. Mathieu don't want I should starve going back to the river. Mathieu—he don't want us to part unfriendly.

Lord, it beat all. If ever he told this to Luce she'd say he was the head liar out of all the liars on the whole river.

He finished one of the fragrant, tender bread cakes and lay down with his back to the fire. It was a long time since he'd felt so happy. Wonderful strange too, how much he and Mathieu had said to each other without words, way off here, never meeting, eating each other's grub.

Toward morning the snow stopped. Just after sunrise the Indian family broke camp and climbed the hill up from the shore. Jan, watching from the opposite hill across the lake, saw them silhouetted, three dark figures on the bare ridge. He pointed his gun at a tree top and let go greeting. Boom-boom . . . Boom. He saw the two women, startled, duck behind their sled.

But Mathieu stood erect against the brightening sky. He raised his rifle and fired one answering shot.

So they stood for a moment, on opposite hills, with up-raised hand. *Good-by. Luck.*

Her feet were the same size as Garbo's

Sixteen

MAUREEN DALY

Now DON'T get me wrong. I mean, I want you to understand
from the beginning that I'm not really so dumb. I know what
a girl should do and what she shouldn't. I get around. I read.
I listen to the radio. And I have two older sisters. So you see,
I know what the score is. I know it's smart to wear tweedish
skirts and shaggy sweaters with the sleeves pushed up and
pearls and ankle-socks and saddle shoes that look as if they've
seen the world. And I know that your hair should be long,
almost to your shoulders, and sleek as a wet seal, just a little
fluffed on the ends, and you should wear a campus hat or a
dink or else a peasant hankie if you've that sort of face.
Properly, a peasant hankie should make you think of edel-
weiss, mist and sunny mountains, yodeling and Swiss cheese.
You know, that kind of peasant. Now, me, I never wear a
hankie. It makes my face seem wide and Slavic and I look
like a picture always in one of those magazine articles that
run—"And Stalin says the future of Russia lies in its women.
In its women who have tilled its soil, raised its children—"
Well, anyway. I'm not exactly too small-town either. I read
Winchell's column. You get to know what New York boy is
that way about some pineapple princess on the West Coast
and what Paradise pretty is currently the prettiest, and why
someone, eventually, will play Scarlett O'Hara. It gives you
that cosmopolitan feeling. And I know that anyone who
orders a strawberry sundae in a drugstore instead of a lemon
coke would probably be dumb enough to wear colored ankle-
socks with high-heeled pumps or use Evening in Paris with
a tweed suit. But I'm sort of drifting. This isn't what I wanted
to tell you. I just wanted to give you the general idea of
how I'm not so dumb. It's important that you understand
that.

You see, it was funny how I met him. It was a winter night
like any other winter night. And I didn't have my Latin done
either. But the way the moon tinseled the twigs and silver-
plated the snow drifts, I just couldn't stay inside. The skating
rink isn't far from our house—you can make it in five minutes

19

if the sidewalks aren't slippery, so I went skating. I remember it took me a long time to get ready that night because I had to darn my skating socks first. I don't know why they always wear out so fast—just in the toes, too. Maybe it's because I have metal protectors on the toes of my skates. That probably is why. And then I brushed my hair—hard, so hard it clung to my hand and stood up around my head in a hazy halo.

My skates were hanging by the back door all nice and shiny, for I'd just gotten them for Christmas and they smelled so queer—just like fresh-smoked ham. My dog walked with me as far as the corner. She's a red chow, very polite and well-mannered, and she kept pretending it was me she liked when all the time I knew it was the ham smell. She panted along beside me and her hot breath made a frosty little balloon balancing on the end of her nose. My skates thumped me good-naturedly on the back as I walked and the night was breathlessly quiet and the stars winked down like a million flirting eyes. It was all so lovely.

It was all so lovely I ran most of the way and it was lucky the sidewalks had ashes on them or I'd have slipped surely. The ashes crunched like crackerjack and I could feel their cindery shape through the thinness of my shoes. I always wear old shoes when I go skating.

I had to cut across someone's back garden to get to the rink and last summer's grass stuck through the thin ice, brown and discouraged. Not many people came through this way and the crusted snow broke through the little hollows between corn stubbles frozen hard in the ground. I was out of breath when I got to the shanty—out of breath with running and with the loveliness of the night. Shanties are always such friendly places. The floor all hacked to wet splinters from skate runners and the wooden wall frescoed with symbols of dead romance. There was a smell of singed wool as someone got too near the glowing isinglass grid of the iron stove. Girls burst through the door laughing with snow on their hair and tripped over shoes scattered on the floor. A pimply-faced boy grabbed the hat from the frizzled head of an eighth-grade blonde and stuffed it into an empty galosh to prove his love and then hastily bent to examine his skate strap with innocent unconcern.

It didn't take me long to get my own skates on and I stuck my shoes under the bench—far back where they wouldn't get knocked around and would be easy to find when I wanted to go home. I walked out on my toes and the shiny runners of my new skates dug deep into the sodden floor.

It was snowing a little outside—quick, eager little Lux-like flakes that melted as soon as they touched your hand. I don't know where the snow came from for there were stars out. Or maybe the stars were in my eyes and I just kept seeing them every time I looked up into the darkness. I waited a moment. You know, to start to skate at a crowded rink is like jumping on a moving merry-go-round. The skaters go skimming round in a colored blur like gaudy painted horses and the shrill musical jabber reechoes in the night from a hundred human calliopes. Once in, I went all right. At least, after I found out exactly where that rough ice was. It was "round, round, jump the rut, round, round, round, jump the rut, round, round—"

And then he came. All of a sudden his arm was around my waist so warm and tight and he said very casually, "Mind if I skate with you?" and then he took my other hand. That's all there was to it. Just that and then we were skating. It wasn't that I'd never skated with a boy before. Don't be silly. I told you before I get around. But this was different. He was a smoothie! He was a big shot up at school and he went to all the big dances and he was the best dancer in town except Harold Wright who didn't count because he'd been to college in New York for two years! Don't you see? This was different.

At first I can't remember what we talked about, I can't even remember if we talked at all. We just skated and skated and laughed every time we came to that rough spot and pretty soon we were laughing all the time at nothing at all. It was all so lovely.

Then we sat on the big snow bank at the edge of the rink and just watched. It was cold at first even with my skating pants on, sitting on that hard heap of snow, but pretty soon I got warm all over. He threw a handful of snow at me and it fell in a little white shower on my hair and he leaned over to brush it off. I held my breath. The night stood still.

The moon hung just over the warming shanty like a big quarterslice of muskmelon and the smoke from the pipe chimney floated up in a sooty fog. One by one the houses around the rink twinked out their lights and somebody's hound wailed a mournful apology to a star as he curled up for the night. It was all so lovely.

Then he sat up straight and said, "We'd better start home." Not "Shall I take you home?" or "Do you live far?" but "We'd better start home." See, that's how I know he wanted to take

me home. Not because he *had* to but because he *wanted* to.
He went to the shanty to get my shoes. "Black ones," I told
him. "Same size as Garbo's." And laughed again. He was still
smiling when he came back and took off my skates and tied
the wet skate strings in a soggy knot and put them over his
shoulder. Then he held out his hand and I slid off the snow
bank and brushed off the seat of my pants and we were ready.

It was snowing harder now. Big, quiet flakes that clung to
twiggy bushes and snuggled in little drifts against the tree
trunks. The night was an etching in black and white. It was
all so lovely I was sorry I lived only a few blocks away. He
talked softly as we walked as if every little word were a secret.
"Did I like Wayne King, and did I plan to go to college next
year and had I a cousin who lived in Appleton and knew his
brother?" A very respectable Emily Post sort of conversation,
and then finally—"how nice I looked with snow in my hair
and had I ever seen the moon so—close?" For the moon was
following us as we walked and ducking playfully behind a
chimney every time I turned to look at it. And then we were
home.

The porch light was on. My mother always puts the porch
light on when I go away at night. And we stood there a moment by the front steps and the snow turned pinkish in the
glow of the colored light and a few feathery flakes settled on
his hair. Then he took my skates and put them over my
shoulder and said, "Good night now. I'll call you," he said.

I went inside then and in a moment he was gone. I watched
him from my window as he went down the street. He was
whistling softly and I waited until the sound faded away so I
couldn't tell if it was he or my heart whistling out there in
the night. And then he was gone, completely gone.

I shivered. Somehow the darkness seemed changed. The
stars were little hard chips of light far up in the sky and the
moon stared down with a sullen yellow glare. The air was
tense with sudden cold and a gust of wind swirled his foot-
prints into white oblivion. Everything was quiet.

But he'd said, "I'll call you." That's what he said, "I'll call
you." I couldn't sleep all night.

And that was last Thursday. Tonight is Tuesday. Tonight
is Tuesday and my homework's done, and I darned some
stockings that didn't really need it, and I worked a cross-word
puzzle, and I listened to the radio and now I'm just sitting.
I'm just sitting because I can't think of anything else to do.
I can't think of anything, anything but snowflakes and ice

skates and yellow moons and Thursday night. The telephone is sitting on the corner table with its old black face turned to the wall so I can't see its leer. I don't even jump when it rings any more. My heart still prays but my mind just laughs. Outside the night is still, so still I think I'll go crazy and the white snow's all dirtied and smoked into grayness and the wind is blowing the arc light so it throws weird, waving shadows from the trees onto the lawn—like thin, starved arms begging for I don't know what. And so I'm just sitting here and I'm not feeling anything, I'm not even sad because all of a sudden I know. I can sit here now forever and laugh and laugh while the tears run salty in the corners of my mouth. For all of a sudden I know, I know what the stars knew all the time—he'll never, never call—never.

Split Cherry Tree

JESSE STUART

I DON'T mind staying after school," I says to Professor Herbert, "but I'd rather you'd whip me with a switch and let me go home early. Pa will whip me anyway for getting home two hours late."

"You are too big to whip," says Professor Herbert, "and I have to punish you for climbing up in that cherry tree. You boys knew better than that! The other five boys have paid their dollar each. You have been the only one who has not helped pay for the tree. Can't you borrow a dollar?"

"I can't," I says. "I'll have to take the punishment. I wish it would be quicker punishment. I wouldn't mind."

Professor Herbert stood and looked at me. He was a big man. He wore a gray suit of clothes. The suit matched his gray hair.

"You don't know my father," I says to Professor Herbert. "He might be called a little old-fashioned. He makes us mind him until we're twenty-one years old. He believes: 'If you spare the rod you spoil the child.' I'll never be able to make him understand about the cherry tree. I'm the first of my people to go to high school."

"You must take the punishment," says Professor Herbert. "You must stay two hours after school today and two hours after school tomorrow. I am allowing you twenty-five cents an hour. That is good money for a high school student. You can sweep the schoolhouse floor, wash the blackboards and clean windows. I'll pay the dollar for you."

I couldn't ask Professor Herbert to loan me a dollar. He never offered to loan it to me. I had to stay and help the janitor and work out my fine at a quarter an hour.

I thought as I swept the floor: "What will Pa do to me? What lie can I tell him when I go home? Why did we ever climb that cherry tree and break it down for anyway? Why did we run crazy over the hills away from the crowd? Why did we do all of this? Six of us climbed up in a little cherry tree after one little lizard! Why did the tree split and fall with

24

us? It should have been a stronger tree! Why did Eif Crabtree just happen to be below us plowing and catch us in his cherry tree? Why wasn't he a better man than to charge us six dollars for the tree?"

It was six o'clock when I left the schoolhouse. I had six miles to walk home. It would be after seven when I got home. I had all my work to do when I got home. It took Pa and me both to do the work. Seven cows to milk. Nineteen head of cattle to feed, four mules, twenty-five hogs. Firewood and stovewood to cut and water to draw from the well. He would be doing it when I got home. He would be mad and wondering what was keeping me!

I hurried home. I would run under the dark leafless trees. I would walk fast uphill. I would run down the hill. The ground was freezing. I had to hurry. I had to run. I reached the long ridge that led to our cow pasture. I ran along this ridge. The wind dried the sweat on my face. I ran across the pasture to the house.

I threw down my books in the chipyard. I ran to the barn to spread fodder on the ground for the cattle. I didn't take time to change my clean school clothes for my old work clothes. I ran out to the barn. I saw Pa spreading fodder on the ground to the cattle. That was my job. I ran up to the fence. I says: "Leave that for me, Pa. I'll do it. I'm just a little late."

"I see you are," says Pa. He turned and looked at me. His eyes danced fire. "What in th' world has kept you so? Why ain't you been here to help me with this work? Make a gentleman out'n one boy in th' family and this is what you get! Send you to high school and you get too onery fer th' buzzards to smell!"

I never said anything. I didn't want to tell why I was late from school. Pa stopped scattering the bundles of fodder. He looked at me. He says: "Why are you gettin' in here this time o' night? You tell me or I'll take a hickory withe to you right here on th' spot!"

I says: "I had to stay after school." I couldn't lie to Pa. He'd go to school and find out why I had to stay. If I lied to him it would be too bad for me.

"Why did you haf to stay atter school?" says Pa.

I says: "Our biology class went on a field trip today. Six of us boys broke down a cherry tree. We had to give a dollar apiece to pay for the tree. I didn't have the dollar. Professor

Herbert is making me work out my dollar. He gives me twenty-five cents an hour. I had to stay in this afternoon. I'll have to stay in tomorrow afternoon!"

"Are you telling me th' truth?" says Pa.

"I'm telling you the truth," I says. "Go and see for yourself."

"That's just what I'll do in th' mornin'," says Pa. "Jist whose cherry tree did you break down?"

"Eif Crabtree's cherry tree!"

"What was you doin' clear out in Eif Crabtree's place?" says Pa. "He lives four miles from th' County High School. Don't they teach you no books at that high school? Do they jist let you get out and gad over th' hillsides? If that's all they do I'll keep you at home, Dave. I've got work here fer you to do!"

"Pa," I says, "spring is just getting here. We take a subject in school where we have to have bugs, snakes, flowers, lizards, frogs and plants. It is biology. It was a pretty day today. We went out to find a few of these. Six of us boys saw a lizard at the same time sunning on a cherry tree. We all went up the tree to get it. We broke the tree down. It split at the forks. Eif Crabtree was plowing down below us. He ran up the hill and got our names. The other boys gave their dollar apiece. I didn't have mine. Professor Herbert put mine in for me. I have to work it out at school."

"Poor man's son, huh," says Pa. "I'll attend to that myself in th' mornin'. I'll take keer o' 'im. He ain't from this county nohow. I'll go down there in th' mornin' and see 'im. Lettin' you leave your books and galavant all over th' hills. What kind of a school is it nohow! Didn't do that, my son, when I's a little shaver in school. All fared alike too."

"Pa, please don't go down there," I says. "Just let me have fifty cents and pay the rest of my fine. I don't want you to go down there! I don't want you to start anything with Professor Herbert!"

"Ashamed of your old Pap, are you, Dave," says Pa, "atter the way I've worked to raise you! Tryin' to send you to school so you can make a better livin' than I've made."

I thought once I'd run through the woods above the barn just as hard as I could go. I thought I'd leave high school and home forever! Pa could not catch me! I'd get away! I couldn't go back to school with him. He'd have a gun and maybe he'd shoot Professor Herbert. It was hard to tell what he would do. I could tell Pa that school had changed in the hills from the way it was when he was a boy, but he wouldn't understand. I could tell him we studied frogs, birds, snakes, lizards, flowers, insects. But Pa wouldn't understand. If I did run away from home it wouldn't matter to Pa. He would see Professor Herbert anyway. He would think that high school and Professor Herbert had run me away from home. There was no need to run away. I'd just have to stay, finish foddering the cattle and go to school with Pa the next morning.

The moon shone bright in the cold March sky. I finished my work by moonlight. Professor Herbert really didn't know how much work I had to do at home. If he had known he would not have kept me after school. He would have loaned me a dollar to have paid my part on the cherry tree. He had never lived in the hills. He didn't know the way the hill boys had to work so that they could go to school. Now he was teaching in a County High School where all the boys who attended were from hill farms.

After I'd finished doing my work I went to the house and ate my supper. Pa and Mom had eaten. My supper was getting cold. I heard Pa and Mom talking in the front room. Pa was telling Mom about me staying in after school.

"I had to do all th' milkin' tonight, chop th' wood myself. It's too hard on me atter I've turned ground all day. I'm goin' to take a day off tomorrow and see if I can't remedy things a little. I'll go down to that high school tomorrow. I won't be a very good scholar fer Professor Herbert nohow. He won't keep me in atter school. I'll take a different kind of lesson down there and make 'im acquainted with it."

"Now, Luster," says Mom, "you jist stay away from there. Don't cause a lot o' trouble. You can be jailed fer a trick like that. You'll get th' Law atter you. You'll jist go down there and show off and plague your own boy Dave to death in front o' all th' scholars!"

"Plague or no plague," says Pa, "he don't take into consideration what all I haf to do here, does he? I'll show 'im it ain't right to keep one boy in and let the rest go scot-free. My boy is good as th' rest, ain't he? A bullet will make a hole in a schoolteacher same as it will anybody else. He can't do me that way and get by with it. I'll plug 'im first. I aim to go down there bright and early in the mo nin' and get all this straight! I aim to see about bug larnin' and this runnin' all over God's creation huntin' snakes, lizards, and frogs. Ransackin' th' country and goin' through cherry orchards and breakin' th' trees down atter lizards! Old Eif Crabtree ought to a-poured th' hot lead into 'em instead o' chargin' six dollars fer th' tree! He ought to a-got old Herbert the first one!"

I ate my supper. I slipped upstairs and lit the lamp. I tried to forget the whole thing. I studied plane geometry. Then I studied my biology lesson. I could hardly study for thinking about Pa. "He'll go to school with me in the morning. He'll take a gun for Professor Herbert! What will Professor Herbert think of me! I'll tell him when Pa leaves that I couldn't help it. But Pa might shoot him. I hate to go with Pa. Maybe he'll cool off about it tonight and not go in the morning."

Pa got up at four o'clock. He built a fire in the stove. Then he built a fire in the fireplace. He got Mom up to get breakfast. Then he got me up to help feed and milk. By the time we had our work done at the barn, Mom had breakfast ready for us. We ate our breakfast. Daylight came and we could see the bare oak trees covered white with frost. The hills were white with frost.

"Now, Dave," says Pa, "let's get ready fer school. I aim to go with you this mornin' and look into bug larnin', frog larnin', lizard and snake larnin' and breakin' down cherry trees! I don't like no sicha foolish way o' larnin' myself!"

Pa hadn't forgot. I'd have to take him to school with me. He would take me to school with him. I was glad we were going early. If Pa pulled a gun on Professor Herbert there wouldn't be so many of my classmates there to see him.

I knew that Pa wouldn't be at home in the high school. He wore overalls, big boots, a blue shirt and a sheepskin coat and a slouched black hat gone to seed at the top. He put his gun in its holster. We started trudging toward the high school across the hill.

It was early when we got to the County High School. Professor Herbert had just got there. I just thought as we walked up the steps into the schoolhouse: "Maybe Pa will find out Professor Herbert is a good man. He just doesn't know him. Just like I felt toward the Lambert boys across the hill. I didn't like them until I'd seen them and talked to them, then I liked them and we were friends. It's a lot in knowing the other fellow."

"You're th' Professor here, ain't you?" says Pa.

"Yes," says Professor Herbert, "and you are Dave's father?"

"Yes," says Pa, pulling out his gun and laying it on the seat in Professor Herbert's office. Professor Herbert's eyes got big behind his black-rimmed glasses when he saw Pa's gun. Color came into his pale cheeks.

"Jist a few things about this school I want to know," says Pa. "I'm tryin' to make a scholar out'n Dave. He's the only one out'n eleven youngins I've sent to high school. Here he comes in late and leaves me all th' work to do! He said you's all out bug huntin' yesterday and broke a cherry tree down. He had to stay two hours atter school yesterday and work out money to pay on that cherry tree! Is that right?"

"W-w-why," says Professor Herbert, "I guess it is."

He looked at Pa's gun.

"Well," says Pa, "this ain't no high school. It's a damn bug school, a lizard school, a snake school! It ain't no damn school nohow!"

"Why did you bring that gun?" says Professor Herbert to Pa.

"You see that little hole," says Pa as he picked up the long blue forty-four and put his finger on the end of the barrel. "A bullet can come out'n that hole that will kill a school-teacher same as it will any other man. It will kill a rich man same as a poor man. It will kill a man. But atter I come in and saw you, I know'd I wouldn't need it. This maul o' mine could do you up in a few minutes."

Pa stood there, big, hard, brown-skinned and mighty beside of Professor Herbert. I didn't know Pa was so much bigger and harder. I'd never seen Pa in a schoolhouse before. I'd seen Professor Herbert. He always looked big before to me. He didn't look big standing beside of Pa.

"I was only doing my duty," says Professor Herbert, "Mr. Sexton, and following the course of study the state provided us with."

"Course o' study!" says Pa. "What study? Bug study? Varmint study? Takin' youngins to th' woods. Boys and girls all out there together a-galavantin' in the brush and kickin' up their heels and their poor old Ma's and Pa's at home a-slavin' to keep 'em in school and give 'em a education!"

Students are coming into the schoolhouse now. Professor Herbert says: "Close the door, Dave, so others won't hear."

I walked over and closed the door. I was shaking like a leaf in the wind. I thought Pa was going to hit Professor Herbert every minute. He was doing all the talking. His face was getting red. The red color was coming through the brown, weather-beaten skin on Pa's face.

"It jist don't look good to me," says Pa, "a-takin' all this swarm of youngins out to pillage th' whole deestrict. Breakin' down cherry trees. Keepin' boys in atter school."

"What else could I have done with Dave, Mr. Sexton?" says Professor Herbert. "The boys didn't have any business all climbing that cherry tree after one lizard. One boy could have gone up the tree and got it. The farmer charged us six dollars. It was a little steep, I think, but we had it to pay. Must I make five boys pay and let your boy off? He said he didn't have the dollar and couldn't get it. So I put it in for him. I'm letting him work it out. He's not working for me. He's working for the school!"

"I jist don't know what you could a-done with 'im," says Pa, "only a-larruped 'im with a withe! That's what he needed!"

"He's too big to whip," says Professor Herbert, pointing at me. "He's a man in size."

"He's not too big fer me to whip," says Pa. "They ain't too big until they're over twenty-one! It jist didn't look fair to me! Work one and let th' rest out because they got th' money. I don't see what bugs has got to do with a high school! It don't look good to me nohow!"

Pa picked up his gun and put it back in its holster. The red color left Professor Herbert's face. He talked more to Pa. Pa softened a little. It looked funny to see Pa in the high school building. It was the first time he'd ever been there.

"We're not only hunting snakes, toads, flowers, butterflies, lizards," says Professor Herbert, "but, Mr. Sexton, I was hunting dry timothy grass to put in an incubator and raise some protozoa."

"I don't know what that is," says Pa. "Th' incubator is th' new-fangled way o' cheatin' th' hens and raisin' chickens. I ain't so sure about th' breed o' chickens you mentioned."

"You've heard of germs, Mr. Sexton, haven't you?" says Professor Herbert.

"Jist call me Luster if you don't mind," says Pa, very casual like.

"All right, Luster, you've heard of germs, haven't you?"

"Yes," says Pa, "but I don't believe in germs. I'm sixty-five years old and I ain't seen one yet!"

"You can't see them with your naked eye," says Professor Herbert. "Just keep that gun in the holster and stay with me in the high school today. I have a few things I want to show you. That scum on your teeth has germs in it."

"What," says Pa, "you mean to tell me I've got germs on my teeth!"

"Yes," says Professor Herbert. "The same kind as we might be able to find in a living black snake if we dissect it!"

"I don't mean to dispute your word," says Pa, "but damned if I believe it. I don't believe I have germs on my teeth!"

"Stay with me today and I'll show you. I want to take you through the school anyway. School has changed a lot in the hills since you went to school. I don't guess we had high schools in this county when you went to school."

"No," says Pa, "jist readin', writin' and cipherin'. We didn't have all this bug larnin', and findin' germs on your teeth and in the middle o' black snakes! Th' world's changin'."

"It is," says Professor Herbert, "and we hope all for the better. Boys like your own there are going to help change it. He's your boy. He knows all of what I've told you. You stay with me today."

"I'll shore stay with you," says Pa. "I want to see th' germs off'n my teeth. I jist want to see a germ. I've never seen one in my life. 'Seein' is believin',' Pap allus told me."

Pa walks out of the office with Professor Herbert. I just hoped Professor Herbert didn't have Pa arrested for pulling his gun. Pa's gun has always been a friend to him when he goes to settle disputes.

The bell rang. School took up. I saw the students when they marched in the schoolhouse look at Pa. They would grin and punch each other. Pa just stood and watched them pass in at the schoolhouse door. Two long lines marched in the house. The boys and girls were clean and well dressed. Pa stood over in the schoolyard under a leafless elm, in his sheepskin coat, his big boots laced in front with buckskin and his heavy socks stuck above his boot tops. Pa's overalls legs were baggy and wrinkled between his coat and boot tops. His blue work shirt showed at the collar. His big black hat showed his gray-streaked black hair. His face was hard and weathertanned to the color of a ripe fodder blade. His hands were big and gnarled like the roots of the elm tree he stood beside.

When I went to my first class I saw Pa and Professor Herbert going around over the schoolhouse. I was in my geometry class when Pa and Professor Herbert came in the room. We were explaining our propositions on the blackboard. Professor Herbert and Pa just quietly came in and sat down for awhile. I heard Fred Wurts whisper to Glenn Armstrong: "Who is that old man? Lord, he's a rough-looking scamp." Glenn whispered back: "I think he's Dave's Pap." The students in geometry looked at Pa. They must have wondered what he was doing in school. Before the class was over, Pa and Professor Herbert got up and went out. I saw them together down

on the playground. Professor Herbert was explaining to Pa.
I could see the outline of Pa's gun under his coat when he'd
walk around.

At noon in the high school cafeteria Pa and Professor Herbert sat together at the little table where Professor Herbert
always ate by himself. They ate together. The students
watched the way Pa ate. He ate with his knife instead of his
fork. A lot of the students felt sorry for me after they found
out he was my father. They didn't have to feel sorry for me.
I wasn't ashamed of Pa after I found out he wasn't going to
shoot Professor Herbert. I was glad they had made friends. I
wasn't ashamed of Pa. I wouldn't be as long as he behaved.

In the afternoon when we went to biology Pa was in the
class. He was sitting on one of the high stools beside the
microscope. We went ahead with our work just as if Pa
wasn't in the class. I saw Pa take his knife and scrape tartar
from one of his teeth. Professor Herbert put it under the lens
and adjusted the microscope for Pa. He adjusted it and worked
awhile. Then he says: "Now, Luster, look! Put your eye right
down to the light. Squint the other eye!"

Pa put his head down and did as Professor Herbert said:
"I see 'im," says Pa. "Who'd a ever thought that? Right on
a body's teeth! Right in a body's mouth! You're right certain
they ain't no fake to this, Professor Herbert?"

"No, Luster," says Professor Herbert. "It's there. That's
the germ. Germs live in a world we cannot see with the naked
eye. We must use the microscope. There are millions of them
in our bodies. Some are harmful. Others are helpful."

Pa holds his face down and looks through the microscope.
We stop and watch Pa. He sits upon the tall stool. His knees
are against the table. His legs are long. His coat slips up behind when he bends over. The handle of his gun shows. Professor Herbert quickly pulls his coat down.

"Oh, yes," says Pa. He gets up and pulls his coat down.
Pa's face gets a little red. He knows about his gun and he
knows he doesn't have any use for it in high school.

"We have a big black snake over here we caught yesterday,"
says Professor Herbert. "We'll chloroform him and dissect
him and show you he has germs in his body too."

"Don't do it," says Pa. "I believe you. I jist don't want to
see you kill the black snake. I never kill one. They are good
mousers and a lot o' help to us on the farm. I like black snakes.
I jist hate to see people kill 'em. I don't allow 'em killed on
my place."

The students look at Pa. They seem to like him better after he said that. Pa with a gun in his pocket but a tender heart beneath his ribs for snakes, but not for man! Pa won't whip a mule at home. He won't whip his cattle.

Professor Herbert took Pa through the laboratory. He showed him the different kinds of work we were doing. He showed him our equipment. They stood and talked while we worked. Then they walked out together. They talked louder when they got out in the hall.

When our biology class was over I walked out of the room. It was our last class for the day. I would have to take my broom and sweep two hours to finish paying for the split cherry tree. I just wondered if Pa would want me to stay. He was standing in the hallway watching the students march out. He looked lost among us. He looked like a leaf turned brown on the tree among the tree top filled with growing leaves.

I got my broom and started to sweep. Professor Herbert walked up and says: "I'm going to let you do that some other time. You can go home with your father. He is waiting out there."

I laid my broom down, got my books, and went down the steps.

Pa says: "Ain't you got two hours o' sweepin' yet to do?"

I says: "Professor Herbert said I could do it some other time. He said for me to go home with you."

"No," says Pa. "You are goin' to do as he says. He's a good man. School has changed from my day and time. I'm a dead leaf, Dave. I'm behind. I don't belong here. If he'll let me I'll get a broom and we'll both sweep one hour. That pays your debt. I'll help you pay it. I'll ast 'im and see if he won't let me hep you."

"I'm going to cancel the debt," says Professor Herbert. "I just wanted you to understand, Luster."

"I understand," says Pa, "and since I understand he must pay his debt fer th' tree and I'm goin' to hep him."

"Don't do that," says Professor Herbert. "It's all on me."

"We don't do things like that," says Pa; "we're just and honest people. We don't want somethin' fer nothin'. Professor Herbert, you're wrong now and I'm right. You'll haf to listen to me. I've larned a lot from you. My boy must go on. Th' world has left me. It changed while I've raised my family and plowed th' hills. I'm a just and honest man. I don't skip debts. I ain't larned 'em to do that. I ain't got much larnin' myself but I do know right from wrong atter I see through a thing."

Professor Herbert went home. Pa and I stayed and swept one hour. It looked funny to see Pa use a broom. He never used one at home. Mom used the broom. Pa used the plow. Pa did hard work. Pa says: "I can't sweep. Durned if I can. Look at th' streaks o' dirt I leave on th' floor! Seems like no work a-tall fer me. Brooms is too light 'r somethin'. I'll jist do th' best I can, Dave. I've been wrong about th' school."

I says: "Did you know Professor Herbert can get a warrant out for you for bringing your pistol to school and showing it in his office! They can railroad you for that!"

"That's all made right," says Pa. "I've made that right. Professor Herbert ain't goin' to take it to court. He likes me. I like 'im. We jist had to get together. He had the remedies. He showed me. You must go on to school. I am as strong a man as ever come out'n th' hills fer my years and th' hard work I've done. But I'm behind, Dave. I'm a little man. Your hands will be softer than mine. Your clothes will be better. You'll allus look cleaner than your old Pap. Jist remember, Dave, to pay your debts and be honest. Jist be kind to animals and don't bother th' snakes. That's all I got agin th' school. Puttin' black snakes to sleep and cuttin' 'em open."

It was late when we got home. Stars were in the sky. The moon was up. The ground was frozen. Pa took his time going home. I couldn't run like I did the night before. It was ten o'clock before we got the work finished, our suppers eaten. Pa sat before the fire and told Mom he was going to take her and show her a germ some time. Mom hadn't seen one either. Pa told her about the high school and the fine man Professor Herbert was. He told Mom about the strange school across the hill and how different it was from the school in their day and time.

After the Ball

SALLY BENSON

No ONE could have guessed her age seeing her drive around town in the cream-colored convertible coupe, its top down. She drove carelessly; one hand resting casually on the wheel. Her lipstick matched her nails and blended with the color of her dress; rust polish with green, red and white, or brown, rose with pastel shades. She was perfect from her smart well-fitting sandals to her seemingly endless supply of small felts. Her manner was perfect, too. She spoke in a tired, low-pitched voice, and she looked at the person she was addressing as though he were very, very far away. Every morning when she strolled in Osborne's Market, she created something of a sensation. The two boys who sold fruit and vegetables simply stared and even old Mr. Osborne who had, as he put it, "seen hundreds of them come and go," was impressed and suggested filet mignon or a nice rib roast, feeling vaguely that chopped round steak or shoulder lamb for stewing was out of the question.

She might have been Joan Crawford, Myrna Loy, or the pampered daughter of a millionaire, home from a winter on the Riviera. She might have been anyone romantic and exciting. But her name was Norma Martin and she was sixteen years old. In her smart little bag with her lipstick and compact was her first driver's license.

She was not the same Norma Martin who had recently been graduated from a school for girls. Her hockey stick had been left to warp in the hall closet at home; her plain white underthings with their name tapes lay packed in a trunk in the attic; her school books had been sold to a child who still believed that being a senior was all that Life could hold. For the Norma Martin summering at Pine Bluffs, school days were gone forever. Pine Bluffs was the Present. It was Life.

The idea of going some place new, some place different had come to her in the Easter vacation. She had caught her mother in the very act of writing old Mrs. Hillis to say that they would take her Spoondrift Cottage at Monroe, Connecticut, as they had done for the last fourteen years, and she realized that

35

never again could she stand Monroe. In the first place, there
was Annie with whom she had played every summer for as
long as she could remember. Annie was nice, she thought, she
was a good kid, but Annie was fifteen. When you were only
fifteen, you were as good as dead. She knew what it was like
to be only fifteen in Monroe. She could see herself as she had
been last summer, being a little noisy on the beach to attract
the attention of the older crowd—the smooth crowd; pretending to think it fun when loathesome little boys threw you off
the raft; dancing with other girls at the Tuesday night dances
at the Yacht Club, being bumped into by rowdy ten-year-olds
who thought a dance floor was meant to slide on; trying to
keep time to the foul four-piece orchestra when your feet
twitched to step to the tropical beat of Hap Harvey's Hey-
Makers who played for the real dances on Saturday nights.
Last summer she and Annie would sit on the fence around the
parking space and look in the windows, content with the
sound of the music and the cool deliciousness of their ice-
cream cones, content with the soft summer nights and
glimpses of the world that revolved before them. But this
summer, she knew, she could never bring herself merely to
look on. She was sixteen. Pretty soon she would be seventeen,
eighteen, nineteen, and then twenty. She would be married
at twenty. Twenty would be the end.

So in a panic she begged her mother not to write for Spoondrift Cottage. In desperation she fished a name from her memory—Pine Bluffs. A girl from school had been there once. It
was awfully smart, the girl said, there were loads of people, the
casino was perfect, there were beach umbrellas and even ca-
banas on the beach—just like Europe. And no one would
know how old she was. She would have her driver's license,
and as far as anyone could tell, she would be as good as eighteen.

Norma didn't paint this picture for her mother. She told
her that there was practically no traffic on the roads, which
would be awfully good since her mother was so nervous in a
car; that it was much cooler, being farther north; that the
cottages were lovely and had gas stoves; that there were beautiful drives, free lectures about wild flowers, no undertow, and
any number of bridge clubs that met once or twice a week, to
say nothing of the duplicate tournaments at the casino.

Mrs. Martin was won over. "I don't know but what I'd
like to change myself," she told her husband. "I feel as though
I knew every cameo pin on every bosom in Monroe. And you

know the bridge I get with Peggy Blake—one spade, two spades, six spades. Goodness! I don't think I could face it again. Besides," she added in her innocence, "it sounds quite different."

Mrs. Martin was a little disappointed when she saw the cottage. They had rented The Breakers, a bare, wind-swept cottage with a view of the ocean from the bathroom, and it was dishearteningly like Spoondrift Cottage in Monroe. It had the same walnut stain on its walls, the same sort of wicker furniture, an identical bridge lamp, similar faded chintz at the windows. But there was a gas stove, the fireplace was large and drew well, and the breeze from the ocean was salt and fresh. Besides, Norma was delighted. She pronounced the cottage perfect, the bathing marvelous, the summer visitors really attractive. And she underwent a great change.

She began to fuss over her appearance, spending hours in the tub, hours over her nails, hours pressing her clothes and getting dressed. It seemed to Mrs. Martin that Norma was always underfoot, fussing with the electric iron, fussing with her hair. It was nice, she thought, that the child was beginning to take an interest in her appearance, but it had been nice, too, in the days when she was up, out of the house and out of the way. She remonstrated with her about it. "I don't see why wearing a dress twice, just twice, without pressing it is going to make you or break you."

Norma answered patiently. "You've got to be well-groomed. Now, you always look all right and sweet, really. But no one could say you were well-groomed. It's a matter of detail."

"Well-groomed!" Mrs. Martin sniffed. "You've been reading the advertisements in the magazines. If you ask me, young lady, I shouldn't say you had much to be well-groomed for!"

The minute she said this, she was sorry. Because, although they had been at Pine Bluff ten days, Norma knew no one. Every morning, after patient hours in front of her mirror, she went to the car, immaculately put together, and drove to the village to do the marketing. This was an innovation, but she was so proud of her driving and there were so few places to drive to that Mrs. Martin had agreed to let her go, a little relieved to be spared a tiresome chore, quite staggered at the amount of stuff Norma sent home. By the time the marketing was done, it was time for lunch—a salad for Norma, a glass of orange juice, a glass of buttermilk. "You've got to eat!" Mrs. Martin cried in desperation over this starvation diet.

"First you tell me I'm too fat, and then you tell me I'm too thin," Norma answered, smoothing her hands over her hips, pulling her stomach in.

Though she did nothing, she seemed strangely contented, during the daytime anyway! She drove around town every spare moment, remembering small errands that had to be done; she dressed and undressed and dressed again; she was practically the girl her mother had hoped she'd be. But somehow it was not quite right. There were the evenings, for instance, when they sat on the porch until dark, and then went in and sat in the wicker chairs in the living-room. They talked a little, or read. At ten they went to bed. Mrs. Martin felt she was living with a beautifully dressed, horribly aloof stranger. Outside in the dark, young people passed the cottage, walking or in cars, talking, laughing, singing, but none of them stopped for Norma. She sat sedately in her wicker chair, determinedly reading, looking pale and very young. The moths beat against the screen door, the wicker furniture creaked, and nothing happened.

Then one day Mrs. Martin came back from the beach, flushed and happy, bearing pleasant news. "Norma!" she called. "What do you think? I met the nicest woman on the beach, and she has a daughter—Jerry, I think they call her. Anyway, she is having a beach picnic tonight and they want you to come."

For a second there was a brief flicker of excitement in Norma's face. But almost immediately she assumed the curiously set expression that lately had been habitual with her. "How old is she?" she asked.

"Oh, I don't know," her mother said. "About your age, I'd say. Fifteen or sixteen."

"Oh, Mother!" Norma exclaimed. "A kid! A perfect child!"

"She's no more a child than you are," Mrs. Martin argued. "What's gotten into you?"

"You haven't found out as much about this place as I have," Norma told her. "There are two sets, not counting the actual babies. There are the kids, fourteen or fifteen, and then there's the older crowd. And if you once go around with the kids, you're absolutely cooked with the older crowd. You might as well be dead."

"Well, those kids, as you call them, look anything but dead. They don't look half as dead as you do. They look to me as though they were having a fine time."

But Norma did not budge. And Mrs. Martin, to teach her

a lesson, left her alone and went to the beach picnic herself. To help out, she said. She returned about ten, conscience-stricken and uneasy, to find Norma patting cold cream on her smooth, young cheeks.

"It was fun!" Mrs. Martin told her brightly. "Loads of fun! Those young people are lovely, really nicer than the crowd at Monroe, I think. They have more get up and go to them."

"Oh, they're all right, I suppose," Norma agreed in her new tired voice. "But they're dreadfully silly. They never say a thing really interesting, though. They just fool all the time."

So things went on as they had been, until Norma met Bill James. He was a blond young man who looked like a composite picture of all the young men in the cigarette advertisements. He had talked to her at the garage where she was having a tire changed, and later that day he had stopped by their cottage with the casual informality, Mrs. Martin thought disapprovingly, of a much older acquaintance.

He was almost as immaculately gotten up as Norma. His grey slacks were spotless, his blond hair was wet and smooth. And he talked unceasingly.

"So this is your first summer here," he said kindly to Mrs. Martin. "Well, you're going to love it. There's a great crowd and the first thing you know you'll be in a whirl. Wait till things get going!" He laughed reminiscently. "The clans haven't gathered yet. Things don't really get started until Scotty MacFarlane and his wife get here. And Ham Brown! He's a great guy! Say, he doesn't have his eyes open, not really open, from the day he comes to the day we pour him on the boat."

"You mean he's—?" Mrs. Martin asked, startled and shocked.

But Bill James knew mothers and how to handle them. "Oh, he acts all right," he assured her. "He knows how to handle it. But he's a riot."

"Goodness!" Mrs. Martin exclaimed. She looked nervously at Norma.

Norma was sitting forward in her chair watching Bill James.

"Yes, it's a great crowd," he went on. "There are the Harrises, the Waites, Dizzy Thomas, the Smith girls—" He reeled off names.

"It's a tight corporation," he told them. But he looked at Norma and his eyes seemed to say, "Don't worry. I'll get you in."

Later, he arose. "We'll call on some of them. They mostly live on the Point."

Mrs. Martin was about to speak when she caught Norma's pleading look. "Well, if you're going to walk to the Point," she said reluctantly, "you'd better change your shoes."

"Oh, nobody walks here," Bill James told her. "You weren't going to use your car, were you, Mrs. Martin?"

For the first time his voice lost some of its brashness.

That night Mrs. Martin wrote her husband. "It's awful here," she wrote. "I don't know what to do. If I put my foot down, Norma will hate me." She went on to tell him about Bill James. "Although I must admit, from what Norma told me, those people don't sound as bad as I'd pictured them. They gave her tea, and I gather all they talk about is the fine time they had last summer. I don't know what they'll find to talk about next summer because, Heaven knows, they don't seem to be doing much now."

To Norma she said, "They sound very dull. I should think you'd be bored. Why, they're older people. Some of them are married, and some are engaged to be married. That Bill James is twenty-six. Ten years older than you. The idea!"

But Norma, it seemed, was not bored. She was impressed and flattered. She allowed Bill James to take her out in her mother's car. She waited in town in the hot sun while he did his errands. He rented, every summer, a small shack near the beach and it was lots of fun there, Norma explained. He kept beer on ice and everyone dropped in.

"Well, don't you drink his beer, young lady," Mrs. Martin said.

"I don't like beer."

Every evening about half-past nine, Bill James dropped in. Sometimes he stayed and talked and Mrs. Martin went tactfully to her room. He smoked their cigarettes, lounged with his feet on their couch and occasionally took Norma places in their car. "I don't want him driving the car," Mrs. Martin protested.

"Oh, Mother, he's a good driver," Norma said impatiently. "He's been driving for years."

"There's to be a dance at the casino this Saturday," Norma announced one day. "It's the first one."

She went to her closet and took out her three evening dresses; the old one from last winter and two new ones.

"Which one would you wear?" she asked.

"Well, I always loved that blue net on you," Mrs. Martin said. "It's a sweet dress."

"It's too sweet. It makes me look about twelve." She laid the blue net aside and studied the others; a flame-colored lace one and a trim black one with a white poplin mess jacket. "The black one's awfully smart," she said vaguely, and hung them up again.

"Are you going with Bill?"

"Oh, I imagine so," Norma answered confidently. "He hasn't said yet. Of course, the tickets are two dollars apiece and he hasn't a lot of money."

"He has enough money to keep himself in beer," Mrs. Martin said acidly.

"He has to keep up his share," Norma explained.

Two nights before the dance, she said unexpectedly to her mother, "Let's go to the movies, the early show."

"What about Bill?"

"Oh, I'm not going to sit here and wait for him to stop by every night. He needn't think I'm just sitting here waiting. Come on, let's go."

They went early and sat in the crowded, hot movie theater a half hour waiting for the pictures to begin. Groups of young girls came in; three or four girls with one young man; couples, young, obviously married. Norma explained them to her mother. "That's Scotty and his wife and the Harrises. Those are the Smith girls and that's Ham Brown with them."

Mrs. Martin looked curiously at Ham Brown, the riot. He was what she called a fat boy, sleepy, dull-looking. He sat with the Smith girls, slouched in his chair, and although Mrs. Martin watched him for quite a while, he never said a word.

"He doesn't look like a ball of fire to me," she said.

"He's awfully funny sometimes," Norma told her.

As people came in, Norma sat forward in her chair and looked eagerly around. She called to people in the rows ahead. "Hello, Diz! Hello, Patty!"

A few negligent heads were turned in their direction, a few casual voices answered, "Oh, hello, Norma."

It was a relief when the house grew dark and the newsreel started. Mrs. Martin was unable to concentrate on the pictures. "What horrid young people," she thought. "How noisy and rude they are."

Afterwards, it was even worse. Norma pulled at sleeves as

she wormed her way up the aisle. She was demanding attention. Mrs. Martin's heart sank for her.

When they got home, Bill James was waiting for them. He was lying on the couch reading a magazine. "Well, where have you been?" he wanted to know.

Norma was animated with him. "To the movies. It was packed. Everybody was there—Ham, and Diz, and Patty, and all the crowd."

Bill James seemed interested. He asked questions about who had been with whom with an almost feminine curiosity. Mrs. Martin went to her room feeling baffled. They were still talking when she went to sleep.

The day before the dance, Norma came home from the beach white and tearful. She came alone and she began talking before she was in the house. "Oh, Mother! The most terrible thing happened! We were sitting around at Bill's, having the grandest time, and Diz got fooling with my bag. She wanted to borrow my lipstick, she said. But I think she was just snooping, because all the girls looked at one another as if they'd put her up to it. And she found my driver's license! And read it!"

"Well, what about it?" Mrs. Martin asked. "There's nothing incriminating on your driver's license as far as I know. You've never been arrested for anything."

"But now they know!" Norma cried. "And they acted so funny!"

"Know what?" Mrs. Martin was puzzled.

"How old I am! They know how old I am!"

"Do you mean to tell me that no one knew how old you are?" Mrs. Martin was aghast.

"Of course not! You don't think for one minute that Bill or any of them would have paid any attention to me for one minute if they'd known I was sixteen, do you? They thought I was about eighteen. I sort of let them think I was."

"Well!" Mrs. Martin exclaimed.

"I'm through," Norma said. "They'll drop me like a hot cake. You ought to hear how they joke about the kids. You ought to have seen how they acted. They said, 'You old cradle-snatcher, you,' to Bill. And he didn't like it, let me tell you."

"Now, now," her mother said. "Bill likes you. Goodness knows he comes around here enough. I *know* he's too old for you. I told you he was. But he seemed to like you, and you

got along together. I mean, why shouldn't he still come
around? If he likes you. After all, it wasn't anything serious.
It was never any life or death matter. I don't see what all
the fuss is about. Maybe the girls did act a little catty. Girls
often do. Especially when there aren't enough boys to go
around."

"You don't understand," Norma said. "It is a matter of
life or death. The summer's just begun and I'm through!"

The rest of the day was awful. Mrs. Martin found herself
listening eagerly for Bill James to call at the front door. She
watched Norma, no longer busy with nail polish and cold
cream, slink about the house, the banner of her lovely youth
pulled down as though she wished to hide it. As though, indeed, she would like to kill her youth. In the evening, Mrs.
Martin suggested the movies again, but Norma shook her
head. "I couldn't," she said.

Bill James did not come that day, nor did he come the
next. "Well, now you know what he's like," Mrs. Martin said
scornfully.

Norma's look was stricken, but her voice was old with understanding. "He can't help it. He couldn't stand the kidding.
He hasn't much money or anything, and all those people have.
And they just kind of let him hang around because he's funny
and fits in with the crowd. He wouldn't dare get them down
on him."

About nine, when the cars began to go by the house and
the music at the casino started, Mrs. Martin pulled down
the shades of the front windows. "Those moths," she said
brightly. "I can't stand hearing them beat their wings off on
the screen. Let's have a fire."

They lit the fire and the room looked more cheerful. Mrs.
Martin tried not to think of the flame-colored dress and the
awfully smart black one hanging in the closet. There was no
shutting out the noise of the cars passing, the laughing, the
sound of the music, the perfectly smooth sax, the gay drum.

At ten she suggested a walk and, surprisingly, Norma
agreed. The night was cool but soft, and the stars were brilliant. They walked along the shore looking at them. "That's
Venus," Mrs. Martin pointed out. "And that's Mars. I wonder if there are people on Mars."

They walked on, looking at the stars, talking about them,
ignoring the deserted look the cottages wore, pretending not

to see the cars that passed them. They walked until after eleven.

"I'm going to sit up a while," Norma said. "I'm going to write some letters. I'm going to write to Annie."

Mrs. Martin brought in a glass of milk and some cookies.

"I was thinking," she said, "that we might hire a sailboat tomorrow and ask that little Jerry to go with us. Or, maybe, you two would rather go alone."

"Mmm, that would be swell," Norma said. She started her letter.

It was about twelve when there was a knock at the door, and Mrs. Martin heard Bill James' voice. He was feeling fine, she heard him say. The party was going like a forest fire, and he had come to take Norma to the dance.

"Hop into your things," he said.

Mrs. Martin waited sickeningly for Norma's answer. "If she is grateful, I'll die," she thought.

Then Norma's voice came to her, cool and fresh. "I couldn't, not possibly. It's late."

"Late!" Bill James laughed. "It's only twelve! We've got three hours! It's the crest of the evening and I'm on the crest of the wave!"

"No, really," Norma said in a prim, schoolgirl's voice. "Thanks just the same."

"Oh, be a sport," Bill James urged. "The whole gang is there—Scotty, Mrs. Scotty, Ham and all the crowd."

"And I suppose Mrs. Scotty is singing with the orchestra the way she sings to that little piano of theirs?"

"She hasn't started yet," Bill James said happily. "But it won't be long now."

"Well, the orchestra will have to go back about six years to play any of the songs she knows. All that old stuff she sings! Why doesn't she get something new for a change?"

"She's all right," Bill James said, surprised. "She's a darn good sport."

There was venom in Norma's voice. "Frankly, she bores me."

There was silence in the living room. "Well, if you won't come—" Bill James said, no longer sounding high.

"No. No, thank you," Norma answered. "I don't feel like it, really. Thanks for dropping by for me."

Mrs. Martin heard the screen door close as Bill James took himself away. "I hope he's miserable," she thought meanly. "I honestly think he liked her. Quite a lot."

Her door opened suddenly and Norma's head looked in. "Did you hear that?" she asked. "Coming around this time of night! Who does he think he is? What does he think I am?"

She smiled suddenly and gaily at her mother. "The old stiff," she said. And added as an afterthought, "The old cripple!"

Kip finds out what 'winning' really means

Eight-Oared Crew

HARRY SYLVESTER

DUSK LAY on the river, making all things its own color. Lights had begun to appear in the other boathouses but where Al Leyden—at 38, the "Old Man"—stood on the landing, there was only the growing shadow, quick-deepening now that the sun had gone out of sight behind the west bank of the Hudson. The shell, moving leisurely toward the landing, was only a darker shadow when it docked. Leyden stood apart from the crew, the mood of the evening heavy in him.

The crew swung the shell out of the water at Kip Grant's command and marched it past Leyden. In the blue light they looked like some giant insect, the shell held over their heads. Kip Grant walked by them, silent now and no longer harrying the crew. Too silent, Leyden thought, but he felt no better for knowing the reason for that silence toward the crew of sophomores.

He touched Kip on the arm and the coxswain turned to him. "How was it?" Leyden said.

In the dusk he could barely see the slight shrug of the other's shoulders. "I don't know. Their form is still good—when they don't have to turn on the heat." He paused and said, again: "What they'll do in the race, I don't know. They learned too quickly. . . ."

Leyden nodded.

"My brothers and some friends are in town for the race," Kip said. "Mind if I run into town for an hour or so?"

"Go ahead," Leyden said. He almost added: "Don't make your going too obvious," but with Grant that wasn't necessary, Leyden knew. These boys from the school's traditional families were mentally precocious. . . .

Leyden watched Kip Grant go into the coaches' room to dress. Grant had begun to do this after Leyden had made the change in the crews. It was not a good thing, Leyden knew, for crew and coxswain to be so sharply divided as they were. Regret stirred in him again at having made that change, but in his mind he knew that he had done the right thing. He came from poor people himself. Even if the university was or

46

had been a "rich man's school," Leyden felt that he himself must be just. His sense of justice lay on him now like a weight. He went wearily up the wooden stairs to his own room.

Two years ago the university had gone out and got some scholarship men to bolster up the football team, which had been bad for three years in a row. They were good boys, the new scholarship men, intelligent enough to get by the stiff entrance exams, but hailing from mine and mill and with names new to the school: Kowalik, Leary and Pivarnik; Granski, Lisbon and Guttman; the Slavs already replacing the Irish among the athletes.

None of them had ever seen a shell; some of them had never seen a river before coming to the school. They came out for crew in the winter of their freshman year and Leyden had watched them that first day in the barge, with the ice still on the river; watched them with pride and with foreboding.

Leyden had two freshman crews that year and the football coach complained that he was keeping the scholarship men from spring practice. So Leyden let them go for spring football practice and they had returned to him after it and said that they still wanted to row. So Leyden had let them row. . . . It was too late to mold them, or some of them, into the freshman crew that would compete at Poughkeepsie that year. So Leyden had let the scholarship men row alone, as a unit . . . and Leyden saw then the thing that might happen.

Leyden had been an athlete and a coach long enough to know that any great team, whether it be a crew or a football eleven, is more than half accident. The unbelievable and precise co-ordination that made a team great, as a team, was largely beyond the ability of any coach to create. He could develop it once the accident had occurred but he could not create it.

What Leyden had seen was that eight of the scholarship men had or were part of that curious accident of co-ordination that might make a great crew. He knew, guiltily, that they, for all their crudeness, could beat the freshman crew already formed. And even when that crew was a close second at Poughkeepsie, Leyden still felt that he had been less than just. Rowing was the traditional sport at the university and, partly by accident, partly by design, the crew was almost always composed of names old in the school's history. Leyden wondered just how much this had affected his judgment.

The next spring he had left the scholarship men together as a unit, as the junior varsity, and he had gone about the always difficult business of making a new crew of some of last year's varsity and some of the freshmen. It was not better than an average crew although it had a great coxswain, the senior, Kip Grant. It was a traditional crew in that it had the old names, Carteret, Grant, Morgan, Fairlee. It won one sprint race, was second in two others and last in a longer race.

That spring it took Leyden a long time to do the thing he felt compelled to do. In May, for the first time, he had the varsity and junior varsity meet in a brush along the river. The junior varsity, the scholarship men, won by a little. They won by a bow a week later, despite having lost their form in the middle of the race. Then, they won by two lengths in a three-mile race with the varsity.

Leyden did then the thing he had to do. He called the varsity together. "The junior varsity," he told them, "has beaten you, decisively. If you want to row at Poughkeepsie as the varsity, go ahead. . . . Knowing you as I do, I don't think you'll want to go to Poughkeepsie that way. The better way is to race the junior varsity the Poughkeepsie distance, four miles . . . and if they beat you, let them go—as the varsity. Tell me tomorrow how you want to go to Poughkeepsie."

So their captain, Jim Fairlee, had come and told Leyden quite gravely that they would go to Poughkeepsie only if they could beat the junior varsity. And they had raced and the junior varsity, stroked by Kowalik, had won by three lengths.

They needed a coxswain and Leyden had asked Kip Grant to go into their boat. And Kip had consented to but he hadn't liked it or them. And so Leyden's varsity was the eight scholarship men and Kip Grant, third generation of his family to sit in one of the university shells.

His dislike for the men he handled the tiller grips for was not unreasonable. They had displaced his friends, had broken a long tradition of which he was a part. Alumni had protested privately and Kip's brothers had even urged him not to sit in the varsity shell. They had done so half humorously, but Kip knew how they felt. He knew, too, how Leyden felt and the weight of the justice that lay heavy on Leyden. . . .

His brothers were awaiting for him now in the private dining room they always had the evening before the race. When he opened the door of the room they were yelling at him:

"The kid himself!"

"Say, Kip, is it really true you had to learn to speak Polish?"

In a way he didn't hear them. For he had seen her face. Among the other women there, among the tall Old Blues, it stood out quietly, as Kip expected that it always might. He greeted the others and sat beside her—Mary Adams, his friend since childhood, now the girl he was going to marry. She took his hand under the table and was silent until the others had stopped shouting at Kip.

"Sure," he kept telling them, "we'll win in a breeze."

"They'll blow up in your face under the bridge," Ad Grant said. "I was watching them from the bank this afternoon through glasses."

"They'll row those other crews into the river," Kip said. Their antagonism, however friendly, did something to him. For the first time, and in surprise, he felt as though he were really part of his crew. . . .

They let him alone after a while and he was able to slip out with Mary Adams. The side streets of the town were quiet under the old trees, the wind from the river rich with spring.

"You seem quiet," Mary Adams said. "I had thought you'd be more nervous with the race so close."

"As I get older I suppose I conceal things better," he said. "If the race has made me nervous, something else has made me quiet. Something else besides you." His hand tightened on her arm. "You can always make me quiet. Just being near you."

"It makes me very happy, Kip," she said.

"The other thing," he went on gravely, "is that I've suddenly realized I've been dishonest. I've snooted those men on the crew when I should have tried to know them better. Why I did, I don't know. They're good men."

"I understand," she said quietly. "I suppose it would have been more honest for you to have resigned from the squad or stroked your—own people on the junior varsity."

"My own people," Kip said. There was an edge to his tone. "They rode me tonight. And they're apt to go haywire and fire Al Leyden after the race."

"I think not," she said. "Coming down in the train, they agreed they'd just let him know that they wanted him not to do anything like it again."

"Even if they win," Kip said.

"None of them expect you to win tomorrow," she said.

An old car squeaked to a stop near them. It had Pennsylvania license plates. A head with a battered hat on it poked out one window and spoke unintelligibly to them. Kip went closer to the car and Mary stood on the curb.

"You know where this faller, Pete Kowalik, he stay at? Faller what row in front in bast crew on here?"

From the curb, Mary saw Kip straighten. "I imagine it's a bit late to see him. All the crew men are in bed."

"All day long, most last night, we drive this flivver," the voice went on in a sing-song. "Stop every garage on road, by damn. Pete Kowalik, he be worried about us. Couldn't phone him, eider, I bet."

"They wouldn't call him to the phone at this time of night," Kip said. He moved back to the curb. Mary touched his arm. "These people—" she hesitated. "They've come a long way. You could take a message to Kowalik. He's your stroke, isn't he?"

"I suppose," he said, "I'll be a snob until I die." He walked back to the old car, which was refusing to start. "I'll see Kowalik—if not tonight, first thing in the morning. I can take a message to him."

"You just him that his brother Joe got here all hokay and that Malie Stefansik, he come too, and we both be there tomorrow, yalling like hell! Say, who are you, mister? Your face, it——"

"I'm one of the managers," Kip said. He turned away.

"I feel better at your having done that," Mary Adams said.

"I feel better myself." They walked a while in silence.

"Something still bothers you," Mary said.

"I know. I don't think we'll win tomorrow. I had to say it in front of the others, but the men are still green for all their power and natural ability."

"No," she said. "It's just the night that makes you think so." She turned to him in the shadow and he kissed her, feeling some old tension in him become lost in another one, renewed. He broke from her. "I have to get back," he said. At the hotel she pressed his hand. "Until after the race," she said.

The boathouse was in darkness when Kip got there. Going up the wooden stairs to the dormitory where the crews slept, the only light he could see was from the crack under the door of Al Leyden's room. Kip was a long time getting to sleep.

After breakfast, Kip said to Kowalik: "I'd like to speak to you on the float." The tall boy looked his surprise but followed Kip outside.

"I ran into your brother last night in town," Kip said. "He had trouble getting here, but he wanted to let you know that he had arrived."

Kowalik looked at once grateful and amused. "Thanks a lot, Grant. I'm glad to hear about my brother getting here all right. But when you called me over here I thought you had something important to say about the race."

"No," Kip said. He turned away, flushing a little. Was he at fault or they? he thought. Was he a snob or were they crude? He had not wanted the others to know that he had spoken even that intimately to Kowalik. Strangely, though, he felt once more his new kinship with the crew, a relation delayed and now hastened by the attitude of his brothers and friends, by the chance meeting with Kowalik's brother, by Mary Adams' quiet words.

A manager came and told Kip that Leyden would like to see him. He found the coach in his room with the crossed oars on the wall. One of them, Kip knew, had been used by Ad Grant six years ago. "Close the door," Leyden said. "Sit down."

"Guess you didn't sleep much," Kip said. "Saw your light on when I came in."

"I never do the night before a race. The crew did, though."

"They all look good," Kip said. His words fell hollowly into a silence created by Leyden's looking away. When he turned to Kip again, Leyden's face showed his weariness.

"They might win," Leyden said, "but probably they won't." Kip nodded once.

"They have stuff," Leyden said, "a lot of it. And guts. They just haven't rowed long enough. They'll try too hard and go to pieces."

"It's a touch late to substitute the jayvee for them," Kip said. "I don't mean to be a wise guy," he added quickly.

"I know," Leyden said. "I made my decision and I'm going to stand by it. About the job I don't have to worry. Your brothers and old man Calder of the crew committee phoned me last night while you were away and said that no matter what happened my job was safe. So it's not me. It's those kids. You don't like them. I can see your point even though I come from the same kind of people they do. But I let them win their place, didn't I?"

"You don't have to talk me into anything," Kip said. "I've changed some. It would be hard to tell you why. But I'll do all I can for them. And I want to win myself. It's my last chance. I'm the only one in the family that never sat in a winning boat at least once at Poughkeepsie."

Leyden nodded. "It's not their last chance," he said. "That's why I called you in here. They have two more big years. What I ask you is this. If they win, all right. If they lose, that's all right, too, in a way, although none of us like to lose. But bring them in a crew—an eight-oared varsity crew." He paused and the two men looked at each other. "You know what I mean," Leyden said. "If they go to pieces today they may never get together again, this year or any other. I don't know what you may have to do . . . but bring them in right—for their sake and the school's . . . if not for anyone else's."

The river was like glass, the stake boats hardly moving in it. Kip's crew had the outside lane, the fastest but also the roughest if the river kicked up. Also the nearest to the line of yachts at the finish.

. The referee called: "Ready all?" and the California cox raised his hand. Kowalik and Guttman cursed at the delay. "Steady," Kip said. It was the first word he had spoken outside of commands since leaving the boathouse. He looked down the line of them and pride in them and what was left of his vanity of class fought in him. They stared at him and formed a curious foreshortened design of white on bronze: the sweatbands sharp against their dark faces, the adhesive tape strapped to their bellies, the heavy wool socks.

"Ready all?" the referee said again and no hand was raised. The little cannon boomed and Kip's "Row!" was lost in its echoes, in the sudden rush of waters as the oars bent in the swift, tremendous beat of the racing start. Something had begun to flow in Kip like his blood, but swifter and more subtle, so that he let them come out of the racing start only gradually, his hands beating out the stroke with the tiller grips at 40 before he consciously knew how high the beat was.

Already they had a quarter length on the others and the lead grew rapidly, was over a length before the mile mark.

"Bring it down! Down, you madmen!" Kip yelled. Something in their eyes dismayed him. They were trying too hard, almost as though they were trying to escape something. . . . He felt older than they . . . but kept shouting at them until they dropped their beat. Still open water showed between them and Navy and California, leading the others.

"Leary——you're shooting your slide!" Kip yelled. Under the excitement, he could marvel at the power they were getting in spite of their form, worse than usual. He saw that Navy was coming up and, with the edge of his eyes, caught the flash of orange-tipped oars, Syracuse making an early bid. "We're not getting much run," he thought. "That's where the bad form counts."

"Get together!" he barked. There was blood on the lips of Lisbon and Guttman. "They're trying too hard," he thought. "If I yell too much they'll blow up."

The beat was up again, he realized, and wondered vaguely whether he was taking the stroke from Kowalik or Kowalik from him. This annoyed him as did their passing the two-mile mark without his knowing it.

"Down, down, you lugs!" he yelled. His voice had risen higher than usual. They eyed him fearfully. They still led, but in dropping the beat they lost ground and Navy's bow was almost even with them, and Syracuse and California less than a length behind.

Kip knew that this crew was in no mood for subtleties, whether of thought or action. He saw the bridge ahead and that decided him. "All right," he called. "Bring it up." He felt the thrill of their tremendous power move through the frail boat and he saw, with pride, the lead begin to grow again. They liked that, he saw, letting them go all out.

"Give it to them!" he called. "Give it to them! Break their damned hearts!"

They liked to hear him talk that way. They had never heard him do it before. Some of them were even grinning. They led by open water again. Something like a coldness dropped on Kip and was gone, and the noise of many voices. They had passed the bridge and the third mile.

Kip turned a little. They had over a length on Syracuse. The others were strung out, Navy and California at Syracuse's bow.

Leary was shooting his slide again, Guttman getting his oar out of the water too fast. "Steady," Kip called, afraid to say more. Still the cedar shell fled like a thing alive, still the long oars bit deeply into the river, shoveling the water back.

Seven bombs had gone off on the bridge when they went under it to tell those at the finish that the crew in the seventh lane was leading. So they would be ready for him, Kip knew, on the yacht. And he would be ready for them. He would bring his crew aboard with him and see how his brothers liked that!

Exultation beat up in him. Half a mile now. The crew's

bodies, sheeted in sweat, gleamed strangely in the twilight. The line of yachts was opening on either side. They were in, Kip thought. "Pick it up," he called. "Pick it up!"

They drove the blades deep, the great bodies bent. "We're in!" he kept thinking in time with the beat of his tiller grips. "We're in! We're in!" The shell trembled as it tore through the water.

Then they blew. Guttman had taken his oar out of the water too soon, had bothered the No. 6 in front of him and made him catch a crab. Leary, shooting his slide, losing power, almost caught one. What he screamed at them, Kip never knew. But when he saw that the bow oar was catching when Kowalik, the stroke, was taking his blade from the water, he knew that it was all over. What boat first slid by them, he did not know. He saw only the strained faces, the terrible confusion in the waist of the shell, and Kowalik's efforts to keep rowing, to pass the rhythm back to the others. The other shells slipped by like ghosts in the deepening twilight.

"Get together," he said, mechanically. Pathetically, they were trying to. The shell had almost lost headway.

People were yelling on the yachts but one voice, out of a megaphone, pierced to Kip's ears. "Leave those punks by themselves," Ad Grant was yelling from the bow of the yacht. Kip turned. They were abreast his brother's yacht, *Cormorant*. He could see them in the bow, yelling and gesturing to him. "Jump in and swim over here," Ad said.

The full meaning of it all came to Kip in a rush. He should abandon these men before him as a last, contemptuous gesture and sign that they did not belong or deserve to belong to that long tradition of which he and his brothers were a part. In doing so, he would appease his brothers and take some of the edge off their sarcasm tonight. His anger at and scorn of the crew returned to him, strong, and Kip half rose to ease himself over the side of the shell. He remembered what Leyden had asked, with curious foresight, of himself— to bring them in an eight-oared crew, so that they would be fully such in the coming years. To hell with them, he thought, and to hell with Leyden. All of them had humiliated him.

Pathetically, they were still rowing, their oars clashing under the sound of the whistles which were already blowing for the winning crew. From his half-crouch, Kip turned to go over the side. He saw them in the bow of the *Cormorant* again . . . this time saw Mary Adams, a little apart from the others as he always liked to think of her. She was shaking her head, almost sadly. When he turned she waved her hand—for him to go on.

He had sat in the shell again before he knew he had done so. Why? he thought and felt stupid. This is silly, he tried to tell himself, but he saw the years that were to come, for them, and some strong, nameless excitement passed over him and left him weak and clear-headed. Sarcasm could never hurt him as much as he had the power to hurt these men before him.

"Way enough!" he called. They looked at him, startled. "Way enough!" His voice bit. The oars came out of the water, hung poised for his command. He made his voice as casual, as even as he could. "Now get together," he said, as though they were just out for a practice paddle. "You've been going like a bunch of washwomen."

"Ready—" he said. Their faces had grown almost composed. He felt pleasantly the sense of his own power, heard Ad Grant's voice through the megaphone, but did not hear Ad's words. . . . "Row!" Kip said. The eight oars took the water like a machine.

Ahead the whistles were screaming for a Navy crew that had come up in the dusk to beat Syracuse and California. And that dusk filled the river, turning the shells into shadows. But those who happened to be looking saw a curious sight— last by almost an eighth of a mile, but moving with a rhythm precise and sure, with unbelievable power; last now, but rich with great promise, an eight-oared varsity shell come home.

Daisy learns the hard way

A Start in Life

RUTH SUCKOW

THE SWITZERS were scurrying around to get Daisy ready by
the time that Elmer Kruse should get through in town. They
had known all week that Elmer might be in for ¹ ˉ any day.
But they hadn't done a thing until he appeared. "Oh, it was
so rainy today, the roads were so muddy, they hadn't thought
he'd get in until maybe next week." It would have been the
same any other day.

Mrs. Switzer was trying now at the last moment to get all
of Daisy's things into the battered telescope that lay on the
bed. The bed had not "got made"; and just as soon as Daisy
was gone, Mrs. Switzer would have to hurry off to the Woodworths, where she was to wash today. Daisy's things were scattered over the dark brown quilt and the rumpled sheet that
were dingy and clammy in this damp weather. So was the
whole bedroom with its sloping ceiling, and old-fashioned
square-paned windows, the commode that they used for a
dresser littered with pin trays, curlers, broken combs, ribbons,
smoky lamp, all mixed up together; the door of the closest
open, showing the confusion of clothes and shabby shoes.
. . . They all slept in this room—Mrs. Switzer and Dwight
in the bed, the two girls in the cot against the wall.

"Mama, I can't find the belt to that plaid dress."

"Oh, ain't it somewheres around? Well, I guess you'll have
to let it go. If I come across it I can send it out to you. Someone'll be going past there."

She had meant to get Daisy all mended and "fixed up" before she went out to the country. But somehow . . . oh,
there was always so much to see to when she came home.
Gone all day, washing and cleaning for other people; it didn't
leave her much time for her own home.

She was late now. The Woodworths liked to have her get
the washing out early so that she could do some cleaning too
before she left. But she couldn't help it. She would have to
get Daisy off first. She had already had on her wraps ready to
go, when Elmer came—her cleaning cap, of a blue faded al-

most gray, and the ancient black coat with gathered sleeves that she wore over her work dress when she went out to wash.

"What's become of all your underclothes? They ain't all dirty, are they?"

"They are, too. You didn't wash for us last week, mama."

"Well, you'll just have to take along what you've got. Maybe there'll be some way of getting the rest to you."

"Elmers come in every week, don't they?" Daisy demanded.

"Yes, but maybe they won't always be bringing you in."

She jammed what she could into the telescope, thinking with her helpless, anxious fatalism that it would have to do somehow.

"Daisy, you get yourself ready now."

"I am ready, mama, I want to put on my other ribbon."

"Oh, that's 'way down in the telescope somewhere. You needn't be so anxious to fix yourself up. This ain't like going visiting."

Daisy stood at the little mirror preening herself—such a homely child, "all Switzer," skinny, with pale sharp eyes set close together and thin, stringy, reddish hair. But she had never really learned yet how homely she was. She was the oldest, and she got the pick of what clothes were given to the Switzers. Goldie and Dwight envied her. She was important in her small world. She was proud of her blue coat that had belonged to Alice Brooker, the town lawyer's daughter. It hung unevenly above her bony little knees, and the buttons came down too far. Her mother had tried to make it over for her.

Mrs. Switzer looked at her, troubled, but not knowing how she could tell her all the things she ought to be told. Daisy had never been away before except to go to her Uncle Fred's at Lehigh. She seemed to think that this would be the same. She had so many things to learn. Well, she would find them out soon enough—only too soon. Working for other people— she would learn what that meant. Elmer and Edna Kruse were nice young people. They would mean well enough by Daisy. It was a good chance for her to start in. But it wasn't the same.

Daisy was so proud. She thought it was quite a thing to be "starting in to earn." She thought she could buy herself so much with her dollar and a half a week. The other children stood back watching her, round-eyed and impressed. They wished that they were going away, like Daisy.

They heard a car come splashing through the mud on low. "There he is back! Have you got your things on? Goldie—go out and tell him she's coming."

"No, me tell him, me!" Dwight shouted jealously.

"Well—both of you tell him. Land! . . ."

She tried hastily to put on the cover of the bulging telescope and to fasten the straps. One of them broke.

"Well, you'll have to take it the way it is."

It was an old thing, hadn't been used since her husband, Mert, had "left off canvassing" before he died. And he had worn it all to pieces.

"Well, I guess you'll have to go now. He won't want to wait. I'll try and send you out what you ain't got with you." She turned to Daisy. Her face was working. There was nothing else to do, as everyone said. Daisy would have to help, and she might as well learn it now. Only, she hated to see Daisy go off, to have her starting in. She knew what it meant. "Well—you try and work good this summer, so they'll want you to stay. I hope they'll bring you in sometimes."

Daisy's homely little face grew pale with awe, suddenly, at the sight of her mother crying, at something that she dimly sensed in the pressure of her mother's thin strong arms. Her vanity in her new importance was somehow shamed and dampened.

Elmer's big new Buick, mud-splashed but imposing, stood tilted on the uneven road. Mud was thick on the wheels. It was a bad day for driving, with the roads a yellow mass, water lying in all the wheel ruts. The little road that led past these few houses on the outskirts of town, and up over the hill, had a cold, rainy loneliness. Elmer sat in the front seat of the Buick, and in the back was a big box of groceries.

"Got any room to sit in there?" he asked genially. "I didn't get out, it's so muddy here."

"No, don't get out," Mrs. Switzer said hastily. "She can put this right on the floor there in the back." She added, with a timid attempt at courtesy, "Ain't the roads pretty bad out that way?"

"Yes, but farmers get so they don't think so much about the roads."

"I s'pose that's so."

He saw the signs of tears on Mrs. Switzer's face, and they made him anxious to get away. She embraced Daisy hastily again. Daisy climbed over the grocery box and scrunched herself into the seat.

"I guess you'll bring her in with you some time when you're coming," Mrs. Switzer hinted.

"Sure. We'll bring her."

He started the engine. It roared, half died down as the wheels of the car spun in the thick wet mud.

In that moment, Daisy had a startled view of home—the small house standing on a rough rise of land, weathered to a dim color that showed dark streaks from the rain; the narrow sloping front porch whose edge had a soaked, gnawed look; the chickens, grayish-black, pecking at the wet ground; their playthings, stones, a wagon, some old pail covers littered about; a soaked, discolored piece of underwear hanging on the line in the back yard. The yard was tussocky and overhung the road with shaggy long grass where the yellow bank was caved in under it. Goldie and Dwight were gazing at her solemnly. She saw her mother's face—a thin, weak, loving face, drawn with neglected weeping, with its reddened eyes and poor teeth . . . in the old coat and heavy shoes and cleaning cap, her work-worn hand with its big knuckles clutching at her coat. She saw the playthings they had used yesterday, and the old swing that hung from one of the trees, the ropes sodden, the seat in crooked. . . .

The car went off, slipping on the wet clay. She waved frantically, suddenly understanding that she was leaving them. They waved at her.

Mrs. Switzer stood there a little while. Then came the harsh rasp of the old black iron pump that stood out under the box elder tree. She was pumping water to leave for the children before she went off to work.

Daisy held on as the car skidded going down the short clay hill. Elmer didn't bother with chains. He was too used to the roads. But her eyes brightened with scared excitement. When they were down, and Elmer slowed up going along the tracks in the deep wet grass that led to the main road, she looked back, holding on her hat with her small scrawny hand.

Just down this little hill—and home was gone. The big car, the feel of her telescope on the floor under her feet, the fact that she was going out to the country, changed the looks of everything. She saw it all now.

Dunkels' house stood on one side of the road. A closed-up white house. The windows stared blank and cold between the old shutters. There was a chair with a broken straw seat under the fruit trees. The Dunkels were old Catholic people who

seldom went anywhere. In the front yard was a clump of tall
pines, the rough brown trunks wet, the green branches, dark
and shining, heavy with rain, the ground underneath mournfully sodden and black.

The pasture on the other side. The green grass, lush, wet
and cold, and the outcroppings of limestone that held little
pools of rain water in all the tiny holes. Beyond, the low hills
gloomy with timber against the lowering sky.

They slid out onto the main road. They bumped over the
small wooden bridge above the swollen creek that came from
the pasture. Daisy looked down. She saw the little swirls of
foam, the long grass that swished with the water, the old
rusted tin cans lodged between the rocks.

She sat up straight and important, her thin, homely little
face strained with excitement, her sharp eyes taking in everything. The watery mud holes in the road, the little thickets of
plum trees, low and wet, in dark interlacings. She held on
fiercely, but made no sound when the car skidded.

She felt the grandeur of having a ride. One wet Sunday,
Mr. Brooker had driven them all home from church, she and
Goldie and Dwight packed tightly into the back seat of the
car, shut in by the side curtains, against which the rain lashed,
catching the muddy scent of the roads. Sometimes they could
plan to go to town just when Mr. Pattey was going to work
in his Ford. Then they would run out and shout eagerly, "Mr.
Pattey! Are you going through town?" Sometimes he said,
with curt good nature, "Well, pile in"; and they all hopped
into the truck back. "He says we can go along with him."

She looked at the black wet fields through which little
leaves of bright green corn grew in rows, at showery bushes
of sumac along the roadside. A gasoline engine pumping water
made a loud desolate sound. There were somber-looking cattle
in the wet grass, and lonely, thick-foliaged trees growing here
and there in the pastures. She felt her telescope on the floor
of the car, the box of groceries beside her. She eyed these with
a sharp curiosity. There was a fresh pineapple—something the
Switzers didn't often get at home. She wondered if Edna
would have it for dinner. Maybe she could hint a little to
Edna.

She was out in the country. She could no longer see her
house even if she wanted to—standing dingy, streaked with
rain, in its rough grass on the little hill. A lump came into
her throat. She had looked forward to playing with Edna's

children. But Goldie and Dwight would play all morning without her. She was still proud of being the oldest, of going out with Elmer and Edna; but now there was a forlornness in the pride.

She wished she were in the front seat with Elmer. She didn't see why he hadn't put her there. She would have liked to know who all the people were who lived on these farms; how old Elmer's babies were; and if he and Edna always went to the movies when they went into town on Saturday nights. Elmer must have lots of money to buy a car like this. He had a new house on his farm, too, and Mrs. Metzinger had said that it had plumbing. Maybe they would take her to the movies, too. She might hint about that.

When she had to visit Uncle Fred, she had had to go on the train. She liked this better. She hoped they had a long way to go. She called out to Elmer:

"Say, how much farther is your place?"

"What's that?" He turned around. "Oh, just down the road a ways. Scared to drive in the mud?"

"No, I ain't scared. I like to drive most any way."

She looked at Elmer's back, the old felt hat crammed down carelessly on his head, the back of his neck with the golden hair on the sunburned skin above the blue of his shirt collar. Strong and easy and slouched a little over the steering wheel that he handled so masterly. Elmer and Edna were just young folks; but Mrs. Metzinger said that they had more to start with than most young farmers did, and that they were hustlers. Daisy felt that the pride of this belonged to her too, now.

"Here we are!"

"Oh, is this where you folks live?" Daisy cried eagerly.

The house stood back from the road, beyond a space of bare yard with a little scattering of grass just starting—small, modern, painted a bright new white and yellow. The barn was new, too, a big splendid barn of frescoed brick, with a silo of the same. There were no trees. A raw, desolate wind blew across the back yard as they drove up beside the back door.

Edna had come out on the step. Elmer grinned at her as he took out the box of groceries, and she slightly raised her eyebrows. She said kindly enough:

"Well, you brought Daisy. Hello, Daisy, are you going to stay with us this summer?"

"I guess so," Daisy said importantly. But she suddenly felt a little shy and forlorn as she got out of the car and stood on the bare ground in the chilly wind.

"Yes, I brought her along," Elmer said.

"Are the roads very bad?"

"Kind of bad. Why?"

"Well, I'd like to get over to mama's some time today."

"Oh, I guess they aren't too bad for that."

Daisy pricked up her sharp little ears. Another ride. That cheered her.

"Look in the door," Edna said in a low fond voice, motioning with her head.

Two little round, blond heads were pressed tightly against the screen door. There was a clamor of "Daddy, daddy!" Elmer grinned with a bashful pride as he stood with the box of groceries, raising his eyebrows with mock surprise and demanding, "Who's this? What you shoutin' 'daddy' for? You don't think daddy's got anything for you, do you?" He and Edna were going into the kitchen together, until Edna remembered and called back hastily:

"Oh, come in, Daisy!"

Daisy stood, a little left out and solitary, there in the kitchen, as Billy, the older of the babies, climbed frantically over Elmer, demanding candy, and the little one toddled smilingly about. Her eyes took in all of it. She was impressed by the shining blue-and-white linoleum, the range with its nickel and enamel, the bright new woodwork. Edna was laughing and scolding at Elmer and the baby. Billy had made his father produce the candy. Daisy's sharp little eyes looked hungrily at the lemon drops and Edna remembered her.

"Give Daisy a piece of your candy," she said.

He would not go up to Daisy. She had to come forward and take one of the lemon drops herself. She saw where Edna put the sack, in a dish high in the cupboard. She hoped they would get some more before long.

"My telescope's out there in the car," she reminded them.

"Oh! Elmer, you go and get it and take it up for her," Edna said.

"What?"

"Her valise—or whatever it is—out in the car."

"Oh, sure," Elmer said with a cheerful grin.

"It's kind of an old telescope," Daisy said conversationally.

"I guess it's been used a lot. My papa used to have it. The strap broke when mama was fastening it this morning. We ain't got any suitcase. I had to take this because it was all there was in the house, and mama didn't want to get me a new one."

Edna raised her eyebrows politely. She leaned over and pretended to spat the baby as he came toddling up to her, then rubbed her cheek against his round head with its funny fuzz of hair.

Daisy watched solemnly. "I didn't know both of your children was boys. I thought one of 'em was a girl. That's what there is at home now—one boy and one girl."

"Um-hm," Edna replied absently. "You can go up with Elmer and take off your things, Daisy," she said. "You can stop and unpack your valise now, I guess, if you'd like to. Then you can come down and help me in the kitchen. You know we got you to help me," she reminded.

Daisy, subdued, followed Elmer up the bright new stairs. In the upper hall, two strips of very clean rag rug were laid over the shining yellow of the floor. Elmer had put her telescope in one of the bedrooms.

"There you are!"

She heard him go clattering down the stairs, and then a kind of murmuring and laughing in the kitchen. The back door slammed. She hurried to the window in time to see Elmer go striding off toward the barn.

She looked about her room with intense curiosity. It, too, had a bright varnished floor. She had a bed all her own—a small, old-fashioned bed, left from some old furnishings, that had been put in this room that had the pipes and the hot water tank. She had to see everything, but she had a stealthy look as she tiptoed about, started to open the drawers of the dresser, looked out of her window. She put her coat and hat on the bed. She would rather be down in the kitchen with Edna than unpack her telescope now.

She guessed she would go down where the rest of them were.

Elmer came into the house for dinner. He brought in a cold, muddy, outdoor breath with him. The range was going, but the bright little kitchen seemed chilly, with the white oilcloth on the table, the baby's varnished high chair and his little fat mottled hands.

Edna made a significant little face at Elmer. Daisy did not

see. She was standing back from the stove, where Edna was at work, looking at the baby.

"He can talk pretty good, can't he? Dwight couldn't say anything but 'mama' when he was that little."

Edna's back was turned. She said meaningly:

"Now, Elmer's come in for dinner, Daisy, we'll have to hurry. You must help me get on the dinner. You can cut bread and get things on the table. You must help, you know. That's what you are supposed to do."

Daisy looked startled, a little scared and resentful. "Well, I don't know where you keep your bread."

"Don't you remember where I told you to put it this morning? Right over in the cabinet, in that big box. You must watch, Daisy, and learn where things are."

Elmer, a little embarrassed at the look that Edna gave him, whistled as he began to wash his hands at the sink.

"How's daddy's old boy?" he said loudly, giving a poke at the baby's chin.

As Edna passed him, she shook her head and her lips just formed, "Been like that all morning!"

He grinned comprehendingly. Then both their faces became expressionless.

Daisy had not exactly heard, but she looked from one to the other, silent and dimly wondering. The queer ache that had kept starting all through the morning, under her interest in Edna's things and doings, came over her again. She sensed something different in the atmosphere than she had ever known before—some queer difference between the position of herself and of the two babies, a faint notion of what mama had meant when she had said that this would not be visiting.

"I guess I'm going to have the toothache again," she said faintly.

No one seemed to hear her.

Edna whisked off the potatoes, drained the water. . . . "You might bring me a dish, Daisy." Daisy searched a long time while Edna turned impatiently and pointed. Edna put the rest of the things on the table herself. Her young, fresh, capable mouth was tightly closed, and she was making certain resolutions.

Daisy stood hesitating in the middle of the room, a scrawny, unappealing little figure. Billy—fat, blond, in funny, dark blue union-alls—was trotting busily about the kitchen. Daisy swooped down upon him and tried to bring him to the table. He set up a howl. Edna turned, looked astonished, severe.

"I was trying to make him come to the table," Daisy explained weakly.

"You scared him. He isn't used to you. He doesn't like it. Don't cry, Billy. The girl didn't mean anything."

"Here, daddy'll put him in his place," Elmer said hastily.

Billy looked over his father's shoulder at Daisy with suffused, resentful blue eyes. She did not understand it, and felt strangely at a loss. She had been left with Goldie and Dwight so often. She had always made Dwight go to the table. She had been the boss.

Edna said in a cool, held-in voice, "Put these things on the table, Daisy."

They sat down. Daisy and the other children had always felt it a great treat to eat away from home instead of at their own scanty, hastily set table. They had hung around Mrs. Metzinger's house at noon, hoping to be asked to stay, not offended when told that "it was time for them to run off now." Her pinched little face had a hungry look as she stared at the potatoes and fried ham and pie. But they did not watch and urge her to have more, as Mrs. Metzinger did, and Mrs. Brooker when she took pity on the Switzers and had them there. Daisy wanted more pie. But none of them seemed to be taking more, and so she said nothing. She remembered what her mother had said, with now a faint comprehension. "You must remember you're out working for other folks, and it won't be like it is at home.

After dinner Edna said, "Now you can wash the dishes, Daisy."

She went into the next room with the children. Daisy, as she went hesitatingly about the kitchen alone, could hear Edna's low contented humming as she sat in there rocking, the baby in her lap. The bright kitchen was empty and lonely now. Through the window, Daisy could see the great barn looming up against the rainy sky. She hoped that they would drive to Edna's mother's soon.

She finished as soon as she could and went into the dining room where Edna was sewing on the baby's rompers. Edna went on sewing. Daisy sat down disconsolately. That queer low ache went all through her. She said in a small dismal voice:

"I guess I got the toothache again."

Edna bit off a thread.

"I had it awful hard awhile ago. Mama come pretty near taking me to the dentist."

"That's too bad," Edna murmured politely. But she offered no other condolence. She gave a little secret smile at the baby asleep on a blanket and a pillow in one corner of the shiny leather davenport.

"Is Elmer going to drive into town tomorrow?"

"Tomorrow? I don't suppose so."

"Mama couldn't find the belt of my plaid dress and I thought if he was, maybe I could go along and get it. I'd like to have it."

Daisy's homely mouth drooped at the corners. Her toothache did not seem to matter to anyone. Edna did not seem to want to see that anything was wrong with her. She had expected Edna to be concerned, to mention remedies. But it wasn't toothache, that strange lonesome ache all over her. Maybe she was going to be terribly sick. Mama wouldn't come home for supper to be told about it.

She saw mama's face as in that last glimpse of it—drawn with crying, and yet trying to smile, under the old cleaning cap, her hand holding her coat together . . .

Edna glanced quickly at her. The child was so mortally unattractive, unappealing even in her forlornness. Edna frowned a little, but said kindly:

"Now you might take Billy into the kitchen out of my way, Daisy, and amuse him."

"Well, he cries when I pick him up," Daisy said faintly.

"He won't cry this time. Take him out and help him play with his blocks. You must help me with the children, you know."

"Well, if he'll go with me."

"He'll go with you, won't he, Billy boy? Won't you go with Daisy, sweetheart?"

Billy stared and then nodded. Daisy felt a thrill of comfort as Billy put his little fat hand in hers and trotted into the kitchen beside her. He had the fattest hands, she thought. Edna brought the blocks and put the box down on the floor beside Daisy.

"Now, see if you can amuse him so that I can get my sewing done."

"Shall you and me play blocks, Billy?" Daisy murmured.

He nodded. Then he got hold of the box with one hand,

tipped out all the blocks on the floor with a bang and a rattle, and looked at her with a pleased proud smile.

"Oh no, Billy. You mustn't spill out the blocks. Look, you're too little to play with them. No, now—now wait! Let Daisy show you. Daisy'll build you something real nice—shall she?"

He gave a solemn nod of consent.

Daisy set out the blocks on the bright linoleum. She had never had such blocks as these to handle before. Dwight's were only a few old, unmatched, broken ones. Her spirit of leadership came back, and she firmly put away that fat hand of Billy's whenever he meddled with her building. She could make something really wonderful with these blocks.

"No, Billy, you mustn't. See, when Daisy's got it all done, then you can see what the lovely building is."

She put the blocks together with great interest. She knew what she was going to make—it was going to be a new house; no, a new church. Just as she got the walls up, in came that little hand again, and then with a delighted grunt Billy swept the blocks pellmell about the floor. At the clatter, he sat back, pursing his mouth to give an ecstatic "Ooh!"

"Oh, Billy—you mustn't, the building wasn't done! Look, you've spoiled it. Now, you've got to sit 'way off here while I try to build it over again."

Billy's look of triumph turned to surprise and then to vociferous protest as Daisy picked him up and firmly transplanted him to another corner of the room. Het set up a tremendous howl. He had never been set aside like that before. Edna came hurrying out. Daisy looked at Edna for justification, but instinctively on the defensive.

"Billy knocked over the blocks. He spoiled the building."

"Wah! Wah!" Billy gave loud heartbroken sobs. The tears ran down his fat cheeks and he held out his arms piteously toward his mother.

"I didn't hurt him," Daisy said, scared.

"Never mind, lover," Edna was crooning. "Of course he can play with his blocks. They're Billy's blocks, Daisy," she said. "He doesn't like to sit and see you put up buildings. He wants to play, too. See, you've made him cry now."

"Do' wanna stay here," Billy wailed.

"Well, come in with mother then." She picked him up, wiping his tears.

"I didn't hurt him," Daisy protested.

"Well, never mind now. You can pick up the blocks and then sweep up the floor, Daisy. You didn't do that when you finished the dishes. Never mind," she was saying to Billy. "Pretty soon daddy'll come in and we'll have a nice ride."

Daisy soberly picked up the blocks and got the broom. What had she done to Billy? He had tried to spoil her building. She had always made Dwight keep back until she had finished. Of course it was Daisy, the oldest, who should lead and manage. There had been no one to hear her side. Everything was different. She winked back tears as she swept, poorly and carelessly.

Then she brightened up as Elmer came tramping up on the back porch and then through the kitchen.

"Edna!"

"She's in there," Daisy offered.

"Want to go now? What? Is the baby asleep?" he asked blankly.

Edna gave him a warning look and the door was closed.

Daisy listened hard. She swept very softly. She could catch only a little of what they said—"Kind of hate to go off . . . I know, but if we once start . . . not a thing all day . . . what we got her for . . ." She had no real comprehension of it. She hurried and put away the broom. She wanted to be sure and be ready to go.

Elmer tramped out, straight past her. She saw from the window that he was backing the car out from the shed. She could hear Edna and Billy upstairs, could hear the baby cry a little as he was wakened. Maybe she ought to go out and get her wraps, too.

Elmer honked the horn. A moment later Edna came hurrying downstairs, in her hat and coat, and Billy in a knitted cap and a red sweater crammed over his union-alls, so that he looked like a little brownie. The baby had on his little coat, too.

Edna called out, "Come in and get this boy, daddy." She did not look at Daisy, but said hurriedly, "We're going for a little ride, Daisy. Have you finished the sweeping? Well, then, you can pick up those pieces in the dining room. We won't be gone so very long. When it's a quarter past five, you start the fire, like I showed you this noon, and slice the potatoes that were left, and the meat. And set the table."

The horn was honked again.

"Yes! Well, we'll be back, Daisy. Come, lover, daddy's in a hurry."

Daisy stood looking after them. Billy clamored to sit beside his daddy. Edna took the baby from Elmer and put him beside her on the back seat. There was room—half of the big back seat. There wasn't anything, really, to be done at home. That was the worst of it. They just didn't want to take her. They all belonged together. They didn't want to take anyone else along. She was an outsider. They all—even the baby—had a freshened look of expectancy.

The engine roared—they had started; slipping on the mud of the drive, then forging straight ahead, around the turn, out of sight.

She went forlornly into the dining room. The light from the windows was dim now in the rainy, late afternoon. The pink pieces from the baby's rompers were scattered over the gay rug. She got down on her hands and knees, slowly picking them up, sniffing a little. She heard the Big Ben clock in the kitchen ticking loudly.

That dreadful ache submerged her. No one would ask about it, no one would try to comfort her. Before, there had always been mama coming home, anxious, scolding sometimes, but worried over them if they didn't feel right, caring about them. Mama and Goldie and Dwight cared about her—but she was away out in the country, and they were at home. She didn't want to stay here, where she didn't belong. But mama had told her that she must begin helping this summer.

Her ugly little mouth contorted into a grimace of weeping. But silent weeping, without any tears; because she already had the cold knowledge that no one would notice or comfort it.

A Student in Economics

GEORGE MILBURN

ALL OF the boys on the third floor of Mrs. Gooch's approved rooms for men had been posted to get Charlie Wingate up that afternoon. He had to go to see the Dean. Two or three of them forgot all about it and two or three of them had other things to do, but Eddie Barbour liked waking people up. Eddie stuck his weasel face in at Charlie's door just as the alarm clock was giving one last feeble tap. The clock stood on the bottom of a tin washpan that was set upside down on a wooden chair beside the bed. The alarm had made a terrific din. Eddie had heard it far down the hall. The hands showed two o'clock. Pale needles from a December sun were piercing the limp green window shade in a hundred places.

Eddie Barbour yelled, "Aw right, Charlie! Snap out of it!" He came into the chilly room and stood for a moment staring vaguely at the ridge of quilts on the sagged iron bed. The only sound was the long, regular sough of Charlie Wingate's breathing. He hadn't heard a thing. Eddie made a sudden grab for the top of the covers, stripped them back and began jouncing the sleeper by the shoulders. Charlie grunted every time the bed springs creaked, but he nuzzled his pillow and went on sleeping. Eddie went over to the study table where a large, white-enameled water pitcher stood and he came back to the bed with the water, breathing giggles. He tipped the water pitcher a little and a few drops fell on the back of Charlie's neck without waking him. Eddie sloshed the icy water up over the pitcher's mouth. A whole cupful splashed on Charlie's head. Charlie sat up quickly, batting his arms about, and Eddie Barbour whinnied with laughter.

"Arise, my lord, for the day is here," he said, going across and ceremoniously raising the crooked window shade. Charlie sat straight up among the rumpled quilts with his head cocked on one side, staring dully. He had slept with his clothes on. He sat up in bed all dressed, in a soldier's brown uniform, all but his shoes and roll puttees.

"You got army today?" asked Eddie, putting the pitcher down.

70

Charlie looked at him for a moment and blinked. Then he said in a voice stuffy with sleep, "Naw. I had army yesterday. I got army make-up today." He worked his mouth, making clopping noises.

"What time you got army make-up, Charlie? When you come in from class you said get you up because you had to go see the Dean at two-thirty."

"Yeah, I do have to go see the Dean at two-thirty. But I got army make-up too. I got to make up drill cuts from three till six." All at once he flopped back down on the bed, sound asleep again.

"Hey! Eddie cried, jumping forward. "Come out of that! Wake up there, Charlie! You can't sleep no more if you got to see the Dean at two-thirty. You just about got time to make it." He jerked him back up in bed.

"Two hours' sleep ain't enough," Charlie said.

"Is two hours all the sleep you got last night?"

"Where you get the 'last night'? I worked all night last night. I had classes till noon today. Two hours' sleep was all I got today. And darn little more yesterday or the day before. When is Sunday? Sunday's the first day I'm due to get any real sleep. Two hours' sleep is not enough sleep for a man to get."

Charlie Wingate loped up the steps of the Administration Building, hurried through the revolving doors, and walked past hissing steam radiators down the long hall to the Dean of Men's office. He was ten minutes late. Before he opened the frosted-glass door he took out a pair of amber-colored spectacles and put them on. Then he went in and handed his summons to the secretary.

"The Dean will see you in a moment," she said. "Please take a chair."

Charlie sat down and gave an amber-hued glance about the outer office. Three dejected freshmen, holding their green caps, were waiting with him. He recognized none of them, so he picked up a week-old copy of the Christian Science Monitor and started to read it. But the room was warm and he immediately went to sleep. He had his head propped back against the wall. The newspaper slipped down into his lap. His amber-colored glasses hid his eyes and no one could see that they were closed. He was awakened by the secretary shaking him. She was smiling and the freshmen were all snickering.

"Wake up and pay for your bed, fella!" one of the freshmen called, and everyone laughed heartily.

"I sort of drowsed off. It's so nice and warm in here," Charlie said, apologizing to the pretty secretary.

The Dean of Men got up as he entered and, with his eyes on the slip bearing Charlie's name, said, "Ah, this is Charles Wingate, isn't it?" He grasped Charlie's hand as if it were an honor and pressed a button under the edge of his desk with his other hand. The secretary appeared at the door. "Miss Dunn, will you bring in Wingate's folder—Charles W-i-n-g-a-t-e. How do you like college by now, Wingate? Eyes troubling you?"

"Pretty well, sir. Yes, sir, a little. I wear these glasses."

The secretary came back with the folder and the Dean looked through it briefly. "Well, Wingate, I suppose you're anxious to know why I sent for you. The unpleasant truth is, Wingate, you don't seem to be doing so well in your college work. Your freshman adviser conferred with you twice about this, and this week he turned your case over to me. My purpose, of course, is to help you. Now, to be quite frank, Wingate, you're on the verge of flunking out. Less than a third of the semester remains, and you have a failing grade in English 101, conditional grades in Psychology 51 and Military Training; three hours of F and four hours of D, almost half your total number of hours. On the other hand, you have an A average in Spanish 1 and a B in Economics 150. Wingate, how do you account for your failing English when you are an A student in Spanish?"

"To tell you the truth, sir, I got behind on my written work in English, and I've never been able to catch up. And I don't really have to study Spanish. My father is a railway section foreman in my home town, and he's always had a gang of Mexicans working for him. I've been speaking Mexican ever since I was a kid. It's not the pure, what they call Castilian, Spanish, but I probably know almost as much Spanish as my professor."

"How about this B in Economics? That's a fairly high grade."

"Yes, sir. Doctor Kenshaw—he's my Ec professor—doesn't give exams. Instead he gives every one a B until he calls for our term papers. We don't recite in his class. We just listen to him lecture. And the grade you get on your term paper is your semester grade."

"Ah! What you students term a pipe course, eh, Wingate?"

"Not exactly, sir. We have to do a lot of outside reading for the term paper. But I'm counting on keeping that B in Ec."

"That's fine, Wingate. But it appears to me that it's high time you were getting busy on some of these other grades, too. Why can't you dig in and pull these D's up to B's, and this F up to at least a C? You've got it in you. You made an unusually high grade on your entrance exams, your record shows. Graduated from high school with honors. What's the trouble, Wingate? Tell me!"

"I don't know, sir, except I work at night and———"

"Oh, I see it here on your enrollment card. Where do you work?"

"I work nights for Nick Pappas, down at The Wigwam."

"How many hours do you work?"

"Ten hours, sir. From nine till seven. The Wigwam stays open all night. I eat and go to eight o'clock class when I get off."

"Very interesting, Wingate. But don't you suppose that it would be advisable to cut down a bit on this outside work and attend a little more closely to your college work? After all, that's what you're here for, primarily—to go to college, not work in a cafe."

"I couldn't work fewer hours and stay in school, sir. I just barely get by as it is. I get my board at The Wigwam, and I pay my room rent, and I've been paying out on a suit of clothes. That leaves only about a dollar a week for all the other things I have to have."

"Wingate, shouldn't you earn more than that, working ten hours?"

"I get the regular, first-year-man rate, sir. Twenty-five cents an hour. It's set by the university. Nick takes out for board."

"Can't you arrange for a little financial support from home?"

"No, sir, I'm afraid I couldn't. I have two brothers and two sisters at home younger than I am. It wouldn't be right for me to ask my father to send money out of what he makes."

"But surely you could get out and land something a little more lucrative than this all-night restaurant job, Wingate."

"No, sir. Twenty-five cents is the standard rate for working students, and I haven't found anything better. Nick says he has at least twenty men on the waiting list for this job I have."

"Well, there's this about it, Wingate. The university is here, supported by the taxpayers of this State, for the purpose of giving the young men and women of this State educational opportunities. The university is not here for the purpose of training young men to be waiters in all-night restaurants. And, so far as I can see, that's about all you are deriving from your university career. So it occurs to me that you should make a choice: either find some way to devote more attention to your college work or drop out of school altogether. We are very loath to encourage students who are *entirely* self-supporting. And yet, I will admit that I know any number of first-rate students who are entirely self-supporting. There's Aubery Carson, for example. Quarterback on the football team, delegate to the Olympics, president of the Student Senate, and he's a straight A student. Aubery Carson was telling me only last week that he hasn't had any financial assistance from home since he enrolled as a freshman. Aubery is a fine example of the working student."

"Yes, sir; but look at the job Carson has. He works for a big tobacco company, and all he has to do is hand out Treasure Trove cigarettes to other students. The tobacco company pays him a good salary for passing out samples of their cigarettes."

"Why, Wingate, you surely must be mistaken about that. I don't believe Aubery Carson smokes. In fact, I know he doesn't smoke. He's one of the finest all-round athletes in this country."

"No, sir; I don't say he smokes either. But that's the straight stuff about his job with the cigarette company. They figure it's a good advertisement to have a popular guy like Aubery Carson passing out Treasure Troves. Sort of an endorsement."

"All the same, Wingate, it doesn't reflect a very good attitude on your part, criticizing the way one of your fellow students earns his college expenses."

"Oh, I didn't mean to criticize him, sir. I was only saying——"

"Yes, yes, I know; but all this is beside the point. We're here to discuss the state of your grades, Wingate. The fact is, you are on probation right now. As you must know, any student who is passing in less than half his work is automatically suspended from the university and must return to his home. Now one F more and out you'll go, Wingate. That's just being frank with you."

"I'd hate to have to go back home like that, sir."

"Well, you'd have to. If you flunk out, the university authorities are obliged to see that you return to your home immediately."

"I'd hate that, sir. I'd hate to go back home and have to live off my family, and that's probably what I'd have to do. I had a letter from mother yesterday, and she says that nearly all the boys who graduated from high school with me are still there, loafing on the streets and living off their old folks. I don't like that idea. Mother's proud of me because I'm working my way through college. You know there are not many jobs to be had nowadays, sir, and I'd hate to have to go back home and loaf."

"It is a problem, I'll confess, Wingate. But what's the point in your coming to the university and working all night in a cafe and then flunking your class work? Moreover, your freshman adviser reports that you make a practice of sleeping in class. Is that true?"

"Well, yes, sir. I suppose I do drop off sometimes."

"Pretty impossible situation, isn't it, Wingate? Well, I've given you the best advice I can. Unless you can alter your circumstances I suggest that you withdraw from the university at once. We have six thousand other students here who need our attention, and the university has to be impartial and impersonal in dealing with these problems. Unless you can find some means to avoid flunking out I suggest withdrawing beforehand."

"Withdrawal would be a disgrace to me, sir. If I withdrew and went back home now, everyone at home would say that I had been expelled. You know how small towns are."

"Ah, now, Wingate, when you begin dealing with small-town gossip, I fear you're really getting outside my province. But I should think you'd prefer honorable withdrawal to flunking out."

"I believe I'll try to stick it through, sir. I'll try to remove the conditional grades, and maybe I can luck through on my finals."

"I hope you can, Wingate. As long as you feel that way about it, good luck to you." The Dean of Men stood up. Charlie stood up too. The Dean put out his hand and showed his teeth in a jovial smile and bore down hard on Charlie's knuckles. "I'm counting on you strong, old man," he said, encircling Charlie's shoulders with his left arm. "I know you have the stuff and that you'll come through with flying colors one of these days."

"Thank you, sir," Charlie said, grinning tearfully while the Dean gave his shoulder little pats. He edged toward the door as soon as the Dean released him, but when he reached it he hesitated and pulled the postal card out of his pocket. "Oh, pardon me, sir, but there's something I forgot to ask you. I got this in the mail today. I've been a little bothered about what to make of it."

The Dean of Men took the mimeographed card and read it quickly. "Why, I should say that you ought to go see what they want, Wingate. You shouldn't ignore things of this sort, you know. It's all a part of the normal activities of college life. No reason for antagonizing your fellow-students."

"All right, sir; I'll go see them."

"Why, to be sure, go see them! Always keep in mind that the university is a social as well as an educational institution, Wingate."

Room 204, Student Union Building, was a newly finished, rather barren office that smelled dankly of lime in the fresh plaster. It was fitted with a metal desk painted to imitate painted walnut, a large brass spittoon, a square metal waste-paper basket, a green metal filing cabinet, a large bank calendar, a huge pasteboard shipping case, and J. Aubery Carson, who had the freshman cap concession.

Charlie Wingate hesitantly opened the door and saw J. Aubery Carson tilted back in a chair, his feet on the metal walnut desk, reading a copy of *Life*.

"Co-ome in! Co-ome in!" J. Aubery Carson called loudly without putting down his magazine. "All right, old timer. What's on your mind?"

Charlie held out the mimeographed card. Carson held his magazine a moment longer before accepting the card. He shoved his hat down over one eye, turning the card, looking first at the back, then at the name on the front. "Um-m-m," he grunted. He reached over to a drawer in the filing cabinet without taking his feet down and flipped through the cards. He looked at the name on the postal card again, pulled his thick lips up into a rosette. He looked at the file card in silence.

"Wingate," he said at last in a severe tone, "you have been dilatory. Indeed, Wingate, I might even go so far as to say you have been remiss. At the beginning of this semester you applied for and received a refund on your student ticket fee. That signifies that you have not attended a single football game this season, and that you have no intention of honoring any of the university's athletic spectacles with your presence this season. Also, the record discloses that you did not register at the Y.M.C.A. freshman mixer. Neither did you respond to polite solicitation for a trifling monetary pledge to the Memorial Stadium Fund.

"And, furthermore, your most heinous offense of all, Wingate, we find that you have yet to pay in one dollar for your freshman cap, prescribed by your seniors and purveyed to you on a nonprofit basis by the Student Committee on Freshman Activities. And yet, Wingate, I find you duly enrolled and attending classes in this here now university. Wingate, what possible excuse do you have for such gross neglect of university tradition? Speak up!"

Charlie said meekly, "Well, I work nights and it's hard for me to get here in the daytime, and I can't afford to buy a cap."

"What's this!" Carson exclaimed, jerking his legs down from the desk top and banging the desk with two flat hands. "Why, boy, this is treason! You mean you can't afford *not* to buy a freshman cap."

"No, I just came to tell you that a dollar has to go a long way with me and that I need every cent I earn to stay in school. So I wish you'd please excuse me from buying a freshman cap."

Carson's lean, florid face suddenly became rigid and he stuck his jaw out with his lower teeth showing and, in spite of his marcelled taffy pompadour and his creased tailored suit, he again looked very much as he did in all the sporting section photographs. "See here, Wingate," he said, hard-lipped, "you're still a freshman at this university. You'll have to wait another year before you can start saying what you will do and won't do, see? Now we've been patient with you. You've been in school here three months without putting on a freshman cap. Do you realize that over eighty-five per cent of the freshman class came in here and bought their caps before the first week of school ended? Now who do you think you are, Wingate? You're going to get you a cap, and you're going to wear it. See? No ifs, ands, or buts about it. And if you don't leave this office with a green cap on your head then I don't mind telling you that we've got ways of getting one on you before another day passes."

"Well, if I buy one it's going to put me in a bad hole. All the money I've got is what I saved out to pay my room rent this week."

"Listen, fella, if we let horsefeathers like that go here, half the freshman class wouldn't be wearing freshman caps right now. Now I've said all I'm going to to you. Do you want your green cap now or will you wait till later? That's all I want to know. I don't aim to give you any highpressure sales talk on something that's already been decided for you. Take it or leave it."

Carson reached over into the large pasteboard box, groped far down in it, and brought forth a small green monkey cap. He tossed it on the desk. Charlie Wingate stuck his forefinger in his watch pocket and pulled out a small pad of three carefully folded dollar bills. He unfolded them and laid one on the desk and picked up the cap. Carson put the dollar in his pocket and stood up.

Charlie stood holding his cap. He scuffed the cement floor with his shoe toe and began doggedly, "The only thing is——"

"Aw, that's O.K., Wingate, old man," Carson said suavely. "No hard feelings whatsoever." He held out a freshly opened pack of cigarettes. "Here, have a Treasure Trove on me before you go."

That night all the stools along the counter at The Wigwam were filled when Charlie Wingate came in, still dusty from the drill field. He got himself a set-up back of the counter and went into the kitchen. He moved about the steamtable, dishing up his dinner. He dragged a stool over to a zinc-covered kitchen table and sat down to eat. The kitchen was warm and steamy and the air was thick with the odors of sour chili grease and yellow soap melting in hot dishwater. Charlie's fork slipped through his fingers and he began nodding over his plate.

Fat Kruger, the night dishwasher and short-order cook, yelled, "Hey, there, wake up and pay for your bed!" Charlie jerked his head up and looked at the ponderous, good-humored cook with half-lidded eyes. "Why'n't you try sleeping in bed once in a while, Charlie?" Fat said in friendly tone. "You're going to kill yourself if you don't watch out, trying to go without sleep."

"Don't worry, Fat. I can take it," Charlie said.

Almost two hours had to pass before it would be the hour for him to come on, but not time enough for him to walk back to his room and catch a nap, so he took the book on which he had to make an outside reading report in Economics 150 and went up to the last booth to study until nine o'clock. He fell asleep and he did not wake up until Red Hibbert, going off, shook him and told him that it was almost time for him to come on. He took down his apron and tied it on over his army breeches. Then he slipped into a white coat.

At one o'clock Charlie finished cleaning off the last of the tables. The Wigwam was empty, so he opened the book he must read for Ec 150. He had read a few lines when a bunch of girls from the Theta house down the street came charging in, giggling and talking in gasps and screams, their fur coats clutched over their sleeping pajamas. It was long after the closing hour, and they told Charlie to keep an eye out for the university night watchman. They took up the two back booths and they consulted The Wigwam's printed menu card without failing to read aloud the lines "Nick (Pericles) Pappas." "We Employ Student Help Exclusively," and "Please Do Not Tip. A Smile Is Our Reward" with the customary shrieks. Nearly all ordered filets mignon and French fries, which were not on the menu, but two or three ordered pecan waffles and coffee, which were. When he had served their orders Charlie went back to his book again, but the low buzz of their talk and their sudden spurts of laughter disturbed him and he could not read. At a quarter of two they began peering round corners of their booths. They asked Charlie in stage whispers if the coast was clear.

Charlie went to the door and looked out on the street and beckoned widely with his arm. They trooped out with their fur coats pulled tight, their fur-trimmed silken mules slapping their bare heels. Charlie went on back to clear away their dishes. They had left about thirty cents as a tip, all in cents and nickels. The coins were carefully imbedded in the cold steak grease and gluey syrup and putty-colored cigarette leavings on their plates. Charlie began stacking the plates without touching the money. He carried the dirty dishes back and set them through the opening in the kitchen wall. Fat Kruger came to the opening and Charlie went back to his book. Fat called, "Hey, Charlie, you leavin' this tip again?"

"You're right, I'm leaving it!" Charlie said. "I can get along without their tips. They leave it that way every time. I guess they think I'll grabble on their filthy plates to get a lousy thirty cents. It takes a woman to think up something like that."

"Charlie, you're too proud. I don't see where you can afford to be so proud. The way I figure it, thirty cents is thirty cents."

"I'm not proud, Fat. I just try to keep my self-respect. When those sorority girls come in and plant their tips in the dirt and grease of their plates, damn' if I'll lower myself to grub it out."

He sat down on a counter stool with the economics book before him, trying to fix his mind on it. He read a page. The print became thin, blurred parallels of black on the page. His eyelids kept drooping shut and he propped the muscles with his palms at his temples, trying to keep his eyes open. His head jerked forward and he caught it and began reading again. Soon his face lowered slowly through his hands and came to rest on the open book.

Fat Kruger came through the kitchen swinging door and tiptoed up front. Fat stood grinning, watching Charlie sleep. Cramped over with his head on the counter, Charlie snored softly. Fat gave his head a gentle shove, and Charlie started up to catch his balance.

"For gosh sakes, guy, you're *dead!*" Fat howled. "Don't you never get no sleep except like that?"

"What time is it?" Charlie said, yawning and arching his back.

"Half-past two."

"Is that all?"

"Charlie, I wouldn't put my eyes out over that book if I was you, when you're dyin' for sleep," Fat said.

"I've got to get it read, Fat. It's my outside reading in Economics and the whole semester grade depends on it. It's the hardest book to keep your mind on you ever saw. I've been reading on it for over a month and I'm only half through, and he's going to call for these reports any day now. If I flunk Ec I flunk out of school."

"Why mess with reading it? I know a guy over at the Masonic Dorm who'll read it and write your report for two bucks. He writes all my English themes for me, and I'm making a straight A in English. He only charges fifty cents for short themes and two bucks for term papers. You ought to try him."

"Well, Fat, you get five dollars a week from home. Where am I going to get two dollars for hiring a guy to read this book?"

"Charlie, I just can't figure you out. You never do get any real sleep. You sure must want a college education bad. It don't look to me like you would figure it's worth it."

"Oh, it's worth it! It's a big satisfaction to my folks to have me in college. And where can a man without a college degree get nowadays? But I'll tell you the truth, I didn't know it was going to be like this when I came down here last fall. I used to read *College Humor* in high school, and when fellows came home from university for the holidays, all dressed up in snappy clothes, talking about dates and football and dances, and using college slang—well, I had a notion I'd be like that when I got down here. The university publicity department sent me a little booklet showing how it was easy to work your way through college. So here I am. I haven't had a date or been to a dance or seen a football game since I enrolled. And there are plenty of others just like me. I guess I'm getting a college education, all right—but the only collegiate thing I've been able to do is go to sleep in class."

"How you get by with sleeping in class, Charlie?"

"I wear those colored spectacles and prop myself, and the profs can't see I've got my eyes closed."

Fat waggled his heavy face mournfully. "Boy, it sure is tough when a man don't get his sleep."

"Yeah, it is," Charlie said, looking down at his book again. "I'll get a break pretty soon, though. I'd rather chop off a hand than to flunk out of university before I'd even finished one semester."

The tardiest of the hundred students enrolled in Dr. Sylvester C. O. Kenshaw's Economics 150 straggled into the lecture room and made their ways to alphabetically assigned chairs with much scuffling and trampling of toes and mumbled apologies. Ec 150, renowned as a pipe course, was always crowded. The only students who ever flunked Ec 150 were those who gave affront to Doctor Kenshaw by neglecting to buy his textbooks or by not laughing at his wit or by being outrageously inattentive to his lectures.

Doctor Kenshaw was late that morning. Charlie Wingate sat in his chair on the back row in an agony of waiting. He had on his amber glasses and he could fall asleep as soon as Doctor Kenshaw opened his lecture. But he had to stay awake until then. There was a slow ache in the small of his back. The rest of his body was numb. He had not taken off his army shoes for twenty hours, and his feet were moist and swollen. Every time he shifted position his arms and legs were bathed in prickling fire. He kept his eyes open behind the amber lenses, watching the clock. Small noises of the classroom came to him as a low, far-off humming.

When the clock on the front wall showed nine after eleven the seated class began stirring as if it were mounted on some eccentric amusement-park device. Excited whispers eddied out on the warm air of the steam-heated lecture room. "He's giving us another cut!" "He's not meeting this class today!" "He's got one more minute to make it!" "Naw; six more! You have to wait fifteen minutes on department heads."

There was a seething argument on this point, but when the clock showed fourteen minutes after eleven a bold leader sprang up and said, "Come on, everybody!" All but five or six especially conscientious students rose and milled after him toward the door. Charlie Wingate followed, thoroughly awakened by the chance of getting to bed so soon. The leader yanked the door open and Doctor Kenshaw stumbled in, all out of breath, his eyeglasses steamed, his pointed gray beard quivering, a vain little man in a greenish-black overcoat.

"Go back to your seats!" Doctor Kenshaw commanded sternly as soon as he could get his breath. He marched over to his lecture table and planked down his leather brief case. He took off his overcoat and began wiping the steam from his eyeglasses while the students hurried back to their chairs. "It does seem to me," he said, his voice quavering with anger, "that it would be no more than courteous for this class to await my arrival on those rare occasions when I am delayed."

A few students exchanged meaning glances. They meant, "Now we're in for it. The old boy has on one of his famous mads."

"Today, I believe I shall forego delivering my prepared lecture," Doctor Kenshaw went on in a more even voice, but with elaborate sarcasm, "and let you do the talking. Perhaps it would be moot to hear a few outside reading reports this morning. All of you doubtless are aware that these reports were due last week, although I had not expected to call for them at once. I trust that I have impressed you sufficiently with the importance of these reports. They represent to me the final result of your semester's work in this course. The grades you receive on these reports will be your grades for the semester. Let us begin forthwith. When your name is called, you will rise and read your report to the class."

"Mr. Abbot!" he called. Mr. Abbot stammered an excuse. Doctor Kenshaw passed coldly on to Miss Adams, making no comment. All through the A's it was the same. But with the B's an ashen, spectacled Miss Ballentyne stood up and began reading in a droning voice her report on "The Economic Consequences of the Peace." Obviously Doctor Kenshaw was not listening to her. His hard little eyes under craggy brows were moving up one row and down the other, eager for a victim. On the back row, Charlie Wingate's propped legs had given way and he had slipped far down into his seat, fast asleep. When Doctor Kenshaw's preying eyes reached Charlie they stopped moving. Someone tittered nervously and then was silent as Doctor Kenshaw jerked his head round in the direction of the noise. Miss Ballentyne droned on.

When she had finished, Doctor Kenshaw said dryly, "Very good, Miss Ballentyne, very good indeed. Er—ah—would someone be kind enough to arouse the recumbent young gentleman in the last row?"

There was a murmur of laughter while everyone turned to look at Milton Weismann nudging Charlie Wingate. Doctor Kenshaw was running down the list of names in his small record book. Milton Weismann gave Charlie another stiff poke in the ribs, and Charlie sprang up quickly. Everyone laughed loudly at that.

"Mr.—ah—Wingate, isn't it? Mr. Wingate, your report."

"Pardon me, sir?"

"Mr. Wingate, what was the title of the book assigned to you for report in this class?"

"*Theory of the Leisure Class* by Veblen, sir."

"Ah, then that's the explanation. So you were assiduously engaged in evolving your own theory of the leisure class. Is that right, Mr. Wingate? You have evidently concluded that Economics 150 is the leisure class."

The class rocked with laughter. Doctor Kenshaw, pleased with his pun and flattered by the response to it, found it hard to keep his face straight. Suddenly he was back in good humor. "Mr. Wingate's theory is quite apparently one to which the majority of this class subscribes. Now I try to be lenient with students in this class. Surely no one could describe me as a hard taskmaster. But I resent your implication that I have been too easygoing. Now these reading reports were assigned to you last September, and you have had ample time to prepare them. I'll not call for any more of them today, but at the next session of this class I expect every one of these papers in. As for you, Mr. Wingate, if you'll see me directly after class, I'll be glad to hear any explanation or apology that you may wish to make. I want most of all to be fair. I have always given every student the benefit of the doubt until a student deliberately flouts me with his indifference. But I am capable of being quite ruthless, I assure you."

"Thank you, sir," Charlie mumbled. He entered a slow torture, trying to keep awake until the class bell rang. He rolled his hot, red-veined eyes up with drunken precision to see the clock. Fifteen minutes had to pass before the bell would ring.

When the bell rang the class arose quickly and began clumping out. Several co-eds and men, politickers and apple-polishers wangling for A's, crowded about the lecture table. Doctor Kenshaw always remained behind after each class to accept their homage. But today he looked up over the heads of the eager group. He silenced their inane questions and flagrant compliments by placing his right forefinger against his thin, unsmiling lips. "Sh-h-h!" he said. The apple-polishers turned their heads in the direction of his gaze and then, giggling softly, tiptoed away. When the last had gone out, Doctor Kenshaw unscrewed his fountain pen and opened his roll book. He ran his finger down the list until he came to "Wingate, C." and in the space opposite under "Smstr Grd" he marked a precise little F.

A whiffling snore escaped Charlie Wingate in the back of the room. Doctor Kenshaw looked back across the varnished chair rows with a frown of annoyance. He took his overcoat from its hanger, slipped into it, and strapped up his brief case. He jammed on his hat and strode out of the lecture room, slamming the door. The noise made a hollow echo in the empty room, but it did not disturb Charlie Wingate. He slept on behind his amber glasses.

Romance

WILLIAM SAROYAN

WOULD YOU rather sit on this side or would you rather sit on the other side? the red-cap said.

Hmm? the young man said.

This side is all right? the red-cap said.

Oh, the young man said. Sure.

He gave the red-cap a dime. The red-cap accepted the small thin coin and folded the young man's coat and placed it on the seat.

Some people like one side, he said, and some like the other.

What? the young man said.

The red-cap didn't know if he ought to go into detail, about some people being used to and preferring certain things in the landscape looking out of the train from one side, and others wanting to get both sides of the landscape all the way down and back, preferring one side going down, usually the shady side, but in some cases the opposite, where a lady liked sunlight or had read it was healthy, and the other side coming up, but he imagined it would take too long to explain everything, especially in view of the fact that he wasn't feeling real well and all morning hadn't been able to give that impression of being on excellent terms with everybody which pleased him so much.

I mean, he said, it's no more than what anybody wants, I guess.

The red-cap figured the young man was a clerk who was going to have a little Sunday holiday, riding in a train from a big city to a little one, going and coming the same day, but what he didn't understand was why the young man seemed so lost, or, as the saying is, dead to the world. The boy was young, not perhaps a college graduate, more likely a boy who'd gone through high school and gotten a job in an office somewhere, maybe twenty-three years old, and perhaps in love. Anyhow, the red-cap thought, the young man looked to be somebody who might at any moment fall in love, without much urging. He had that sad or dreamy look of the potential

85

adorer of something in soft and colorful cloth with long hair and smooth skin.

The young man came to an almost violent awakening which very nearly upset the red-cap.

Oh, he said, I've been sort of day-dreaming.

He wiggled the fingers of his right hand near his head, or where people imagined one day-dreamed.

Have I given you a tip? he said.

The red-cap felt embarrassed.

Yes, sir, he said.

The young man wiggled the fingers of his left hand before his face.

I very often forget what I'm doing, he said, until long afterwards—sometimes years. May I ask how much I gave you?

The red-cap couldn't figure it out at all. If the young man was being funny or trying to work some sort of racket, it was just too bad because the red-cap wasn't born yesterday. The young man had given him a dime and if the young man came out with the argument that he had given the red-cap some such ridiculous coin as a five-dollar gold piece the red-cap would simply hold his ground and say, this is all you gave me —this dime.

You gave me a dime, he said.

I'm sorry, the young man said, here.

He gave the red-cap another dime.

Thank you, sir, the red-cap said.

Were you saying something while we were coming down the aisle? the young man said.

Nothing important, the red-cap said. I was only saying how some folks liked to sit on one side and others on the other.

Oh, the young man said. Is this side all right?

Yes, it is, the red-cap said. Unless of course you prefer not getting the sunshine.

No, the young man said, I kind of like the sunshine.

It's a fine day too, the red-cap said.

The young man looked out the window as if at the day. There was nothing but trains to see, but he looked out the window as if he were looking to see how fine a day it was.

The sun don't get in here where it's covered up, the red-cap said, but no sooner than you get out of here into the open you'll be running into a lot of sunshine. Most California folks get tired of it and get over on the other side. You from New York?

There was nothing about the young man to suggest that he was from New York or for that matter from anywhere else either, but the red-cap wondered where the young man was from, so he asked.

No, the young man said, I've never been out of California.

The red-cap was in no hurry, although there was considerable activity everywhere, people piling into the car, other red-caps rushing about, helping with bags, and hurrying away. Nevertheless, he lingered and carried on a conversation. There was a girl across the aisle who was listening to the conversation and the red-cap fancied he and the young man were cutting quite a figure with her, one way or another. It was charming conversation, in the best of spirits, and, although between men in different stations of life, full of that fraternal feeling which is characteristic of westerners and Americans.

I've never been out of California myself, the red-cap said.

You'd think you'd be the sort of man to travel a good deal, the young man said.

Yes, you would at that, the red-cap said. Working on trains, or least-aways near them, on and off most of my life since I was eighteen, which was thirty years ago, but it's true, I haven't set foot outside the boundary lines of this state. I've met a lot of travelers though, he added.

I wouldn't mind getting to New York some day, the young man said.

I don't blame a young man like you for wanting to get to New York, the red-cap said. New York sure must be an interesting place down around in there.

Biggest city in the world, the young man said.

It sure is, the red-cap said, and then he made as if to go, dragging himself away as it were, going away with tremendous regret.

Well, he said, have a pleasant journey.

Thanks, the young man said.

The red-cap left the car. The young man looked out the window and then turned just in time to notice that the girl across the aisle was looking at him and was swiftly turning her head away, and he himself, so as not to embarrass her, swiftly continued turning his head so that something almost happened to his neck. Almost instantly he brought his head all the way back to where it had been, near the window, looking out, and felt an awful eagerness to look at the girl again and at the same time a wonderful sense of at last beginning to go places, in more ways than one, such as meeting people like her and marrying one of them and settling down in a house somewhere.

He didn't look at the girl again, though, for some time but kept wanting to very eagerly, so that finally when he did look at her he was embarrassed and blushed and gulped and tried very hard to smile but just couldn't quite make it. The girl just couldn't make it either.

That happened after they'd been moving along for more than ten minutes, the train rolling out among the hills and rattling pleasantly and making everything everywhere seem pleasant and full of wonderful potentialities, such as romance and a good deal of good humor and easy-going naturalness, especially insofar as meeting her and being friendly and pleasant and little by little getting to know her and falling in love.

They saw one another again after about seven minutes more, and then again after four minutes, and then they saw one another more steadily by pretending to be looking at the landscape on the other side, and finally they just kept seeing one another steadily for a long time, watching the landscape.

At last the young man said, are you from New York?

He didn't know what he was saying. He felt foolish and unlike young men in movies who do such things on trains.

Yes, I am, the girl said.

What? the young man said.

Didn't you ask if I was from New York? the girl said.

Oh, the young man said. Yes, I did.

Well, the girl said, I am.

I didn't know you were from New York, the young man said.

I know you didn't, the girl said.

The young man tried very hard to smile the way they smiled in pictures.

How did you know? he said.

Oh, I don't know, the girl said. Are you going to Sacramento?

Yes, I am, the young man said. Are you?

Yes, I am, the girl said.

What are you doing so far from home? the young man said.

New York isn't my home, the girl said. I was born there, but I've been living in San Francisco most of my life.

So have I most of mine, the young man said. In fact all of it.

I've lived in San Francisco practically all of my life too, the girl said, with the possible exception of them few months in New York.

Is that all the time you lived in New York? the young man said.

Yes, the girl said, only them first five months right after I was born in New York.

I was born in San Francisco, the young man said. There's lots of room on these two seats, he said with great effort. Wouldn't you like to sit over here and get the sun?

All right, the girl said.

She stepped across the aisle and sat across from the young man.

I just thought I'd go down to Sacramento on the special Sunday rate, the young man said.

I've been to Sacramento three times, the girl said.

The young man began to feel very happy. The sun was strong and warm and the girl was wonderful. Unless he was badly mistaken, or unless he got fired Monday morning, or unless America got into a war and he had to become a soldier and go away and get himself killed for no good reason, he had a hunch some day he would go to work and get acquainted with the girl and marry her and settle down.

He sat back in the sunlight while the train rattled along and smiled romantically at the girl, getting ready for the romance.

Clothe the Naked

DOROTHY PARKER

BIG LANNIE went out by the day to the houses of secure and leisured ladies, to wash their silks and their linens. She did her work perfectly; some of the ladies even told her so. She was a great, slow mass of a woman, colored a sound brown-black save for her palms and the flat of her fingers that were like gutta-percha from steam and hot suds. She was slow because of her size, and because the big veins in her legs hurt her, and her back ached much of the time. She neither cursed her ills nor sought remedies for them. They had happened to her; there they were.

Many things had happened to her. She had had children, and the children had died. So had her husband, who was a kind man, cheerful with the little luck he found. None of their children had died at birth. They had lived to be four or seven or ten, so that they had had their ways and their traits and their means of causing love; and Big Lannie's heart was always wide for love. One child had been killed in a street accident and two others had died of illnesses that might have been no more than tedious, had there been fresh food and clear spaces and clean air behind them. Only Arlene, the youngest, lived to grow up.

Arlene was a tall girl, not so dark as her mother but with the same firm flatness of color. She was so thin that her bones seemed to march in advance of her body. Her little pipes of legs and her broad feet with jutting heels were like things a child draws with crayons. She carried her head low, her shoulders scooped around her chest, and her stomach slanted forward.

Big Lannie did not know it, when Arlene was going to have a baby. Arlene had not been home in nearly half a year; Big Lannie told the time in days. There was no news at all of the girl until the people at the hospital sent for Big Lannie to come to her daughter and grandson. She was there to hear Arlene say the baby must be named Raymond, and to see the girl die.

He was a long, light-colored baby, with big, milky eyes that

90

looked right back at his grandmother. It was several days before the people at the hospital told her he was blind.

Big Lannie went to each of the ladies who employed her and explained that she could not work for some while; she must take care of her grandson. The ladies were sharply discommoded, after her steady years, but they dressed their outrage in shrugs and cool tones. Each arrived, separately, at the conclusion that she had been too good to Big Lannie, and had been imposed upon, therefore. "Honestly, those people!" each said to her friends. "They're all alike."

Big Lannie sold most of the things she lived with, and took one room with a stove in it. There, as soon as the people at the hospital would let her, she brought Raymond and tended him. He was all her children to her.

She had always been a saving woman, with few needs and no cravings, and she had been long alone. Even after Arlene's burial, there was enough left for Raymond and Big Lannie to go on for a time. Big Lannie was slow to be afraid of what must come; fear did not visit her at all, at first, and then it slid in only when she waked, when night hung motionless before another day.

Raymond was a good baby, a quiet, patient baby, lying in his wooden box and stretching out his delicate hands to the sounds that were light and color to him. It seemed but a little while, so short to Big Lannie, before he was walking about the room, his hands held out, his feet quick and sure. Those of Big Lannie's friends who saw him for the first time had to be told that he could not see.

Then, and it seemed again such a little while, he could dress himself, and open the door for his granny, and unlace the shoes from her tired feet, and talk to her in his soft voice. She had occasional employment—now and then a neighbor would hear of a day's scrubbing she could do, or sometimes she might work in the stead of a friend who was sick—infrequent, and not to be planned on. She went to the ladies for whom she had worked, to ask if they might not want her back again; but there was little hope in her, after she had visited the first one. Well, now, really, said the ladies; well really, now.

The neighbors across the hall watched over Raymond while Big Lannie looked for work. He was no trouble to them, nor to himself. He sat and crooned at his chosen task. He had been given a wooden spool around the top of which were driven little brads, and over these with a straightened hairpin he looped bright worsted, working faster than sight until a long tube of woven wool fell through the hole in the spool. The neighbors threaded big, blunt needles for him, and he coiled the woolen tubes and sewed them into mats. Big Lannie called them beautiful, and it made Raymond proud to have her tell him how readily she sold them. It was hard for her, when he was asleep at night, to unravel the mats and wash the worsted and stretch it so straight that even Raymond's shrewed fingers could not tell, when he worked with it next day, that it was not new.

Fear stormed in Big Lannie and took her days and nights. She might not go to any organization dispensing relief for fear that Raymond would be taken from her and put in—she would not say the word to herself, and she and her neighbors lowered their voices when they said it to one another—an institution. The neighbors wove lingering tales of what happened inside certain neat, square buildings on the cindery skirts of the town, and, if they must go near them, hurried as if passing graveyards, and came home heroes. When they got you in one of those places, whispered the neighbors, they laid your spine open with whips, and then when you dropped, they kicked your head in. Had anyone come into Big Lannie's room to take Raymond away to an asylum for the blind, the neighbors would have fought for him with stones and rails and boiling water.

Raymond did not know about anything but good. When he grew big enough to go alone down the stairs and into the street, he was certain of delight each day. He held his head high, as he came out into the little yard in front of the flimsy wooden house, and slowly turned his face from side to side, as if the air were soft liquid in which he bathed it. Trucks and wagons did not visit the street, which ended in a dump for rusted bedsprings and broken boilers and staved-in kettles; children played over its cobbles, and men and women sat talking in open windows and called across to one another in gay, rich voices. There was always laughter for Raymond to hear, and he would laugh back, and hold out his hands to it.

At first, the children stopped their play when he came out, and gathered quietly about him, and watched him, fascinated. They had been told of his affliction, and they had a sort of sickened pity for him. Some of them spoke to him, in soft, careful tones. Raymond would laugh with pleasure, and stretch his hands, the curious smooth, flat hands of the blind, to their voices. They would draw sharply back, afraid that his strange hands might touch them. Then, somehow ashamed because they had shrunk from him and he could not see that they had done so, they said gentle good-bys to him, and backed away into the street again, watching him steadily.

When they were gone, Raymond would start on his walk to the end of the street. He guided himself lightly touching the broken fences along the dirt sidewalk, and as he walked he crooned little songs with no words to them. Some of the men and women at the windows would call hello to him, and he would call back and wave and smile. When the children, forgetting him, laughed again at their games, he stopped and turned to the sound as if it were the sun.

In the evening, he would tell Big Lannie about his walk, slapping his knee and chuckling at the memory of the laughter he had heard. When the weather was too hard for him to go out in the street, he would sit at his worsted work, and talk all day of going out the next day.

The neighbors did what they could for Raymond and Big Lannie. They gave Raymond clothes their own children had not yet worn out, and they brought food, when they had enough to spare and other times. Big Lannie would get through a week, and would pray to get through the next one; and so the months went. Then the days on which she could find work fell farther and farther apart, and she could not pray about the time to come because she did not dare to think of it.

It was Mrs. Ewing who saved Raymond's and Big Lannie's lives, and let them continue together. Big Lannie said that then and ever after; daily she blessed Mrs. Ewing, and nightly she would have prayed for her, had she not known, in some dimmed way, that any intercession for Mrs. Delabarre Ewing must be impudence.

Mrs. Ewing was a personage in the town. When she went to Richmond for a visit, or when she returned from viewing the azalea gardens in Charleston, the newspaper always printed the fact. She was a woman rigorously conscious of her noble obligation; she was prominent on the Community Chest committee, and it was she who planned and engineered the annual Bridge Drive to raise funds for planting salvia around the cannon in front of the D.A.R. headquarters. These and many others were her public activities, and she was no less exacting of herself in her private life. She kept a model, though childless, house for her husband and herself, relegating the supervision of details to no domestic lieutenant, no matter how seemingly trustworthy.

Back before Raymond was born, Big Lannie had worked as laundress for Mrs. Ewing. Since those days, the Ewing wash tubs had witnessed many changes, none for the better. Mrs. Ewing took Big Lannie back into her employment. She apologized for this step to her friends by the always winning method of self-deprecation. She knew she was a fool, she said, after all that time, and after the way that Big Lannie had treated her. But still, she said, and she laughed a little at her own ways. Anyone she felt kind of sorry for could always get around her, she said. She knew it was awful foolish, but that, she said, was the way she was. Mr. Ewing, she said outside her husband's hearing, always called her just a regular little old easy mark.

Two days' work in the week meant money for rent and stovewood and almost enough food for Raymond and Big Lannie. She must depend, for anything further, on whatever odd jobs she could find, and she must not stop seeking them. Pressed on by fear and gratitude, she worked so well for Mrs. Ewing that there was sometimes expressed satisfaction at the condition of the lady's household linen and her own and her husband's clothing. Big Lannie had a glimpse of Mr. Ewing occasionally, leaving the house as she came, or entering it as she was leaving. He was a bit of a man, not much bigger than Raymond.

Raymond grew so fast that he seemed to be taller each morning. Every day he had his walk in the street to look forward to and experience and tell Big Lannie about at night. He had ceased to be a sight of the street; the children were so used to him that they did not even look at him, and the men and women at the windows no longer noticed him enough to hail him. He did not know. He would wave to any gay cry he heard, and go on his way, singing his little songs and turning toward the sound of laughter.

Then his lovely list of days ended as sharply as if ripped from some bright calendar. A winter came, so sudden and savage as to find no comparison in the town's memories, and Raymond had no clothes to wear out in the street. Big Lannie mended his outgrown garments as long as she could, but the stuff had so rotted with wear that it split in new places when she tried to sew together the ragged edges of rents.

The neighbors could give no longer; all they had they must keep for their own. A demented colored man in a near-by town had killed the woman who employed him, and terror had spread like brush fire. There was a sort of panic in reprisal; colored employees were dismissed from their positions, and there was no new work for them. But Mrs. Ewing, admittedly soft-hearted certainly to a fault and possibly to a peril, kept her black laundress on. More than ever Big Lannie had reason to call her blessed.

All winter, Raymond stayed indoors. He sat at his spool and worsted, with Big Lannie's old sweater about his shoulders and, when his tattered knickerbockers would no longer hold together, a calico skirt of hers lapped around his waist. He lived, at his age, in the past; in the days when he had walked, proud and glad, in the street, with laughter in his ears. Always, when he talked of it, he must laugh back at that laughter.

Since he could remember, he had not been allowed to go out when Big Lannie thought the weather unfit. This he had accepted without question, and so he accepted his incarceration through the mean weeks of the winter. But then one day it was spring, so surely that he could tell it even in the smoky, stinking rooms of the house, and he cried out with joy because now he might walk in the street again. Big Lannie had to explain to him that his rags were too thin to shield him, and that there were no odd jobs for her, and so no clothes and shoes for him.

Raymond did not talk about the street any more, and his fingers were slow at his spool.

Big Lannie did something she had never done before; she begged of her employer. She asked Mrs. Ewing to give her some of Mr. Ewing's old clothes for Raymond. She looked at the floor and mumbled so that Mrs. Ewing requested her to talk up. When Mrs. Ewing understood, she was, she said, surprised. She had, she said, a great, great many demands on her charity, and she would have supposed that Big Lannie, of all people, might have known that she did everything she could, in fact, a good deal more. She spoke of inches and ells. She said that if she found she could spare anything, Big Lannie was kindly to remember it was to be just for this once.

When Big Lannie was leaving at the end of her day's work, Mrs. Ewing brought her a package with her own hands. There, she said, was a suit and a pair of shoes; beautiful, grand things that people would think she was just crazy to be giving away like that. She simply didn't know, she said, what Mr. Ewing would say to her for being such a crazy. She explained that that was the way she was when anyone got around her, all the while Big Lannie was trying to thank her.

Big Lannie had never before seen Raymond behave as he

did when she brought him home the package. He jumped
and danced and clapped his hands, he tried to squeak and
squealed instead, he tore off the paper himself, and ran his
fingers over the close-woven cloth and held it to his face
and kissed it. He put on the shoes and clattered about in
them, digging with his toes and heels to keep them on; he
made Big Lannie pin the trousers around his waist and roll
them up over his shins. He babbled of the morrow when he
would walk in the street, and could not say his words for
laughing.

Big Lannie must work for Mrs. Ewing the next day, and
she had thought to bid Raymond wait until she could stay
at home and dress him herself in his new garments. But she
heard him laugh again; she could not tell him he must wait.
He might go out at noon next day, she said, when the sun
was so warm that he would not take cold at his first outing;
one of the neighbors across the hall would help him with
the clothes. Raymond chuckled and sang his little songs until
he went to sleep.

After Big Lannie left in the morning, the neighbor came
in to Raymond, bringing a pan of cold pork and corn bread
for his lunch. She had a call for a half-day's work, and she
could not stay to see him start out for his walk. She helped
him put on the trousers and pinned and rolled them for him,
and she laced the shoes as snug as they would go on his feet.
Then she told him not to go out till the noon whistles blew,
and kissed him, and left.

Raymond was too happy to be impatient. He sat and
thought of the street and smiled and sang. Not until he
heard the whistles did he go to the drawer where Big Lannie
had laid the coat, and take it out and put it on. He felt it
soft on his bare back, he twisted his shoulders to let it fall
warm and loose from them. As he folded the sleeves back over
his thin arms, his heart beat so that the cloth above it
fluttered.

The stairs were difficult for him to manage, in the big
shoes, but the very slowness of the descent was delicious to
him. His anticipation was like honey in his mouth.

Then he came out into the yard, and turned his face in
the gentle air. It was all good again; it was all given back
again. As quickly as he could, he gained the walk and set
forth, guiding himself by the fence. He could not wait; he
called out, so that he would hear gay calls in return, he
laughed so that laughter would answer him.

He heard it. He was so glad that he took his hand from the fence and turned and stretched out his arms and held up his smiling face to welcome it. He stood there, and his smile died on his face, and his welcoming arms stiffened and shook.

It was not the laughter he had known; it was not the laughter he had lived on. It was like great flails beating him flat, great prongs tearing his flesh from his bones. It was coming at him, to kill him. It drew slyly back, and then it smashed against him. It swirled around and over him, and he could not breathe. He screamed and tried to run through it, and fell, and it licked over him, howling higher. His clothes unrolled, and his shoes flapped on his feet. Each time he could rise, he fell again. It was as if the street were perpendicular before him, and the laughter leaping at his back. He could not find the fence, he did not know which way he was turned. He lay screaming, in blood and dust and darkness.

When Big Lannie came home, she found him on the floor in a corner of the room, moaning and whimpering. He still wore his new clothes, cut and torn and dusty, and there was dried blood on his mouth and his palms. Her heart had leapt in alarm when he had not opened the door at her footstep, and she cried out so frantically to ask what had happened that she frightened him into wild weeping. She could not understand what he said; it was something about the street, and laughing at him, and make them go away, and don't let him go in the street no more, never in the street no more. She did not try to make him explain. She took him in her arms and rocked him, and told him, over and over, never mind, don't care, everything's all right. Neither he nor she believed her words.

But her voice was soft and her arms warm. Raymond's sobs softened, and trembled away. She held him, rocking silently and rhythmically, a long time. Then gently she set him on his feet, and took from his shoulders Mr. Ewing's old full-dress coat.

Grandpa really *knew how to live!*

The Heyday of the Blood

DOROTHY CANFIELD FISHER

THE OLDER professor looked up at the assistant, fumbling fretfully with a pile of papers. "Farrar, what's the matter with you lately?" he said sharply.

The younger man started. "Why . . . why . . ." the brusqueness of the other's manner shocked him suddenly into confession. "I've lost my nerve. Professor Mallory, that's what's the matter with me. I'm frightened to death," he said melodramatically.

"What of?" asked Mallory, with a little challenge in his tone.

The floodgates were open. The younger man burst out in exclamations, waving his thin, nervous, knotted fingers, his face twitching as he spoke. "Of myself . . . no, not myself, but my body; I'm not well. . . . I'm getting worse all the time. The doctors can't make out what is the matter . . . I don't sleep. . . . I worry. . . . I forget things. I take no interest in life . . . the doctors intimate a nervous breakdown ahead of me . . . and yet I rest. . . . I rest . . . more than I can afford to! I never go out. Every evening I'm in bed by nine o'clock. I take no part in college life beyond my work, for fear of the nervous strain. I've refused to take charge of that summer school in New York, you know, that would be such an opportunity for me . . . if I could only sleep! But though I never do anything exciting in the evening . . . heavens! what nights I have. Black hours of seeing myself in a sanitarium, dependent on my brother. I never . . . that's what's the matter with me!"

He sat silent, his drawn face turned to the window. The older man looked at him speculatively. When he spoke it was with a cheerful, casual quality in his voice which made the other look at him surprised.

"You don't suppose those great friends of yours, the nerve specialists, would object to my telling you a story, do you? It's very quiet and unexcited. You're not too busy?"

"Busy! I've forgotten the meaning of the word! I don't dare to be!"

"Very well, then; I mean to carry you back to the stony little farm in the Green Mountains, where I had the extreme good luck to be born and raised. You've heard me speak of Hillsboro; and the story is all about my great-grandfather, who came to live with us when I was a little boy."

"Your great-grandfather?" said the other incredulously. "People don't remember their great-grandfathers!"

"Oh, yes they do, in Vermont. There was my father on one farm, and my grandfather on another, without a thought that he was no longer young, and there was 'Gran'ther' as we called him, eighty-eight years old and just persuaded to settle back, let his descendants take care of him, and consent to be an old man. He had been in the War of 1812—think of that, you mushroom!—and had lost an arm and a good deal of his health there. He had lately begun to get a pension of twelve dollars a month, so that for an old man he was quite independent financially, as poor Vermont farmers look at things; and he was a most extraordinary character, so that his arrival in our family was quite an event.

"He took precedence at once of the oldest man in the township, who was only eighty-four and not very bright. I can remember bragging at school about Gran'ther Pendleton, who'd be eighty-nine come next Woodchuck Day, and could see to read without glasses. He had been ailing all his life, ever since the fever he took in the war. He used to remark triumphantly that he had now outlived six doctors who had each given him but a year to live; 'and the seventh is going downhill fast, so I hear!' This last was his never-failing answer to the attempt of my conscientious mother and anxious, dutiful father to check the old man's reckless indifference to any of the rules of hygiene.

"They were good disciplinarians with their children, and this naughty old man, who would give his weak stomach frightful attacks of indigestion by stealing out to the pantry and devouring a whole mince pie because he had been refused two pieces at the table—this rebellious, unreasonable, whimsical old madcap was an electric element in our quiet, orderly life. He insisted on going to every picnic and church sociable, where he ate recklessly of all the indigestible dainties he could lay his hands on, stood in drafts, tired himself to the verge of fainting away by playing games with the children, and returned home, exhausted, animated, and quite ready to pay the price of a day in bed, groaning and screaming out with pain as heartily and unaffectedly as he had laughed with the pretty girls the evening before.

"The climax came, however, in the middle of August, when he announced his desire to go to the county fair, held some fourteen miles down the valley from our farm. Father never dared let gran'ther go anywhere without himself accompanying the old man, but he was perfectly sincere in saying that it was not because he could not spare a day from the haying that he refused point-blank to consider it. The doctor who had been taking care of gran'ther since he came to live with us said that it would be crazy to think of such a thing. He added that the wonder was that gran'ther lived at all, for his heart was all wrong, his asthma was enough to kill a young man, and he had no digestion; in short, if father wished to kill his old grandfather, there was no surer way than to drive fourteen miles in the heat of August to the noisy excitement of a county fair.

"So father for once said 'No,' in the tone that we children had come to recognize as final. Gran'ther grimly tied a knot in his empty sleeve—a curious, enigmatic mode of his to express strong emotion—put his one hand on his cane, and his chin on his hand, and withdrew himself into that incalculable distance from the life about him where very old people spend so many hours.

"He did not emerge from this until one morning toward the middle of fair week, when all the rest of the family were away—father and the bigger boys on the far-off upland meadows haying and mother and the girls off blackberrying. I was too little to be of any help, so I had been left to wait on gran'ther, and to set out our lunch of bread and milk and huckleberries. We had not been alone half an hour when gran'ther sent me to extract, from under the mattress of his bed, the wallet in which he kept his pension money. There was six dollars and forty-three cents—he counted it over carefully, sticking out his tongue like a schoolboy doing a sum, and when he had finished he began to laugh and snap his fingers and sing out in his high, cracked old voice:

" 'We're goin' to go a skylarkin'! Little Jo Mallory is goin' to the county fair with Gran'ther Pendleton, an' he's goin' to have more fun than ever was in the world, and he——' "

" 'But, gran'ther, father said we mustn't!' I protested, horrified.

" 'But I say we *shall!* I was your gre't-gran'ther long be-

fore he was your feyther, and anyway I'm here and he's not
—so, *march!* Out to the barn!'

"He took me by the collar, and, executing a shuffling
fandango of triumph, he pushed me ahead of him to the
stable, where old white Peggy, the only horse left at home,
looked at us amazed.

" 'But it'll be twenty-eight miles, and Peg's never driven
over eight!' I cried, my old-established world of rules and
orders reeling before my eyes.

" 'Eight—and—twenty-eight!
But I—am—*eighty*-eight!

"Gran'ther improvised a sort of whooping chant of scorn
as he pulled the harness from the peg. 'It'll do her good to
drink some pink lemonade—old Peggy! An' if she gits tired
comin' home, I'll git out and carry her part way myself!'

"His adventurous spirit was irresistible. I made no further
objection and we hitched up together, I standing on a chair
to fix the check-rein, and gran'ther doing wonders with his
one hand. Then, just as we were—gran'ther in a hickory shirt,
and with an old hat flopping over his wizened face, I bare-
legged, in ragged old clothes—so we drove out of the grassy
yard, down the steep, stony hill that led to the main valley
road, and along the hot, white turnpike, deep with the dust
which had been stirred up by the teams on their way to the
fair. Gran'ther sniffed the air jubilantly, and exchanged hilarious greetings with the people who constantly overtook old
Peg's jogging trot. Between times he regaled me with spicy
stories of the hundreds of thousands—they seemed no less
numerous to me then—of county fairs he had attended in his
youth. He was horrified to find that I had never been even to
one.

" 'Why, Joey, how old be ye? 'Most eight, ain't it? When
I was your age I had run away and been to two fairs an' a
hangin'.'

" 'But didn't they lick you when you got home?" I asked
shudderingly.

" 'You *bet* they did!' cried gran'ther with gusto.

"I felt the world changing into an infinitely larger place
with every word he said.

" 'Now, this is somethin' *like!*' he exclaimed, as we drew
near to Granville and fell into a procession of wagons all filled

with country people in their best clothes, who looked with friendly curiosity at the little, shriveled cripple, his face shining with perspiring animation, and at the little boy beside him, his bare feet dangling high above the floor of the battered buckboard, overcome with the responsibility of driving a horse for the first time in his life, and filled with such a flood of new emotions and ideas that he must have been quite pale."

Professor Mallory leaned back and laughed aloud at the vision he had been evoking—laughed with so joyous a relish in his reminiscences that the drawn, impatient face of his listener relaxed a little. He drew a long breath, he even smiled a little absently.

"Oh, that was a day!" went on the professor, still laughing and wiping his eyes. "Never will I have such another! At the entrance to the grounds gran'ther stopped me while he solemnly untied the knot in his empty sleeve. I don't know what kind of hair-brained vow he had tied up in it, but with the little ceremony disappeared every trace of restraint, and we plunged head over ears into the saturnalia of delights that was an old-time county fair.

"People had little cash in those days, and gran'ther's six dollars and forty-three cents lasted like the widow's cruse of oil. We went to see the fat lady, who, if she was really as big as she looked to me then, must have weighed at least a ton. My admiration for gran'ther's daredevil qualities rose to infinity when he entered into free-and-easy talk with her, about how much she ate, and could she raise her arms enough to do up her own hair, and how many yards of velvet it took to make her gorgeous, gold-trimmed robe. She laughed a great deal at us, but she was evidently touched by his human interest, for she confided to him that it was not velvet at all, but furniture covering; and when he went away she pressed on us a bag of peanuts. She said she had more peanuts than she could eat—a state of unbridled opulence which fitted in for me with all the other superlatives of that day.

"We saw the dog-faced boy, whom we did not like at all; gran'ther expressing, with a candidly outspoken cynicism, his belief that 'them whiskers was glued to him.' We wandered about the stock exhibit, gazing at the monstrous oxen, and hanging over the railings where the prize pigs lived to scratch their backs. In order to miss nothing, we even conscientiously passed through the Woman's Building, where we were very much bored by the serried ranks of preserve jars.

" 'Sufferin' Hezekiah!' cried gran'ther irritably. 'Who cares how gooseberry jel *looks*. If they'd give a felly a taste, now——'

"This reminded him that we were hungry, and we went to a restaurant under a tent, where, after taking stock of the wealth that yet remained of gran'ther's hoard, he ordered the most expensive things on the bill of fare."

Professor Mallory suddenly laughed out again. "Perhaps in heaven, but certainly not until then, shall I ever taste anything so ambrosial as that fried chicken and coffee ice cream! I have not lived in vain that I have such a memory back of me!"

This time the younger man laughed with the narrator, settling back in his chair as the professor went on:

"After lunch we rode on the merry-go-round, both of us, gran'ther clinging desperately with his one hand to his red camel's wooden hump, and crying out shrilly to me to be sure and not lose his cane. The merry-go-round had just come in at that time, and gran'ther had never experienced it before. After the first giddy flight we retired to a lemonade-stand to exchange impressions, and finding that we both alike had fallen completely under the spell of the new sensation, gran'-ther said that we sh'd keep on-a-ridin' till we'd had enough! King Solomon couldn't tell when we'd ever git a chance again!' So we returned to the charge, and rode and rode and rode, through blinding clouds of happy excitement, so it seems to me now, such as I was never to know again. The sweat was pouring off from us, and we had tried all the different animals on the machine before we could tear ourselves away to follow the crowd to the race-track.

"We took reserved seats, which cost a quarter apiece, instead of the unshaded ten-cent benches, and gran'ther began at once to pour out to me a flood of horse talk and knowing race-track aphorisms, which finally made a young fellow sitting next to us laugh superciliously. Gran'ther turned on him heatedly.

" 'I bet-che fifty cents I pick the winner in the next race!' he said sportily.

" 'Done!' said the other, still laughing.

"Gran'ther picked a big black mare, who came in almost last, but he did not flinch. As he paid over the half-dollar he said: 'Everybody's likely to make mistakes about *some* things; King Solomon was a fool in the head about women folks! I bet-che a dollar I pick the winner in *this* race! and 'Done!'

said the disagreeable young man, still laughing. I gasped, for I knew we had only eighty-seven cents left, but gran'ther shot me a command to silence out of the corner of his eyes, and announced that he bet on the sorrel gelding.

"If I live to be a hundred and break the bank at Monte Carlo three times a week," said Mallory, shaking his head reminiscently, "I could not know a tenth part of the frantic excitement of that race or of the mad triumph when our horse won. Gran'ther cast his hat upon the ground, screaming like a steam caliope with exultation as the sorrel swept past the judges' stand ahead of all the others, and I jumped up and down in an agony of delight.

"After that we went away, feeling that the world could hold nothing more glorious. It was five o'clock and we decided to start back. We paid for Peggy's dinner out of the dollar we had won on the race—I say 'we,' for by that time we were welded into one organism—and we still had a dollar and a quarter left. 'While ye're about it, always go the whole hog!' said gran'ther, and we spent twenty minutes in laying out that money in trinkets for all the folks at home. Then, dusty, penniless, laden with bundles, we bestowed our exhausted bodies and our uplifted hearts in the old buckboard, and turned Peg's head toward the mountains. We did not talk much during that drive, and though I thought at the time only of the carnival of joy we had left, I can now recall every detail of the trip—how the sun sank behind Indian Mountain, a peak I had known before only through distant views; then, as we journeyed on, how the stars came out above Hemlock Mountain—our own home mountain behind our house, and later, how the fireflies filled the darkening meadows along the river below us, so that we seemed to be floating between the steady stars of heaven and their dancing, twinkling reflection in the valley.

"Gran'ther's dauntless spirit still surrounded me. I put out of mind doubts of our reception at home, and lost myself in delightful ruminatings on the splendors of the day. At first, every once in a while, gran'ther made a brief remark, such as, ' 'Twas the hind-quarters of the sorrel I bet on. He was the only one in the hull kit and bilin' of 'em that his quarters didn't fall away'; or, 'You needn't tell me that them Siamese twins ain't unpinned every night as separate as you and me!' But later on, as the damp evening air began to bring on his asthma, he subsided into silence, only broken by great gasping coughs.

"These were heard by the anxious, heartsick watchers at home, and, as old Peg stumbled wearily up the hill, father came running down to meet us. 'Where you be'n?' he demanded, his face pale and stern in the light of his lantern. 'We be'n to the county fair!' croaked gran-ther with a last flare of triumph, and fell over sideways against me. Old Peg stopped short, hanging her head as if she, too, were at the limit of her strength. I was frightfully tired myself, and frozen with terror of what father would say. Gran'ther's collapse was the last straw. I began to cry loudly, but father ignored my distress with an indifference which cut me to the heart. He lifted gran'ther out of the buckboard, carrying the unconscious little old body into the house without a glance backward at me. But when I crawled down to the ground sobing, I felt mother's arms around me.

"'Oh, poor, naughty little Joey!' she said 'Mother's bad, dear little boy!'"

Professor Mallory stopped short.

"Perhaps that's something else I'll know again in heaven," he said soberly, and waited a moment before he went on: "Well, that was the end of our day. I was so worn out that I fell asleep over my supper, in spite of the excitement in the house about sending for a doctor for gran'ther, who was so one of my awestruck sisters told me, having some kind of 'fits.' Mother must have put me to bed, for the next thing I remember, she was shaking me by the shoulder and saying, 'Wake up, Joey. Your great-grandfather wants to speak to you. He's been suffering terribly all night, and the doctor thinks he's dying.'

"I followed her into gran'ther's room, where the family was assembled about the bed. Gran'ther lay drawn up in a ball, groaning so dreadfully that I felt a chill like cold water at the roots of my hair; but a moment or two after I came in, all at once he gave a great sigh and relaxed, stretching out his legs and attempting to smile at me.

"'Well, it was wuth it, warn't it, Joey?' he said gallantly, and closed his eyes peacefully to sleep."

"Did he die?" asked the younger professor, leaning forward eagerly.

"Die? Gran'ther Pendleton? Not much! He came tottering down to breakfast the next morning, as white as an old ghost, with no voice left, his legs trembling under him, but he kept the whole family an hour and a half at the table, telling them in a loud whisper all about the fair, until father said really he would have to take us to the one next year. Afterward he sat out on the porch watching old Peg graze around the yard. I thought he was in one of his absent-minded fits, but when I came out, he called me to him, and, setting his lips to my ear, he whispered:

" 'An' the seventh is a-goin' downhill fast, so I hear!' He chuckled to himself over this for some time, wagging his head feebly, and then he said: 'I tell ye, Joey, I've lived a long time, and I've larned a lot about the way folks is made. The trouble with most of 'em is, they're 'fraid-cats! As Jeroboam Warner used to say—he was in the same regiment with me in 1812—the only way to manage this business of livin' is to give a hoop and let her rip! If ye just about half-live, ye just the same as half-die; and if ye spend yer time half-dyin' some day ye turn in and die all over, without rightly meanin' to at all—just a kind o' bad habit ye've got yerself inter.' Gran'ther fell into a meditative silence for a moment. 'Jeroboam, he said that the evenin' before the battle of Lundy's Lane, and he got killed the next day. Some live, and some die; but folks that live all over die happy, anyhow! Now I tell you what's my motto, an' what I've lived to be eighty-eight on——' "

Professor Mallory stood up and, towering over the younger man, struck one hand into the other as he cried: "This was the motto he told me: 'Live while you live, and then die and be done with it!' "

Rope

KATHERINE ANNE PORTER

On the third day after they moved to the country he came walking back from the village carrying a basket of groceries and a twenty-four-yard coil of rope. She came out to meet him, wiping her hands on her green smock. Her hair was tumbled, her nose scarlet with sunburn; he told her that already she looked like a born country woman. His gray flannel shirt stuck to him, his heavy shoes were dusty. She assured him he looked like a rural character in a play.

Had he brought the coffee? She had been waiting all day long for coffee. They had forgot it when they ordered at the store the first day.

Gosh, no, he hadn't. Lord, now he'd have to go back. Yes, he would if it killed him. He thought, though, he had everything else. She reminded him it was only because he didn't drink coffee himself. If he did he would remember it quick enough. Suppose they ran out of cigarettes? Then she saw the rope. What was that for? Well, he thought it might do to hang clothes on, or something. Naturally she asked him if he thought they were going to run a laundry? They already had a fifty-foot line hanging right before his eyes. Why, hadn't he noticed it, really? It was a blot on the landscape to her.

He thought there were a lot of things a rope might come in handy for. She wanted to know what, for instance. He thought for a few seconds, but nothing occurred. They could wait and see, couldn't they? You need all sorts of strange odds and ends around a place in the country. She said, yes, that was so; but she thought just at that time, when every penny counted, it seemed funny to buy more rope. That was all. She hadn't meant anything else. She hadn't just seen, not at first, why he felt it was necessary.

Well, thunder, he had bought it because he wanted to, and that was all there was to it. She thought that was reason enough, and couldn't understand why he hadn't said so, at first. Undoubtedly it would be useful, twenty-four yards of rope, there were hundreds of things, she couldn't think of any

107

at the moment, but it would come in. Of course. As he had said, things always did in the country.

But she was a little disappointed about the coffee, and oh, look, look, look at the eggs! Oh, my, they're all running! What had he put on top of them? Hadn't he known eggs mustn't be squeezed? Squeezed, who had squeezed them, he wanted to know. What a silly thing to say. He had simply brought them along in the basket with the other things. If they got broke it was the grocer's fault. He should know better than to put heavy things on top of eggs.

She believed it was the rope. That was the heaviest thing in the pack; she saw him plainly when he came in from the road, the rope was a big package on top of everything. He desired the whole wide world to witness that this was not a fact. He had carried the rope in one hand and the basket in the other, and what was the use of her having eyes if that was the best they could do for her?

Well, anyhow, she could see one thing plain: no eggs for breakfast. They'd have to scramble them now, for supper. It was too damned bad. She had planned to have steak for supper. No ice, meat wouldn't keep. He wanted to know why she couldn't finish breaking the eggs in a bowl and set them in a cool place.

Cool place! If he could find one for her, she'd be glad to set them there. Well, then, it seemed to him they might very well cook the meat at the same time they cooked the eggs and then warm up the meat for tomorrow. The idea simply choked her. Warmed-over meat, when they might as well have had it fresh. Second-best and scraps and makeshifts, even to the meat! He rubbed her shoulder a little. It doesn't really matter so much, does it, darling? Sometimes when they were playful, he would rub her shoulder and she would arch and purr. This time she hissed and almost clawed. He was getting ready to say that they could surely manage somehow when she turned on him and said, if he told her they could manage somehow she would certainly slap his face.

He swallowed the words red hot, his face burned. He picked up the rope and started to put it on the top shelf. She would not have it on the top shelf, the jars and tins belonged there; positively she would not have the top shelf cluttered up with a lot of rope. She had borne all the clutter she meant to bear in the flat in town, there was space here at least and she meant to keeps things in order.

Well, in that case, he wanted to know what the hammer

and nails were doing up there? And why had she put them
there when she knew very well he needed that hammer and
those nails upstairs to fix the window sashes? She simply
slowed down everything and made double work on the place
with her insane habit of changing things around and hiding
them.

She was sure she begged his pardon and if she had had
any reason to believe he was going to fix the sashes this summer she would have left the hammer and nails right where
he put them; in the middle of the bedroom floor where they
could step on them in the dark. And now if he didn't clear
the whole mess out of there she would throw them down the
well.

Oh, all right, all right—could he put them in the closet?
Naturally not, there were brooms and mops and dustpans in
the closet, and why couldn't he find a place for his rope outside her kitchen? Had he stopped to consider there were
seven rooms in the house and only one kitchen?

He wanted to know what of it? And did she realize she
was making a complete fool of herself? And what did she
take him for, a three-year-old idiot? The whole trouble with
her was she needed something weaker than she was to heckle
and tyrannize over. He wished now they had a couple of children she could take it out on. Maybe he'd get some rest.

Her face changed at this, she reminded him he had forgot
the coffee and had bought a worthless piece of rope. And
when she thought of all the things they actually needed to
make the place even decently fit to live in, well, she would cry,
that was all. She looked so forlorn, so lost and despairing he
couldn't believe it was only a piece of rope that was causing
all the racket. What was the matter?

Oh, would he please hush and go away, and stay away, if
he could, for five minutes. By all means, yes, he would. He'd
stay away indefinitely if she wished. Lord, yes, there was
nothing he'd like better than to clear out and never come
back. She couldn't for the life of her see what was holding
him, then. It was a swell time. Here she was, stuck, miles from
a railroad, with a half-empty house on her hands, and not a
penny in her pocket, and everything on earth to do; it seemed
the moment for him to get out from under. She was surprised
he hadn't stayed in town as it was until she had come out
and done the work and got things straightened out. It was
his usual trick.

It appeared to him that this was going a little far. Just a

touch out of bounds, if she didn't mind his saying so. Why had he stayed in town the summer before? To do a half-dozen extra jobs to get the money he had sent her. That was it. She knew perfectly well they couldn't have done it otherwise. She had agreed with him at the time. And that was the only time, so help him, he had ever left her to do anything by herself.

Oh, he could tell that to his great-grandmother. She had her notion of what had kept him in town. Considerably more than a notion, if he wanted to know. So, she was going to bring all that up again, was she? Well, she could just think what she pleased. He was tired of explaining. It may have looked funny but he had simply got hooked in, and what could he do? It was impossible to believe that she was going to take it seriously. Yes, yes, she knew how it was with a man: if he was left by himself a minute, some woman was certain to kidnap him. And naturally he couldn't hurt her feelings by refusing!

Well, what was she raving about? Did she forget she had told him those two weeks alone in the country were the happiest she had known for four years? And how long had they been married when she said that? All right, shut up! If she thought that hadn't stuck in his craw.

She hadn't meant she was happy because she was away from him. She meant she was happy getting the devilish house nice and ready for him. That was what she meant, and now look! Bringing up something she had said a year ago simply to justify himself for forgetting her coffee and breaking the eggs and buying a wretched piece of rope they couldn't afford. She really thought it was time to drop the subject, and now she wanted only two things in the world. She wanted him to get that rope from underfoot, and go back to the village and get her coffee, and if he could remember it, he might bring a metal mitt for the skillets, and two more curtain rods, and if there were any rubber gloves in the village, her hands were simply raw, and a bottle of milk of magnesia from the drugstore.

He looked out at the dark blue afternoon sweltering on the slopes, and mopped his forehead and sighed heavily and said, if only she could wait a minute for anything, he was going back. He had said so, hadn't he, the very instant they found he had overlooked it?

Oh, yes, well . . . run along. She was going to wash windows. The country was so beautiful. She doubted they'd have

a moment to enjoy it. He meant to go, but he could not until
he had said that if she wasn't such a hopeless melancholiac she
might see that this was only for a few days. Couldn't she remember anything pleasant about the other summers? Hadn't
they ever had any fun? She hadn't time to talk about it, and
now would he please not leave that rope lying around for her
to trip on? He picked it up, somehow it had toppled off the
table, and walked out with it under his arm.

Was he going this minute? He certainly was. She thought
so. Sometimes it seemed to her he had second sight about the
precisely perfect moment to leave her ditched. She had meant
to put the mattresses out to sun, if they put them out
this minute they would get at least three hours, he must have
heard her say that morning she meant to put them out. So
of course he would walk off and leave her to do it. She supposed he thought the exercise would do her good.

Well, he was merely going to get her coffee. A four-mile
walk for two pounds of coffee was ridiculous, but he was perfectly willing to do it. The habit was making a wreck of her,
but if she wanted to wreck herself there was nothing he could
do about it. If he thought it was coffee that was making a
wreck of her, she congratulated him: he must have an easy
conscience.

Conscience or no conscience, he didn't see why the mattresses couldn't very well wait until tomorrow. And, anyhow,
were they living in the house, or were they going to let the
house ride them to death? She paled at this, her face grew
livid about the mouth, she looked quite dangerous, and reminded him that housekeeping was no more her work than it
was his: she had other work to do as well, and when did he
think she was going to find time to do it at this rate?

Was she going to start on that again? She knew as well as
he did that his work brought in the regular money, hers was
only occasional, if they depended on what she made—and she
might as well get straight on this question once for all!

That was positively not the point. The question was, when
both of them were working on their own time, was there
going to be a division of the housework, or wasn't there? She
merely wanted to know, she had to make her plans. Why,
he thought that was all arranged. It was understood that he
was to help. Hadn't he always, in summer?

Hadn't he, though? Oh, just hadn't he? And when, and
where, and doing what? Lord, what an uproarious joke!

It was such a very uproarious joke that her face turned

slightly purple, and she screamed with laughter. She laughed
so hard she had to sit down, and finally a rush of tears spurted
from her eyes and poured down into the lifted corners of her
mouth. He dashed toward her and dragged her up to her feet
and tried to pour water on her head. The dipper hung by a
string on a nail and he broke it loose. Then he tried to pump
water with one hand while she struggled in the other. So he
gave it up and shook her instead.

She wrenched away, crying out for him to take his rope and
get out, she had simply given him up; and ran. He heard her
high-heeled bedroom slippers clattering and stumbling on the
stairs.

He went out around the house and into the lane; he suddenly realized he had a blister on his heel and his shirt felt
as if it were on fire. Things broke so suddenly you didn't
know where you were. She could work herself into a fury
about simply nothing. She was terrible, not an ounce of reason. You might as well talk to a sieve as that woman when she
got going. Darned if he'd spend his life humoring her! Well,
what to do now? He would take back the rope and exchange it
for something else. Things accumulated, things were moun-
tainous, you couldn't move them or sort them out or get rid of
them. They just lay and rotted around. He'd take it back.
Why should he? He wanted it. What was it anyhow? A
piece of rope. Imagine anybody caring more about a piece of
rope than about a man's feelings. What earthly right had she
to say a word about it? He remembered all the useless, mean-
ingless things she bought for herself: Why? because I wanted
it, that's why! He stopped and selected a large stone by the
road. He would put the rope behind it. He would put it in the
toolbox when he got back. He'd heard enough about it to last
him a lifetime.

When he came back she was leaning against the post box
beside the road waiting. It was pretty late, the smell of broiled
steak floated nose high in the cooling air. Her face was young
and smooth and fresh-looking. Her unmanageable funny black
hair was all on end. She waved to him from a distance, and
he speeded up. She called out that supper was ready and
waiting, was he starved?

You bet he was starved. Here was the coffee. He waved it
at her. She looked at his other hand. What was that he had
there?

Well, it was the rope again. He stopped short. He had

meant to exchange it but forgot. She wanted to know why he should exchange it, if it was something he really wanted. Wasn't the air sweet now, and wasn't it fine to be here?

She walked beside him with one hand hooked into his leather belt. She pulled and jostled him a little as he walked, and leaned against him. He put his arm clear around her and patted her stomach. They exchanged wary smiles. Coffee, coffee for the Ootsum-Wootums! He felt as if he were bringing her a beautiful present.

He was a love, she firmly believed, and if she had had her coffee in the morning, she wouldn't have behaved so funny. . . . There was a whippoorwill still coming back, imagine, clear out of season, sitting in the crab-apple tree calling all by himself. Maybe his girl stood him up. Maybe she did. She hoped to hear him once more, she loved whippoorwills. . . . He knew how she was didn't he?

Sure, he knew how she was.

Can a toothache change a man's life?

A Tooth for Paul Revere

STEPHEN VINCENT BENÉT

I

SOME SAY it all happened because of Hancock and Adams
(said the old man, pulling at his pipe), and some put it back
to the Stamp Act and before. Then there's some hold out for
Paul Revere and his little silver box. But the way I heard it, it
broke loose because of Lige Butterwick and his tooth.

What's that? Why, the American Revolution, of course.
What else would I be talking about? Well, your story about
the land down South that they had to plough with alligators
reminded me.

No, this is a true story—or at least that's how I heard it
told. My great-aunt was a Butterwick and I heard it from her.
And, every now and then, she'd write it out and want to get
it put in the history books. But they'd always put her off
with some trifling sort of excuse. Till, finally, she got her
dander up and wrote direct to the President of the United
States. Well, no, he didn't answer himself exactly—the President's apt to be a pretty busy man. But the letter said he'd
received her interesting communication and thanked her for
it, so that shows you. We've got it framed, in the trailer—the
ink's a little faded, but you can make out the man's name
who signed it. It's either Bowers or Thorpe and he wrote a
very nice hand.

You see, my great-aunt, she wasn't very respectful to the
kind of history that does get into the books. What she liked
was the queer corners of it and the tales that get handed down
in families. Take Paul Revere, for instance—all most folks
think about, with him, is his riding a horse. But when she
talked about Paul Revere—why, you could just see him in his
shop, brewing the American Revolution in a silver teapot and
waiting for it to settle. Oh yes, he was a silversmith by trade—
but she claimed he was something more. She claimed there
was a kind of magic in that quick, skillful hand of his—and
that he was one of the kind of folks that can see just a little bit

114

farther into a millstone than most. But it was when she got to Lige Butterwick that she really turned herself loose.

For she claimed that it took all sorts to make a country—and that meant the dumb ones, too. I don't mean ijits or nincompoops—just the ordinary folks that live along from day to day. And that day may be a notable day in history—but it's just Tuesday to them, till they read all about it in the papers. Oh, the heroes and the great men—they can plan and contrive and see ahead. But it isn't till the Lige Butterwicks get stirred up that things really start to happen. Or so she claimed. And the way that they do get stirred up is often curious, as she'd tell this story to prove.

For, now you take Lige Butterwick—and, before his tooth started aching, he was just like you and me. He lived on a farm about eight miles from Lexington, Massachusetts, and he was a peaceable man. It was troubled times in the American colonies, what with British warships in Boston Harbor and British soldiers in Boston and Sons of Liberty hooting the British soldiers—not to speak of Boston tea parties and such. But Lige Butterwick, he worked his farm and didn't pay much attention. There's lots of people like that, even in troubled times.

When he went into town, to be sure, there was high talk at the tavern. But he bought his goods and came home again —he had ideas about politics, but he didn't talk about them much. He had a good farm and it kept him busy—he had a wife and five children and they kept him humping. The young folks could argue about King George and Sam Adams —he wondered how the corn was going to stand that year. Now and then, if somebody said that this and that was a burning shame, he'd allow as how it might be, just to be neighborly. But, inside, he was wondering whether next year he mightn't make an experiment and plant the west field in rye.

Well, everything went along for him the way that it does for most folks with good years and bad years, till one April morning, in 1775, he woke up with a toothache. Being the kind of man he was, he didn't pay much attention to it at first. But he mentioned it that evening, at supper, and his wife got a bag of hot salt for him. He held it to his face and it seemed to ease him, but he couldn't hold it there all night, and, next morning, the tooth hurt worse than ever.

Well, he stood it the next day and the next, but it didn't

improve any. He tried tansy tea and other remedies—he tried
tying a string on it and having his wife slam the door. But,
when it came to the pinch, he couldn't quite do it. So, finally,
he took the horse and rode into Lexington town to have it
seen to. Mrs. Butterwick made him—she said it might be an
expense, but anything was better than having him act as if
he wanted to kick the cat across the room every time she put
her feet down hard.

When he got into Lexington, he noticed that folks there
seemed kind of excited. There was a lot of talk about muskets
and powder and a couple of men called Hancock and Adams
who were staying at Parson Clarke's. But Lige Butterwick had
his own business to attend to—and, besides, his tooth was
jumping so he wasn't in any mood for conversation. He set
off for the local barber's, as being the likeliest man he knew
to pull a tooth.

The barber took one look at it and shook his head.

"I can pull her, Lige," he said. "Oh, I can pull her, all
right. But she's got long roots and strong roots and she's going
to leave an awful gap when she's gone. Now, what you really
need," he said, kind of excited, for he was one of those perky
little men who's always interested in the latest notion, "what
you really need—though it's taking away my business—is one
of these-here artificial teeth to go in the hole."

"Artificial teeth!" said Lige. "It's flying in the face of Nature!"

The barber shook his head. "No, Lige," he said, "that's
where you're wrong. Artificial teeth is all the go these days,
and Lexington ought to keep up with the times. It would do
me good to see you with an artificial tooth—it would so."

"Well, it might do you good," said Lige, rather crossly, for
his tooth was jumping, "but, supposing I did want one—how
in tunket will I get one in Lexington?"

"Now, you just leave that to me," said the barber, all excited, and he started to rummage around. "You'll have to go
to Boston for it, but I know just the man." He was one of
those men who can always tell you where to go and it's usually
wrong. "See here," he went on. "There's a fellow called Revere in Boston that fixes them and they say he's a boss work-
man. Just take a look at this prospectus"—and he started to
read from a paper: " 'Whereas many persons are so unfortu-
nate as to lose their fore-teeth'—that's you, Lige—'to their
great detriment, not only in looks but in speaking, both in
public and private, this is to inform all such that they may

have them replaced by artificial ones'—see?—'that look as well as the natural and answer the end of speaking to all intents'—and then he's got his name—Paul Revere, goldsmith, near the head of Dr. Clarke's wharf, Boston.''

"Sounds well enough," said Lige, "but what's it going to cost?"

"Oh, I know Revere," said the barber, swelling up like a robin. "Comes through here pretty often, as a matter of fact. And he's a decent fellow, if he is a pretty big gun in the Sons of Liberty. You just mention my name."

"Well, it's something I hadn't thought of," said Lige, as his tooth gave another red-hot jounce, "but in for a penny, in for a pound. I've missed a day's work already and that tooth's got to come out before I go stark, staring mad. But what sort of man is this Revere, anyway?"

"Oh, he's a regular wizard!" said the barber. "A regular wizard with his tools."

"Wizard!" said Lige. "Well, I don't know about wizards. But if he can fix my tooth I'll call him one."

"You'll never regret it," said the barber—and that's the way folks always talk when they're sending someone else to the dentist. So Lige Butterwick got on his horse again and started out for Boston. A couple of people shouted at him as he rode down the street, but he didn't pay any attention. And, going by Parson Clarke's, he caught a glimpse of two men talking in the Parson's front room. One was a tallish, handsomish man in pretty fine clothes and the other was shorter and untidy, with a kind of bulldog face. But they were strangers to him and he didn't really notice them—just rode ahead.

II

But as soon as he got into Boston he started to feel queer —and it wasn't only his tooth. He hadn't been there in four years and he'd expected to find it changed, but it wasn't that. It was a clear enough day and yet he kept feeling there was thunder in the air. There'd be knots of people, talking and arguing, on street corners, and then, when you got closer to them, they'd kind of melt away. Or, if they stayed, they'd look at you, out of the corners of their eyes. And there, in the Port of Boston, were the British warships, black and grim. He'd known they'd be there, of course, but it was different, seeing them. It made him feel queer to see their guns pointed at the town. He'd known there was trouble and dispute, in

Boston, but the knowledge had passed over him like rain and hail. But now here he was in the middle of it—and it smelt like earthquake weather. He couldn't make head or tail of it, but he wanted to be home.

All the same, he'd come to get his tooth fixed, and, being New England, he was bound to do it. But first he stopped at a tavern for a bite and a sup, for it was long past his dinnertime. And there, it seemed to him, things got even more curious.

"Nice weather we're having, these days," he said, in a friendly way, to the barkeep.

"It's bitter weather for Boston," said the barkeep, in an unfriendly voice, and a sort of low growl went up from the boys at the back of the room and every eye fixed on Lige.

Well, that didn't help the toothache any, but, being a sociable person, Lige kept on.

"May be, for Boston," he said, "but out in the country we'd call it good planting weather."

The barkeep stared at him hard.

"I guess I was mistaken in you," he said. "It is good planting weather—for some kinds of trees."

"And what kind of trees were you thinking of?" said a sharp-faced man at Lige's left and squeezed his shoulder.

"There's trees and trees, you know," said a red-faced man at Lige's right, and gave him a dig in the ribs.

"Well, now that you ask me—" said Lige, but he couldn't even finish before the red-faced man dug him hard in the ribs again.

"The liberty tree!" said the red-faced man. "And may it soon be watered in the blood of tyrants!"

"The royal oak of England!" said the sharp-faced man. "And God save King George and loyalty!"

Well, with that it seemed to Lige Butterwick as if the whole tavern kind of riz up at him. He was kicked and pummeled and mauled and thrown into a corner and yanked out of it again, with the red-faced man and the sharp-faced man and all the rest of them dancing quadrilles over his prostrate form. Till, finally, he found himself out in the street with half his coat gone galley-west.

"Well," said Lige to himself, "I always heard city folks were crazy. But politics must be getting serious in these American colonies when they start fighting about trees!"

Then he saw the sharp-faced man was beside him, trying to shake his hand. He noticed with some pleasure that the sharp-faced man had the beginnings of a beautiful black eye.

"Nobly done, friend," said the sharp-faced man, "and I'm glad to find another true-hearted loyalist in this pestilent, rebellious city."

"Well, I don't know as I quite agree with you about that," said Lige. "But I came here to get my tooth fixed, not to talk politics. And as long as you've spoken so pleasant, I wonder if you could help me out. You see, I'm from Lexington way— and I'm looking for a fellow named Paul Revere——"

"Paul Revere!" said the sharp-faced man, as if the name hit him like a bullet. Then he began to smile again—not a pleasant smile.

"Oh, it's Paul Revere you want, my worthy and ingenuous friend from the country," he said. "Well, I'll tell you how to find him. You go up to the first British soldier you see and ask the way. But you better give the password first."

"Password?" said Lige Butterwick, scratching his ear.

"Yes," said the sharp-faced man, and his smile got wider. "You say to that British soldier, 'Any lobsters for sale today?' Then you ask about Revere."

"But why do I talk about lobsters first?" said Lige Butterwick, kind of stubborn.

"Well, you see," said the sharp-faced man, "the British soldiers wear red coats. So they like being asked about lobsters. Try it and see." And he went away, with his shoulders shaking.

Well, that seemed queer to Lige Butterwick, but no queerer than the other things that had happened that day. All the same, he didn't quite trust the sharp-faced man, so he took care not to come too close to the British patrol when he asked them about the lobsters. And it was lucky he did, for no sooner were the words out of his mouth than the British soldiers took after him and chased him clear down to the wharves before he could get away. At that, he only managed it by hiding in an empty tar barrel, and when he got out he was certainly a sight for sore eyes.

"Well, I guess that couldn't have been the right password," he said to himself, kind of grimly, as he tried to rub off some of the tar. "All the same, I don't think soldiers ought to act like that when you ask them a civil question. But, city folks or soldiers, they can't make a fool out of me. I came here to get my tooth fixed and get it fixed I will, if I have to surprise the whole British Empire to do it."

And just then he saw a sign on a shop at the end of the wharf. And, according to my great-aunt, this was what was on

the sign. It said 'PAUL REVERE, SILVERSMITH' at the
top, and then, under it in smaller letter, 'Large and small
bells cast to order, engraving and printing done in job lots,
artificial teeth sculptured and copper boilers mended, all
branches of goldsmith and silversmith work and revolutions
put up to take out. Express Service, Tuesdays and Fridays, to
Lexington, Concord and Points West.'

"Well," said Lige Butterwick, "kind of Jack-of-all-trades.
Now maybe I can get my tooth fixed." And he marched up
to the door.

III

Paul Revere was behind the counter when Lige came in,
turning a silver bowl over and over in his hands. A man of
forty-odd he was, with a quick, keen face and snapping eyes.
He was wearing Boston clothes, but there was a French look
about him—for his father was Apollos Rivoire from the
island of Guernsey, and good French Huguenot stock. They'd
changed the name to Revere when they crossed the water.

It wasn't such a big shop, but it had silver pieces in it that
people have paid thousands for, since. And the silver pieces
weren't all. There were prints and engravings of the Port of
Boston and caricatures of the British and all sorts of goldsmith work, more than you could put a name to. And Paul
Revere moved about it, quick and keen, with his eyes full of
life and hot temper—the kind of man who knows what he
wants to do and does it the next minute.

There were quite a few customers there when Lige Butterwick first came in—so he sort of scrooged back in a corner
and waited his chance. For one thing, after the queer sign
and the barber's calling him a wizard, he wanted to be sure
about this fellow, Revere, and see what kind of customers
came to his shop.

Well, there was a woman who wanted a christening mug
for a baby and a man who wanted a print of the Boston Mas-
sacre. And then there was a fellow who passed Revere some
sort of message, under cover—Lige caught the whisper, "powder" and "Sons of Liberty," though he couldn't make out the
rest. And finally, there was a very fine silk-dressed lady who
seemed to be giving Revere considerable trouble. Lige peeked
at her round the corner of his chair, and, somehow or other,
she reminded him of a turkey-gobbler, especially the strut.

She was complaining about some silver that Paul Revere

had made for her—expensive silver it must have been. And "Oh, Master Revere, I'm so disappointed!" she was saying. "When I took the things from the box, I could just have cried!"

Revere drew himself up a little at that, Lige noticed, but his voice was pleasant.

"It is I who am disappointed, madam," he said, with a little bow. "But what was the trouble? It must have been carelessly packed. Was it badly dented? I'll speak to my boy."

"Oh, no, it wasn't dented," said the turkey-gobbler lady. "But I wanted a really impressive silver service—something I can use when the Governor comes to dinner with us. I certainly paid for the best. And what have you given me?"

Lige waited to hear what Paul Revere would say. When he spoke, his voice was stiff.

"I have given you the best work of which I am capable, madam," he said. "It was in my hands for six months—and I think they are skillful hands."

"Oh," said the woman, and rustled her skirts, "I know you're a competent artisan, Master Revere——"

"Silversmith, if you please——" said Paul Revere, and the woman rustled again.

"Well, I don't care what you call it," she said, and then you could see her fine accent was put on like her fine clothes. "But I know I wanted a real service—something I could show my friends. And what have you given me? Oh, it's silver, if you choose. But it's just as plain and simple as a picket fence!"

Revere looked at her for a moment and Lige Butterwick thought he'd explode.

"Simple?" he said. "And plain? You pay me high compliments, madam!"

"Compliments indeed!" said the woman, and now she was getting furious. "I'm sending it back tomorrow! Why, there isn't as much as a lion or a unicorn on the cream jug. And I told you I wanted the sugar bowl covered with silver grapes! But you've given me something as bare as the hills of New England! And I won't stand it, I tell you! I'll send to England instead."

Revere puffed his cheeks and blew, but his eyes were dangerous.

"Send away, madam," he said. "We're making new things in this country—new men—new silver—perhaps, who knows, a new nation. Plain, simple, bare as the hills and rocks of New England—graceful as the boughs of her elm trees—if my silver were only like that indeed! But that is what I wish to make it. And, as for you, madam"—he stepped toward her like a cat—"with your lions and unicorns and grape leaves and your nonsense of bad ornament done by bad silversmiths —your imported bad taste and your imported British manners—puff!" And he blew at her, just the way you blow at a turkey-gobbler, till she fairly picked up her fine silk skirts and ran. Revere watched her out of the door and turned back, shaking his head.

"William!" he called to the boy who helped him in the shop. "Put up the shutters—we're closing for the day. And William—no word yet from Dr. Warren?"

"Not yet, sir," said the boy, and started to put up the shutters. Then Lige Butterwick thought it was about time to make his presence known.

So he coughed, and Paul Revere whirled and Lige Butterwick felt those quick, keen eyes boring into his. He wasn't exactly afraid of them, for he was stubborn himself, but he knew this was an unexpected kind of man.

"Well, my friend," said Revere, impatiently, "and who in the world are you?"

"Well, Mr. Revere," said Lige Butterwick. "It is Mr. Revere, isn't it? It's kind of a long story. But, closing or not, you've got to listen to me. The barber told me so."

"The barber!" said Revere, kind of dumbfounded.

"Uh-huh," said Lige, and opened his mouth. "You see, it's my tooth."

"Tooth!" said Revere, and stared at him as if they were both crazy. "You'd better begin at the beginning. But wait a minute. You don't talk like a Boston man. Where do you come from?"

"Oh, around Lexington way," said Lige. "And, you see——"

But the mention of Lexington seemed to throw Revere into a regular excitement. He fairly shook Lige by the shoulders.

"Lexington!" he said. "Were you there this morning?"

"Of course I was," said Lige. "That's where the barber I told you about——"

"Never mind the barber!" said Revere. "Were Mr. Hancock and Mr. Adams still at Parson Clarke's?"

"Well, they might have been, for all I know," said Lige. "But I couldn't say."

"Great heaven!" said Revere. "Is there a man in the American colonies who doesn't know Mr. Hancock and Mr. Adams?"

"There seems to be me," said Lige. "But, speaking of strangers—there was two of them staying at the parsonage, when I rode past. One was a handsomish man and the other looked more like a bulldog——"

"Hancock and Adams!" said Revere. "So they are still there." He took a turn or two up and down the room. "And the British ready to march!" he muttered to him. "Did you see many soldiers as you came to my shop, Mr. Butterwick?"

"See them?" said Lige. "They chased me into a tar-barrel. And there was a whole passel of them up by the Common with guns and flags. Looked as if they meant business."

Revere took his hand and pumped it up and down.

"Thank you, Mr. Butterwick," he said. "You're a shrewd observer. And you have done me—and the colonies—an invaluable service."

"Well, that's nice to know," said Lige. "But, speaking about this tooth of mine——"

Revere looked at him and laughed, while his eyes crinkled.

"You're a stubborn man, Mr. Butterwick," he said. "All the better. I like stubborn men. I wish we had more of them. Well, one good turn deserves another—you've helped me and I'll do my best to help you. I've made artificial teeth—but drawing them is hardly my trade. All the same, I'll do what I can for you."

So Lige sat down in a chair and opened his mouth.

"Whew!" said Revere, with his eyes dancing. His voice grew solemn. "Mr. Butterwick," he said, "it seems to be a compound, agglutinated infraction of the upper molar. I'm afraid I can't do anything about it tonight."

"But——" said Lige.

"But here's a draught—that will ease the pain for a while," said Revere, and poured some medicine into a cup. "Drink!" he said, and Lige drank. The draught was red and spicy, with a queer, sleepy taste, but pungent. It wasn't like anything Lige had ever tasted before, but he noticed it eased the pain.

"There," said Revere. "And now you go to a tavern and get a good night's rest. Come back to see me in the morning— I'll find a tooth-drawer for you, if I'm here. And—oh yes— you'd better have some liniment."

He started to rummage in a big cupboard at the back of the shop. It was dark now, with the end of day and the shutters up, and whether it was the tooth, or the tiredness, or the draught Paul Revere had given him, Lige began to feel a little queer. There was a humming in his head and a lightness in his feet. He got up and stood looking over Paul Revere's shoulder, and it seemed to him that things moved and scampered in that cupboard in a curious way, as Revere's quick fingers took down this box and that. And the shop was full of shadows and murmurings.

"It's a queer kind of shop you've got here, Mr. Revere," he said, glad to hear the sound of his own voice.

"Well, some people think so," said Revere—and that time Lige was almost sure he saw something move in the cupboard. He coughed. "Say—what's in that little bottle?" he said, to keep his mind steady.

"That?" said Paul Revere, with a smile, and held the bottle up. "Oh, that's a little chemical experiment of mine. I call it Essence of Boston. But there's a good deal of East Wind in it."

"Essence of Boston!" said Lige with his eyes bulging. "Well, they did say you was a wizard. It's gen-u-wine magic, I suppose?"

"Genuine magic, of course," said Revere, with a chuckle. "And here's the box with your liniment. And here——"

He took down two little boxes—a silver and a pewter one —and placed them on the counter. But Lige's eyes went to the silver one—they were drawn to it, though he couldn't have told you why.

"Pick it up," said Paul Revere, and Lige did so and turned it in his hands. It was a handsome box. He could make out a growing tree and an eagle fighting a lion. "It's mighty pretty work," he said.

"It's my own design," said Paul Revere. "See the stars around the edge—thirteen of them? You could make a very pretty design with stars—for a new country, say—if you wanted to—I've sometimes thought of it."

"But what's in it?" said Lige.

"What's in it?" said Paul Revere, and his voice was light but steely. "Why, what's in the air around us? Gunpowder and war and the making of a new nation. But the time isn't quite ripe yet—not quite ripe."

"You mean," said Lige, and he looked at the box very respectful, "that this-here revolution folks keep talking about——"

"Yes," said Paul Revere, and he was about to go on. But just then his boy ran in, with a letter in his hand.

"Master!" he said. "A message from Dr. Warren!"

IV

Well, with that Revere started moving, and, when he started to move, he moved fast. He was calling for his riding boots in one breath and telling Lige Butterwick to come back tomorrow in another—and, what with all the bustle and confusion, Lige Butterwick nearly went off without his liniment after all. But he grabbed up a box from the counter, just as Revere was practically shoving him out of the door—and it wasn't till he'd got to his tavern and gone to bed for the night that he found out he'd taken the wrong box.

He found it out then because, when he went to bed, he couldn't get to sleep. It wasn't his tooth that bothered him —that had settled to a kind of dull ache. But his mind kept going over all the events of the day—the two folks he'd seen at Parson Clarke's, and being chased by the British and what Revere had said to the turkey-gobbler woman—till he couldn't get any peace. He could feel something stirring in him, though he didn't know what it was.

" 'Tain't right to have soldiers chase a fellow down the street," he said to himself. "And 'taint right to have people like that woman run down New England. No, it ain't. Oh me —I better look for that liniment of Mr. Revere's."

So he got up from his bed and went over and found his coat. Then he reached his hand in the pocket and pulled out the silver box.

Well, at first he was so flustrated that he didn't know rightly what to do. For here, as well as he could remember it, was gunpowder and war and the makings of a new nation—the revolution itself, shut up in a silver box by Paul Revere. He mightn't have believed there could be such things before he came to Boston. But now he did.

The draught was still humming in his head, and his legs felt a mite wobbly. But, being human, he was curious. "Now, I wonder what is inside that box," he said.

He shook the box and handled it, but that seemed to make it warmer, as if there was something alive inside it, so he stopped that mighty quick. Then he looked all over it for a keyhole, and, if there had been, he didn't have a key.

Then he put his ear to the box and listened hard. And it seemed to him that he heard, very tiny and far away, inside the box, the rolling fire of thousands of tiny muskets and the tiny, far-away cheers of many men. "Hold your fire!" he heard a voice say. "Don't fire till you're fired on—but, if they want a war, let it begin here!" And then there was a rolling of drums and a squeal of fifes. It was small, still, and far away, but it made him shake all over, for he knew he was listening to something in the future—and something that he didn't have a right to hear. He sat down on the edge of his bed, with the box in his hands.

"Now, what am I going to do with this?" he said. "It's too big a job for one man."

Well, he thought, kind of scared, of going down to the river and throwing the box in, but, when he thought of doing it, he knew he couldn't. Then he thought of his farm near Lexington and the peaceful days. Once the revolution was out of the box, there'd be an end to that. But then he remembered what Revere had said when he was talking with the woman about the silver—the thing about building a new country and building it clean and plain. "Why, I'm not a Britisher," he thought. "I'm a New Englander. And maybe there's something beyond that—something people like Hancock and Adams know about. And, if it has to come with a revolution —well, I guess it has to come. We can't stay Britishers forever, here in this country."

He listened to the box again, and now there wasn't any shooting in it—just a queer tune played on a fife. He didn't know the name of the tune, but it lifted his heart.

He got up, sort of slow and heavy. "I guess I'll have to take this back to Paul Revere," he said.

Well, the first place he went was Dr. Warren's, having heard Revere mention it, but he didn't get much satisfaction there. It took quite a while to convince them that he wasn't a spy, and, when he did, all they'd tell him was that Revere had gone over the river to Charlestown. So he went down to the waterfront to look for a boat. And the first person he met was a very angry woman.

"No," she said, "you don't get any boats from me. There was a crazy man along here an hour ago and he wanted a boat, too, and my husband was crazy enough to take him. And then, do you know what he did?"

"No, ma'am," said Lige Butterwick.

"He made my husband take my best petticoat to muffle the

oars so they wouldn't make a splash when they went past that Britisher ship," she said, pointing out where the man-of-war *Somerset* lay at anchor. "My best petticoat, I tell you! And when my husband comes back he'll get a piece of my mind!"

All the same, Lige managed to get a boat at last—the story doesn't say how—and row across the river. The tide was at young flood and the moonlight bright on the water, and he passed under the shadow of the *Somerset*, right where Revere has passed. When he got to the Charlestown side, he could see the lanterns in North Church, though he didn't know what they signified. Then he told the folks at Charlestown he had news for Revere and they got him a horse and so he started to ride. And, all the while, the silver box was burning in his pocket.

Well, he lost his way more or less, as you well might in the darkness, and it was dawn when he came into Lexington by a side road. He was feeling the box burn his pocket and thinking hard.

Then, all of a sudden, he reined up his tired horse. For there, on the side road, were two men carrying a trunk—and one of them was Paul Revere.

They looked at each other and Lige began to grin. For Revere was just as dirty and mud-splashed as he was—he'd warned Hancock and Adams all right, but then, on his way to Concord, he'd got caught by the British and turned loose again. So he'd gone back to Lexington to see how things were there—and now he and the other fellow were saving a trunk of papers that Hancock had left behind, so they wouldn't fall into the hands of the British.

Lige swung off his horse. "Well, Mr. Revere," he said, "you see, I'm on time for that little appointment about my tooth. And, by the way, I've got something for you." He took the box from his pocket. And then he looked over toward Lexington Green and caught his breath. For, on the Green, there was a little line of Minute Men—neighbors of his, as he knew—and, in front of them, the British regulars. And, even as he looked, there was the sound of a gunshot, and, suddenly, smoke wrapped the front of the British line and he heard them shout as they ran forward.

Lige Butterwick took the silver box and stamped on it with his heel. And with that the box broke open—and there was a dazzle in his eyes for a moment and a noise of men shouting—and then it was gone.

"Do you know what you've done?" said Revere. "You've let out the American Revolution!"

"Well," said Lige Butterwick, "I guess it was about time. And I guess I'd better be going home now. I've got a gun on the wall there. And I'll need it."

"But what about your tooth?" said Paul Revere.

"Oh, a tooth's a tooth," said Lige Butterwick. "But a country's a country. And, anyhow, it's stopped aching."

All the same, they say Paul Revere made a silver tooth for him, after the war. But my great-aunt wasn't quite sure of it, so I won't vouch for that.

Love spikes an inferiority complex

Fumble

KATHARINE BRUSH

THE LAMPS were not lighted in the room; but light from the street, falling through the double casement windows, cascading over the cushioned window seat to a wide white pool on the floor, illumined it faintly. You could tell that it was a college room, a careless and a gay room. There were Morris chairs. There were smoking stands. There were photographs of girls. On the couch in the corner a large young man lay. Face downward. Motionless.

That day, in the concrete horseshoe that loomed at the edge of the town, a game had been played; and eighty-five thousand people had watched it. They were trying to go home now. "Let us out," snarled their horns. "Out of this town! We're cold! We're tired! Let us o-o-o-u-u-ut!" Whole car-loads went by, singing and shouting. Car-loads of the conquerors. Triumphant. Pitiless. Howling defiance to the campus of the conquered. "Team! Team! Team!" Bawling the score: "Nine to seven! Y-a-a-ay! Nine to seven!"

A tea dance was going on in the Beta house next door. The throb of the jazz came, muffled by walls, like a beaten jungle tom-tom miles away. Nearer were the sounds of sociability downstairs. Collegians and their girls, grads and their wives, warming themselves before the fire in the living room, sipping drinks, eating sandwiches. Discussing the game.

The young man above heard only their voices; but he knew. He knew what they said. It was the thing they were saying tonight all over the campus, all over the town. It was the thing that, in the basement of the telegraph office on High Street, the newspaper men from the cities were saying, rattling it out on their portable typewriters, handing it page by yellow page to the telegraph operators, so that, tomorrow morning, headlines wide and black might cry it to the world at large: "Evans' Fumble Loses to the Scarlet in Final Minutes of Gridiron Classic. . . ."

He stirred, and dug his face deeper in the damp, warm curve of the pillow. He was back at the field. The dusk of two hours earlier was graying all around him, the ceaseless raucous roar of just two hours ago was crashing on his heedless ears. The game was almost over. It was almost their game, seven to three. All they had to do was hold 'em, hold 'em. Seated on a bench in a dark blue blanket, hunched like a crippled thing, he was holding 'em, from the sidelines. His cleated shoes were clawing the sod beneath him, his fists were flaying wildly, pounding his knees; his breath was short. Every muscle of him, every sinew and nerve, was fighting with the team. . . . Now he was darting out onto the field, carrying his right arm high, feeling on his jerseyed back the sting of the coach's hand. His heart bursting, bursting. Now he was there. He was saying two quick choked words to the referee, and Andrews was pulling off his headguard. Andrews, mud-streaked, bloody, going to the bench—so that Jeffry Evans, substitute, might win his letter before it was forever too late.

You had to play in this game, or the Army game, to win a letter. Lesser games didn't count. Jeffry Evans was a senior, and in three aching years he had only played in the games that didn't count. Or none at all.

Three minutes more. They were huddled for signals again. Bending very low, heads together, quick breaths mingling white in the tight little circle they made. Le Marr coughing and Caprou dashing the perspiration from his eyes. Himself pulling at a dislocated thumb with his other hand. The thirty-five-yard line. First down. "Formation left! Evans! Off tackle!"

He had leaped into place, he had received the ball, he had carried it—how far? A couple of yards maybe, three, four. Then he had fallen, struggling, sobbing for breath, under three men. And the ball——

This was his zero-hour. In all his life to come (he was twenty-two) he would never quite again know such despair. He always failed. Not pettily and inconspicuously, at the very start; but terribly, later, when it mattered. As now. How much, how infinitely better never to have made the football squad than to have made it and toiled on and on—to this!

"Fumble." Butter-fingered word. Thick and slow and stupid word. It had branded him at last, stamped itself upon him. Now all men should know him for the sorry thing he was, the almost good, the near-do-well. . . .

His mind was momentarily diverted from himself by a sudden commotion at the door. Someone was trying to get in. He had forgotten that the door was locked.

"Hey, Jeff! Lemme in, will you, Jeff? It's Weary."

The identification was necessary. Jeffry's roommate, "Weary" Haynes—so called because of his habit of napping in classes, in chapel, and elsewhere where the world was rather dull—had led cheers from two until half-past five that afternoon. His voice was now not a voice but a guttural wheeze, quite unrecognizable.

Jeffry rose from the couch. He had an impulse to tell Weary to go away and stay away and let him alone. This impulse was babyish. He drew a quick sleeve across his eyes, humiliated at the gesture even though there was none but himself to witness it.

"Hullo," he said.

"Hullo," said Weary hoarsely. "Why the bolts and bars?"

"No special reason. I—just thought I'd lock it."

This was lame, and Weary's eyes upon him were wise and rather uncomfortably sympathetic. Weary shut the door and dropped into a chair.

"Hey! Hey! I'm done up."

"I'll bet. It sounded great, though," said Jeffry, who had not really heard a single rah of it.

"Fair," Weary nodded, "fair."

Constraint between them, born of the things that had not been said but must be said, was increasing. "Well, say it," thought Jeffry ahead. "Go on, let's get it over with."

He stole a glance at his roommate, and felt an abrupt new pang. Here was a man who was all the things that he himself was not. Here was a man who never fumbled. His progress through the university had been strewn with laurels, attended with hysterical hosannas. He was not athletic, but it came to Jeffry now that if he had been—if Weary had been the substitute put into today's game in the last five minutes—he would have made a touchdown, like the substitutes of fiction, and emerged trailing clouds of glory. "But," thought Jeffry, "he wouldn't have been a substitute. . . ."

Weary broadcast a small cough into the silence—a sort of preparatory "Stand by!"

"I think it's fine, Jeff, getting your letter."

Jeffry was silent.

"If ever a guy deserved one," Weary continued warmly, "you deserved one. Every day for three years, all through the fall, working out there like a horse—Lord! I'll say you deserved it! They should've given it to you years ago."

"I wish they had," said Jeffry. "If I'd copped it before, they wouldn't have put me in the game today, and we'd have won."

"Bilge!" exploded Weary promptly, loyally. "That's no way to look at it, Jeff."

"How else can I look at it?" Jeffry turned from the window, presenting a tragic face. "I threw the game away. I know it and you know it." He turned back. "Everybody knows it."

"Everybody doesn't know it!" Weary cried out, sitting erect in his earnestness. "In the first place, it isn't so! That is—well, a fumble—that might happen to anybody, mightn't it? Sure it might! Happens all the time!"

Weary cleared his throat hurriedly, risking no interruption. "And in the second place, Jeff, you haven't any idea how—how anonymous the players are on a football field! Why, I'll bet you money that out of those eighty or ninety thousand people in the stadium this afternoon, only a few knew who it was who—fumbled. I'll bet you!"

"They'll know tomorrow," Jeffry said in the same low voice. "Leave it to the sporting writers! They never heard of Jeff Evans till this afternoon—but they found out. And so will everybody. Anyway, what difference does it make whether everybody knows or doesn't? I know. I knew beforehand."

"What?"

"I mean," explained Jeffry patiently, quietly, "I might've. I ought to have known. It was just like me, what I did. I would do something like that. I'm one of those people."

"Oh, listen!" Weary was dismayed. "Don't talk like that, Jeff! Forget it!"

Jeffry smiled a twisted smile. He looked straight at Weary and said, "Yes, you know how soon I'll forget it, don't you?"

And Weary was silenced.

He didn't forget it. Other people did, as other people do; but Jeffry forgot it never at all, nor did he comprehend that others had forgotten. He had always been a sensitive boy; now he was hypersensitive, almost quite truly mad with brooding and grieving. He went looking for wounds, and thought he found in the eyes of his fellows daggers of unforgiveness, and in their casual tongue, lashes of scorn.

The night of the football banquet, when they gave him his letter—with careful words anent his three-year service to the team—he died a little. The applause which was generous seemed merciless; hands slapping him on the raw—and so interminably! Perspiration was chill on his face, his fingers nagged and worried his napkin; he could not look up.

"Fellows," he said, "you—you all know whose fault—" He couldn't go on. They were very kind to him afterward, they shook his hand and mumbled things about not being an ass. But he was not comforted. Pity—he felt it was nothing else—is never comforting to strong men.

He tried to wear the letter; not to wear it seemed absurd when all the campus knew he had it. But wearing it meant minutes of screwing up his courage, meant agonies of sharp self-consciousness. Everybody eyed it. Freshmen, classmates, townspeople. That their eyes were envious, impressed or interested, according to their several stations, he never dreamed. To him the glances leveled at his chest were jeering glances, "Look-at-that-you've-got-a-nerve" glances. . . . He took to wearing the sweater with a buttoned coat above it, and finally he stopped wearing it altogether.

There was one good result of all this. Because he was so much alone in his room, avoiding companionship, he studied; and his grades achieved unprecedented heights. He had never been a brilliant student; he was not now; but he had become a diligent one, and it told. He passed his examinations in June, his final finals, easily; though not as easily as Weary Haynes, who seldom, in the vernacular, "cracked" a book.

It was a relief to graduate, to go away from there, even though the pall of that ruined year went with him. It was a relief to leave Weary, whom he loved.

The first of July found him in New York, which, because of its cruelty, its colossal carelessness, its myriads who are cleverer, stronger, richer, higher up—no matter how high or rich or strong or clever one may be—was the very worst place in the world for him.

He had an uncle in New York, his mother's brother, Peter Lambert, of Lambert and Company, publishers. For years it had been casually understood that when Jeffry finished college he would go to work for his uncle; and lately they had had some definite correspondence on the matter. "The job," Peter Lambert had written, a month before commencement, "awaits you. That's all it is, Jeff—a 'job.' Whether or not it becomes in due time a 'position' depends on you, precisely as if you and I were strangers."

This was strategic, but not altogether true. Peter Lambert was a bachelor, and owner of the business. Jeffry, fatherless since childhood, was his favorite among several nephews. He thought of him paternally, with fondness and with faith. He planned, as he had always planned, to bring Jeffry up and up, until he was of the firm; until, indeed, Jeffry was the firm, carrying on after him.

Unfortunately, Jeffry divined these things, aided by hints from his mother; and in his new frame of mind they distressed and frightened him. He pondered them long. And in the end, deciding that he could not disappoint his uncle by falling down on the job, he hurt him sorely by declining to try it at all, on the ground that he didn't believe the publishing game appealed to him.

He took a very small apartment, and went hunting for work. He thought he would sell bonds. Everybody did. Almost anybody, apparently, could. Accordingly, every morning for many successive mornings, he subwayed down to Wall Street and lower Broadway, and knocked at various and sundry doors. Sometimes he gained admittance, oftener he did not. Two things militated against him. One was that summer's bumper campus crop of would-be bond salesmen; a supply far in excess of the demand. The other was his manner of approach. He always entered thinking, "I suppose I won't get this," "Not a chance here, of course," and this showed in his bearing, which was timid, even apologetic, so that office boys dared to bully him and stenographers to say at once, "No. Sorry. They're not taking anybody now." Feeling, as he felt, the worthlessness of the commodity, he could not even sell Jeffry Evans.

At the end of several weeks his uncle, who had watched from afar, repeated his offer, albeit this time rather gruffly. This time Jeffry accepted. He had to accept. He was down to his last ten dollars.

The thing was too bad all around. Jeffry now firmly believed that nobody but a relative would employ him. And Peter Lambert was now convinced that this pet nephew of his would have gone to work for almost anyone rather than for him. So neither was content.

Futile as he had come to believe himself, Jeffry found that the work was fascinating, and often it absorbed him so he quite forgot to watch the chip on his shoulder. He was very busy. In line with Peter Lambert's plan to teach him the business from every angle, from the ground up, he belonged to no set department, but labored in them all by turns.

Sometimes he read manuscript, sometimes proof. Sometimes he wrote advertisements. He spent whole days at the printing plant in Brooklyn, seeing books made; he packed books for shipment, delivered copies to spectacled reviewers in newspaper offices, sold novels across the counter at one or another of the several little shops maintained and managed by the firm. Once he accompanied the firm's star salesman on a trip through the Middle West, listening and learning, and lugging the sample case.

His salary to start was forty dollars a week. At the end of six months it was forty dollars a week. At the end of a year it still was. He was doing well, he deserved more, and his uncle was aware that he did. But Peter Lambert had got everything he had by asking for it, not by keeping quiet and waiting for it. He believed in demand—provided, of course, there was justice to back it up. Jeffry had not approached him on the subject of a raise.

"And," vowed Jeffry's uncle to himself, "he won't get one till he does."

This was a matter of discipline, a lesson. Lambert did not guess that to Jeffry it was simply another proof of his hopeless inefficiency. A whole year—and he was worth no more than when he started! Not even worth that, probably. Had you encountered him about this time, you would have seen a serious, unsmiling big fellow, young except for the slight, beaten droop of his splendid shoulders. Had you met him, shaken his hand, you would have found him polite, but unresponsive; either preoccupied, or—or what?

Then he fell in love. It happened without preamble, without warning; and that was the worst of it. Afterward Jeffry told himself that if he had only seen it coming, he could have headed it off—and would have. But he didn't see it.

On a morning in September he was called on the telephone by a half-forgotten classmate named Caruthers, who, it appeared, had written a book. Caruthers was on from his home town, which Jeffry's mind dimly identified as Johnstown, or possibly Williamsburg, for the purpose of placing his book with a New York publishing house; and he wanted to know whether if he submitted the manuscript to Jeffry's uncle's firm, Jeffry would personally guarantee that somebody—preferably his uncle, but failing that, "somebody who means something"—read it.

"All I ask," Caruthers said, "is a reading. That's all. Just a reading. You see, I know this publishing racket. If I simply send it in without a word it won't be read. They never are. Don't tell me!"

Jeffry promised that *Clinging Vines*, by Rodney H. Caruthers, would be read, thoroughly and discerningly; and he also agreed, albeit without undue enthusiasm, to be taken to luncheon that day by the grateful author. They met in the lobby of the Cherokee, where Caruthers (having heard that it was literary) was staying, and exchanged the feverish "Well—well—wells" of two who never knew one another well at all, but are striving to overlook the fact.

Toward the end of a meal which seemed to Jeffry doomed to endlessness, Caruthers interrupted himself long enough to inquire what his old classmate was going to do that evening. Jeffry said, after only a tiny pause, "Why—nothing." He heard himself saying it with astonishment. It, of course, committed him to the further society of this merciless egotist; he could have fibbed out of it with ease and he was at a loss to understand why he had not. The truth was that Caruthers was flattering Jeffry. He felt that Jeffry was important to him, and he treated him with deference and respect. Jeffry in his sore heart wanted more of this—much more, at whatever cost.

"I know a little girl," observed Caruthers now (and Jeffry had a quick, bleak picture of the kind of little girl Caruthers would know), "from my home town, Barbara Kincaid, her name is. Awfully nice kid. She has an apartment down in Greenwich Village—she's here designing, or something. I'm going to take her to dinner tonight. Like to have you join us."

"Thanks," said Jeffry. "I—I'd like to."

Her apartment was the first shock. Huge studio room, rough-walled, high-ceilinged, tasteful and beautiful. Lamps under odd-shaped parchment shades, diffusing low soft gold. Dark things, velvet things to sit on and lie on, and sudden flaming gorgeous splashes of color. Books in long cases, unglassed.

Her voice was the second shock. Soft and laughing—cool, and just a trifle breathless, as if she feared she might be interrupted before the end of each sentence. "Hello, ol' Rod Caruthers!" she said. And then, "Oh! How nice. You've brought someone——"

The third shock was dizzying. Not the studio, the setting, not even the voice had prepared him properly. Blonde she was, slim, wrapped tight with cloth-of-silver, tinted like a gay bouquet in which an artist-florist had blended yellow, scarlet, pink and gray, exquisitely. A glamorous person. At first glance a light and frivolous person, belonging to the world of shine and bubbles and string bands. Then you saw her eyes. And her peaked, firm chin. And the eyebrows, dark and straight and rather heavy. And the hands, intelligent, restless, pale. Hands with temperament.

"I should think," observed Barbara at the first break in Caruthers' monologue, "that the publishing business would be awfully interesting. Isn't it?"

"It certainly is," Jeffry said.

"Tell me about it."

He told her. He described, he explained, he gesticulated. Eucouraged and drawn out of himself by Barbara's eyes, her intentness, her questions, he talked glibly and well, without diffidence. At least he knew that nothing he said was as idiotic as anything and everything said by Caruthers.

"You really ought to see for yourself," he wound up. "You ought to let me take you through our plant, and show you."

During dinner he was reminded, by a chance remark of Barbara's about her shop, that Caruthers had told him she did designing. This suddenly became exceedingly important. Just what did she do? What sort of designing? Where was the shop? How long had she had it?

"The shop," replied Barbara, "is on Madison Avenue, between Fifty-second and Fifty-third. It's the very littlest shop in New York, and the cutest, if I do say so as I shouldn't. I've had it three years, and it's called Bal Masqué, and we make fancy-dress costumes."

"Who's we?"

"I am we," Barbara said. "Then I've three girls who sew. I design, and they manufacture."

"Fancy-dress costumes," mused Jeffry aloud.

Barbara nodded. "And original ones. I have never in my life," she added, buttering a roll, "turned out a Pierrette, and so help me, I never shall."

They went from dinner to a play, and from the theater to a supper club, and from that to another, and thence to a third. This was known as "giving Rod a whirl," and was done by Barbara and Jeffry with the customary relentlessness of New Yorkers entertaining out-of-towners.

"See here!" said Jeffry, sitting bolt upright excitedly, turning to her, "maybe you don't have to go home yet, hmm? You haven't had a thing to eat since dinner, and now it's——"

"Four A.M.," Barbara laughed. "I'd love to, Jeff. But—ask me again. I'm a business woman, you know. With an alarm clock."

It was plain that she was not to be persuaded. By forcing Barbara to repeat her refusal twice, thrice, more and more firmly, he reminded himself that she probably didn't like him, really; he had been merely the lesser of two evils, after all.

There was a moment at the door of her apartment house when he thought he might have been mistaken. Her lifted gray eyes were so seemingly sincere, her voice when she said, "I'll see you soon, Jeff?" sounded so as if she wanted to, that his breath came short, his pulses pounded, and he hoped again.

"But tonight's tonight!" he cried desperately. "How do I know I'll ever—" He broke off. Stared at her. Flung down her hands. He picked up his hat from the parquet floor where it had fallen, and rammed it on. "I'm sorry you were bored," he said bitterly and strode to his cab and slammed himself in.

An absurd performance. Two seconds afterward he knew that it had been; and shame boiled in him, and he writhed. What must she think of him now? Oh, fool! Fathead!

He decided to forget her. He said to himself naively that there wasn't any use getting interested in her. A girl like that, who counted her income in five figures and her suitors in three. He would put her out of his mind. And for all time.

Having settled this, and emphasized it with a blow of his fist on the desk, he telephoned her and asked her to dine with him that evening. She couldn't, or wouldn't. She had, she said, a previous engagement. She was terribly sorry; and would Jeffry surely try her again very soon?

The next day, however, the sun was shining and the air was tonic and brisk, and it came to Jeffry, returning from an errand downtown in midmorning, that maybe she really had had an engagement, after all. She would. She was the kind that of necessity kept a little gilt-edged date book: "Bill, tea, Friday, five." "Jimmy, luncheon, Monday, twelve." You couldn't expect to get her on two hours' notice—or on two days' notice, even.

In the office he sought a telephone behind a door that would lock and rang her at her place of business. He said, "This is Jeff Evans again," and she said, "Oh, hel-lo there!" as if she were delighted that it was.

"Listen," he said, "when can you go to dinner, hmm?"

"We-ell," Barbara said, "let's see. How is Saturday?"

Saturday was not very good, because it was four days off; but Jeffry took it without argument. "Write me down," he directed, "in the little book."

Jeffry's party for two was a smooth and flawless and wonderful thing, even surpassing anticipation. One couldn't, of course, anticipate Barbara. She was lovelier than one's most bewitching visions of her, more gracious than one's fondest, brightest hopes.

It was dawn when he took her home. They had been, as Barbara said, "Pretty nearly everywhere." They had danced miles on rhythmic, obedient feet, called by the silver horns.

Barbara said, "I don't feel like talking."

"I don't either."

After a moment her hand pressed his. "You're so—comfortable, Jeff. It's as if I'd known you—almost always."

Their kiss was brief, unpremeditated. One instant they were smiling at one another, blue eyes into gray in the half light. The next their lips were touching, softly, swiftly like children's lips. A kiss to remember the night, and to go with the dawn.

Afterward they rode a little closer together, they held hands a little tighter. But there were no more kisses. Jeffry in that moment was wise with a wisdom that later he marveled at. Too very wise to lose a fragrance in a flame.

When he reached home, Weary's telegram was waiting:

Kill the fatted calf Stop Dress the Avenue in flags and wrestle down the Murphy bed for good Stop I arrive tomorrow Century to take charge promotion our New York office Stop Appointment very sudden but permanent and boy how swell Stop Meet me

(Signed) Weary

Jeffry met him. He had had no sleep to speak of, and perhaps this fact accounted for the barely perceptible listlessness of his welcome, the lack, in a degree or two, of the fervor that was fitting. Weary himself was looking very striking, very picturesque and brown and debonair. Jeff had forgotten that he looked like that.

They taxied to Jeffry's apartment, hemmed in by incredible baggage. Weary talked all the way, occasionally thumping and pummeling Jeffry, now and then uttering a war whoop of sheer young animal glee. They were going to have, he announced, the time of their lives. Parties? Hey! Hey! Jeffry would see. For a starter, they were going to give up Jeffry's apartment, and get a bigger and better one.

"How, by the way," said Weary as an afterthought, "are you fixed for women?"

"I don't know any," said Jeffry.

"Wh-at?"

"Fact. I don't."

"Not a one?" Weary was appalled and unbelieving. "Who were you out with last night, then?" he demanded.

Jeffry bent over the pile of lugage. "Just some fellows. Fellows from the office."

Early in the morning, Weary betook himself to his new office; and when they parted, Jeffry said, "If you get a chance during the day, drop over. I want you to meet my uncle, and see where I slave, and all."

Weary arrived about four in the afternoon. Jeffry, performing some duty in an outer office in which there were numbers of youthful feminine clerks, was apprised of his coming by the little flutter that began at the door and went through the room like a breeze, tilting faces, sending hands to coiffures in a hurry. Weary was radiant, buoyant. He had much to tell, and when he and Jeffry were shut into privacy, he told it joyously. Everything was great. Everybody had been fine to him, and he was to have a corking private office with his name on the door—"the fellow was lettering it when I blew in—and what a secretary! And really very little to do. Really a pipe job, absolutely."

He broke off and regarded the door, and Jeffry also regarded the door, saying, "Come in," because someone had knocked.

Barbara came in. Barbara in a tan dress and a small enchanting hat, with a pair of former foxes, the teeth of one sunk forever into the flank of the other, slanted around her shoulder.

"Am I—interrupting?" she asked hesitantly from the threshold.

"Not at all," said Weary before Jeffry could speak.

Barbara smiled at him; smiled at Jeffry; came all the way in, and closed the door. "I was going by"—she addressed Jeffry—"and I thought I'd stop. You know you said any time I wanted to see the office——"

"Of course," agreed Jeffry, stiff-lipped. He looked at Weary. "This is Weary Haynes. Miss Kincaid."

"How-do-you-do?" said Barbara.

"I'm very happy to meet you," Weary said.

They looked so like a magazine cover, that beautiful pair, shaking hands. . . .

"Take this chair," directed Weary. He had become master of ceremonies, naturally and at once.

"You're not interrupting," he repeated, beaming down at

her. "I should say not! This isn't a business conference—it's part of a reunion! To join which," he assured her, "you are invited. Not to say urged."

"A reunion?"

Weary nodded. "Jeff and I used to room together."

"Oh, really?"

"He hasn't told you about me," Weary deduced mournfully. "But then he didn't tell me about you either. In fact"—here Weary fixed Jeffry with a stern accusing eye—"in fact I seem to recall his telling me, not twenty-four hours ago, that he didn't know any girls in New York. How 'bout that, Jeff?"

"He forgot me," Barbara proclaimed. She made a little face. "Just a girl that men forget," she sighed mock-tragically.

"Not men of sanity," Weary said. "Never. Never in the world."

Jeffry showed them through the plant. He did it mechanically, stalking in and out of elevators, down long corridors ahead of them—pausing and turning when occasion demanded, saying, "This is the business office." "Proofreaders in this room"—mere statements without elaboration.

Every time he spoke he interrupted something amusing and bright that Weary was saying. Weary would cease, he and Barbara would look in and murmur appropriate comments; then they would move on, Weary resuming, Barbara listening appreciatively. The inspection tour took twenty minutes. Jeffry was glad when it was over, and felt that they were glad. It had been flat.

Then Barbara consulted a dot of a watch set in diamonds and platinum, and said she must go.

"So must I," Weary echoed, rising instantly. He took up his hat and confronted Jeffry. "Can you break off now, old man? Or will I see you later?"

"Later," Jeffry said, because he could feel that they wanted him to say that.

He gave them a ten-minute start. Then he, too, left, and went home. Weary's trunks had been delivered at the apartment and dumped in the living room. Two of them. Very big ones. He sat and gazed at them.

Weary joined him. He was in high spirits. "Hullo!" he said. "What ho! And how is Lambert and Company's pride?" He began ridding his pockets of letters and change, his watch and his wallet, laying them all on Jeffry's chiffonier. "I'm late," he observed, "because I took the Glorious Baby to tea."

"You did?" said Jeffry.

"Yeah. I did." Weary, in the act of unfastening the fraternity pin from his vest, wheeled around. "Say," he said, "what was the idea? Why didn't you tell me about her?"

"I—didn't think," Jeffry answered with difficulty. "I don't know her very well——"

"Don't you like her?"

For a racking instant Jeffry thought he was going to make a fool of himself, going to throw himself on Weary's mercy, crying, "Like her? I love her! Oh, let her alone, will you, Weary? Give me a chance!" He had to fight himself to keep this back.

"She's all right," he said indifferently.

"She's marvelous!" Weary declared. "If you weren't such an old woman-hater——" He left the sentence there. He thought a minute, unbuttoning his vest with absent fingers. "Well," he said, "then there's no reason why I shouldn't press my suit, as they say in the subtitles? . . . Much as it needs it," he added, holding out the corners of his vest, "I do not mean the suit you see before you."

"No reason," said Jeffry tonelessly, "as far as I'm concerned."

Then he was the onlooker. He was the confidant, the ear, for Weary's detailed reports of progress. He was the mutual friend to whom they said, "Come on along with us, Jeff. We'd love to have you!" He rarely went. The pain of staying at home alone and following them in his mind was tortuous; but the pain of watching them—so magnificent, so *right* together— was worse.

They were together constantly, tea-ing, dining, dancing. They went to football games away from town; they motored far in Weary's new machine. Once they attended a week-end party in Connecticut. It was during this week-end that Jeffry went one night and looked at the river. He did it because it seemed the thing for a man as wretched as he was to do; he was amazed to find when he got there that he had no real inclination to throw himself in.

Weary was always talking about her. Discussing, speculating, asking advice.

"She's the funniest girl," he assured Jeffry once. "No fooling now, she is. For instance—she won't let me kiss her. Can you imagine a girl like that?"

"No," said Jeffry.

Weary reddened. "Rats!" he said. "I didn't mean—I didn't mean *me*, for heaven's sake! I meant, can you imagine a girl that simply won't be kissed in this age of quick and easy osculation?" He grew reflective. "Sometimes," he remarked, "sometimes I think she must be in love with somebody."

"Who?"

"I haven't an idea. Have you?"

"No," said Jeffry. And he hadn't.

His lease expired on the first of November, and he and Weary moved. The new apartment was spacious and expensive—too expensive, Jeffry thought. Weary, however, was deaf to all protests.

"Pipe down," he said. "It's a short life. Why spend it where the plaster's dirty?"

They bought new furniture, carpets and curtains, and the effect was good. But it didn't suit Weary. On the Sunday afternoon when they were finally settled, their last book tucked in place, their final picture hung, he paced around, hands in his trousers' pockets, scowling into corners and at the walls.

"It could be better," he said. "It needs something. I don't know just exactly what, but something—Barbara'll know," he concluded. "By the way, have we got cakes, and all that junk? She's coming to tea to look the place over."

Jeffry sat motionless for a moment. Then he shambled to his feet. "We've got cakes, I guess. There's tea in that can marked 'Sugar,' and sugar around somewhere. Cream on the ice. If you want lemons, I'll stop at Luigi's on my way out and have some sent——"

"You're not going out?"

"Sure. Why not?"

"Oh, now, Jeff," said Weary earnestly, "stick around. You ought to be here. It's your place as well as mine, you know."

"But it's—your girl."

There was a slight pause. Then Jeffry strolled on into his bedroom, rolling down his sleeves as he went. He felt aimless. He had to tell himself, with words in his mind, just what to do. Snap cuff links. Comb hair. Tie tie. . . .

"Jeff!"

"What?"

Weary was sitting on the divan, looking solemn. Looking at Jeffry. "You ass," he said, "she's in love with you."

Jeffry merely stared at him.

"Heaven help me," said Weary, "for telling you. She made me swear I wouldn't—but you'll never wake up and hear the birdies sing unless I do. I'm convinced of that."

"What," asked Jeffry, "are you talking about?"

"I'm talking about Barbara. She's in love with you. *Love*,"

Weary repeated. "L-o-v-e. Amo, amas, amat—and all that sort of thing." He moaned abruptly, and seized his banjo from a neighboring chair, brandishing it aloft. "Gosh! Have I got to *beat* it in? What is that object you call your head? Just a parking place for teeth? Or does it work?"

"Say what you said again," said Jeffry.

"She's in love with you."

"What makes you think so?"

"She told me!" said Weary, his patience frayed. "She told me the first—no, the second time I ever saw her. I tried to sell myself—and what happened? I got enlisted! Committee of one, to try to make you jealous—so you'd wake up." He made a wry face. "She picked me," he said, "because I'd be the most conspicuous—to you, d'you see? But *you!*—blind, dumb and unconscious you——"

"Wait," begged Jeffry, "wait a minute." He was thinking hard; his lips were moving. "She—she could have had——"

He stopped, overcome; and in that dazzling split second, all his ideas about himself shifted as a backfield shifts, in one swift simultaneous leap. He was in place again, mentally. He had courage once more, and faith in himself. For the man whom Barbara preferred to Weary—to *Weary!*—well, that man could not be such a dud, after all.

He lifted his gleaming eyes and met Weary's eyes, which had watched him with affection from the divan.

"Eureka!" said Weary. "It penetrates. At last it penetrates! And"—his voice softened—"you're crazy about her, aren't you? I wasn't sure. She was pretty sure, but I wasn't absolutely. I see now." He stood up. "*This* baby," he declared, tapping his chest, "will get the lemons. He may even pick them, so don't expect him soon."

For fully three minutes after the door banged shut, Jeffry stayed in his chair. He was seeing things he had not seen. He was understanding things he had misunderstood. He was steeping himself in heavenly realization. Then he thought of the time.

He bolted into his bedroom, changed his suit, borrowed a shirt of Weary's, shaved. He emerged immaculate, rushed to the kitchenette, and there wildly broke things and upset things. Presently his jaw set hard, and he marched to the telephone. He called up his uncle.

"Listen," he said, "I've just been thinking, and—well, the fact is—I've got to have more money. A whole lot more," he insisted stubbornly. "I—" He swallowed. "I'll quit if I don't——"

"Now why," crowed his uncle, "why in tarnation didn't you say so before?"

When his feet moved again, it was off at a tangent into his bedroom. He dug into the depths of his lowest bureau drawer, and by and by he dragged out something. Something woolen and blue. And lettered in white.

He bore this into the living room and arranged it on a chair back. Carelessly, as if he had just taken it off. Yet carefully, with the letter showing . . . so that, in case no one had told her, she would know that he had been a football player.

Prelude

ALBERT HALPER

I WAS coming home from school, carying my books by a strap, when I passed Gavin's poolroom and saw the big guys hanging around. They were standing in front near the windows, looking across the street. Gavin's has a kind of thick window curtain up to eye level, so all I saw was their heads. The guys were looking at Mrs. Oliver, who lately has started to get talked about. Standing in her window across the street, Mrs. Oliver was doing her nails. Her nice red hair was hanging loose down her back. She certainly is a nice-looking woman. She comes to my father's newspaper stand on the corner and buys five or six movie magazines a week, also the afternoon papers. Once she felt me under the chin, and laughed. My father laughed, too, stamping about in his old worn leather jacket to keep warm. My old man stamps a lot because he has leg pains and he's always complaining about a heavy cold in his head.

When I passed the poolroom one or two guys came out. "Hey, Ike, how's your good-looking sister?" they called, but I didn't turn around. The guys are eighteen or nineteen and haven't ever had a job in their life. "What they need is work," my father is always saying when they bother him too much. "They're not bad; they get that way because there's nothing to do," and he tries to explain the meanness of their ways. But I can't see it like my father. I hate those fellas and I hope every one of them dies under a truck. Every time I come home from school past Lake Street they jab me, and every time my sister Syl comes along they say things. So when one of them, Fred Gooley, calls, "Hey, Ike, how's your sister?" I don't answer. Besides, Ike isn't my name anyway. It's Harry.

I passed along the sidewalk, keeping close to the curb. Someone threw half an apple but it went over my head. When I went a little farther someone threw a stone. It hit me in the back of the leg and stung me but it didn't hurt much. I kept a little toward the middle of the sidewalk because I saw a woman coming the other way and I knew they wouldn't throw.

When I reached the corner under the Elevated two big

146

news trucks were standing with their motors going, giving my father the latest editions. The drivers threw the papers onto the sidewalk with a nice easy roll so the papers wouldn't get hurt. The papers are bound with that heavy yellow cord which my father saves and sells to the junkyard when he fills up a bag. "All right, Silverstein," a driver called out. "We'll give you a five-star at six," and both trucks drove off.

The drivers are nice fellas and when they take back the old papers they like to kid my old man. They say, "Hey, you old banker, when are you gonna retire?" or, "Let's roll him, boys, he's got bags of gold in his socks." Of course they know my old man isn't wealthy and that the bags in the inside of the newsstand hold only copper pennies. But they like to kid him and they know he likes it. Sometimes the guys from Gavin's pitch in, but the truck drivers would flatten them if they ever got rough with my old man.

I came up to the newsstand and put my school books inside. "Well, Pa," I said, "you can go to Florida now." So my Pa went to "Florida," that is, a chair near the radiator that Nick Pappas lets him use in his restaurant. He has to use Nick's place because our own flat is too far away, almost a quarter-mile off.

While my father was in Nick's place another truck came to a stop. They dropped off a big load of early sport editions and yelled, "Hey, there, Harry, how's the old man?" I checked off the papers, yelling back, "He's okay, he's in Nick's." Then the truck drove away and the two helpers waved.

I stood around, putting the papers on the stand and making a few sales. The first ten minutes after coming home from school and taking care of the newsstand always excites me. Maybe it's the traffic. The trucks and cars pound along like anything and of course there's the Elevated right up above you which thunders to beat the band. We have our newsstand right up against a big El post and the stand is a kind of cabin which you enter from the side. But we hardly use it, only in the late morning and around two P.M., when business isn't very rushing. Customers like to see you stand outside over the papers ready for business and not hidden inside where they can't get a look at you at all. Besides, you have to poke your head out and stretch your arm to get the pennies, and kids can swipe magazines from the sides, if you don't watch. So we most always stand outside the newsstand, my father, and me, and my sister. Anyhow, I like it. I like everything about selling papers for my father. The fresh air gets me and I like to

talk to customers and see the rush when people are let out
from work. And the way the news trucks bring all the new
editions so we can see the latest headlines, like a bank got
held up on the South Side on Sixty-third Street, or the Cubs
are winning their tenth straight and have a good chance to
cop the pennant, is exciting.

The only thing I don't like is those guys from Gavin's. But
since my father went to the police station to complain they
don't come around so often. My father went to the station a
month ago and said the gang was bothering him, and Mr.
Fenway, he's the desk sergeant there, said, "Don't worry any
more about it, Mr. Silverstein, we'll take care of it. You're a
respectable citizen and taxpayer and you're entitled to protec-
tion. We'll take care of it." And the next day they sent over
a patrolman who stood around almost two hours. The gang
from Gavin's saw him and started to go away, but the cop
hollered, "Now listen, don't bother this old fella. If you bother
him any I'll have to run some of you in."

And then one of the guys recognized that the cop was Butch,
Fred Gooley's cousin. "Listen who's talkin'," he yells back.
"Hey, Fred, they got your cousin Butch takin' care of the
Yid." They said a lot of other things until the cop got mad
and started after them. They ran faster than lightning,
separating into alleys. The cop came back empty-handed and
said to my father, "It'll blow over, Mr. Silverstein; they won't
give you any more trouble." Then he went up the street, turning into Steuben's bar.

Well, all this happened three or four weeks ago and so far
the gang has let us alone. They stopped pulling my sixteen-
year-old sister by her sweater and when they pass the stand
going home to supper all they give us is dirty looks. During the
last three or four days, however, they passed by and kinda muttered, calling my father a communist banker and me and my
sister reds. My father says they really don't mean it, it's the
hard times and bad feelings, and they got to put the blame on
somebody, so they put the blame on us. It's certain speeches
on the radio and the pieces in some of the papers, my father
told us. "Something is happening to some of the people and
we got to watch our step," he says.

I am standing there hearing the traffic and thinking it over
when my little fat old man comes out from Nick's looking like
he liked the warm air in Nick's place. My old man's cheeks
looked rosy, but his cheeks are that way from high blood pres-
sue and not from good health. "Well, colonel," he says smil-

ing, "I am back on the job." So we stand around, the two of us, taking care of the trade. I hand out change snappy and say thank you after each sale. My old man starts to stamp around in a little while and, though he says nothing, I know he's got pains in his legs again. I look at the weather forecast in all the papers and some of them say flurries of snow and the rest of them say just snow. "Well, Pa," I tell my old man, "maybe I can go skating tomorrow if it gets cold again."

Then I see my sister coming from high school carrying her briefcase and heading this way. Why the heck doesn't she cross over so she won't have to pass the poolroom, I say to myself; why don't she walk on the other side of the street? But that's not like Sylvia; she's a girl with a hot temper, and when she thinks she is right you can't tell her a thing. I knew she wouldn't cross the street and then cross back, because according to her, why, that's giving in. That's telling those hoodlums that you're afraid of their guts. So she doesn't cross over but walks straight on. When she comes by the pool hall two guys come out and say something to her. She just holds herself tight and goes right on past them both. When she finally comes up she gives me a poke in the side. "Hello, you mickey mouse, what mark did you get in your algebra exam?" I told her I got A, but the truth is I got a C.

"I'll check up on you later," she says to me. "Pa, if he's lying to us we'll fine him ten years!"

My father started to smile and said, "No, Harry is a good boy, two years is enough."

So we stand around kidding and pretty soon, because the wind is coming so sharp up the street, my old man has to "go to Florida" for a while once more. He went into Nick's for some "sunshine," he said, but me and Syl could tell he had the pains again. Anyway, when he was gone we didn't say anything for a while. Then Hartman's furniture factory, which lately has been checking out early, let out and we were busy making sales to the men. They came up the sidewalk, a couple of hundred, all anxious to get home, so we had to work snappy. But Syl is a fast worker, faster than me, and we took care of the rush all right. Then we stood waiting for the next rush from the Hillman's cocoa factory up the block to start.

We were standing around when something hit me in the head, a half of a rotten apple. It hurt a little. I turned quick but didn't see anybody, but Syl started yelling. She was pointing to a big El post across the street behind which a guy was hiding.

"Come on, show your face," my sister was saying. "Come on, you hero, show your yellow face!" But the guy sneaked away, keeping the post between. Syl turned to me and her face was boiling. "The rats! It's not enough with all the trouble over in Europe; they have to start it here."

Just then our old man came out of Nick's and when he saw Syl's face he asked what was the matter.

"Nothing," she says. "Nothing, I'm just thinking."

But my old man saw the half of a rotten apple on the sidewalk, and at first he didn't say anything but I could see he was worried. "We just have to stand it," he said, like he was speaking to himself, "we just have to stand it. If we give up the newsstand where else can we go?"

"Why do we have to stand it?" I exploded, almost yelling. "Why do we——"

But Mrs. Oliver just then came up to the stand, so I had to wait on her. Besides, she's a good customer and there's more profit on two or three magazines than from a dozen papers.

"I'll have a copy of *Film Fan*, a copy of *Breezy Stories* and a copy of *Movie Stars on Parade*," she says. I go and reach for the copies.

"Harry is a nice boy," Mrs. Oliver told my father, patting my arm. "I'm very fond of him."

"Yes, he's not bad," my father answered smiling. "Only he has a hot temper once in a while."

But who wouldn't have one, that's what I wanted to say! Who wouldn't? Here we stand around minding our own business and the guys won't let us alone. I tell you sometimes it almost drives me crazy. We don't hurt anybody and we're trying to make a living, but they're always picking on us and won't let us alone. It's been going on for a couple of years now, and though my old man says it'll pass with the hard times, I know he's worried because he doesn't believe what he says. He reads the papers as soon as he gets them from the delivery trucks and lately the news about Europe is all headlines and I can see that it makes him sick. My old man has a soft heart and every time he sees in the papers that something bad in Europe has happened again he seems to grow older and he stands near the papers kind of small and all alone. I tell you, sometimes it almost drives me crazy. My old man should be down in Florida, where he can get healthy, not in Nick Pappas' "Florida," but down in real Florida where you have to go by train. That's where he should be. Then maybe his legs would be all right and he wouldn't have that funny color in his cheeks. Since our mother died last year it seems the doctor's treatments don't make him any better, and he has to skip a treatment once in a while because he says it costs too much. But when he stands there with a customer chuckling you think he's healthy and hasn't got any worries and you feel maybe he has a couple thousand in the bank.

And another thing, what did he mean when he said something two days ago when the fellas from Gavin's passed by and threw a stone at the stand? What did he mean, that's what I want to know. Gooley had a paper rolled up with some headlines about Europe on it and he wiggled it at us and my father looked scared. When they were gone my father said something to me, which I been thinking and thinking about. My Pa said we got to watch our step extra careful now because there's no other place besides this country where we can go. We've always been picked on, he said, but we're up against the last wall now, he told me, and we got to be calm because if they start going after us here there's no other place where we can go. I been thinking and thinking about that, especially the part about the wall. When he said that, his voice sounded funny and I felt like our newsstand was a kind of island and if that went we'd be under the waves.

"Harry, what are you thinking of?" Mrs. Oliver asked me. "Don't I get any change?" She was laughing.

And then I came down from the clouds and found she had given me two quarters. I gave her a nickel change. She laughed again. "When he looks moody and kind of sore like that, Mr. Silverstein, I think he's cute."

My old man crinkled up his eyes and smiled. "Who can say, Mrs. Oliver. He should only grow up to be a nice young man and a good citizen and a credit to his country. That's all I want."

"I'm sure Harry will." Mrs. Oliver answered, then talked to Syl a while and admired Syl's new sweater and was about to go away. But another half of a rotten apple came over and splashed against the stand. Some of it splashed against my old man's coat sleeve. Mrs. Oliver turned around and got mad.

"Now you boys leave Mr. Silverstein alone! You've been pestering him long enough! He's a good American citizen who doesn't hurt anybody! You leave him alone!"

"Yah!" yelled Gooley, who ducked behind an El post with two other guys. "Yah! Sez you!"

"You leave him alone!" hollered Mrs. Oliver.

"Aw, go peddle your papers," Gooley answered. "Go run up a rope."

"Don't pay any attention to them," Syl told Mrs. Oliver. "They think they're heroes, but to most people they're just yellow rats."

I could tell by my old man's eyes that he was nervous and wanted to smooth things over, but Syl didn't give him a chance. When she gets started and knows she's in the right not even the Governor of the State could make her keep quiet.

"Don't pay any attention to them," she said in a cutting voice while my old man looked anxious. "When men hide behind Elevated posts and throw rotten apples at women you know they're not men but just things that wear pants. In Europe they put brown shirts on them and call them saviors of civilization. Here they haven't got the shirts yet and hang around poolrooms."

Every word cut like a knife and the guys ducked away. If I or my father would have said it we would have been nailed with some rotten fruit, but the way Syl has of getting back at those guys makes them feel like yellow dogs. I guess that's why they respect her even though they hate her, and I guess that's why Gooley and one or two of his friends are always trying to get next to her and date her up.

Mrs. Oliver took Syl's side and was about to say something more when Hillman's cocoa factory up the block let out and the men started coming up the street. The 4:45 rush was on and we didn't have time for anything, so Mrs. Oliver left, saying she'd be back when the blue-streak edition of the *News* would arrive. Me and Syl were busy handing out the papers and making change and our Pa helped us while the men took their papers and hurried for the El. It started to get darker and colder and the traffic grew heavier along the street.

Then the *Times* truck, which was a little late, roared up and dropped a load we were waiting for. I cut the strings and stacked the papers and when my father came over and read the first page he suddenly looked scared. In his eyes there was that hunted look I had noticed a couple of days ago. I started to look at the first page of the paper while my old man didn't say a word. Nick came to the window and lit his new neon light and waved to us. Then the light started flashing on and off, flashing on the new headlines. It was all about Austria and how people were fleeing toward the borders and trying to get

out of the country before it was too late. My old man grew
sick and looked kind of funny and just stood there. Sylvia,
who is active in the high-scohol social science club, began to
read the *Times* out loud and started analyzing the news to us;
but our Pa didn't need her analysis and kept standing there
kind of small with that hunted look on his face. He looked
sick all right. It almost drove me crazy.

"For Pete's sake," I yelled at Syl. "Shut up, shut up!"

Then she saw our Pa's face, looked at me, and didn't say
anything more.

In a little while it was after five and Syl had to go home and
make supper. "I'll be back in an hour," she told me. "Then Pa
can go home and rest a bit and me and you can take care of
the stand." I said all right.

After she was gone it seemed kind of lonesome. I couldn't
stop thinking about what my father had said about this being
our last wall. It got me feeling funny and I didn't want to read
the papers any more. I stood there feeling queer, like me and
my old man were standing on a little island and the waves
were coming up. There was still a lot of traffic and a few people
came up for papers, but from my old man's face I could tell
he felt the same as me.

But pretty soon some more editions began coming and we
had to check and stack them up. More men came out from
factories on Walnut Street and we were busy making sales.
It got colder than ever and my old man began to stamp
again. "Go into Nick's, Pa," I told him. "I can handle it out
here." But he wouldn't do it because just then another factory
let out and we were swamped for a while. "Hi, there, Silverstein," some of the men called to him, "what's the latest news,
you king of the press?" They took the papers, kidding him,
and hurried up the stairs to the Elevated, reading all about
Austria and going home to eat. My father kept staring at the
headlines and couldn't take his eyes off the print where it said
that soldiers were pouring across the border and mobs were
robbing people they hated and spitting on them and making
them go down on their hands and knees to scrub the streets.
My old man's eyes grew small, like he had the toothache and
he shook his head like he was sick. "Pa, go into Nick's," I told
him. He just stood there, sick over what he read.

Then the guys from Gavin's poolroom began passing the
stand on their way home to supper after a day of just killing
time. At first they looked as if they wouldn't bother us. One
or two of them said something mean to us, but my old man

and me didn't answer. If you don't answer hoodlums, my father once told me, sometimes they let you alone.

But then it started. The guys who passed by came back and one of them said: "Let's have a little fun with the Yids." That's how it began. A couple of them took some magazines from the rack and said they wanted to buy a copy and started reading.

In a flash I realized it was all planned out. My father looked kind of worried but stood quiet. There were about eight or nine of them, all big boys around eighteen and nineteen, and for the first time I got scared. It was just after six o'clock and they had picked a time when the newspaper trucks had delivered the five-star and when all the factories had let out their help and there weren't many people about. Finally one of them smiled at Gooley and said, "Well, this physical culture magazine is mighty instructive, but don't you think we ought to have some of the exercises demonstrated?" Gooley said, "Sure, why not?"

So the first fella pointed to some pictures in the magazine and wanted me to squat on the sidewalk and do the first exercise. I wouldn't do it. My father put his hand on the fella's arm and said, "Please, please." But the guy pushed my father's hand away.

"We're interested in your son, not you. Go on, squat."

"I won't," I told him.

"Go on," he said. "Do the first exercise so that the boys can learn how to keep fit."

"I won't," I said.

"Go on," he said, "do it."

"I won't."

Then he came over to me smiling, but his face looked nasty. "Do it. Do it if you know what's good for you."

"Please, boys," said my Pa. "Please go home and eat and don't make trouble. I don't want to have to call a policeman——"

But before I knew it someone got behind me and tripped me so that I fell on one knee. Then another of them pushed me, trying to make me squat. I shoved someone and then someone hit me, and then I heard someone trying to make them stop. While they held me down on the sidewalk I wiggled and looked up. Mrs. Oliver, who had come for the blue-flash edition, was bawling them out.

"You let him alone! You tramps, you hoodlums, you let him alone!" She came over and tried to help me, but they pushed her away. Then Mrs. Oliver began to yell as two guys twisted my arm and told me to squat.

By this time a few people were passing and Mrs. Oliver called at them to interfere. But the gang were big fellows and there were eight or nine of them, and the people were afraid.

Then while they had me down on the sidewalk Syl came running up the street. When she saw what was happening she began kicking them and yelling and trying to make them let me up. But they didn't pay any attention to her, merely pushing her away.

"Please," my Pa kept saying. "Please let him up; he didn't hurt you, I don't want to have to call the police——"

Then Syl turned to the people who were watching and yelled at them. "Why don't you help us? What are you standing there for?" But none of them moved. Then Syl began to scream:

"Listen, why don't you help us? Why don't you make them stop picking on us? We're human beings the same as you!"

But the people just stood there afraid to do a thing. Then while a few guys held me, Gooley and about four others went for the stand, turning it over and mussing and stamping on all the newspapers they could find. Syl started to scratch them, so they hit her, then I broke away to help her, and then they started socking me too. My father tried to reach me, but three guys kept him away. Four guys got me down and started kicking me and all the time my father was begging them to let me up and Syl was screaming at the people to help. And while I was down, my face was squeezed against some papers on the sidewalk telling about Austria and I guess I went nuts while they kept hitting me, and I kept seeing the headlines against my nose.

Then someone yelled, "Jiggers, the cops!" and they got off of me right away. Nick had looked out the window and had called the station, and the guys let me up and beat it away fast.

But when the cops came it was too late; the stand was a wreck. The newspapers and magazines were all over the sidewalk and the rack that holds the Argosy and Western Aces was all twisted up. My Pa, who looked sicker than ever, stood there crying and pretty soon I began to bawl. People were standing looking at us like we were some kind of fish, and I just couldn't help it, I started to bawl.

Then the cops came through the crowd and began asking questions right and left. In the end they wanted to take us to the station to enter a complaint, but Syl wouldn't go. She looked at the crowd watching and she said, "What's the use? All those people standing around and none of them would help!" They were standing all the way to the second El post, and when the cops asked for witnesses none of them except Mrs. Oliver offered to give their names. Then Syl looked at Pa and me and saw our faces and turned to the crowd and began to scream.

"In another few years, you wait! Some of you are working people and they'll be marching through the streets and going after you too! They pick on us Jews because we're weak and haven't any country; but after they get us down they'll go after you! And it'll be your fault; you're all cowards, you're afraid to fight back!"

"Listen," one of the cops told my sister, "are you coming to the station or not? We can't hang around here all evening."

Then Syl broke down and began to bawl as hard as me. "Oh, leave us alone," she told them and began wailing her heart out. "Leave us alone. What good would it do?"

By this time the crowd was bigger, so the cops started telling people to break it up and move on. Nick came out and took my father by the arm into the lunchroom for a drink of hot tea. The people went away slowly and then, as the crowd began to dwindle, it started to snow. When she saw that, Syl started bawling harder than ever and turned her face to me. But I was down on my hands and knees with Mrs. Oliver, trying to save some of the magazines. There was no use going after the newspapers, which were smeared up, torn, and dirty from the gang's feet. But I thought I could save a few, so I picked a couple of them up.

"Oh, leave them be," Syl wept at me. "Leave them be, leave them be!"

One with Shakespeare

MARTHA FOLEY

YES, MISS COX was there, sitting at her desk in the almost empty classroom. Elizabeth took in the theme she had written to make up for a class missed because of illness.

A description of people under changing circumstances was the assignment.

Elizabeth had chosen immigrants arriving at a Boston dock. She had got quite excited as she wrote about the black-eyed women and their red and blue dresses, the swarthy men and their earrings, and the brightness of a faraway Mediterranean land slipping off a rocking boat to be lost in the grayness of Boston streets.

Elizabeth had liked writing this theme better than anything she had done since the description of a sunset. Amethyst and rose with a silver ribbon of river. Elizabeth shivered. A silver ribbon—that was lovely. And so was "scarlet kerchief in the night of her hair" in this theme. Words were so beautiful.

Miss Cox read the new theme, a red pencil poised in her authoritative fingers. Miss Cox was so strong. She was strongest of all the teachers in the school. Stronger even that the two men teachers, Mr. Carpenter of physics and Mr. Cattell of math. A beautiful strongness. Thought of Miss Cox made Elizabeth feel as she did when two bright shiny words suddenly sprang together to make a beautiful, a perfect phrase.

Elizabeth was glad she had Miss Cox as an English teacher and not Miss Foster any more. Miss Foster had made the class last year count the number of times certain words occurred in *Poor Richard's Almanac*, to be sure they read the book right through word for word. And the words were all so ugly. Like the picture of Benjamin Franklin. But Miss Cox made you feel the words. As when she read from *The Tale of Two Cities* in her singing voice, "This is a far, far better thing than I have ever done." Poor Sydney Carton.

Miss Cox had finished the second page of the theme. She was looking up at Elizabeth, her small dark blue eyes lighting up her glasses.

"Let me give you a pointer, my dear."

Elizabeth automatically looked toward the blackboard ledge at the chalky pointer until the words "my dear" bit into her mind. My dear! Miss Cox had called her "My dear."

"You have a spark of the divine fire," Miss Cox said. "You should make writing your vocation."

Elizabeth flamed. Miss Cox, "my dear," themes about immigrants, blackboards, and desks whirled and fused in the divine fire.

Miss Cox marked "A" in the red pencil at the top of the theme and Elizabeth said "thank you" and went away.

Elizabeth went back to her desk in the IIIA class room which was in charge of Miss Perry. Miss Perry was her Greek teacher as well as her room teacher. Somehow Miss Perry made Elizabeth hate Greek. Elizabeth liked to think of Greece. White and gold in a blue Aegean. I, Sappho. Wailing Trojan women. Aristotle and Plato and Socrates. Grace and brains, said her father, of the men. But that was outside of Greek class. To Miss Perry, Greece was the aorist of *tithemi* and Xenonphon's march in the *Anabasis*. Elizabeth always said to herself as she came into the IIIA room, "I hate Miss Perry, the aorist, and Xenonphon. Oh, how I hate them!"

But this morning Elizabeth only pitied Miss Perry. She had no spark of the divine fire, poor thing.

Greek was the first class this morning. Elizabeth didn't care. She should make writing her vocation. That was something Miss Perry could never do. If she were called on for the list of irregular verbs this morning, she would like to tell Miss Perry that. It would explain why she hadn't studied her Greek home-lesson. Why should she be bothered with conjugations when she had to describe blue and red men arriving on an alien shore?

"Now, Miss Morris, will you please give me the principal parts of the verb *to give*."

That was *didomi*. But what was the perfect tense? Divine fire, divine fire.

"If you don't know, you may sit down. But I warn you that unless you do your home-lessons better you are not going to pass this month."

Divine fire, divine fire.

The second hour was study class. Under Miss Pratt with the ugly bulb of a nose, splotchy face, and eternal smile. Miss Pratt taught something or other to the younger girls down in the sixth class. She always smiled at Elizabeth but Elizabeth

seldom smiled back. Her smile never means anything, thought
Elizabeth.

Elizabeth dumped her books down in her desk in Miss
Pratt's room. She opened Vergil at the part she liked—where
Aeneas told Dido the story of his wandering while the stars
waned and drooped in the sky. It was not her lesson. She had
had that months ago. But she liked going back over it, just as
she liked the beginning of the first book. Great bearded Aeneas rang out in arma virumque cano. That was strong. She
would write strong some day. Strong like Vergil, and fine like
Swinburne:

> "I will go back to the great sweet mother,
>   Mother and lover of men, the sea."

Swinburne had divine fire. Keats. Shelley: "Hail to thee,
blithe spirit." And Masefield whose autograph she had bought
for five shillings, not to help the British but to have a bit of
the man who wrote The Widow in Bye Street.

Elizabeth looked out into the school courtyard. Fine green
shoots. Yellow on the laburnum. Spring was here. Divine fire,
divine fire.

"Miss Morris, haven't you any work to do?" Miss Pratt smiling. Nasty, nasty, smiling. Didn't she know whom she was
talking to like that? A great writer. A girl who would be famous. Let her ask Miss Cox. Why, I have a spark of the
divine fire. I am one with Shakespeare and Keats, Thackeray
and Brontë, and all the other great writers.

Elizabeth plumped her head in her hands and stared at the
Latin page. Opposite was an illustration of an old statue, supposed to be Dido. Further on was a pen-an-ink sketch of Dido
mounting the funeral pyre. Further on was a sketch of Aeneas
nearing Rome. Further on was the vocabulary. Then the end
of the book. Elizabeth turned, page by page. She could not
study, and if she looked out the window at spring again Miss
Pratt would be nasty.

"Please, Miss Pratt, may I go to the library?"

"Must you go to the library? What for?"

"I have a reference in my history lesson to look up in the
encyclopedia."

"Very well."

The library was large and quiet—a whole floor above Miss
Pratt and the study class. It was divided off into alcoves. History in one. Encyclopedias in another. Languages, sciences.

Fiction and poetry were in the farthest end which opened out toward the Fenway. The Fenway with its river and wide sky where Elizabeth liked to walk alone.

Elizabeth had read all the fiction and all the poetry. All of Jane Austen and *The Sorrows of Werther* and lots of other books which had nothing to do with her classes. She was always afraid one of her teachers would come in some day during study class and ask her what she was reading that book for. But that had never happened. And the librarian never paid any attention to her.

Now she went into the fiction and poetry alcove and sat on a small shelf ladder. She looked out the window at the long line of poplars rimming the fens. What would she call them if she were writing about them? Black sentinels against the sky. Oh beautiful, oh beautiful! That was the divine fire.

There was ancient history with Miss Tudor, who had had the smallpox and it showed all over her face; and geometry with Mr. Cattell who had a gray beard and gray eyes and gray clothes and gray manner. Elizabeth liked that—gray manner. That was what the Advanced English Composition called penetrating analysis of character. She would do lots of penetrating analysis when she wrote in earnest.

She would write novels, the greatest, most moving novels ever written, like *Jean Christophe*, Elizabeth was deciding when the bell rang for the end of the history lesson. And in between the novels she would write fine medallions of short stories like Chekhov's, Elizabeth told herself when the bell rang for the end of the geometry lesson. And she would always write lovely poems in between the novels and the short stories, she was thinking when the bell rang for the end of the school day.

Elizabeth walked past Miss Cox's room on her way out of the building. She slowed down her steps as she came to the door. Miss Cox was putting away her things in the drawer of her desk. Elizabeth would dedicate her first book to Miss Cox. "To Miss Eleanor G. Cox this book is gratefully dedicated by the author."

Eileen and Ruth were waiting for Elizabeth at the entrance. Eileen was the cousin of a famous poet and her mother was an Anarchist. Elizabeth liked the thought of anyone being an Anarchist. It sounded so much more beautiful than being a Democrat or a Republican. And Ruth, who was a class ahead, had already had her poems printed in the *Transcript*. Four times. And one of the poems had been reprinted by William

Stanley Braithwaite, in his anthology. Oh, they were going to be great and famous, all three.

"Let's walk home and save our fares for fudge sundaes," said Eileen.

"All right, only I am going to have pineapple," said Ruth.

"I'll go with you but I won't have any sundae," Elizabeth said." I'm going to save my fares this week and buy Miss Cox flowers."

"You have a crush on Miss Cox."

"Perhaps I have and perhaps I haven't. Anyway she said something wonderful to me this morning. She said I had a spark of divine fire and should make writing my vocation."

"Oh, that is wonderful. She never told me that, not even after Mr. Braithwaite took one of my poems for his anthology."

"This is the happiest day of my life. Even when I have written many books and proved Miss Cox's faith in me, I shall always look back to this day. I never expected to be so wonderfully happy."

The three girls, arm in arm, walked through the Fenway.

"I tell you, let's not get sundaes. Since Elizabeth's saving her money, it isn't fair to go in and eat them right before her. Let's you, Ruth, and I buy some of those big frosted doughnuts and some bananas and eat them on the Charles River esplanade. Then Elizabeth can have some too."

"All right, and we can watch the sun set."

"Oh, but that's what isn't fair. To save my money and then eat up what you buy."

"Next time you can give us something."

Elizabeth loved the Charles River. It always hurt her to think that it was on a Charles River bridge that Longfellow should have made up "I stood on the bridge at midnight." Perhaps that wasn't so bad, but so many parodies of the poem had ridiculed the river. Once Elizabeth had written a "Letter to a River." Elizabeth pretended she was away off somewhere like in New York and was writing to the river to tell how much she missed its beauty. She had put so many lovely phrases in it, she thought, and she couldn't understand why the editor of the *Atlantic Monthly* had sent it back to her. But great writers always had many rejections first. That Scottish writer in whose eyes Ruth said she saw his soul, had said in his lecture that to write gently, one must first suffer greatly.

How she had suffered, thought Elizabeth. Her math and Greek teachers were so cruel to her. She who had a spark of divine fire to be treated as they treated her. Tears came to her eyes. And now, when she was tired, she was walking home instead of riding so she could buy Miss Cox flowers. Pink sweetheart roses. Little tight knots of flowers. That was suffering and sacrifice. But it was for love as well as for literature.

"I felt the rhythm of the universe last night," Ruth was saying; "I was sitting on the roof in the dark and I felt the night all around me."

"That makes me think of 'swiftly walk over the western wave, spirit of Night.' But it always bothers me that the wave is to the east in Boston," said Eileen. "Otherwise I like that poem very much."

"The rhythm of the universe? What do you mean?"

"Oh, you know. The way someone said the stars swing round in their courses. And that's why I never, never want to study astronomy. I want only to imagine the stars. That's so much more beautiful than any facts about them can ever be."

"I don't agree with you at all. Why, when you think that the light of the nearest star started coming to you three years ago and what you were doing then and how this minute some star is starting to send you light that may not get to you until far away and old and . . ."

"Stop! Don't give me facts about the stars! You can have those facts about your stars, if you want. But leave me my stars to love as I please."

"Oh, very well. There, now the sky is coloring. See that lovely clear green high up. Pretty soon the deep colors will come. My, these frosted doughnuts are good! Much better than any near where we live."

"There's the first light on the other bank. Over near the Tech building."

That was what it was to have a spark of divine fire. Elizabeth's thoughts flowed on with the darkening river. She could put all this, the river and the sky colors and the lights, into writing. People would feel the loveliness of the world as they had never felt it before. People would no longer walk with their heads bent to the street when there was a sunset to be seen. What have you done to her, masters of men, that her head should be bowed down thus, thus in the deepening twilight and golden angelus? Her father said Noyes wrote maudlin sing-song. It was jingly sometimes but she did like it. And too many heads were bowed down, you masters of men.

"Mother'll scold me if I stay any later," said Eileen.

"And my mother said she wouldn't get me a new dress for the class party if I came home late again."

"Yes, we must all be going. But isn't it nice to think when you wake up at home in bed at night that the river is out here, creeping on and on under the stars?"

"No wonder Miss Cox said you had divine fire. Let's put our banana peels in here. This is Spring Clean-up Week, you know."

"Good night."

"Good night."

"Good night."

Holding the thought of her own greatness close to her, Elizabeth went home. A sliver of moon curled in the sky. That is the moon Shelley, Shakespeare, Spenser and yes, 'way back, Chaucer looked at. And now I am looking at it.

"Mother, Miss Cox says I have a spark of divine fire. I am to be a great writer some day."

"Isn't that nice? Did you remember not to wipe your pen point on your petticoat today?"

"Oh, mother, you know that's not a question of remembering. I never do it when I'm thinking about it. But you didn't half listen to what Miss Cox said about me."

"Indeed I did. She said you had a divine spark of fire. That means you'll get another A in English this month on your report card."

"It means more than any old report card. It means my whole life. I'm to be a writer, a great writer."

"But first you must finish school and college. And that means you have to do your mathematics better. Remember how angry your father was about that E in geometry last month."

Elizabeth sighed. She went out on the back porch which looked across the city. Lights pricked the blackness. Like a necklace which had spilled over velvet. Oh, words were lovely.

The moon was still there, a more emphatic sliver now. "Moon of Shelley and Keats and Shakespeare, and my moon," said Elizabeth and went in to dinner.

The Chrysanthemums

JOHN STEINBECK

THE HIGH gray-flannel fog of winter closed the Salinas Valley from the sky and from all the rest of the world. On every side it sat like a lid on the mountains and made of the great valley a closed pot. On the broad, level land floor the gang plows bit deep and left the black earth shining like a metal where the shares had cut. On the foothill ranches across the Salinas River the yellow stubble fields seemed to be bathed in pale cold sunshine; but there was no sunshine in the valley now in December. The thick willow scrub along the river flamed with sharp and positive yellow leaves.

It was a time of quiet and of waiting. The air was cold and tender. A light wind blew up from the southwest so that the farmers were mildly hopeful of a good rain before long; but fog and rain do not go together.

Across the river, on Henry Allen's foothill ranch there was little work to be done, for the hay was cut and stored and the orchards were plowed up to receive the rain deeply when it should come. The cattle on the higher slopes were becoming shaggy and rough-coated.

Elisa Allen, working in her flower garden, looked down across the yard and saw Henry, her husband, talking to two men in business suits. The three of them stood by the tractor shed, each man with one foot on the side of the Little Fordson. They smoked cigarettes and studied the machine as they talked.

Elisa watched them for a moment and then went back to her work. She was thirty-five. Her face was lean and strong and her eyes were as clear as water. Her figure looked blocked and heavy in her gardening costume, a man's black hat pulled low down over her eyes, clodhopper shoes, a figured print dress almost completely covered by a big corduroy apron with four big pockets to hold the snips, the trowel and scratcher, the seeds and the knife she worked with. She wore heavy leather gloves to protect her hands while she worked.

She was cutting down the old year's chrysanthemum stalks with a pair of short and powerful scissors. She looked down toward the men by the tractor shed now and then. Her face was eager and mature and handsome; even her work with the scissors was overeager, overpowerful. The chrysanthemum stems seemed too small and easy for her energy.

She brushed a cloud of hair out of her eyes with the back of her glove, and left a smudge of earth on her cheek in doing it. Behind her stood the neat white farmhouse with red geraniums close-banked round it as high as the windows. It was a hard-swept looking little house, with hard-polished windows, and a clean mat on the front steps.

Elisa cast another glance toward the tractor shed. The stranger men were getting into their Ford coupe. She took off a glove and put her strong fingers down into the forest of new green chrysanthemum sprouts that were growing round the old roots. She spread the leaves and looked down among the close-growing stems. No aphids were there, no sow bugs nor snails nor cutworms. Her terrier fingers destroyed such pests before they could get started.

Elisa started at the sound of her husband's voice. He had come near quietly and he leaned over the wire fence that protected her flower garden from cattle and dogs and chickens. "At it again," he said. "You've got a strong new crop coming."

Elisa straightened her back and pulled on the gardening glove again. "Yes. They'll be strong this coming year." In her tone and on her face there was a little smugness.

"You've got a gift with things," Henry observed. "Some of those yellow chrysanthemums you had last year were ten inches across. I wish you'd work out in the orchard and raise some apples that big."

Her eyes sharpened. "Maybe I could do it too. I've a gift with things all right. My mother had it. She could stick anything in the ground and make it grow. She said it was having planters' hands that knew how to do it."

"Well, it sure works with flowers," he said.

"Henry, who were those men you were talking to?"

"Why, sure, that's what I came to tell you. They were from the Western Meat Company. I sold those thirty head of three-year-old steers. Got nearly my own price too."

"Good," she said. "Good for you."

"And I thought," he continued, "I thought how it's Saturday afternoon, and we might go into Salinas for dinner at a restaurant and then to a picture show—to celebrate, you see."

"Good," she repeated. "Oh, yes. That will be good."

Henry put on his joking tone. "There's fights tonight. How'd you like to go to the fights?"

"Oh, no," she said breathlessly. "No, I wouldn't like fights."

"Just fooling, Elisa. We'll go to a movie. Let's see. It's two now. I'm going to take Scotty and bring down those steers from the hill. It'll take us maybe two hours. We'll go in town about five and have dinner at the Cominos Hotel. Like that?"

"Of course I'll like it. It's good to eat away from home."

"All right then. I'll go get up a couple of horses."

She said, "I'll have plenty of time to transplant some of these sets, I guess."

She heard her husband calling Scotty down by the barn. And a little later she saw the two men ride up the pale-yellow hillside in search of the steers.

There was a little square sandy bed kept for rooting the chrysanthemums. With her trowel she turned the soil over and over and smoothed it and patted it firm. Then she dug ten parallel trenches to receive the sets. Back at the chrysanthemum bed she pulled out the little crisp shoots, trimmed off the leaves of each one with her scissors, and laid it on a small orderly pile.

A squeak of wheels and plod of hoofs came from the road. Elisa looked up. The country road ran along the dense bank of willows and cottonwoods that bordered the river, and up this road came a curious vehicle, curiously drawn. It was an old spring-wagon, with a round canvas top on it like the cover of a prairie schooner. It was drawn by an old bay horse and a little gray-and-white burro. A big stubble-bearded man sat between the cover flaps and drove the crawling team. Underneath the wagon, between the hind wheels, a lean and rangy mongrel dog walked sedately. Words were painted on the canvas in clumsy crooked letters. "Pots, pans, knives, sisors, lawn mores, Fixed." Two rows of articles, and the triumphantly definitive "Fixed" below. The black paint had run down in little sharp points beneath each letter.

Elisa, squatting on the ground, watched to see the crazy loose-jointed wagon pass by. But it didn't pass. It turned into the farm road in front of her house, crooked old wheels skirling and squeaking. The rangy dog darted from beneath the wheels and ran ahead. Instantly the two ranch shepherds flew out at him. Then all three stopped, and with stiff and quivering tails, with taut straight legs, with ambassadorial dignity, they slowly circled, sniffing daintily. The caravan pulled up to Elisa's wire fence and stopped. Now the newcomer dog, feeling outnumbered, lowered his tail and retired under the wagon with raised hackles and bared teeth.

The man on the wagon seat called out, "That's a bad dog in a fight when he gets started."

Elisa laughed. "I see he is. How soon does he generally get started?"

The man caught up her laughter and echoed it heartily. "Sometimes not for weeks and weeks," he said. He climbed stiffly down over the wheel. The horse and the donkey drooped like unwatered flowers.

Elisa saw that he was a very big man. Although his hair and beard were graying, he did not look old. His worn black suit was wrinkled and spotted with grease. The laughter had disappeared from his face and eyes the moment his laughing voice ceased. His eyes were dark and they were full of the brooding that gets in the eyes of teamsters and of sailors. The calloused hands he rested on the fence were cracked, and every crack was a black line. He took off his battered hat.

"I'm off my general road, ma'am," he said. "Does this dirt road cut over across the river to the Los Angeles highway?"

Elisa stood up and shoved the thick scissors in her apron pocket. "Well, yes, it does, but it winds around and then fords the river. I don't think your team could pull through the sand."

He replied with some asperity, "It might surprise you what them beasts can pull through."

"When they get started?" she asked.

He smiled for a second. "Yes. When they get started."

"Well," said Elisa, "I think you'll save time if you go back to the Salinas road and pick up the highway there."

He drew a big finger down the chicken wire and made it sing. "I ain't in any hurry, ma'am. I go from Seattle to San Diego and back every year. Takes all my time. About six months each way. I aim to follow nice weather."

Elisa took off her gloves and stuffed them in the apron pocket with the scissors. She touched the under edge of her man's hat, searching for fugitive hairs. "That sounds like a nice kind of a way to live," she said.

He leaned confidentially over the fence. "Maybe you noticed the writing on my wagon. I mend pots and sharpen knives and scissors. You got any of them things to do?"

"Oh, no," she said quickly. "Nothing like that." Her eyes hardened with resistance.

"Scissors is the worst thing," he explained. "Most people just ruin scissors trying to sharpen 'em, but I know how. I got a special tool. It's a little bobbit kind of thing and patented. But it sure does the trick."

"No. My scissors are all sharp."

"All right then. Take a pot," he continued earnestly, "a bent pot or a pot with a hole. I can make it like new so you don't have to buy no new ones. That's a saving for you."

"No," she said shortly. "I tell you I have nothing like that for you to do."

His face fell to an exaggerated sadness. His voice took on a whining undertone. "I ain't had a thing to do today. Maybe I won't have no supper tonight. You see I'm off my regular road. I know folks on the highway clear from Seattle to San Diego. They save their things for me to sharpen up because they know I do it so good and save them money."

"I'm sorry," Elisa said irritably. "I haven't anything for you to do."

His eyes left her face and fell to searching the ground. They roamed about until they came to the chrysanthemum bed where she had been working. "What's them plants, ma'am?"

The irritation and resistance melted from Elisa's face. "Oh, those are chrysanthemums, giant whites and yellows. I raise them every year, bigger than anybody around here."

"Kind of a long-stemmed flower? Looks like a quick puff of colored smoke?" he asked.

"That's it. What a nice way to describe them."

"They smell kind of nasty till you get used to them," he said.

"It's a good bitter smell," she retorted, "not nasty at all."

He changed his tone quickly ."I like the smell myself."

"I had ten-inch blooms this year," she said.

The man leaned farther over the fence. "Look. I know a lady down the road a piece has got the nicest garden you ever seen. Got nearly every kind of flower but no chrysanthemums. Last time I was mending a copper-bottom wash tub for her (that's a hard job but I do it good), she said to me, 'If you ever run acrost some nice chrysanthemums I wish you'd try to get me a few seeds.' That's what she told me."

Elisa's eyes grew alert and eager. "She couldn't have known much about chrysanthemums. You can raise them from seed, but it's much easier to root the little sprouts you see there."

"Oh," he said. "I s'pose I can't take none to her then."

"Why yes, you can," Elisa cried. "I can put some in damp sand, and you can carry them right along with you. They'll take root in the pot if you keep them damp. And then she can transplant them."

"She'd sure like to have some, ma'am. You say they're nice ones?"

"Beautiful," she said. "Oh, beautiful." Her eyes shone. She tore off the battered hat and shook out her dark pretty hair. "I'll put them in a flowerpot, and you can take them right with you. Come into the yard."

While the man came through the picket gate Elisa ran excitedly along the geranium-bordered path to the back of the house. And she returned carrying a big red flowerpot. The gloves were forgotten now. She kneeled on the ground by the starting bed and dug up the sandy soil with her fingers and scooped it into the bright new flowerpot. Then she picked up the little pile of shoots she had prepared. With her strong fingers she pressed them into the sand and tamped round them with her knuckles. The man stood over her. "I'll tell you what to do," she said. "You remember so you can tell the lady."

"Yes, I'll try to remember."

"Well, look. These will take root in about a month. Then she must set them out, about a foot apart in good rich earth like this, see?" She lifted a handful of dark soil for him to look at. "They'll grow fast and tall. Now remember this. In July tell her to cut them down, about eight inches from the ground."

"Before they bloom?" he asked.

"Yes, before they bloom." Her face was tight with eagerness. "They'll grow right up again. About the last of September the buds will start."

She stopped and seemed perplexed. "It's the budding that takes the most care," she said hesitantly. "I don't know how to tell you." She looked deep into his eyes searchingly. Her mouth opened a little, and she seemed to be listening. "I'll try to tell you," she said. "Did you ever hear of planting hands?"

"Can't say I have, ma'am."

"Well, I can only tell you what it feels like. It's when you're picking off the buds you don't want. Everything goes right down into your fingertips. You watch your fingers work. They do it themselves. You can feel how it is. They pick and pick the buds. They never make a mistake. They're with the plant. Do you see? Your fingers and the plant. You can feel that, right up your arm. They know. They never make a mistake. You can feel it. When you're like that you can't do anything wrong. Do you see that? Can you understand that?"

She was kneeling on the ground looking up at him. Her breast swelled passionately.

The man's eyes narrowed. He looked away self-consciously. "Maybe I know," he said. "Sometimes in the night in the wagon there——"

Elisa's voice grew husky. She broke in on him. "I've never lived as you do, but I know what you mean. When the night is dark—the stars are sharp-pointed, and there's quiet. Why, you rise up and up!"

Kneeling there, her hand went out toward his legs in the greasy black trousers. Her hesitant fingers almost touched the cloth. Then her hand dropped to the ground.

He said, "It's nice, just like you say. Only when you don't have no dinner it ain't."

She stood up then, very straight, and her face was ashamed. She held the flowerpot out to him and placed it gently in his arms. "Here. Put it in your wagon, on the seat, where you can watch it. Maybe I can find something for you to do."

At the back of the house she dug in the can pile and found two old and battered aluminum saucepans. She carried them back and gave them to him, "Here, maybe you can fix these."

His manner changed. He became professional. "Good as new I can fix them." At the back of his wagon he set a little anvil, and out of an oily toolbox dug a small machine hammer. Elisa came through the gate to watch him while he pounded out the dents in the kettles. His mouth grew sure and knowing. At a difficult part of the work he sucked his underlip.

"You sleep right in the wagon?" Elisa asked.

"Right in the wagon, ma'am. Rain or shine I'm dry as a cow in there."

"It must be nice," she said. "It must be very nice. I wish women could do such things."

"It ain't the right kind of a life for a woman."

Her upper lip raised a little, showing her teeth. "How do you know? How can you tell?" she said.

"I don't know, ma'am," he protested. "Of course I don't know. Now here's your kettles, done. You don't have to buy no new ones."

"How much?"

"Oh, fifty cents'll do. I keep my prices down and my work good. That's why I have all them satisfied customers up and down the highway."

Elisa brought him a fifty-cent piece from the house and dropped it in his hand. "You might be surprised to have a rival sometime. I can sharpen scissors too. And I can beat the dents out of little pots. I could show you what a woman might do."

He put his hammer back in the oily box and shoved the little anvil out of sight. "It would be a lonely life for a woman, ma'am, and a scary life, too, with animals creeping under the wagon all night." He climbed over the singletree, steadying himself with a hand on the burro's white rump. He settled himself in the seat, picked up the lines. "Thank you kindly, ma'am," he said. "I'll do like you told me; I'll go back and catch the Salinas road."

"Mind," she called, "if you're long in getting there, keep the sand damp."

"Sand, ma'am?—Sand? Oh, sure. You mean around the chrysanthemums. Sure I will." He clucked his tongue. The beasts leaned luxuriously into their collars. The mongrel dog took his place between the back wheels. The wagon turned and crawled out the entrance road and back the way it had come, along the river.

Elisa stood in front of her wire fence watching the slow progress of the caravan. Her shoulders were straight, her head thrown back, her eyes half-closed, so that the scene came vaguely into them. Her lips moved silently, forming the words "Good-by—good-by." Then she whispered, "That's a bright direction. There's a glowing there." The sound of her whisper startled her. She shook herself free and looked about to see whether anyone had been listening. Only the dogs had heard. They lifted their heads toward her from their sleeping in the dust, and then stretched out their chins and settled asleep again. Elisa turned and ran hurriedly into the house.

In the kitchen she reached behind the stove and felt the water tank. It was full of hot water from the noonday cooking. In the bathroom she tore off her soiled clothes and flung them into the corner. And then she scrubbed herself with a little block of pumice, legs and thighs, loins and chest and arms, until her skin was scratched and red. When she had dried herself she stood in front of a mirror in her bedroom and looked at her body. She tightened her stomach and threw out her chest. She turned and looked over her shoulder at her back.

After a while she began to dress slowly. She put on her newest underclothing and her nicest stockings and the dress which was the symbol of her prettiness. She worked carefully on her hair, penciled her eyebrows, and rouged her lips.

Before she was finished she heard the little thunder of hoofs and the shouts of Henry and his helper as they drove the red steers into the corral. She heard the gate bang shut and set herself for Henry's arrival.

His step sounded on the porch. He entered the house calling, "Elisa, where are you?"

"In my room, dressing. I'm not ready. There's hot water for your bath. Hurry up. It's getting late."

When she heard him splashing in the tub. Elisa laid his dark suit on the bed, and shirt and socks and tie beside it. She stood his polished shoes on the floor beside the bed. Then she went to the porch and sat primly and stiffly down. She looked toward the river road where the willow-lane was still yellow with frosted leaves so that under the high gray fog they seemed a thin band of sunshine. This was the only color in the gray afternoon. She sat unmoving for a long time.

Henry came banging out of the door, shoving his tie inside his vest as he came. Elisa stiffened and her face grew tight. Henry stopped short and looked at her. "Why—why, Elisa. You look so nice!"

"Nice? You think I look nice? What do you mean by 'nice'?"

Henry blundered on. "I don't know. I mean you look different, strong and happy."

"I am strong? Yes, strong. What do you mean 'strong'?"

He looked bewildered. "You're playing some kind of a game," he said helplessly. "It's a kind of play. You look strong enough to break a calf over your knees, happy enough to eat it like a watermelon."

For a second she lost her rigidity. "Henry! Don't talk like that. You didn't know what you said." She grew complete again. "I am strong," she boasted. "I never knew before how strong."

Henry looked down toward the tractor shed, and when he brought his eyes back to her, they were his own again. "I'll get out the car. You can put on your coat while I'm starting."

Elisa went into the house. She heard him drive to the gate and idle down his motor, and then she took a long time to put on her hat. She pulled it here and pressed it there. When Henry turned the motor off she slipped into her coat and went out.

The little roadster bounced along on the dirt road by the river, raising the birds and driving the rabbits into the brush. Two cranes flapped heavily over the willow-line and dropped into the river-bed.

Far ahead on the road Elisa saw a dark speck in the dust. She suddenly felt empty. She did not hear Henry's talk. She tried not to look; she did not want to see the little heap of sand and green shoots, but she could not help herself. The chrysanthemums lay in the road close to the wagon tracks. But not the pot; he had kept that. As the car passed them she remembered the good bitter smell, and a little shudder went through her. She felt ashamed of her strong planter's hands, that were no use, lying palms up in her lap.

The roadster turned a bend and she saw the caravan ahead. She swung full round toward her husband so that she could not see the little covered wagon and the mismatched team as the car passed.

In a moment they had left behind them the man who had not known or needed to know what she said, the bargainer. She did not look back.

To Henry she said loudly, to be heard above the motor. "It will be good, tonight, a good dinner."

"Now you're changed again," Henry complained. He took one hand from the wheel and patted her knee. "I ought to take you in to dinner oftener. It would be good for both of us. We get so heavy out on the ranch."

"Henry," she asked, "could we have wine at dinner?"

"Sure. Say! That will be fine."

She was silent for a while; then she said, "Henry, at those prize fights do the men hurt each other very much?"

"Sometimes a little, not often. Why?"

"Well, I've read how they break noses, and blood runs down their chests. I've read how the fighting gloves get heavy and soggy with blood."

He looked round at her. "What's the matter, Elisa? I didn't know you read things like that." He brought the car to a stop, then turned to the right over the Salinas River bridge.

"Do any women ever go to the fights?" she asked.

"Oh, sure, some. What's the matter, Elisa? Do you want to go? I don't think you'd like it, but I'll take you if you really want to go."

She relaxed limply in the seat. "Oh, no. I don't want to go. I'm sure I don't." Her face was turned away from him. "It will be enough if we can have wine. It will be plenty." She turned up her coat collar so he could not see that she was crying weakly—like an old woman.

Young Man Axelbrod

SINCLAIR LEWIS

THE COTTONWOOD is a tree of a slovenly and plebeian habit.
Its woolly wisps turn gray the lawns and engender neighbor-
hood hostilities about our town. Yet it is a mighty tree, a ref-
uge and an inspiration; the sun flickers in its towering foliage,
whence the tattoo of locusts enlivens our dusty summer after-
noons. From the wheat country out to the sagebrush plains
between the buttes and the Yellowstone it is the cottonwood
that keeps a little grateful shade for sweating homesteaders.

In Joralemon we called Knute Axelbrod "Old Cottonwood." As a matter of fact, the name was derived not so much
from the quality of the man as from the wide grove about his
gaunt white house and red barn. He made a comely row of
trees on each side of the country road, so that a humble,
daily sort of man, driving beneath them in his lumber wagon
might fancy himself lord of a private avenue. And at sixty-five
Knute was like one of his own cottonwoods, his roots deep in
the soil, his trunk weathered by rain and blizzard and baking
August noons, his crown spread to the wide horizon of day
and the enormous sky of a prairie night.

This immigrant was an American even in speech. Save for
a weakness about his j's and w's, he spoke the twangy Yankee
English of the land. He was the more American because, in
his native Scandinavia, he had dreamed of America as a land of
light. Always, through disillusion and weariness, he beheld
America as the world's nursery for justice, for broad, fair
towns, and eager talk; and always he kept a young soul that
dared to desire beauty.

As a lad Knute Axelbrod had wished to be a famous scholar,
to learn the ease of foreign tongues, the romance of history,
to unfold in the graciousness of the wise books. When he first
came to America he worked in a sawmill all day and studied
all evening. He mastered enough book learning to teach district school for two terms; then when he was only eighteen,
a great-hearted pity for faded Lena Wesselius moved him to
marry her. Gay enough, doubtless, was their hike by prairie

schooner to new farm lands, but Knute was promptly caught in a net of poverty and family. From eighteen to fifty-eight he was always snatching children away from death or the farm away from mortgages.

He had to be content—and generously content he was—with the second-hand glory of his children's success and, for himself, with pilfered hours of reading—that reading of big, thick, dismal volumes of history and economics which the lone, mature learner chooses. Without ever losing his desire for strange cities and the dignity of towers, he stuck to his farm. He acquired a half-section, free from debt, fertile, well-stocked, adorned with a cement silo, a chicken-run, a new windmill. He became comfortable, secure, and then he was ready, it seemed, to die; for at sixty-three his work was done, and he was unneeded and alone.

His wife was dead. His sons had scattered afar, one a dentist in Fargo, another a farmer in the Golden Valley. He had turned over his farm to his daughter and son-in-law. They had begged him to live with them, but Knute refused.

"No," he said, "you must learn to stand on your own feet. I vill not give you the farm. You pay me four hundred dollars a year rent, and I live on that and vatch you from my hill."

On a rise beside the lone cottonwood which he loved best of all his trees Knute built a tar-paper shack, and here he "bached it": cooked his meals, made his bed—sometimes, sat in the sun, read many books from the Joralemon library, and began to feel that he was free of the yoke of citizenship which he had borne all his life.

For hours at a time he sat on a backless kitchen chair before the shack, a wide-shouldered man, white-bearded, motionless; a seer despite his grotesquely baggy trousers, his collarless shirt. He looked across the miles of stubble to the steeple of the Jack-rabbit Forks church and meditated upon the uses of life. At first he could not break the rigidity of habit. He rose at five, found work in cleaning his cabin and cultivating his garden, had dinner exactly at twelve, and went to bed by afterglow. But little by little he discovered that he could be irregular without being arrested. He stayed abed till seven or even eight. He got a large, deliberate tortoise-shell cat, and played games with it; let it lap milk upon the table, called it the Princess, and confided to it that he had a "sneaking idee" that men were fools to work so hard. Around this coatless old man, his stained waistcoat flapping about a huge torso, in a shanty of rumpled bed and pine table covered with sheets of food-daubed newspaper, hovered all the passionate aspiration of youth and the dreams of ancient beauty.

He began to take long walks by night. In his necessitous life, night had ever been a period of heavy slumber in close rooms. Now he discovered the mystery of the dark; saw the prairies wide flung and misty beneath the moon, heard the voices of grass and cottonwoods and drowsy birds. He tramped for miles. His boots were dew-soaked, but he did not heed. He stopped upon hillocks, shyly threw wide his arms, and stood worshiping the naked, slumbering land.

These excursions he tried to keep secret, but they were bruited abroad. Neighbors, good, decent fellows with no nonsense about walking in the dew at night, when they were returning late from town, drunk, lashing their horses, and flinging whisky bottles from their racing democrat wagons, saw him, and they spread the tiding that Old Cottonwood was "getting nutty since he give up his farm to that son-in-law of his and retired. Seen the old codger wandering around at midnight. Wish I had his chance to sleep. Wouldn't catch me out in the night air."

Any rural community from Todd Center to Seringapatam is resentful of any person who varies from its standard, and is morbidly fascinated by any hint of madness. The countryside began to spy on Knute Axelbrod, to ask him questions, and to stare from the road at his shack. He was sensitively aware of it, and inclined to be surly to inquisitive acquaintances. Doubtless that was the beginning of his great pilgrimage.

As a part of the general wild license of his new life—really, he once roared at that startled cat, the Princess: "By gollies! I ain't going to brush my teeth tonight. All my life I've brushed 'em, and alvays vanted to skip a time vunce"—Knute took considerable pleasure in degenerating in his taste in scholarship. He wilfully declined to finish *The Conquest of Mexico*, and began to read light novels borrowed from the Joralemon library. So he rediscovered the lands of dancing and light wines, which all his life he had desired. Some economics and history he did read, but every evening he would stretch out in his buffalo-horn chair, his feet on the cot and the princess in his lap, and invade Zenda or fall in love with Trilby.

Among the novels, he chanced upon a highly optimistic story of Yale in which a worthy young man "earned his way through" college, stroked the crew, won Phi Beta Kappa, and had the most entertaining, yet moral, conversations on or adjacent to "the dear old fence."

As a result of this chronicle, at about three o'clock one morning when Knute Axelbrod was sixty-four years of age, he decided that he would go to college! All his life he had wanted to. Why not do it?

When he awoke in the morning he was not so sure about it as when he had gone to sleep. He saw himself as ridiculous, a ponderous, oldish man among clean-limbed youths, like a dusty cottonwood among silver birches. But for months he wrestled and played with that idea of a great pilgrimage to the Mount of Muses; for he really supposed college to be that sort of place. He believed that all college students, except for the wealthy idlers, burned to acquire learning. He pictured Harvard and Yale and Princeton as ancient groves set with marble temples, before which large groups of Grecian youths talked gently about astronomy and good government. In his picture they never cut classes or ate.

With a longing for music and books and graciousness such as the most ambitious boy could never comprehend, this thick-faced prairie farmer dedicated himself to beauty, and defied the unconquerable power of approaching old age. He sent for college catalogues and schoolbooks, and diligently began to prepare himself for college.

He found Latin irregular verbs and the whimsicalities of algebra fiendish. They had nothing to do with actual life as he had lived it. But he mastered them; he studied twelve hours a day, as once he had plodded through eighteen hours a day in the hayfield. With history and English literature he had comparatively little trouble; already he knew much of them from his recreative reading. From German neighbors he had picked up enough Plattdeutsch to make German easy. The trick of study began to come back to him from his small schoolteaching of forty-five years before. He began to believe that he could really put it through. He kept assuring himself that in college, with rare and sympathetic instructors to help him, there would not be this baffling search, this nervous strain.

But the unreality of the things he studied did disillusion him, and he tired of his new game. He kept it up chiefly because all his life he had kept up onerous labor without any taste for it. Toward the autumn of the second year of his eccentric life he no longer believed that he would ever go to college.

Then a busy little grocer stopped him on the street in Joralemon and quizzed him about his studies, to the delight of the informal club which always loafs at the corner of the hotel.

Knute was silent, but dangerously angry. He remembered just in time how he had once laid wrathful hands upon a hired man, and somehow the man's collarbone had been broken. He turned away and walked home, seven miles, still boiling. He picked up the Princess, and, with her mewing on his shoulder, tramped out again to enjoy the sunset.

He stopped at a reedy slough. He gazed at a hopping plover without seeing it. He plucked at his beard. Suddenly he cried: "I am going to college. It opens next week. I t'ink that I can pass the examinations."

Two days later he had moved the Princess and his sticks of furniture to his son-in-law's house, had bought a new slouch hat, a celluloid collar, and a solemn suit of black, had wrestled with God in prayer through all of a star-clad night, and had taken the train for Minneapolis, on the way to New Haven.

While he stared out of the car window Knute was warning himself that the millionaires' sons would make fun of him. Perhaps they would haze him. He bade himself avoid all these sons of Belial and cleave to his own people, those who "earned their way through."

At Chicago he was afraid with a great fear of the lightning flashes that the swift crowds made on his retina, the batteries of ranked motorcars that charged at him. He prayed, and ran for his train to New York. He came at last to New Haven.

Not with gibing rudeness, but with politely quizzical eyebrows, Yale received him, led him through entrance examinations, which, after sweaty plowing with the pen, he barely passed, and found for him a roommate. The roommate was a large-browed, soft white grub named Ray Gribble, who had been teaching school in New England, and seemed chiefly to desire college training so that he might make more money as a teacher. Ray Gribble was a hustler; he instantly got work tutoring the awkward son of a steel man, and for board he waited on table.

He was Knute's chief acquaintance. Knute tried to fool himself into thinking he liked the grub, but Ray couldn't keep his damp hands off the old man's soul. He had the skill of a professional exhorter of young men in finding out Knute's motives, and when he discovered that Knute had a hidden desire to dabble in gay, polite literature, Ray said in a shocked way:

"Strikes me a man like you, that's getting old, ought to be thinking more about saving your soul than about all these frills. You leave this poetry and stuff to these foreigners and artists, and you stick to Latin and math and the Bible. I tell you, I've taught school, and I've learned by experience."

With Ray Gribble, Knute lived grubbily, an existence of torn comforters and a smelly lamp, of lexicons and logarithm tables. No leisurely loafing by fireplaces was theirs. They roomed in West Divinity, where gather the theologues, the lesser sort of law students, a whimsical genius or two, and a horde of unplaced freshmen and "scrub seniors."

Knute was shockingly disappointed, but he stuck to his room because outside of it he was afraid. He was a grotesque figure, and he knew it, a white-polled giant squeezed into a small seat in a classroom, listening to instructors younger than his own sons. Once he tried to sit on the fence. No one but "ringers" sat on the fence any more, and at the sight of him trying to look athletic and young, two upperclassmen snickered, and he sneaked away.

He came to hate Ray Gribble and his voluble companions of the submerged tenth of the class, the hewers of tutorial wood. It is doubtless safer to mock the flag than to question that best-established tradition of our democracy—that those who "earn their way through" college are necessarily stronger, braver, and more assured of success than the weaklings who talk by the fire. Every college story presents such a moral. But tremblingly the historian submits that Knute discovered that waiting on table did not make lads more heroic than did football or happy loafing. Fine fellows, cheerful and fearless, were many of the boys who "earned their way," and able to talk to richer classmates without fawning; but just as many of them assumed an abject respectability as the most convenient pose. They were pickers-up of unconsidered trifles; they toadied to the classmates whom they tutored; they wriggled before the faculty committee on scholarships; they looked pious at Dwight Hall prayer meetings to make an impression on the serious-minded; and they drank one glass of beer at Jake's to show the light-minded that they meant nothing offensive by their piety. In revenge for cringing to the insolent athletes whom they tutored, they would, when safe among their own kind, yammer about the "lack of democracy in colleges today." Not that they were so indiscreet as to do anything about it. They lacked the stuff of really rebellious souls. Knute listened to them and marveled. They sounded like young hired men talking behind his barn at harvest time.

This submerged tenth hated the dilettantes of the class even more than they hated the bloods. Against one Gilbert Washburn, a rich esthete with more manner than any freshman ought to have, they raged righteously. They spoke of seriousness and industry till Knute, who might once have desired to know lads like Washburn, felt ashamed of himself as a wicked, wasteful old man.

With the friends of his roommate began Knute's series of disillusions. Humbly though he sought, he found no inspiration and no comradeship. He was the freak of the class, and aside from the submerged tenth, his classmates were afraid of being "queered" by being seen with him.

As he was still powerful, one who could take up a barrel of pork on his knees, he tried to find friendship among the athletes. He sat at Yale Field, watching the football tryouts, and tried to get acquainted with the candidates. They stared at him and answered his questions grudgingly—beefy youths who in their simple-hearted way showed that they considered him plain crazy.

The place itself began to lose the haze of magic through which he had first seen it. Earth is earth, whether one sees it in Camelot or Joralemon or on the Yale campus—or possibly even in the Harvard yard! The buildings ceased to be temples to Knute; they became structures of brick or stone, filled with young men who lounged at windows and watched him amusedly as he tried to slip by.

The Gargantuan hall of Commons became a tri-daily horror because at the table where he dined were two youths, who, having uncommonly penetrating minds, discerned that Knute had a beard, and courageously told the world about it. One of them, named Atchison, was a superior person, very industrious and scholarly, glib in mathematics and manners. He despised Knute's lack of definite purpose in coming to college. The other was a play boy, a wit and a stealer of street signs, who had a wonderful sense for a subtle jest; and his references to Knute's beard shook the table with jocund mirth three times a day. So these youths of gentle birth drove the shambling, wistful old man away from Commons, and thereafter he ate at the lunch counter at the Black Cat.

Lacking the stimulus of friendship, it was the harder for Knute to keep up the strain of studying the long assignments. What had been a week's pleasure reading in his shack was now thrown at him as a day's task. But he would not have minded the toil if he could have found one as young as himself. They

were all so dreadfully old, the money-earners, the serious labor-
ers at athletics, the instructors who worried over their life
work of putting marks in class-record books.

Then, on a sore, bruised day, Knute did meet one who was
young.

Knute had heard that the professor who was the idol of the
college had berated the too-earnest lads in his Browning class,
and insisted that they read *Alice in Wonderland*. Knute
floundered dustily about in a second-hand bookshop till he
found an *Alice*, and he brought it home to read over his lunch
of a hot-dog sandwich. Something in the grave absurdity of
the book appealed to him, and he was chuckling over it when
Ray Gribble came into the room and glanced at the reader.

"Huh!" said Mr. Gribble.

"That's a fine, funny book," said Knute.

"Huh! *Alice in Wonderland!* I've heard of it. Silly nonsense. Why don't you read something really fine, like Shakespeare or *Paradise Lost?*"

"Vell—" said Knute, but that was all he could find to say.

With Ray Gribble's glassy eye on him, he could no longer
roll and roar with the book. He wondered if indeed he ought
not to be reading Milton's pompous anthropological miscon-
ceptions. He went unhappily out to an early history class, ably
conducted by Blevins, Ph.D.

Knute admired Blevins, Ph.D. He was so tubbed and eye-
glassed and terribly right. But most of Blevins' lambs did not
like Blevins. They said he was a "crank." They read newspapers
in his class and covertly kicked one another.

In the smug, plastered classroom, his arm leaning heavily
on the broad tablet-arm of his chair, Knute tried not to miss
one of Blevins' sardonic proofs that the correct date of the
second marriage of Themistocles was two years and seven days
later than the date assigned by that illiterate ass, Frutari of
Padua. Knute admired young Blevins' performance, and he
felt virtuous in application to these hard, unnonsensical facts.

He became aware that certain lewd fellows of the lesser
sort were playing poker just behind him. His prairie-trained
ear caught whispers of "Two to dole," and "Raise you two
beans." Knute revolved, and frowned upon these mockers of
sound learning. As he turned back he was aware that the of-
fenders were chuckling, and continuing their game. He saw
Blevins as merely a boy. He was sorry for him. He would do
the boy a good turn.

When the class was over he hung about Blevins' desk till the other students had clattered out. He rumbled:

"Say, Professor, you're a fine fellow. I do something for you. If any of the boys make themselves a nuisance, you yust call on me, and I spank the son of a guns."

Blevins, Ph.D., spake in a manner of culture and nastiness:

"Thanks so much, Axelbrod, but I don't fancy that will ever be necessary. I am supposed to be a reasonably good disciplinarian. Good day. Oh, one moment. There's something I've been wishing to speak to you about. I do wish you wouldn't try quite so hard to show off whenever I call on you during quizzes. You answer at such needless length, and you smile as though there were something highly amusing about me. I'm quite willing to have you regard me as a humorous figure, privately, but there are certain classroom conventions, you know, certain little conventions."

"Why, Professor!" wailed Knute. "I never make fun of you! I didn't know I smile. If I do, I guess it's yust because I am so glad when my stupid old head gets the lesson good."

"Well, well, that's very gratifying, I'm sure. And if you will be a little more careful——"

Blevins, Ph.D., smiled a toothy, frozen smile, and trotted off to the Graduates' Club, to be witty about old Knute and his way of saying "yust," while in the deserted classroom Knute sat chill, an old man and doomed. Through the windows came the light of Indian summer; clean, boyish cries rose from the campus. But the lover of autumn smoothed his baggy sleeve, stared at the blackboard, and there saw only the gray of October stubble about his distant shack. As he pictured the college watching him, secretly making fun of him and his smile, he was now faint and ashamed, now bull-angry. He was lonely for his cat, his fine chair of buffalo horns, the sunny doorstep of his shack, and the understanding land. He had been in college for about one month.

Before he left the classroom he stepped behind the instructor's desk and looked at an imaginary class.

"I might have stood there as a prof if I could have come earlier," he said softly to himself.

Calmed by the liquid autumn gold that flowed through the streets, he walked out Whitney Avenue toward the butte-like hill of East Rock. He observed the caress of the light upon the scarped rock, heard the delicate music of leaves, breathed in air pregnant with tales of old New England. He exulted:

"I could write poetry now if I yust—if I yust could write poetry!"

He climbed to the top of East Rock, whence he could see the Yale buildings like the towers of Oxford, Long Island Sound, and the white glare of Long Island itself beyond the water. He marveled that Knute Axelbrod of the cottonwood country was looking across an arm of the Atlantic to New York State.

He noticed a freshman on a bench at the edge of the rock, and he became irritated. The freshman was Gilbert Washburn, the snob, the dilettante, of whom Ray Gribble had once said: "That guy is the disgrace of the class. He doesn't go out for anything, high stand or Dwight Hall or anything else. Thinks he's so doggone much better than the rest of the fellows that he doesn't associate with anybody. Thinks he's literary, they say, and yet he doesn't even heel the 'lit,' like the regular literary fellows! Got no time for a loafing, mooning snob like that."

As Knute stared at the unaware Gil, whose profile was fine in outline against the sky, he was terrifically public-spirited and disapproving and that sort of moral thing. Though Gil was much too well-dressed, he seemed moodily discontented.

"What he needs is to work in a thrashing-crew and sleep in the hay," grumbled Knute almost in the virtuous manner of Gribble. "Then he vould know when he vas vell off, and not like he had the earache. Pff!"

Gil Washburn rose, trailed toward Knute, glanced at him, hesitated, sat down on Knute's bench.

"Great view!" he said. His smile was eager.

That smile symbolized to Knute all the art of life he had come to college to find. He tumbled out of his moral attitude with ludicrous haste, and every wrinkle of his weathered face creased deep as he answered:

"Yes; I t'ink the Acropolis must be like this here."

"Say, look here, Axelbrod; I've been thinking about you."

"Yas?"

"We ought to know each other. We two are the class scandal. We came here to dream, and these busy little goats like Atchison and Giblets, or whatever your roommate's name is, think we're fools not to go out for marks. You may not agree with me, but I've decided that you and I are precisely alike."

"What makes you t'ink I come here to dream?" bristled Knute.

"Oh, I used to sit near you at Commons and hear you try to quell jolly old Atchison whenever he got busy discussing the reasons for coming to college. That old, motheaten topic! I wonder if Cain and Abel didn't discuss it at the Eden Agricultural College. You know, Abel the mark-grabber, very pious and high stand, and Cain wanting to read poetry."

"Yes," said Knute, "and I guess Prof Adam say, 'Cain, don't you read this poetry; it von't help you in algebry.' "

"Of course. Say, wonder if you'd like to look at this volume of Musset I was sentimental enough to lug up here today. Picked it up when I was abroad last year."

From his pocket Gil drew such a book as Knute had never seen before, a slender volume, in a strange language, bound in hand-tooled, crushed levant, an effeminate bibelot over which the prairie farmer gasped with luxurious pleasure. The book almost vanished in his big hands. With a timid forefinger he stroked the levant, ran through the leaves.

"I can't read it, but that's the kind of book I alvays t'ought there must be some like it," he sighed.

"Let me read you a little. It's French poetry."

Gill read aloud. He made of the alien verses a music which satisfied Knute's sixty-five years of longing for he had never known what.

"That's—that's fine," he said.

"Listen!" cried Gil. "Ysaye is playing up at Hartford tonight. Let's go hear him. We'll trolley up, make it in plenty of time. Tried to get some of the fellows to come, but they thought I was a nut."

What an Ysaye was, Knute Axelbrod had no notion, but "Sure!" he boomed.

When they got to Hartford they found that between them they had just enough money to get dinner, hear Ysaye from gallery seats, and return only as far as Meriden.

At Meriden, Gil suggested:

"Let's walk back to New Haven, then. Can you make it?"

Knute had no knowledge as to whether it was four miles or forty miles back to the campus, but "Sure!" he said. For the last few months he had been noticing that, despite his bulk, he had to be careful, but tonight he could have flown.

In the music of Ysaye, the first real musician he had ever heard, Knute had found all the incredible things of which he had slowly been reading in William Morris and Idylls of the King. Tall knights he had beheld, and slim princesses in white samite, the misty gates of forlorn towns, and the glory of the chivalry that never was.

They did walk, roaring down the road beneath the October moon, stopping to steal apples and to exclaim over silvered fanedog. It was Gill who talked, and Knute who listened, for the most part; but Knute was lured into tales of the pioneer days, of blizzards, of harvesting, and of the first flame of the green wheat. Regarding the Atchisons and Gribble of the class, both of them were youthfully bitter and supercilious. They were wandering minstrels, Gilbert the troubadour with his man-at-arms.

They reached the campus at about five in the morning.

Fumbling for words that would express his feeling, Knute stammered:

"Vell, it vas fine. I go to bed now and I dream about——"

"Bed? Rats! Never believe in winding up a party when it's going strong. Too few good parties. Besides, it's only the shank of the evening. Besides, we're hungry. Besides—oh, besides! Wait here a second. I'm going up to my room to get some money, and we'll have some eats. Wait! Please do!"

Knute would have waited all night. He had lived sixty-five years and traveled fifteen hundred miles and endured Ray Gribble to find Gil Washburn.

Policemen wondered to see the celluloid-collared old man and the expensive-looking boy rolling arm in arm down Chapel Street in search of a restaurant suitable to poets. They were all closed.

"The Ghetto will be awake by now," said Gil. "We'll go buy some eats and take 'em up to my room. I've got some tea there."

Knute shouldered through dark streets beside him as naturally as though he had always been a nighthawk, with an aversion to anything as rustic as beds. Down on Oak Street, a place of low shops, smoky lights, and alley mouths, they found the slum already astir. Gil contrived to purchase boxed biscuits, cream cheese, chicken loaf, a bottle of cream. While Gil was chaffering, Knute stared out into the street milkily lighted by wavering gas and the first feebleness of coming day; he gazed upon Kosher signs and advertisements in Russian letters, shawled women and bearded rabbis; and as he looked he gathered contentment which he could never lose. He had traveled abroad tonight.

The room of Gil Washburn was all the useless, pleasant

things Knute wanted it to be. There was more of Gil's Paris days in it than of his freshmanhood: cloisonné on the mantel-piece, Persian rugs, a silver tea service, etchings, and books. Knute Axelbrod of the tar-paper shack and piggy farmyards gazed in satisfaction. Vast-bearded, sunk in an easy chair, he clucked amiably while Gil lighted a fire and spread a wicker table.

Over supper they spoke of great men and heroic ideals. It was good talk, and not unspiced with lively references to Grib-ble and Atchison and Blevins, all asleep now in their correct beds. Gill read snatches of Stevenson and Anatole France; then at last he read his own poetry.

It does not matter whether that poetry was good or bad. To Knute it was a miracle to find one who actually wrote it.

The talk grew slow and they began to yawn. Knute was sensitive to the lowered key of their Indian-summer madness, and he hastily rose. As he said good-by he felt as though he had but to sleep a little while and return to this unending night of romance.

But he came out of the dormitory upon day. It was six-thirty of the morning, with a still, hard light upon red-brick walls.

"I can go to his room plenty times now; I find my friend," Knute said. He held tight the volume of Musset, which Gil had begged him to take.

As he started to walk the few steps to West Divinity, Knute felt very tired. By daylight the adventure seemed more and more incredible.

As he entered the dormitory he sighed heavily:

"Age and youth, I guess they can't team together long." As he mounted the stairs he said: "If I saw the boy again, he vould get tired of me. I tell him all I got to say." And as he opened his door, he added: "This is what I come to college for—this one night; I live for it sixty-five years. I go avay be-fore I spoil it."

He wrote a note to Gil, and began to pack his telescope. He did not even wake Ray Gribble, sonorously sleeping in the stale air.

At five that afternoon, on the day coach of a westbound train, an old man sat smiling. A lasting content was in his eyes, and in his hands a small book in French, though the curious fact is that this man could not read French.

Lawrence redeems his honor

Strawberry Ice Cream Soda

IRWIN SHAW

EDDIE BARNES looked at the huge Adirondack hills, browning in the strong summer afternoon sun. He listened to his brother Lawrence practice finger-exercises on the piano inside the house, onetwothreefourfive, onetwothreefourfive, and longed for New York. He lay on his stomach in the long grass of the front lawn and delicately peeled his sunburned nose. Morosely he regarded a grasshopper, stupid with sun, wavering on a bleached blade of grass in front of his nose. Without interest he put out his hand and captured it.

"Give honey," he said, listlessly. "Give honey or I'll kill yuh . . ."

But the grasshopper crouched unmoving, unresponsive, oblivious to Life or Death.

Disgusted, Eddie tossed the grasshopper away. It flew uncertainly, wheeled, darted back to its blade of grass, alighted and hung there dreamily, shaking a little in the breeze in front of Eddie's nose. Eddie turned over on his back and looked at the high blue sky.

The country! Why anybody ever went to the country . . . What things must be doing in New York now, what rash, beautiful deeds on the steaming, rich streets, what expeditions, what joy, what daring sweaty adventure among the trucks, the trolley cars, the baby-carriages! What cries, hoarse and humorous, what light laughter outside the red-painted shop where lemon ice was sold at three cents the double scoop, true nourishment for a man at fifteen.

Eddie looked around him, at the silent, eternal, granite-streaked hills. Trees and birds, that's all. He sighed, torn with thoughts of distant pleasure, stood up, went over to the window behind which Lawrence seriously hammered at the piano, onetwothreefourfive.

"Lawrrrence," Eddie called, the rrr's rolling with horrible gentility in his nose, "Lawrrrence, you stink."

Lawrence didn't even look up. His thirteen-year-old fingers, still pudgy and babyish, went onetwothreefourfive, with unswerving precision. He was talented and he was dedicated to

188

his talent and someday they would wheel a huge piano out onto the stage of Carnegie Hall and he would come out and bow politely to the thunder of applause and sit down, flipping his coat-tails back, and play, and men and women would laugh and cry and remember their first loves as they listened to him. So now his fingers went up and down, up and down, taking strength against the great day.

Eddie looked through the window a moment more, watching his brother, sighed and walked around to the side of the house, where a crow was sleepily eating the radish seeds that Eddie had planted three days ago in a fit of boredom. Eddie threw a stone at the crow and the crow silently flew up to the branch of an oak and waited for Eddie to go away. Eddie threw another stone at the crow. The crow moved to another branch. Eddie wound up and threw a curve, but the crow disdained it. Eddie picked his foot up the way he'd seen Carl Hubbell do and sizzled one across not more than three feet from the crow. Without nervousness the crow walked six inches up the branch. In the style now of Dizzy Dean, with terrifying speed, Eddie delivered his fast one. It was wild and the crow didn't even cock his head. You had to expect to be a little wild with such speed. Eddie found a good round stone and rubbed it professionally on his back pocket. He looked over his shoulder to hold the runner close to the bag, watched for the signal. Eddie Hubbell Dean Mungo Feller Ferrell Warnecke Gomez Barnes picked up his foot and let go his high hard one. The crow slowly got off his branch and regretfully sailed away.

Eddie went over, kicked away the loose dirt, and looked at his radish seeds. Nothing was happening to them. They just lay there, baked and inactive, just as he had placed them. No green, no roots, no radishes, no anything. He was sorry he'd ever gone in for farming. The package of seeds had cost him a dime, and the only thing that happened to them was that they were eaten by crows. And now he could use that dime. Tonight he had a date.

"I got a date," he said aloud, savoring the words. He went to the shade of the grape arbor to think about it. He sat down on the bench under the cool flat leaves, and thought about it. He'd never had a date before in his life. He had thirty-five cents. Thirty-five cents ought to be enough for any girl, but if he hadn't bought the radish seeds, he'd have had forty-five cents, really prepared for any eventuality. "Damn crow," he said, thinking of the evil black head feeding on his dime.

Many times he'd wondered how you managed to get a

date. Now he knew. It happened all of a sudden. You went
up to a girl where she was lying on the raft in a lake and you
looked at her, chubby in a blue bathing suit, and she looked
seriously at you out of serious blue eyes where you stood dripping with lake water, with no hair on your chest, and suddenly
you said, "I don't s'pose yuh're not doing anything t'morra
night, are yuh?" You didn't know quite what you meant, but
she did, and she said, "Why, no, Eddie. Say about eight
o'clock?" And you nodded and dived back into the lake and
there you were.

Still, those radish seeds, that crow-food, that extra dime . . .

Lawrence came out, flexing his fingers, very neat in clean
khaki shorts and a white blouse. He sat down next to Eddie
in the grape arbor.

"I would like a strawberry ice cream soda," he said.

"Got any money?" Eddie asked, hopefully.

Lawrence shook his head.

"No strawberry ice cream soda," Eddie said.

Lawrence nodded seriously. "You got any money?" he
asked.

"Some," Eddie said carefully. He pulled down a grape leaf
and cracked it between his hands, held up the two parts and
looked at them critically.

Lawrence didn't say anything, but Eddie sensed a feeling
developing in the grape arbor, like a growth. "I gotta save my
money," Eddie said harshly. "I got a date. I got thirty-five
cents. How do I know she won't want a banana-split tonight?"

Lawrence nodded again, indicating that he understood, but
sorrow washed up in his face like a high tide.

They sat in silence, uncomfortably, listening to the rustle
of the grape leaves.

"All the time I was practicing," Lawrence said, finally, "I
kept thinking, 'I would like a strawberry ice cream soda, I
would like a strawberry ice cream soda . . .' "

Eddie stood up abruptly. "Aaah, let's get outa here. Let's
go down to the lake. Maybe something's doing down the lake."

They walked together through the fields to the lake, not
saying anything, Lawrence flexing his fingers mechanically.

"Why don't yuh stop that fer once?" Eddie asked, with
distaste. "Just fer once?"

"This is good for my fingers. It keeps them loose."

"Yuh give me a pain."

"All right," Lawrence said, "I won't do it now."

They walked on again, Lawrence barely up to Eddie's chin, frailer, cleaner, his hair mahogany dark and smooth on his high, pink, baby brow. Lawrence whistled. Eddie listened with disguised respect.

"That's not so bad," Eddie said. "You don't whistle half bad."

"That's from the Brahms second piano concerto." Lawrence stopped whistling for a moment. "It's easy to whistle."

"Yuh give me a pain," Eddie said, mechanically, "a real pain."

When they got to the lake, there was nobody there. Flat and unruffled it stretched across, like a filled blue cup, to the woods on the other side.

"Nobody here," Eddie said, staring at the raft, unmoving and dry in the still water. "That's good. Too many people here all the time." His eyes roamed the lake, to the farthest corner, to the deepest cove.

"How would yuh like to go rowing in a boat out in that old lake?" Eddie asked.

"We haven't got a boat," Lawrence answered reasonably.

"I didn't ask yuh that. I asked, 'How'd yuh like to go rowing?'"

"I'd like to go rowing if we had a . . ."

"Shut up!" Eddie took Lawrence's arm, led him through tall grass to the water's edge, where a flat-bottomed old boat was drawn up, the water just lapping at the stern, high, an old red color, faded by sun and storm. A pair of heavy oars lay along the bottom of the boat.

"Jump in," Eddie said, "when I tell yuh to."

"But it doesn't belong to us."

"Yuh want to go rowing, don't yuh?"

"Yes, but . . ."

"Then jump in when I give yuh the word."

Lawrence neatly took off his shoes and socks while Eddie hauled the boat into the water.

"Jump in!" Eddie called.

Lawrence jumped. The boat glided out across the still lake. Eddie rowed industriously once they got out of the marsh grass.

"This isn't half bad, is it?" He leaned back on his oars for a moment.

"It's nice," Lawrence said. "It's very peaceful."

"Aaah," said Eddie, "yuh even talk like a pianist." And

he rowed. After a while he got tired and let the boat go with the wind. He lay back and thought of the night to come, dabbling his fingers in the water, happy. "They oughta see me now, back on a Hunnerd and Seventy-third Street," he said. "They oughta see me handle this old boat."

"Everything would be perfect," Lawrence agreed, picking his feet up out of the puddle that was collecting on the bottom of the boat, "if we only knew that when we got out of this boat, we were going to get a strawberry ice cream soda."

"Why don't yuh think of somethin' else? Always thinkin' of one thing! Don't yuh get tired?"

"No," Lawrence said, after thinking it over.

"Here!" Eddie pushed the oars toward his brother. "Row! That'll give yuh somethin' else t' think about."

Lawrence took the oars gingerly. "This is bad for my hands," he explained as he pulled dutifully on the oars. "It stiffens the fingers."

"Look where yuh're goin'!" Eddie cried impatiently. "In circles! What the hell's the sense in goin' in circles?"

"That's the way the boat goes," Lawrence said, pulling hard. "I can't help it if that's the way the boat goes."

"A pianist. A regular pianist. That's all yuh are. Gimme those oars."

Gratefully Lawrence yielded the oars up.

"It's not my fault if the boat goes in circles. That's the way it's made," he persisted quietly.

"Aaah, shut up!" Eddie pulled savagely on the oars. The boat surged forward, foam at the prow.

"Hey, out there in the boat! Hey!" A man's voice called over the water.

"Eddie," Lawrence said, "there's a man yelling at us."

"Come on in here, before I beat your pants off!" the man called. "Get out of my boat!"

"He wants us to get out of his boat," Lawrence interpreted. "This must be his boat."

"You don't mean it," Eddie snorted with deep sarcasm. He turned around to shout at the man on the shore, who was waving his arms now. "All right," Eddie called. "All right. We'll give yuh yer old boat. Keep your shirt on."

The man jumped up and down. "I'll beat yer heads off," he shouted.

Lawrence wiped his nose nervously. "Eddie," he said, "why don't we row over to the other side and walk home from there?"

Eddie looked at his brother contemptuously. "What're yuh —afraid?"

"No," Lawrence said, after a pause. "But why should we get into an argument?"

For answer Eddie pulled all the harder on the oars. The boat flew through the water. Lawrence squinted to look at the rapidly nearing figure of the man on the bank.

"He's a great big man, Eddie," Lawrence reported. "You never saw such a big man. And he looks awfully sore. Maybe we shouldn't've gone out in this boat. Maybe he doesn't like people to go out in his boat. Eddie, are you listening to me?"

With a final heroic pull, Eddie drove the boat into the shore. It grated with a horrible noise on the pebbles of the lake bottom.

"That," the man said, "is the end of that boat."

"That doesn't really hurt it, mister," Lawrence said. "It makes a lot of noise, but it doesn't do any damage."

The man reached over and grabbed Lawrence by the back of his neck with one hand and placed him on solid ground. He was a very big man, with tough bristles that grew all over his double chin and farmer's muscles in his arms that were quivering with passion now under a mat of hair. There was a boy of about thirteen with him, obviously, from his look, his son, and the son was angry, too.

"Hit 'im, Pop," the son kept calling. "Wallop 'im!"

The man shook Lawrence again and again. He was almost too overcome with anger to speak. "No damage, eh? Only noise, eh!" he shouted into Lawrence's paling face. "I'll show you damage. I'll show you noise."

Eddie spoke up. Eddie was out of the boat now, an oar gripped in his hand, ready for the worst. "That's not fair," he said. "Look how much bigger yuh are than him. Why'n't yuh pick on somebody yuh size?"

The farmer's boy jumped up and down in passion, exactly as his father had done. "I'll fight him, Pop! I'll fight 'im! I'm his size! Come on, kid, put yer hands up!"

The farmer looked at his son, looked at Lawrence. Slowly he released Lawrence. "O.K.," he said. "Show him, Nathan."

Nathan pushed Lawrence. "Come into the woods, kid," he said belligerently. "We cin settle it there."

"One in the eye," Eddie whispered out of the corner of his mouth. "Give 'im one in the eye, Larry!"

But Lawrence stood with eyes lowered, regarding his hands. "Well?" the farmer asked.

Lawrence still looked at his hands, opening and closing them slowly.

"He don't wanna fight," Nathan taunted Eddie. "He just wants t' row in our boat, he don't wanna fight."

"He wants to fight, all right," Eddie said staunchly, and under his breath, "Come on, Larry, in the kisser, a fast one in the puss . . ."

But Larry stood still, calmly, seeming to be thinking of Brahms and Beethoven, of distant concert halls.

"He's yella, that's what's the matter with him," Nathan roared. "He's a coward, all city kids're cowards!"

"He's no coward," Eddie insisted, knowing in his deepest heart that his brother was a coward. With his knees he nudged Lawrence. "Bring up yuh left! Please, Larry, bring up yuh left!"

Deaf to all pleas, Lawrence kept his hands at his sides.

"Yella! Yella! Yella!" Nathan screamed loudly.

"Well," the farmer wanted to know, "is he goin' to fight or not?"

"Larry!" Fifteen years of desperation was in Eddie's voice, but it made no mark on Lawrence. Eddie turned slowly toward home. "He's not goin' to fight," he said flatly. And then, as one throws a bone to a neighbor's noisy dog, "Come on, you . . ."

Slowly Lawrence bent over, picked up his shoes and socks, took a step after his brother.

"Wait a minute, you!" the farmer called. He went after Eddie, turned him around. "I want to talk to ye."

"Yeah?" Eddie said sadly, with little defiance. "What do yuh wanna say?"

"See that house over there?" the farmer asked, pointing.

"Yeah," Eddie said. "What about it?"

"That's my house," the farmer said. "You stay away from it. See?"

"O.K. O.K.," Eddie said wearily, all pride gone.

"See that boat there?" the farmer asked, pointing at the source of all the trouble.

"I see it," Eddie said.

"That's my boat. Stay away from it or I'll beat hell outa ye. See?"

"Yeah, yeah, I see," Eddie said. "I won't touch yer lousy boat." And once more, to Lawrence, "Come on, you. . . ."

"Yella! Yella! Yella!" Nathan kept roaring, jumping up and

down, until they passed out of earshot, across the pleasant fields, ripe with the soft sweet smell of clover in the late summer afternoon. Eddie walked before Lawrence, his face grimly contracted, his mouth curled in shame and bitterness. He stepped on the clover blossoms fiercely, as though he hated them, wanted to destroy them, the roots under them, the very ground they grew in.

Holding his shoes in his hands, his head bent on his chest, his hair still mahogany smooth and mahogany dark, Lawrence followed ten feet back in the footsteps, plainly marked in the clover, of his brother.

"Yella," Eddie was muttering, loud enough for the villain behind him to hear clearly. "Yella! Yella as a flower. My own brother," he marveled. "If it was me I'da been glad to get killed before I let anybody call me that. I would let 'em cut my heart out first. My own brother. Yella as a flower. Just one in the eye! Just one! Just to show 'im . . . But he stands there, takin' guff from a kid with holes in his pants. A pianist. Lawrrrrence! They knew what they were doin' when they called yuh Lawrrrrence! Don't talk to me! I don't want yuh ever to talk to me again as long as yuh live! Lawrrrrence!"

In sorrow too deep for tears, the two brothers reached home, ten feet, ten million miles apart.

Without looking around, Eddie went to the grape arbor, stretched out on the bench. Lawrence looked after him, his face pale and still, then went into the house.

Face downward on the bench, close to the rich black earth of the arbor, Eddie bit his fingers to keep the tears back. But he could not bite hard enough, and the tears came, a bitter tide, running down his face, dropping on the black soft earth in which the grapes were rooted.

"Eddie!"

Eddie scrambled around, pushing the tears away with iron hands. Lawrence was standing there, carefully pulling on doeskin gloves over his small hands. "Eddie," Lawrence was saying, stonily disregarding the tears. "I want you to come with me."

Silently, but with singing in his heart so deep it called new tears to his wet eyes, Eddie got up, blew his nose, and followed after his brother, caught up with him, walked side by side with him across the field of clover, so lightly that the red and purple blossoms barely bent in their path.

Eddie knocked sternly at the door of the farm house, three

knocks, solid, vigorous, the song of trumpets caught in them.

Nathan opened the door. "What do ye want?" he asked suspiciously.

"A little while ago," Eddie said formally, "yuh offered to fight my brother. He's ready now."

Nathan looked at Lawrence, standing there, straight, his head up, his baby lips compressed into a thin tight line, his gloved hands creased in solid fists. He started to close the door. "He had his chance," Nathan said.

Eddie kept the door open firmly. "Yuh offered, remember that," he reminded Nathan politely.

"He shoulda fought then," Nathan said stubbornly. "He had his chance."

"Come on," Eddie almost begged. "Yuh wanted to fight before."

"That was before. Lemme close the door."

"Yuh can't do this!" Eddie was shouting desperately. "Yuh offered!"

Nathan's father, the farmer, appeared in the doorway. He looked bleakly out. "What's goin' on here?" he asked.

"A little while ago," Eddie spoke very fast, "this man here offered to fight this man here." His eloquent hand indicated first Nathan, then Lawrence. "Now we've come to take the offer."

The farmer looked at his son. "Well?"

"He had his chance," Nathan grumbled sullenly.

"Nathan don't want t' fight," the farmer said to Eddie. "Get outa here."

Lawrence stepped up, over to Nathan. He looked Nathan squarely in the eye. "Yella," he said to Nathan.

The farmer pushed his son outside the door. "Go fight him," he ordered.

"We can settle it in the woods," Lawrence said.

"Wipe him up, Larry!" Eddie called as Lawrence and Nathan set out for the woods, abreast, but a polite five yards apart. Eddie watched them disappear behind trees, in silence.

The farmer sat down heavily on the porch, leaned back against a pillar, stretched comfortably.

'Sit down," the farmer said, "ye cin never tell how long kids'll fight."

In silence they both looked across the field to the woods that shielded the battlefield. The tops of the trees waved a little in the wind and the afternoon was collecting in deep blue shadows among the thick brown tree-trunks where they gripped the ground. A chicken hawk floated lazily over the field, banking and slipping with the wind. The farmer regarded the chicken hawk without malice.

"Some day," the farmer said, "I'm going to get that son of a gun."

"What is it?" Eddie asked.

"Chicken hawk. You're from the city, ain't ye?"

"Yeah."

"Like it in the city?"

"Nothing like it."

The farmer puffed reflectively. "Some day I'm goin' to live in the city. No sense in livin' in the country these days."

"Oh, I don't know," Eddie said. "The country's very nice. There's a lot to be said for the country."

The farmer nodded, weighing the matter in his own mind. "Say," he said, "do you think your brother'll damage my kid?"

"It's possible," Eddie said. "He's very tough, my brother. He has dozens a' fights, every month. Every kid back home's scared stiff a' him. Why," said Eddie, sailing full into fancy, "I remember one day, Larry fought three kids all in a row. In a half a hour. He busted all their noses. In a half a hour! He's 'got a terrific left jab—one, two, bang! like this—and it gets 'em in the nose."

"Well, he can't do Nathan's nose any harm." The farmer laughed. "No matter what you did to a nose like that it'd be a improvement."

"He's got a lot of talent, my brother," Eddie said, proud of the warrior in the woods. "He plays the piano. He's a very good piano-player. You ought to hear him."

"A little kid like that," the farmer marveled. "Nathan can't do nothing."

Off in the distance, in the gloom under the trees, two figures appeared, close together, walked slowly out into the sunlight of the field. Eddie and the farmer stood up. Wearily the two fighters approached, together, their arms dangling at their sides.

Eddie looked first at Nathan. Nathan's mouth had been bleeding and there was a lump on his forehead and his ear was red. Eddie smiled with satisfaction. Nathan had been in a fight. Eddie walked slowly toward Lawrence. Lawrence approached with head high. But it was a sadly battered head. The hair was tangled, an eye was closed, the nose was bruised and still bled. Lawrence sucked in the blood from his nose from time to time with his tongue. His collar was torn, his pants covered with forest loam, with his bare knees skinned and raw. But in the one eye that still could be seen shone a clear light, honorable, indomitable.

"Ready to go home now, Eddie?" Lawrence asked.

"Sure." Eddie started to pat Lawrence on the back, pulled his hand back. He turned and waved to the farmer. "So long."

"So long," the farmer called. "Any time you want to use the boat, just step into it."

"Thanks." Eddie waited while Lawrence shook hands gravely with Nathan.

"Good night," Lawrence said. "It was a good fight."

"Yeah," Nathan said.

The two brothers walked away, close together, across the field of clover, fragrant in the long shadows. Half the way they walked in silence, the silence of equals, strong men communicating in a language more eloquent than words, the only sound the thin jingle of the thirty-five cents in Eddie's pocket.

Suddenly Eddie stopped Lawrence. "Let's go this way," he said, pointing off to the right.

"But home's this way, Eddie."

"I know. Let's go into town. Let's get ice cream sodas," Eddie said; "let's get strawberry ice cream sodas."

I Can't Breathe

RING LARDNER

I AM staying here at the Inn for two weeks with my Uncle Nat and Aunt Jule and I think I will keep a kind of a diary while I am here to help pass the time and so I can have a record of things that happen though goodness knows there isn't likely to anything happen, that is, anything exciting with Uncle Nat and Aunt Jule making the plans as they are both at least 35 years old and maybe older.

Dad and mother are abroad to be gone a month and me coming here is supposed to be a recompense from them not taking me with them. A fine recompense to be left with old people that come to a place like this to rest. Still it would be a heavenly place under different conditions, for instance, if Walter were here, too. It would be heavenly if he were here, the very thought of it makes my heart stop.

I can't stand it. I won't think about it.

This is our first separation since we have been engaged, nearly 17 days. It will be 17 days tomorrow. And the hotel orchestra at dinner this evening played that old thing "Oh how I miss you tonight" and it seemed as if they must be playing it for my benefit though, of course, the person in that song is talking about how they miss their mother though, of course, I miss mother, too, but a person gets used to missing their mother and it isn't like Walter or the person you are engaged to.

But there won't be any more separations much longer, we are going to be married in December even if mother does laugh when I talk to her about it because she says I am crazy to even think of getting married at 18.

She got married herself when she was 18, but of course that was "different," she wasn't crazy like I am, she knew whom she was marrying. As if Walter were a policeman or a foreigner or something. And she says she was only engaged once while I have been engaged at least five times a year since I was 14, of course, it really isn't as bad as that and I have really only been really what I call engaged six times altogether, but is getting

engaged my fault when they keep insisting and hammering at
you and if you didn't say yes they would never go home.

But it is different with Walter. I honestly believe if he had
not asked me I would have asked him. Of course I wouldn't
have, but I would have died. And this is the first time I have
even been engaged to be really married. The other times when
they talked about when should we get married I just laughed
at them, but I hadn't been engaged to Walter ten minutes
when he brought up the subject of marriage and I didn't laugh.
I wouldn't be engaged to him unless it was to be married. I
couldn't stand it.

Anyway mother may as well get used to the idea because it
is "No Foolin' " this time and we have got our plans all made
and I am going to be married at home and go out to California and Hollywood on our honeymoon. December, five
months away. I can't stand it. I can't wait.

There were a couple of awfully nice looking boys sitting together alone in the dining room tonight. One of them wasn't
so much, but the other was cute. And he——

There's the dance orchestra playing "Always," what they
played at the Biltmore the day I met Walter. "Not for just
an hour not for just a day." I can't live. I can't breathe.

July 13

This has been a much more exciting day than I expected
under the circumstances. In the first place I got two long night
letters, one from Walter and one from Gordon Flint. I don't
see how Walter ever had the nerve to send his, there was
everything in it and it must have been horribly embarrassing
for him while the telegraph operator was reading it over and
counting the words to say nothing of embarrassing for the
operator.

But the one from Gordon was a kind of a shock. He just
got back from a trip around the world, left last December to
go on it and got back yesterday and called up our house and
Helga gave him my address, and his telegram, well it was
nearly as bad as Walter's. The trouble is that Gordon and I
were engaged when he went away, or at least he thought so
and he wrote to me right along all the time he was away and
sent cables and things and for a while I answered his letters,
but then I lost track of his itinery and couldn't write to him
any more and when I got really engaged to Walter I couldn't
let Gordon know because I had no idea where he was besides
not wanting to spoil his trip.

And now he still thinks we are engaged and he is going to call me up tomorrow from Chicago and how in the world can I explain things and get him to understand because he is really serious and I like him ever and ever so much and in lots of ways he is nicer than Walter, not really nicer but better looking and there is no comparison between their dancing. Walter simply can't learn to dance, that is really dance. He says it is because he is flat footed, he says that as a joke, but it is true and I wish to heavens it wasn't.

All afteroon I thought and thought and thought about what to say to Gordon when he calls up and finally I couldn't stand thinking about it any more and just made up my mind I wouldn't think about it any more. But I will tell the truth though it will kill me to hurt him.

I went down to lunch with Uncle Nat and Aunt Jule and they were going out to play golf this afternoon and were insisting that I go with them, but I told them I had a headache and then I had a terrible time getting them to go without me. I didn't have a headache at all and just wanted to be alone to think about Walter and besides when you play with Uncle Nat he is always correcting your stance or your swing or something and always puts his hands on my arms and shoulders to show me the right way and I can't stand it to have old men touch me, even if they are your uncle.

I finally got rid of them and I was sitting watching the tennis when that boy that I saw last night, the cute one, came and sat right next to me and of course I didn't look at him. So we got to talking and he is even cuter than he looks, the most original and wittiest person I believe I ever met and I haven't laughed so much in I don't know how long.

For one thing he asked me if I had heard Rockefeller's song and I said no and he began singing "Oil alone." Then he asked me if I knew the orange juice song and I told him no again and he said it was "Orange juice sorry you made me cry." I was in hysterics before we had been together ten minutes.

His name is Frank Caswell and he has been out of Dartmouth a year and is 24 years old. That isn't so terribly old, only two years older than Walter and three years older than Gordon. I hate the name Frank, but Caswell is all right and he is so cute.

He was out in California last winter and visited Hollywood and met everybody in the world and it is fascinating to listen to him. He met Norma Shearer and he said he thought she was the prettiest thing he had ever seen. What he said was "I did think she was the prettiest girl in the world, till today." I was going to pretend I didn't get it, but I finally told him to be sensible or I would never be able to believe anything he said.

Well, he wanted me to dance with him tonight after dinner and the next question was how to explain how we had met each other to Uncle Nat and Aunt Jule. Frank said he would fix that all right and sure enough he got himself introduced to Uncle Nat when Uncle Nat came in from golf and after dinner Uncle Nat introduced him to me and Aunt Jule and we danced together all evening, that is not Aunt Jule. They went to bed, thank heavens.

He is a heavenly dancer, as good as Gordon. One dance we were dancing and for one of the encores the orchestra played "In a cottage small by a waterfall" and I simply couldn't dance to it. I just stopped still and said "Listen, I can't bear it, I can't breathe" and poor Frank thought I was sick or something and I had to explain that that was the tune the orchestra played the night I sat at the next table to Jack Barrymore at Barney Gallant's.

I made him sit out that encore and wouldn't let him talk till they got through playing it. Then they played something else and I was all right again and Frank told me about meeting Jack Barrymore. Imagine meeting him. I couldn't live.

I promised Aunt Jule I would go to bed at eleven and it is way past that now, but I am all ready for bed and have just been writing this. Tomorrow Gordon is going to call up and what will I say to him? I just won't think about it.

July 14

Gordon called up this morning from Chicago and it was wonderful to hear his voice again though the connection was terrible. He asked me if I still loved him and I tried to tell him no, but I knew that would mean an explanation and the connection was so bad that I never could make him understand so I said yes, but I almost whispered it purposely, thinking he wouldn't hear me, but he heard me all right and he said that made everything all right with the world. He said he thought I had stopped loving him because I had stopped writing.

I wish the connection had been decent and I could have told him how things were, but now it is terrible because he is planning to get to New York the day I get there and heaven knows what I will do because Walter will be there, too. I just won't think about it.

Aunt Jule came in my room just after I was through talking to Gordon, thank heavens. The room was full of flowers. Walter had sent me some and so had Frank. I got another long night letter from Walter, just as silly as the first one. I wish he would say those things in letters instead of night letters so everybody in the world wouldn't see them. Aunt Jule wanted me to read it aloud to her. I would have died.

While she was still in the room, Frank called up and asked me to play golf with him and I said all right and Aunt Jule said she was glad my headache was gone. She was trying to be funny.

I played golf with Frank this afternoon. He is a beautiful golfer and it is thrilling to watch him drive, his swing is so much more graceful than Walter's. I asked him to watch me swing and tell me what was the matter with me, but he said he couldn't look at anything but my face and there wasn't anything the matter with that.

He told me the boy who was here with him had been called home and he was glad of it because I might have liked him, the other boy, better than himself. I told him that couldn't be possible and he asked me if I really meant that and I said of course, but I smiled when I said it so he wouldn't take it too seriously.

We danced again tonight and Uncle Nat and Aunt Jule sat with us a while and danced a couple of dances themselves, but they were really there to get better acquainted with Frank and see if he was all right for me to be with. I know they certainly couldn't have enjoyed their own dancing, no old people really can enjoy it because they can't really do anything.

They were favorably impressed with Frank I think, at least Aunt Jule didn't say I must be in bed at eleven, but just not to stay up too late. I guess it is a big surprise to a girl's parents and aunts and uncles to find out that the boys you go around with are all right, they always seem to think that if I seem to like somebody and the person pays a little attention to me, why he must be a convict or a policeman or a drunkard or something queer.

Frank had some more songs for me tonight. He asked me if I knew the asthma song and I said I didn't and he said "Oh, you must know that. It goes, Yes, sir, asthma baby." Then he told me about the underwear song, "I underwear my baby is tonight." He keeps you in hysterics and yet he has his serious side, in fact he was awfully serious when he said good night to me and his eyes simply shone. I wish Walter were more like him in some ways, but I mustn't think about that.

July 15

I simply can't live and I know I'll never sleep tonight. I am in a terrible predicament or rather I won't know whether I really am or not till tomorrow and that is what makes it so terrible.

After we had danced two or three dances, Frank asked me to go for a ride with him and we went for a ride in his car and finally he told me he loved me and I said not to be silly, but he said he was perfectly serious and he certainly acted that way. He asked me if I loved anybody else and I said yes and he asked if I didn't love him more than anybody else and I said yes, but only because I thought he wouldn't remember it anyway and the best thing to do was humor him under the circumstances.

Then all of a sudden he asked me when I could marry him and I said, just as a joke, that I couldn't possibly marry him before December. He said that was a long time to wait, but I was certainly worth waiting for and he said a lot of other things and maybe I humored him a little too much, but that is just the trouble, I don't know.

I was absolutely sure he would forget the whole thing. If he doesn't remember anything about it, of course I am all right. But if he does remember and if he took me seriously, I will simply have to tell him about Walter and maybe about Gordon, too. And it isn't going to be easy. The suspense is what is maddening and I know I'll never live through this night.

July 16

I can't stand it, I can't breathe, life is impossible. Frank remembered everything about last night and firmly believes we are engaged and going to be married in December. His people live in New York and he says he is going back when I do and have them meet me.

Of course it can't go on and tomorrow I will tell him about Walter or Gordon or both of them. I know it is going to hurt him terribly, perhaps spoil his life and I would give anything in the world not to have had it happen. I hate so to hurt him because he is so nice besides being so cute and attractive.

He sent me the loveliest flowers this morning and called up at ten and wanted to know how soon he could see me and I hope the girl wasn't listening in because the things he said were, well, like Walter's night letters.

And that is another terrible thing, today I didn't get a night letter from Walter, but there was a regular letter instead and I carried it around in my purse all this afternoon and evening and never remembered to read it till ten minutes ago when I came up in the room. Walter is worried because I have only sent him two telegrams and written him one letter since I have been here. He would be a lot more worried if he knew what has happened now, though of course it can't make any difference because he is the one I am really engaged to be married to and the one I told mother I was going to marry in December and I wouldn't dare tell her it was somebody else.

I met Frank for lunch and we went for a ride this afternoon and he was so much in love and so lovely to me that I simply did not have the heart to tell him the truth, I am surely going to tell him tomorrow and telling him today would have just meant one more day of unhappiness for both of us.

He said his people had plenty of money and his father had offered to take him into partnership and he might accept, but he thinks his true vocation is journalism with a view to eventually writing novels and if I was willing to undergo a few hardships just at first we would probably both be happier later on if he was doing something he really liked. I didn't know what to say, but finally I said I wanted him to suit himself and money wasn't everything.

He asked me where I would like to go on my honeymoon and I suppose I ought to have told him my honeymoon was all planned, that I was going to California, with Walter, but all I said was that I had always wanted to go to California and he was enthusiastic and said that is where we would surely go and he would take me to Hollywood and introduce me to all those wonderful people he met there last winter. It nearly takes my breath away to think of it, going there with someone who really knows people and has the entrée.

We danced again tonight, just two or three dances, and then went out and sat in the tennis court, but I came upstairs early because Aunt Jule had acted kind of funny at dinner. And I wanted to be alone, too, and think, but the more I think the worse it gets.

Sometimes I wish I were dead, maybe that is the only solution and it would be best for everyone concerned. I *will* die if things keep on the way they have been. But of course tomorrow it will be all over, with Frank I mean, for I must tell him the truth no matter how much it hurts us both. Though I don't care how much it hurts me. The thought of hurting him is what is driving me mad. I can't bear it.

July 18

I have skipped a day. I was busy every minute of yesterday and so exhausted when I came upstairs that I was tempted to fall into bed with all my clothes on. First Gordon called me up from Chicago to remind me that he would be in New York the day I got there and that when he comes he wants me all to himself all the time and we can make plans for our wedding. The connection was bad again and I just couldn't explain to him about Walter.

I had an engagement with Frank for lunch and just as we were going in another long distance call came, from Walter this time. He wanted to know why I haven't written more letters and sent him more telegrams and asked me if I still loved him and of course I told him yes because I really do. Then he asked me if I had met any men here and I told him I had met one, a friend of Uncle Nat's. After all it was Uncle Nat who introduced me to Frank. He reminded me that he would be in New York on the 25th which is the day I expect to get home, and said he would have theater tickets for that night and we would go somewhere afterwards and dance.

Frank insisted on knowing who had kept me talking so long and I told him it was a boy I had known a long while, a very dear friend of mine and a friend of my family's. Frank was jealous and kept asking questions till I thought I would go mad. He was so serious and kind of cross and gruff that I gave up the plan of telling him the truth till some time when he is in better spirits.

I played golf with Frank in the afternoon and we took a ride last night and I wanted to get in early because I had promised both Walter and Gordon that I would write them long letters, but Frank wouldn't bring me back to the Inn till I had named a definite date in December. I finally told him the 10th, and he said all right if I was sure that wasn't a Sunday. I said I would have to look it up, but as a matter of fact I know the 10th falls on a Friday because the date Walter and I have agreed on for our wedding is Saturday the 11th.

Today has just been the same thing over again, two more night letters, a long distance call from Chicago, golf and a ride with Frank, and the room full of flowers. But tomorrow I am going to tell Frank, and I am going to write Gordon a long letter and tell him, too, because this simply can't go on any longer. I can't breathe. I can't live.

July 21

I wrote to Gordon yesterday, but I didn't say anything about Walter because I don't think it is a thing a person ought to do by letter. I can tell him when he gets to New York and then I will be sure that he doesn't take it too hard and I can promise him that I will be friends with him always and make him promise not to do anything silly, while if I told it to him in a letter there is no telling what he would do, there all alone.

And I haven't told Frank because he hasn't been feeling well, he is terribly sunburned and it hurts him terribly so he can hardly play golf or dance, and I want him to be feeling his best when I do tell him, but whether he is all right or not I simply must tell him tomorrow because he is actually planning to leave here on the same train with us Saturday night and I can't let him do that.

Life is so hopeless and it could be so wonderful.

It is only half past ten, the earliest I have gone to bed in weeks, but I am worn out and Frank went to bed early so he could put cold cream on his sunburn.

Listen, diary, the orchestra is playing "Limehouse Blues," the first tune I danced to with Merle Oliver, two years ago. I can't stand it. And how funny that they should play that old tune tonight of all nights, when I have been thinking of Merle off and on all day, and I hadn't thought of him before in weeks and weeks. I wonder where he is, I wonder if it is just an accident or if it means I am going to see him again. I simply mustn't think about it or I'll die.

July 22

I knew it wasn't an accident. I knew it must mean something, and it did.

Merle is coming here today, here to this Inn, and just to see me. And there can only be one reason. And only one answer, I knew that when I heard his voice calling from Boston. How could I ever have thought I loved anyone else? How could he ever have thought I meant it when I told him I was engaged to George Morse?

A whole year and he still cares and I still care. That shows we were always intended for each other and for no one else.

I won't make *him* wait till December. I doubt if we even wait till dad and mother get home. And as for a honeymoon I will go with him to Long Beach or the Bronx Zoo, wherever he wants to take me.

After all, this is the best way out of it, the only way. I won't have to say anything to Frank, he will guess when he sees me with Merle. And when I get home Sunday and Walter and Gordon call me up, I will invite them both to dinner and Merle can tell them himself. With two of them there it will only hurt each one half of much as if they were alone.

The train is due at 2:40, almost three hours from now. I can't wait. And what if it should be late? I can't stand it.

About the Authors

About the Authors

MARJORIE KINNAN RAWLINGS

MARJORIE KINNAN RAWLINGS was born in Washington, D. C. (1896), where her father was in the government service. Her childhood was spent in Washington and on her father's Maryland farm. After graduating from the University of Wisconsin she did newspaper work for ten years—in Louisville, New York, and Rochester. Then, in 1928, she left the North and made her way to a "jungle edge between two lakes" at isolated Cross Creek, in Florida. The autobiographical *Cross Creek* tells the story of her contented and full life there.

Before she went to Florida Mrs. Rawlings had written stories, but not with much success. Once in the back country of Florida, however, she had a remarkable experience which, she says, made all the difference. One day out hunting in the pine scrub she got lost, sat down to wait until she was discovered. Alone there in the great silence she "felt a profound peace and fell to wondering who lived in such a country." Out of that mood of peace and harmony with her environment Mrs. Rawlings began to write the books that have made her famous. *South Moon Under* (a Book-of-the-Month selection reprinted by Bantam Books) was the first, followed by *Golden Apples*. Then came the delightful story of Jody and his pet fawn which, under the title of *The Yearling*, won the Pulitzer Prize in 1939. Her short stories which had appeared in the magazines were collected into one volume, under the title *When the Whippoorwill*. Bantam Books has reprinted some of the most memorable of these stories, plus a chapter from *Cross Creek*, under the title *Gal Young Un*.

In her last novel, *The Sojourner*, she departed from her usual Florida background and set the story in New York State. At the time of her death on December 15, 1953, Mrs. Rawlings was working on a life of the novelist Ellen Glasgow.

Mrs. Rawlings had identified herself so closely with Florida that she has been called a regional writer. She is much more than that. Just to prove it, here's *A Mother in Mannville*, a story without the familiar Florida background, but with the same universal quality that distinguishes all of Mrs. Rawlings' work.

ELLIOTT MERRICK

ELLIOTT MERRICK is a writer from whom not enough has
been heard—especially in short stories. You'll see what we
mean when you read "Without Words"—one of the most
popular stories that has appeared in *Scholastic*. And you'll be
interested to discover that although "Without Words" is a
perfectly good short story as it stands, it has since appeared as
a chapter in Mr. Merrick's novel, *Frost and Fire*. We are particularly happy to preserve it here, in this collection of bests,
in its original form.

After graduating from Yale, Elliott Merrick worked as newspaper reporter and publicity man in New York, then pulled
up stakes and went to Labrador where for more than two years
he taught at Indian Harbor, the most northerly station of the
famous Grenfell Mission. During that time he took many a
trek with the fur trappers up Grand River into the interior,
where he endured the intense cold and hardship of the Labrador winter—and liked it. Out of this experience and out of
his dislike for the warmth and softness of city life, have come
Mr. Merrick's books—*True North* (a description of his Labrador travels); *Ever the Wind Blows; From This Hill Look
Down; Frost and Fire*, and *Northern Nurse* (all novels). In
Labrador Mr. Merrick married a girl from Australia, also of the
Grenfell Mission, who went on his treks with him, and is as
enthusiastic about the country as he is. From 1942 to 1944
Elliott Merrick wrote for the Office of War Information.

MAUREEN DALY

MAUREEN DALY was just sixteen years old when her story,
"Sixteen," won first prize in *Scholastic's* annual short-story
contest. Since its appearance in the magazine, "Sixteen" has
had a remarkable career. It was snapped up by Harry Hansen
for the *O. Henry Memorial Award Prize Stories of 1938* (the
first time a high school student has been included in that annual selection of the year's "bests"); it was later reprinted in
Redbook Magazine and now appears in about a dozen anthologies.

She won the first Intercollegiate Literary Fellowship established by Dodd Mead with her novel *Seventeeth Summer*.
It's the story of a boy and girl in love for the first time, and
the setting is Maureen Daly's own background—the Wisconsin Lake Country.

Maureen Patricia Daly was born, as her name hints, in
Castlecanfield, County Tyrone, Ireland (1921). When she
was two years old her family came to this country and, after a

short stay in New York, moved on to Fond du Lac, Wisconsin. Miss Daly was graduated from Rosary College, River Forest, Illinois, where she was interested in dramatics, writing, and sports. She has been on the staff of the *Ladies' Home Journal* for many years, and she edited a book called *Profile of Youth*—a collection of studies of American youth which had appeared in the *Ladies' Home Journal*. She's written several personality and etiquette books, among them *The Perfect Hostess* and *What's Your P.Q.?*

She is married to mystery-writer William P. McGivern. They are now living in New York with their two children.

JESSE STUART

JESSE STUART is a big, husky man who divides his time and energy between running his 500-acre farm in the Kentucky hills, and singing of those hills in prose and poetry. He is a regional writer, and proud of it.

Mr. Stuart is a native of the Kentucky he loves so much. He was born near Riverton (1907), rode muleback or walked to the country school when chores on the home farm permitted, had to stop school entirely when he was eleven to help the family. At fifteen he gave his grammar a sixty-day brush, then entered high school where, he says, he was like a mule in a new pasture. From there he went to work in the steel mills, later worked his way through Lincoln Memorial University in three years—the first of his people to achieve and to finish college. He was also the first to write a book.

The Man with a Bull-Tongue Plow, published in 1934, was a volume of poems which wrote themselves as the young farmer worked in the woods, the fields, the barnyard, and behind the mule hitched to that famous plow.

Taps for Private Tussie won the Thomas Jefferson Southern award of $2500. *Men of the Mountain* is a collection of tales about his hill neighbors. *Foretaste of Glory* and *Tales from the Plum Grove Hills* were published in 1946.

Stuart has also written his personal history, *Thread That Runs So True*. In it he traces his career from the day when he first taught in a one-room rural school in Kentucky, through his years in various teaching positions, to the time nearly twenty years later when he went back to the land.

Stuart has written many, many short stories in a wide variety of magazines. "Split Cherry Tree" is typical of these, reflecting as it does his own background and strenuous experience in getting an education. His two most recent books are *Hie to the Hunter* and *Beatinest Boy*.

A few years before he retired to his life as farmer-writer, Stuart was awarded a Guggenheim Fellowship for a year's travel in Europe—and headed straight for Scotland, home of the Stuart clan. For several years, *Scholastic* claimed him as one of the judges in its annual Writing Awards.

SALLY BENSON

WHEN SALLY BENSON learned that her collection of short stories, *Junior Miss*, had been selected as a Book-of-the-Month and had sold 40,000 copies in advance of publication, she said she felt as if she'd been hit by a truck. But she shouldn't have been that surprised. During the ten years she had been writing stories for the *New Yorker*, Sally Benson had garnered just one rejection slip from that particular magazine, which is probably a record. And that one slip was for the story, "The Overcoat," which she later sent to the *American Mercury*, from which it was reprinted in Edward J. O'Brien's annual *Best Short Stories* collection.

Mrs. Benson is one of those born writers, apparently, whose stories come out of their heads and lie flat and obedient on the paper, ready for the printer. No second, third, twentieth revision. No rewriting. Her average for a story is about two hours. She says she writes quickly to get it over with—much as other women attack the dinner dishes. Her sister says that she doesn't really write her stories at all—that she gets them from the ouija board. Whatever the explanation, Mrs. Benson's witty and tightly written stories have been delighting readers as they appeared in the magazines, and have created a ready audience for her as the stories were bound into book form. Besides the highly successful *Junior Miss*, Mrs. Benson has two other collections: *People Are Fascinating* and *Emily*. Her book about home life in Missouri was made into the diverting film, *Meet Me in St. Louis*. In 1940 she published another kind of collection—*Stories of Gods and Heroes*—in which she retold the stories of the Greek and Roman world of mythology.

Sara Mahala Redway Smith was born in St. Louis, Missouri (1900), moved to New York when she was ten years old. When she was nineteen she married Reynolds Benson, graduate Manager of athletics at Columbia University. The Bensons have one daughter, Barbara. Mrs. Benson does not want Barbara confused with Judy Graves, the lumpy little thirteen-year-old heroine of *Junior Miss*. "Barbara's five feet nine and she's very pretty," she says. "She isn't Judy—at least she hasn't been for a long time."

HARRY SYLVESTER

HARRY SYLVESTER is a past master at writing that particularly difficult kind of tale to come across—the good sports story. Not for him the impossible and sentimental fairy tale of the poor sub, ignored through the season, who goes in during the last two minutes of play to make at least seven touchdowns and win the game for good old ivy-covered Alma Mater. His heroes are made of much better and more human stuff. Sometimes they win, sometimes they lose, but that's incidental. The story itself is a story of character, as you'll see in "Eight-Oared Crew."

Mr. Sylvester was born in Brooklyn, New York (1908); graduated from Notre Dame in 1930. The next year while he was doing post-graduate work in English at the university he worked as staff correspondent for the New York *Evening Post* covering football throughout the entire Middle West. Later he was on the staffs of the New York *Herald Tribune* and the Brooklyn *Eagle*. He sold his first short story while he was a senior in college, since then has published a hundred more in *Collier's*, *Scribner's*, *Story*, *The Commonweal*, *Pictorial Review*, *The American Mercury*. One of his best-known, "A Boxer: Old," was reprinted from *Story* magazine in the *O. Henry Memorial Award Prize Stories of 1934*; three of his stories appeared in the O'Brien collection of the year's bests; still others have been reprinted in England and Scandinavia.

Mr. Sylvester is the author of three novels which together constitute a trilogy about the Catholic Church in the United States: *Dearly Beloved*, *Dayspring*, and *Moon Gaffney*. He also had published a collection of short stories, *All Your Idols*, in addition to the novel, *A Golden Girl*.

RUTH SUCKOW

WHEN RUTH SUCKOW was a little girl, her father, who was a Congregational minister, traveled from church to church across the broad state of Iowa, from small village to big city. His daughter grew up to know and love her native state thoroughly, and eventually to write about it and its people in short stories and novels that show her complete understanding of her subject.

Miss Suckow was born in Hawarden, Iowa (1892). After graduating from Grinnell College she took another degree at the University of Denver and taught there for an interval. This, however, left little time for the writing she wanted to do, so she gave up teaching, established the Orchard Apiary back in Earlville, Iowa, and supported herself by selling honey while she was making a fine reputation as an author. She was discovered by H. L. Mencken, who published many of her early stories in Smart Set, and later in the American Mercury. After that she had no trouble in getting recognition, and gave up bees for stories. She has published five novels (Country People, The Odyssey of a Nice Girl, The Bonney Family, Cora, The Kramer Girls—all about Iowa) and one book of short stories were bound into an omnibus volume, under the title, Carry-Over. Since then she has written a novel called New Hope. It too is about Iowa. In 1952 Rinehart published Some Others and Myself: Seven Stories and a Memoir.

GEORGE MILBURN

GEORGE MILBURN is the author of the hilarious novel, Catalogue, and many short stories—some very funny, some, like "Student in Economics," movingly serious. Milburn was born (1906) in Coweta, Oklahoma. His career as a writer started when he was sixteen, with a job as correspondent for the Pawhuska Daily Capitol. His course at the University of Oklahoma was interrupted by two years of hack writing in Chicago, where he worked for a publisher of paper-bound books, and by a year's wandering. Back at the university again, he made a living writing jokes until he finished college.

All this time Milburn had been writing stories, and when H. L. Mencken, then editor of the American Mercury, saw three of those stories in the magazine Folksay, he promptly bought all the manuscripts Milburn had on hand. After that it was clear sailing, and stories by George Milburn began to appear and kept on appearing in such magazines as Harper's, Scribner's, the New Yorker, and Story. His stories were collected in the two volumes, Oklahoma Town and No More Trumpets. Blackjack Country and The Uncommon Man came out later. His most recent book is the novel Flannigan's Folly.

George Milburn is an author who writes with honesty and sincerity about life as he sees it in America. Most of his stories have their setting in his native Oklahoma and retain the distinct flavor of that part of our country. Some, however, like "A Student in Economics," could have happened anywhere, as anyone who has hashed his way through college knows.

WILLIAM SAROYAN

WILLIAM SAROYAN flashed into the short-story scene in 1933 with his "The Daring Young Man on the Flying Trapeze" (published in Story Magazine), thereby starting a commotion that hasn't died down since. The trapeze is still swinging, and the daring young Saroyan on it still flies through the air, attracting the attention of the beholder with the greatest of ease. Mr. Saroyan's mind is as nimble as any trapeze performer, sometimes doing tricks, sometimes indulging in antics, but always swift, alive and full of grace.

William Saroyan was born (1908) in the vineyard country near Fresno, California, and grew up there. He comes by his gift for writing quite naturally. His father, a native of Armenia, was himself a writer and a teacher. His grandmother was a story-teller and a source of many of Saroyan's tales. Since the publication of "The Daring Young Man" Saroyan has published enough short stories to put his name in a long, long list of magazines, and to fill more than half a dozen books. Best known of these are probably his collections, *Little Children; Three Times Three; Love, Here Is My Hat; Peace, It's Wonderful*, and (a Book-of-the-Month) *My Name Is Aram*. His four plays produced on Broadway have had a lot to do with keeping the Saroyan trapeze swinging. Like the readers of his stories, critics like his plays either very much, or not at all. At any rate, in 1940 his *The Time of Your Life* was awarded the Pulitzer Prize as the best play of the year (which Saroyan turned down) and the Critics' Circle Prize (which he accepted). It was made into a movie. Perhaps you read *The Human Comedy* or saw the movie made from it. *The Adventure of Wesley Jackson*, a book inspired by Mr. Saroyan's army experiences, won the author more blame than praise. Two of his most recent books are *Laughing Matter* and *Bicycle Rider in Beverly Hills*.

The warm sympathy for people which marks all of Mr. Saroyan's work flows out over everyone he meets and everything he sees, transforming the most ordinary scene—this journey in a train for example—into something new and exciting.

DOROTHY PARKER

Up until the time Dorothy Parker's "Clothe the Naked" appeared, people had become used to thinking of her as a satirist and a deadly wit, as the national champion of the smart crack. She was famous for her stories which showed their hapless subjects up in an unpleasantly revealing light. It was clear that the author didn't think very highly of the people she wrote about. They were wonderful stories to read, but they didn't leave you with much of a feeling for your fellow man. Then along came a most un-Parkerish story, "Clothe the Naked," written with sympathy and understanding and compassion—one of the best stories Dorothy Parker ever wrote.

Dorothy Rothschild Parker was born (1893) in West End, New Jersey. Her first job in the literary world was writing fashion captions for *Vogue* at ten dollars a week. A job as dramatic critic on *Vanity Fair* a few years later was a step up, but ended abruptly when her criticisms of the current theatrical season proved a little too strong for those concerned—but it did a lot toward building up the Parker legend. When, for instance, she did some pinch-hitting for Robert Benchley, then drama critic for the *New Yorker*, her old friend Alexander Woollcott, was moved to remark, "It would be her idea of her duty to catch up the torch as it fell from his hand—and burn someone with it."

Mrs. Parker is equally known for her stories and her poetry. They can be found in the two Modern Library volumes, *Collected Stories*, and *Collected Poetry*, and also in *The Portable Dorothy Parker*. Mrs. Parker has often lent her touch for light and witty dialogue to Hollywood script writing, and recently she co-authored the Broadway play *Ladies of the Corridor*. She and the co-author, Arnold d'Usseau, are now working on another play.

DOROTHY CANFIELD FISHER

DOROTHY CANFIELD FISHER, whose foreword introduces this collection of the best short stories published in *Scholastic*, needs no introduction herself. Her name has long been associated with the literature of this country, with education, and with good works in general. She has written many fine novels, short stories, articles, plays; was for some time, one of the judges who make the Book-of-the-Month Club selections that guide other people to good reading; she was for years the only woman member of the Vermont State Board of Education; she was a member of the American Youth Commission; she has served as a hard-working and enthusiastic judge in *Scholastic*'s annual Writing Awards.

Anyone who has read her books will know that Mrs. Fisher is an American of New England stock, but he may not realize how far that heritage goes back. Her family came to this country in 1636, moved to Vermont in 1764, and Canfields have owned land there ever since. What she sees now when she looks out of her door at her home in Arlington, Vermont, is the same changeless and ever-changing view of the Green Mountains, their valleys and rocky pastures and little rivers, that the early Canfields saw almost two hundred years ago.

She herself hasn't always lived there. Dorothy Canfield was born in Kansas (1879), where her father was president of the

State University at Lawrence. She was educated in France and in America, dividing her time from the age of ten between schools in the two countries, where she was and is equally at home. Her education has been cosmopolitan, but at rock bottom as American as her Vermont hills. Her stories, by the way, usually have their setting in those Vermont hills, but her values are always the ordinary human values of universal experience.

Best known of her books are *The Bent Twig, The Brimming Cup, Rough-hewn, The Deepening Stream, Seasoned Timber* (all novels); her collections of short stories, *Hillsboro People* and *Made-to-Order Stories;* her translation of Giovanni Papini's *Life of Christ;* and her recent *Vermont Tradition: Biography of an Outlook on Life.*

KATHERINE ANNE PORTER

KATHERINE ANNE PORTER is rated by most critics as the outstanding stylist among living American writers. She gives us a clue to some of the reasons why in the following autobiographical paragraph:

"As soon as I learned to form letters on paper, at about three years, I began to write stories, and this has been the basic and absorbing occupation, the intact line of my life which directs my actions, determines my point of view, profoundly affects my character and personality, my social beliefs and economic status, and the kind of friendships I form. I did not choose this vocation, and if I had had any sense in the matter, I would not have chosen it . . . Yet for this vocation I was and am willing to live and die, and I consider very few other things of the slightest importance."

Miss Porter was born in Indian Creek, Texas (1894), the great-great-great-great-granddaughter of Daniel Boone. Even as a child she never stayed in one spot for long, so that her experience is spread over places as varied as Chicago and Mexico City; New York and Berlin; Paris and Bermuda.

After a handful of her early stories had appeared in the magazines they were collected in a limited edition, in 1930, under the title *Flowering Judas*—which promptly became a collector's item. Shortly after, she received a Guggenheim Fellowship and went to Europe where she lived for a number of years. She returned to America, where her *Flowering Judas* was reissued, in 1935, with two short and two long stories added. That book brought her a Book-of-the-Month Fellowship and, in 1938, another Guggenheim grant. *Pale Horse, Pale Rider* (a collection of three novelettes), published in

1939, was awarded the gold medal of the Society for the Libraries of New York University, and *The Leaning Tower*, a book of short stories, excited critics. In 1944 Katherine Anne Porter was elected a Fellow of Regional American Literature in the Library of Congress.

Her most recent book is *Days Before*, a collection of papers that have appeared in various periodicals and as book prefaces over the last thirty years. About a third of them are critical articles and reviews.

STEPHEN VINCENT BENÉT

MOST OF the stories in this book were chosen because of the picture they present of life in America today. We feel sure, however, that this story by Stephen Vincent Benét belongs here too, along with the rest, to remind us of the kind of men who did so much to establish the traditions of American democracy we hold so dear. The setting of the story is around 1775, but the fundamental truths in it are timeless and as universal as Lige Butterwick's toothache.

Stephen Vincent Benét, poet, short story writer, novelist, was born in Bethlehem, Pennsylvania (1898), because his army family happened to be stationed there at the time. Like most military households, they roved about the country from post to post, and the three Benét children grew up in a constantly changing scene—New England, California, and points in between. For generations the Benét men had belonged to the army, first in Spain, then in America. The present generation of Benét sons, however, broke away from that tradition and, with their sister, turned unanimously and successfully to writing. Soon all three, William Rose, Stephen Vincent, and Laura Benét, presented a triple threat on another kind of front—literature.

Stephen Benét began publishing when he was twelve and kept steadily at it. His first poems won him gold and silver badges from the old *St. Nicholas Magazine*; his later writings have gone on winning him prizes of distinction. In 1928 his book-length poem about our Civil War, *John Brown's Body*, was awarded the Pulitzer Prize; more recently his short story, "The Devil and Daniel Webster," was tapped as the best short story of its year and was not only snapped up by Hollywood, but has also been made into an opera! You'll find a collection of Mr. Benét's best short stories (including "A Tooth for Paul Revere") bound into his volume, *Thirteen O'Clock*. His *Selected Works* came out in 1942. Stephen Vincent Benét died March 13, 1943.

KATHARINE BRUSH

KATHARINE INGHAM BRUSH was born in Middletown, Connecticut (1902), lived in Washington, D. C., and in Baltimore until her father was made headmaster at a boys' preparatory school in Newbury, Massachusetts. Like so many other authors, her introduction to writing was a newspaper job—mostly drama and movie reviews. Later she tried a bit of poetry, then discovered herself (and alert magazine editors discovered her) in the field of popular fiction. She published some hundred-odd short stories, more than half a dozen books, wrote occasional screen originals (about two a year), and a weekly syndicated newspaper column called *Out of My Mind*. One of her earliest novels was the highly popular *Young Man of Manhattan*; the last was *This Man and This Woman*. She also wrote *Boy from Maine* and *You Go Your Way*. The only non-fiction book on her list is her autobiography, *This Is On Me*, which she herself termed hodgepodge, but which critics called a frank stock taking, full of good sense and good humor. Katharine Brush died June 10, 1952.

"Fumble," the story included in this collection, tells of a young man and his inferiority complex. It is one of Miss Brush's earliest stories and one of her best.

ALBERT HALPER

ALBERT HALPER is the author of seven novels and many short stories, written out of his experience and observation of the life and people around him. He was born in Chicago (1904), where his father ran a small general store; grew up there in the slum district near the railroad tracks and stockyards. After graduating from high school he worked for seven years at various jobs. He was order-picker in a large mail-order house, jewelry clerk, advance agent for a tobacco company, shipping clerk in an electrotype foundry, and night clerk at the Chicago Central Post Office before he decided to come to New York and write. That was in 1928. He has been writing ever since.

On the merits of his two first novels (*Union Square*, a Literary Guild choice, and *The Foundry*), and the many short stories which had appeared in magazines and were later collected in the volume, *On the Shore*, Mr. Halper was awarded a Guggenheim Fellowship in 1934. Since his return from a year's stay in Europe he has published *The Chute* (which goes back to his mail-order days); *Sons of the Fathers*, the story of a Jewish family in Chicago; *The Little People* and *Only an Inch from Glory*.

He also edited an anthology called *This Is Chicago*, and his latest book is the novel *The Golden Watch*, about a boy growing up in Chicago.

What Mr. Halper has to say in "Prelude" can be summed up in one sentence of warning, "Look out, America, here comes Fascism!" It's the story of one family in one large American city, but what happens to the Silversteins in Chicago in this tale could happen in any place in our country unless we all do what we can to stamp out any sign of anti-Semitism whenever or wherever it raises its un-American head. When this story appeared in *Scholastic* a few years ago we received a letter from a high school boy which said simply: "I have never read anything else of Albert Halper's, but I think that on the basis of this one short story he should be given the Nobel Prize for Literature at once."

MARTHA FOLEY

MARTHA FOLEY's fame, as a writer and editor, has risen steadily with the result that she now holds one of the very top positions in the short story field. Miss Foley is the editor of the annual Best Short Stories anthologies which for twenty-six years were edited by that late, great short story expert Edward J. O'Brien. Miss Foley has continued to keep up the fine quality of these volumes. She says in her introduction to *The Best American Short Stories 1953*: "One of the most important services a volume like this can perform is to bring to intelligent readers stories of permanent literary value they otherwise would miss."

Miss Foley was born in Boston, where she went to the Girls' Latin School, later studied at Boston University. She began her writing career as a reporter and caption writer on the staffs of San Francisco, Los Angeles, and New York papers before she went to Europe (1926). There she worked on the Paris edition of the New York *Herald*, later was sent to the Balkans as foreign correspondent. In Vienna in 1931, she and Whit Burnett—newspaperman and short story writer—founded the magazine, *Story*. She began editing the short story annual in 1942.

Miss Foley has lectured extensively on the short story at Columbia University, the University of Colorado and New York University. She has also helped *Scholastic* judge its annual Writing Awards.

JOHN STEINBECK

WHEN JOHN STEINBECK was writing his first novel he got a job in a fish hatchery at Lake Tahoe, California. He liked that job, but when asked why, he could only reply vaguely, "Oh, all the little fishes." That answer explains a lot about John Steinbeck. Little fishes—little people—simple lives, are what interest him most; are what he writes about with deep understanding. His first successful book, *Tortilla Flat*, was about the Mexican paisanos of Monterey; his next, *Of Mice and Men*, told the story of two migratory farm hands on a California ranch; his most talked-about book, *The Grapes of Wrath* (which won him the Pulitzer Prize in 1940), was an earnest and compelling saga of the westward trek of the small farmers and sharecroppers of our Dust Bowl in search of a self-respecting way of life. In *The Moon Is Down*, Mr. Steinbeck extended his faith in freedom-loving people to another country by telling us the story of the betrayal of a little town in an unnamed European country. Some of his other famous books are: *Cannery Row*, *The Wayward Bus*, *The Pearl*, and *The Red Pony*. His bestseller *East of Eden* was published in 1952.

John Ernst Steinbeck was born (1902) and grew up in Salinas, in the heart of the lettuce-growing country of California. Like so many other boys, he worked while he was going to the Salinas High School, running cultivators, bucking grainbags, doing odd jobs on the surrounding cattle ranches among the people he was to write about later. After attending Stanford University off and on for a number of years he moved on to New York, where he held down a reporter's job until he got fired, then carried bricks to help build Madison Square Garden. When there were no more bricks to carry he went back to California and started work on his first novel, *Cup of Gold*, which is where we (and the little fishes) came in.

SINCLAIR LEWIS

SINCLAIR LEWIS, novelist, short story writer, playwright and sometime actor, was born (1885) in Sauk Center, Minnesota, better known to the millions of readers of *Main Street* as Gopher Prairie. The neighbors who saw the lanky red-headed Lewis kid jogging around the country with his doctor father (sometimes holding the horses, sometimes holding the instruments in emergency operations) little suspected then that this young mind was photographing everything it came in contact with for future reference. The boy himself couldn't have suspected that some day he was to write a book that would make Sauk Center famous; that he was to be the first American to receive the Nobel Prize for Literature; that he would spurn a Pulitzer Prize; and that, all in all, he would become one of America's best-known writers.

After graduating from Yale, Sinclair Lewis tried out a few

ideas by living in Upton Sinclair's Utopian colony in New Jersey; went to sea on a cattle boat (which was what all the young men were doing in those days); traveled to Panama on a wild goose chase to help dig the canal; finally turned up in San Francisco with a job as reporter. Later he took six months off for serious writing; sold one item—a joke to *Judge*. Then, in 1920, after publishing five novels which didn't cause a ripple, *Main Street* came out and the resulting tidal wave of pros and cons was felt around the world.

Sinclair Lewis published a long list of novels, some adding to his stature as a man with a peculiar genius for isolating the germ of American culture, some run-of-the-mill. Best on the list are *Arrowsmith*, in which Lewis showed us (among other things) his idea of the stuff heroes are made of; *Babbitt*, which did for the average American businessman what *Main Street* had done for the average American town; *Dodsworth*, a great success as novel, play and movie; and *It Can't Happen Here*, a book about the threat of Fascism in this country.

More recent were: *Prodigal Parents*, *Bethel Merriday*, *Gideon Planish*, *Cass Timberlane*, and *Kingsblood Royal*. Since his death in 1951, Random House has published *Man from Main Street: A Sinclair Lewis Reader, 1903-1950*, edited by Melville H. Cane and H. E. Maule.

IRWIN SHAW

Irwin Shaw, short story writer, novelist, movie scenarist and playwright, was born (1913) in Brooklyn, New York, where he started his literary career at the age of twelve with a series of essays published in the school paper. At Brooklyn College he divided his extra-curricular time between more writing and four years of varsity football, baseball, and basketball. On leaving school he carried his talent for, and interest in, the theater to the radio, where he met with great success in writing serial dramatizations of the famous comic strips, *Dick Tracy* and *The Gumps*.

In 1936 he was in Hollywood, where his flair for rich and telling dialogue had inevitably led him, when his now famous one-act play, *Bury the Dead*, opened in New York. He flew East for the opening. The success of the play and the critics' praise that met his ears were enough to cheer any young writer's heart—especially a young writer whose first eighteen stories had been turned down. Since then Irwin Shaw has had four other plays produced. His brilliant novel of World War II, *The Young Lions*, was very well received, and in 1951 his novel about the red witch hunts in radio, "*The Troubled Air*," was published.

Irwin Shaw's short stories, among them "Strawberry Ice Cream Soda," have been collected in the volume *Mixed Company*. He is now living in Europe.

RING LARDNER

WHEN RING LARDNER first began writing short stories, people didn't take him seriously. They thought of him as just another funny man who could spin entertaining tales better than most. But nowadays when critics are judging and praising new writers they often use such phrases as "satire as penetrating as Ring Lardner's," "an ear for the American dialect as keen as Ring Lardner's," "impatience with frauds, snobs, and hypocrites as deep as Ring Lardner's." Lardner loved generosity and truth in all things, hated human depravity, and expressed his resentment by using the writer's most powerful weapon—laughter. His stories are funny, whether he's letting a baseball rookie, a small town barber, an old man vacationing in Florida, or a high school girl tell the tale. But they're more than funnybone ticklers.

Ringgold Wilmer Lardner, newspaperman, sports editor, short story writer, playwright, was born in Niles, Michigan (1885), graduated from the high school there, and then attended Armour Institute in Chicago for a year. From 1904 until 1919 he wrote and edited sports columns on newspapers all the way from Chicago to Boston. It was at this time that he began writing his bitingly realistic baseball columns. It was natural therefore that his first stories should have been about a baseball rookie: later they turned into the *You Know Me, Al* series that introduced the racy baseball vernacular later known as "Lardner's Ringlish." In his stories (the best of which have been collected in the volume *Round Up*), as well as in the play *June Moon* which he wrote with George S. Kaufman, you'll find the same Lardner—a man with a sad face and a witty and devastating way of pointing out the foibles of the human race. Mr. Lardner died in 1933.

In "I Can't Breathe" he shakes his finger, and his head, at puppy-love.

UNFORGETTABLE READING

THE INCREDIBLE JOURNEY by SHEILA BURNFORD. The heart warming story of a Labrador retriever, a bull terrier, and a Siamese cat and their epic journey across the Canadian wilderness in the dead of winter to return to the family they love. **50c** ☐

APRIL MORNING by HOWARD FAST. The exciting story of a young boy living in revolutionary America who suddenly becomes a man during the battle of Lexington. **60c** ☐

If you enjoyed this book, you'll want to read these other exciting Bantam Pathfinder Editions.

Other Bantam titles you are certain to enjoy